D1646076

Raised in Langholm, Dumfries & Galloway – 'the indisputable centre of the Universe' - Barbara Morris has written for her own enjoyment since she was at school.

With both her children now having left the nest, she has finally committed most of her free time to writing and *One Missed Step* is her first published work.

Although now living and working in rural north Northumberland, where the idyllic Cheviot Hills are her escape from the world, she is a regular visitor to Langholm and her second love, the Isle of Skye.

ONE MISSED STEP

Barbara Morris

One Missed Step

Vanguard Press

VANGUARD PAPERBACK

ISBN 978 184386 810 1

Vanguard Press is an imprint of
Pegasus Elliot MacKenzie Publishers Ltd.
www.pegasuspublishers.com

First Published in 2013

Vanguard Press
Sheraton House, Castle Park
Cambridge, England

Printed & Bound in Great Britain

Acknowledgements

Firstly, I owe a huge thank you to Pegasus Elliot MacKenzie Publishers for giving me this opportunity and for all their hard work in producing this book. Every member of every department was professional, pleasant and efficient, treating this nervous new author with respect at every turn. Thank you for that.

I am also indebted to Monica Finn and the staff at Vancouver Island Regional Library, Duncan, for providing information with courtesy and interest, and I would like to point out that any inaccuracies are down to me alone. Also people of Duncan, Portree and Camastianavaig, please forgive any liberties I may have taken with locations and descriptions.

Thanks to Jake for leaving the indescribable voice message for me on finishing the book, I wish I had kept it, auld freen! Also to Rachel, Jill, Emma, Sally and Jayne for their genuine views and enthusiasm – you all made me a little less scared. Aeneas, thanks for letting me use your name!

I have to thank the group Runrig, whose music has inspired me since I saw them at the Scottish College of Textiles in 1984. You made each visit to Skye even better, if that is possible. Thanks also to Dan Harmon, creator of 'Community'. Without Community I would not have seen Joel McHale. Without Joel McHale, 'my' David Wilder would not have had a face or a body and I might still be struggling on Chapter 3. Thanks to you both.

Finally, thanks to Geoff, Rowan and Rhuraidh for giving me the time to do this. You could have moaned, you could have laughed out loud, you could have told me to get a grip, but you did none of the above. You just let me get on with it and enjoy myself. Thank you.

For Geoff, Rowan and Rhuraidh with much love.

And for Jacqueline – every step of the way.

PART 1
23rd September 1993 – Late Afternoon

Chapter 1
23rd September 1993 – Late Afternoon

The words on the gravestone were simple and concise:

Fiona Mary Wilder - nee Mackinnon
Born 10.03.53   Died 17.09.93
Mother of Hazel and Kathryn
Wife of David

They told little of the subject herself however, giving no hint to her character, her painful illness or her willpower. Any stranger, any visitor-of-graveyards would perhaps comment on her age, or the sparsely worded inscription but would then pass, judging the lettering on the different granite headstones or the flowers on view. They were unaware that the ordinary grey slab had been worded by the subject herself in the months before she died. It merely stood there, proclaiming death where there had once been life, its gleaming surface signalling its recent arrival.

Kate Wilder, stooping to fill a jug with water from the tap by the gate, noticed just such a group of observers pause by her mother's stone. She straightened immediately, resentment raising the fine hairs on her arms. She wanted to scream at them to take their half-interest elsewhere, that if they were not here to grieve then to get the hell away. She almost did, but the atmosphere in this place was too reverent to be shattered by anything so harsh. Even the rising wind seemed to be stilled inside these gates and the Ben in the distance would not have approved. Instead, Kate gathered her roses and water and marched over to where the people murmured and pointed.

At her approach, a woman in glasses and raincoat turned to acknowledge her, but had no time to utter a word before Kate had brushed past her and picked her way through the already wilting wreaths to the flower vase. She said nothing as she snipped and arranged the roses, but her arrival caused embarrassed coughs and shuffling amongst the company. They had all but drifted away when Kate faced them.

"If you're interested," she began quite calmly, "She was my mother. This stone tells you nothing much except her age and her name but she was the most amazing person. Funny, really pretty and I can't believe ....Well, if you'd known her, you would know why there are so many wreaths." Red-faced now, Kate hastily gathered the discarded rose stems and tapped the headstone with her scissors. "I'm the Kathryn, by the way."

As she strode off, staring straight ahead, one of the silenced group hurried after her. It was Mrs Thomson, the wife of the undertaker. She put her hand on Kate's shoulder.

"Wait, Kate," she implored.

At the mention of her name, Kate stopped and looked at the woman.

"Oh, it's you, Mrs Thomson," she breathed, recognising the face behind the glasses for the first time. "I thought you were all strangers coming to gawp. Sorry."

"No, let *me* apologise," Mrs Thomson extended her arm around Kate's shoulder. "If I'd known you were coming again today, we would never have walked this way." She gestured back towards the group, who were now huddled sheepishly together, the sea restless and grey behind them. "My cousin and family are over for the weekend, we were just out for a stroll, and the view across the bay is so nice. But we'll leave you now. Don't let us stop you... you know. I'm sorry."

As Mrs Thomson walked back down the gravel path, Kate let out a laboured sigh and realised that, her show of bravado over, she had begun to shiver inside her fleecy jacket. She no longer even had the ability to return to the graveside for her daily chat with her mother and although her outburst had been a release of some tension, she had not benefitted from it at all. She merely felt cold and on the brink of more tears, and with these feelings came the leaden realisation that this would always be the case. She could communicate with people, talk, argue, shout, but when it was over, her mother would still be missing. Her heart would once again lurch downwards, and it was beginning to feel at home in that place. Inevitably, it would settle there.

Unlocking her bike from the cemetery's iron gates, she struggled with the unfairness of inevitability. In Kate's experience, if something was inevitable, it was usually negative and unjust. No choice, no ability to fight, 'nothing you can do' – inevitable. She could think of no example when the word meant anything other than something to be dreaded and feared. But she didn't want to be stuck here, didn't want to be governed by these circumstances. She shook her head to stop herself going any deeper into this area and clenched her hands around the handlebars. She would take control of this. She would *demand* that she be given some choices in life. Surely she was old enough now to qualify for that privilege?

Kate was almost glad that the cycle home would be a chore in the keen breeze. She could fight her present injustices by gritting her teeth and forcing her legs to pump faster and harder, putting the steep rises behind her and freewheeling down to the village, through the now buffeting rain. Indeed, the three miles or so to Camastianavaig did seem shorter than normal although that may have been due to the satisfaction she had gained from screaming obscenities at the top of her voice. The recipient had been a passing tourist bus who had caused her to wobble and swerve as it misjudged the width of the road, and for once she had been exhilarated as she tried to match its speed in retaliation. However, by the time she was wheeling her bike up the path to the cottage, her looks were blacker than the western sky. Yet the place was welcoming. The lamp shone in the far bedroom and Beth was at the kitchen window. She lifted her hand to Kate as she stacked a wet plate on the drainer. Kate managed a vague smile in return.

"You should have had a coat on, pet," began Beth, before Kate had even crossed the threshold, "There's a real chill in that wind... oh, and you're soaked!"

"I know," mumbled Kate, rubbing her hands over the gas heater, shaking the worst drops of water from her hair. "And the light's starting to go already."

As Kate pulled a chair nearer to the heater, Beth filled the kettle and switched it on. She glanced at her niece, who had laid her head on her folded arms across the table, and sighed. The funeral had been two days previously but Kate seemed even more out of sorts. She was lethargic, yet restless and seemed only interested in either visiting Fiona or sleeping. Beth could not find fault with her, however. They had all known Fiona was dying and the only remaining mystery was the actual date. Now that it was past, there was no focus, no point to anything.

"Where's Hazel?" muttered Kate into her arms.

"Stuart has taken her to Portree."

"Och, they could have given me a lift!" There was a moment's silence and then Kate sat up, blinking. "You don't think they're buying a ring, do you?" Her voice was suspicious, not excited.

"Good God, no," laughed Beth, and then turned to Kate, frowning. "At least, I hope not. Do you know something I don't? But that's ridiculous. And yet, just the kind of thing Stu would do to try and cheer her up. But never! If she thinks she could be happy settling - "

"Beth, I haven't a clue why they've gone. I just don't see the attraction of Portree on a filthy day. There must be something going on."

Beth's brow creased even deeper. This concern for her nieces' welfare was not new. She had shared the girls' lives since Fiona had returned from Canada, white-faced, pregnant and with Hazel clasped to her hip, more than seventeen years previously. Beth had cried at Kate's birth, had nursed both youngsters through chicken pox and was an endless source of advice on how the mind of a teenage boy might work. The emotion and stress of the last few months had blown them apart, and then almost instantly seared them back together. Now they were a closed unit. Three raw, grieving females under one roof, daring God to throw something else their way. He had not disappointed them.

Kate pushed her chair away from the table and leaned back in it. Passively, she looked around the room. "So. Where's everybody's favourite Canadian, then?"

At once, Beth was agitated.

"Sshh! He's next door," she shushed, her eyes flashing a warning. "And I'm not in the mood for a confrontation. Not today. Haze and I are perfectly aware of how you feel, but if it's on your mind so much, its time you talked to him about it."

Kate leapt out of her chair. "On my *mind* so much? How can it *not* be on my mind?"

"Talk to him, Kate. Hazel's made the effort, why can't you?"

"Because I don't think he should be here!" Kate hissed. "I shouldn't have to see him. I didn't ask him to come." Pause. "And if you want my opinion, the whole thing is a completely insane situation."

Beth, wiping dishes vigorously with a checked cloth, seemed on the point of arguing, then her face cleared.

"Fair enough.Cup of tea?"

Breathing heavily, Kate reached for two mugs on her way to the kettle. "I'll do it."

"I think we couldalldo with a cup, don't you?" said Beth, pointedly, handing Kate a third mug.

Scowling, Kate took it. She absently dropped a tea-bag in each of the mugs, her neck already beginning to prickle with anxiety. Beth poked her shoulder with a teaspoon. "Maybe he'd prefer a coffee?"

Kate looked steadily at Beth, wondering how far she would push it. The slate-grey eyes regarded the older, bluer pair, neither gaze wavering. Slowly, Beth folded her arms. Kate, not renowned for her meekness, now gritted her teeth and headed towards the door. It was a shallow victory however, and rather than smile, Beth simply sighed and rubbed her neck.

The corridor between the kitchen and sitting room was cool and comforting but Kate would rather have been anywhere else in the world at that moment. The rooms of the one-storey cottage had been built around this space, and so the long passageway boasted no natural light, but as the doors were only ever closed at night, it had never caused a problem. Kate now leaned against the wall, hidden from view, frustration rising to choke her. Why was he in their house? Why, when everyone was at their most vulnerable? She listened, but there was no sound from the sitting room. She could sense him there, however, and tried to prepare herself for what the sight of him would do to her. It always followed the same pattern. His eyes on her, partly wary, partly apologetic but always anxious would set her jaw and twist her stomach. Her feelings were a brew of extremes. Amid the annoyance and hostility which years of his 'neglect' had caused, curiosity and wonder would surface against her will. She wanted to harbour zero feelings for this man because he was nothing to her and this would be infinitely easier if he was not here. After a moment, Kate realised that he would have heard the kitchen door open and was probably waiting for someone to make an appearance. Silently cursing her own stupidity, Kate walked boldly into the room.

David Wilder was perched on the arm of a chair, silhouetted against the window's autumn light. His long, lean body was completely motionless and he appeared to be studying a well-thumbed photo album, although there was scarcely

18

enough light to do so. Another number of albums lay scattered around. Kate faltered as the silence and dimness engulfed her, but was almost instantly defensive. Had he asked if he could look at those? She flicked on the ceiling light and made one determined step towards him, but was halted once again as David's head snapped up, startled from his stupor. Kate, for once, had no idea what to say.

His face was as pale as bleached bone but this alone did not cause the shuddering shock within Kate. It was the bleak agony in his eyes. His pupils were so black that she could see no life in them and he seemed frozen in position by her scrutiny of him. Kate hesitated, looked away, and then felt her shoulders sink as the familiar heaviness descended. Oddly, David did not try to engage her in conversation, but placed the album respectfully on the floor and stood with his back to her, staring out at the discontented sky.

She watched him scratch his wrist then fold his arms, his head dipped slightly forward into his chest. Still, he said nothing, didn't even clear his throat. Kate suddenly felt exhausted. This was too much. At seventeen she shouldn't have to cope with this. This tall, strong, living being, who should have been her whole world up to this point, was a total stranger to her and he was standing in her home, making her feel very uncomfortable. Yet, he too seemed to be grieving for all those years; she had just seen it in his expression. Maybe it was a bond of some sort and yet Kate could not conceive that this outsider had once been connected to any of them.

Carefully, Kate picked up the albums and stacked them neatly on the coffee table. She plumped one of the cushions on the sofa, switched on the standard lamp and turned off the harsh ceiling light. Finally, she wandered over to the window where David had made his retreat, and stood as near to him as she could bear to. He took one small step away from her, possibly not wanting to intimidate her with his height, but there could have been a multitude of reasons behind the action. Kate was unaffected by it anyway.

From the window, they watched the bluish-purple clouds begin their journey across the bay. The sea was now undeniably choppy in appearance and the rain marched across their view, turning it to a blurry dusk. Stormy, thought Kate. When David finally turned to face her, Kate absently brushed a straying cobweb from the window pane and shook it from her sleeve. As it floated to the floor, some of it landed on the arm of his jumper. Her objective complete, she took a breath and stared straight back up at him. His face was now hopeful, which caused another twinge of annoyance.

"I don't know you," Kate explained, her tone sufficient to alter David's expression. "You're a visitor in this house, that's all." Pause. "So, would you like a cup of something? Beth's put the kettle on."

David watched Kate as she spoke. Even after three days in her company, he was still catching his breath at the similarities between the girl and Fiona. Facially, there was a certain resemblance, but Kate's heavy eyebrows and angular chin gave her a permanently solemn look which he could barely associate with the laughing, bubbling power-pack of energy he had married. Kate's eyes were more grey than blue, but the small hands and feet which turned in slightly, were all Fiona. The lilting voice, which barely rose above a quiet monotone in his company, but was strong and melodic when speaking to Hazel or Beth, had stirred countless memories. Now he was aware of something more. In this, their first actual conversation, he realised how disturbingly little she thought of him.

"Well?"

David cleared his throat. "No. Thanks anyway, Kathryn."

Immediately, Kate turned away from the window. David closed his eyes in despair as she marched from the room, but snapped them open as she spoke from the corridor.

"It's *Kate*, by the way."

Alone, David leaned his face against the glass, unable to ignore the accusation in her last remark. He felt completely disorientated, staring out at the spectacular but unfamiliar, acutely aware that the last time he had surveyed this landscape his wife had been at this side.

"God, Fiona. What made you think I could do it?" he whispered.

* * * *

"All I said was that I didn't get it. Don't go all moody on me, Haze."

"Then just shut up about it," snapped Hazel, facing Stuart's growing irritation. "Let's go for a coffee, I'm frozen."

Slipping her arm through his, Hazel steered her reluctant boyfriend in the direction of the nearest cafe. The evening was rapidly becoming less than pleasant, and not what Hazel had planned. It had started fairly well, with an afternoon walk round Scorrybreac, dodging the last of the summer tourists and enjoying the relatively warm weather; a break from the surreal atmosphere of the house. Now it had begun to pour, the streets emptying rapidly as the light disappeared and the wind rendered umbrellas useless, and Stuart kept asking the most ridiculous questions, to which she had not one answer.

Nicolson's Coffee Shop was overwhelmingly stuffy, full of steaming, sheltering couples and the odd whingeing child. As Hazel fought her way to a window seat, Stuart ordered two coffees and tried to decide which cake would cheer her up the most. She had become a bit of a mystery to him lately, and he was not afraid to admit that this whole bereavement thing was beyond him. He had thought the world of Fiona but had decided to ignore his own grief in favour of healing Hazel. Instead, he seemed continually to get on her nerves.

Hazel drew a five-pointed star in some spilled sugar, tried to transform it into a three-dimensional version of itself, and then failed to wipe it up with a napkin, cursing how sticky it had made her fingers. She watched Stuart edge his way carefully through the occupied chairs with a tray of two mugs and a plate of cakes.

"I didn't know what you fancied, so I brought two of three different kinds."

Hazel stared at the plate, starting to shake with suppressed laughter. She put her hand over the mouth, and then let out a shriek of mirth which caused many a turned head and the odd drop of spilled tea.

"Wha-at?" Stuart grinned uncertainly.

"You," giggled Hazel, rescuing the tray from his hands. "I suddenly saw you in a cap and frilly apron. Quite suited you actually."

"Well, I'm glad I can still make you laugh. I wondered if ....sorry."

"Och, it's alright, Stuey," sighed Hazel, inspecting the cakes on offer. "I know I've been a complete pain." Pause. "But believe me, I've been a pure pleasure compared with Kate. Horrendous."

"Tell me more," said Stuart, sipping his coffee.

Hazel shook her head in despair and tried to convey what the past few days had been like. The periods of united grief interspersed with hours of avoiding issues and the occasional barbed comment, usually directed at David. Then there was Kate's sporadic refusal to even acknowledge their Dad's existence. But Hazel was caught in a trap. This man fascinated her.

Each night she lay awake, trying to separate actual recollections from those of her imagination. He was so familiar and yet, surely she could not remember him? Fiona had brought her home from Canada when she was barely three and she could not picture the place or anyone who lived there. Yet she *knew* David Wilder. When they had stood in the graveyard, heads bent as Fiona was laid to rest, Hazel had edged closer to his tall frame. It had been an instinctive movement and she had become light-headed, as his presence had been so absurdly familiar. It had caused her to sway a little and his hand on her shoulder had not felt out of place. She had leaned against him without giving it a lot of thought.

"She's not giving him a chance," sighed Hazel.

"Well," replied Stuart, gently spraying sponge crumbs across the table, and causing Hazel to smile, "I don't really blame her for that. It's not like she ever met the man. You at least had a few years with him."

"Yeah, but I can't remember much. I don't really know him at all."

Except that she *did*. However, these were not feelings that Hazel was about to discuss with Stuart. She hoped that she would address them some day with the person concerned. But for now, she wanted to cherish them a bit longer, maybe try and make a bit of sense out of them.

"What do you think of him, Stu?"

Stuart's face fell as he laid down his cup. It was one thing to try and cheer Hazel up, to take her out of the house and ply her with pieces of millionaire shortbread. But to express opinions on her father, when he could turn out to be the best or worst thing that ever happened to her, was a game even he found too dangerous to play. His hesitation and startled expression made Hazel lean back in her chair. She released his hand from hers.

"It's alright," Hazel said softly. "I'll ask you when you know him better. Come on, it's getting late."

Chapter 2
17th September 1993 - Six Days Earlier

Kate's eyelids started to droop. Every few seconds she had to actively will them to stay open. For mid-September on Skye, it was a sticky afternoon and even the prospect of double English, her favourite subject, could not prevent Kate from adopting the recently familiar position of head on folded arms. Her stomach was in permanent spasm, she could not remember the last time that food had held any interest and there was a density brewing in her head which she knew would not leave her that day. For a moment or two, she watched chalk dust rise from where Mr Ellis had dropped the board cleaner, before she gave up the fight and allowed her eyes to close.

Within seconds she was winging her way through a multi-coloured universe. Vivid blue and bright green clouds bombarded her vision, before plunging her into a sea of pink, prawn-like creatures. Mr Ellis' voice was a comfortable accompaniment to this fantastic journey and occasionally the words he spoke would appear superimposed on the pink ocean. She felt herself physically relax. It was her last conscious movement.

Kate stood at the edge of a sea of blue crystal. It was calm, completely flat and there appeared to be only two layers of colour before her, the sky a paler version of the water. She dipped her toe into the liquid and was surprised at how warm it felt, so warm that it began to creep up her skin like the sun's rays and it seemed the most natural thing to simply throw her body forwards. She wanted to be engulfed by that warmth and float in its embryonic fluid. Still, she hesitated.

"Go on, Katy."

Kate turned to see her mother – young, glowing, healthy – waving at her from her seat on a sandy dune. She wore a floral dress and her hair was waist-length, the dark strands being picked and up distributed by the breeze.

"Go on, you'll love it!"

She took a step forward and sank into the water's embrace. It lapped at Kate's chin and was an altogether becalming and peaceful sensation. The sunshine was angelic on her face and it did not sting nor blind; her legs were weightless, blending with the water around them. She raised her hand to where Fiona had been, but her mother was no longer seated or alone. Fear tightened around Kate's throat. A dark-haired, clear-eyed man was standing beside Fiona. They stood perfectly still in a formal pose, both grinning at Kate. Fiona held flowers, the man wore a suit. They looked like black and white cardboard cut-outs.

"Mum!" yelled Kate, choking on the tepid, salty water. The figures on the shore were frozen to the spot. They grinned on.

"Mum?"

Now Kate's legs felt heavy, the water she trod in as thick and as black as oil. Desperately, she kicked towards the shore, but made no progress. As she forced her arms and legs to plough through the thickening sludge, she saw the two-dimensional couple sway in the breeze. She couldn't reach them and they were going to topple. They would fall into the water and disintegrate unless she could reach them and prevent it. She couldn't quite…

"Kate?"

Kate was on her feet in a moment, sending her chair careering backwards. Temporarily blinded by the brightness of the room, she gradually became aware of many pairs of eyes on her. Mr Ellis stood beside her desk. Gently he laid his hand on her shoulder and spoke quietly.

"Easy now. Are you okay?"

Kate could feel her heart racing and the blood swishing in her ears. Her face hot with shame, she bent to pick up her chair.

"Sorry," she mumbled, unable to look at anyone. "My head hurts."

The class watched with varied interest as Kate sat down, but remained upright in her seat. Somewhere a boy sniggered. She wiped her damp brow but could not raise her eyes from her desk. There was not one person in the High School who was unaware of her personal circumstances and if she saw one more sympathetic look, she thought she might actually throw her chair through the window.

"Take it easy," Mr Ellis repeated, then made his way back to the front of the class. "Graeme, open that window. The rest of you, back to it."

Kate forced herself to breathe slowly and deeply, which helped, but she remained mortified. It was not the fact that she had fallen asleep, but rather that she had done it in Mr Ellis' class. He was one of the few teachers she respected and really worked for. Now, without a doubt, she had offended him. Miserably, she flicked through her textbook to the appropriate page and tried to concentrate on the black print before her. The heat was intolerable. Her classmates coughed and shuffled and she was aware of their occasional glances. But when at last Kate raised her head, it was to look, sheepishly, at her teacher. Mr Ellis, without wavering from the point he was making, winked quickly at her. Everything was fine.

"So, Catriona, question one. I'd rather hear your thoughts on it than watch you chew that ruler."

The lesson crept on, Kate trying to lose herself in the comprehension task. She was grateful for the challenge, it would see her through to the end of another day, but as she dotted her last 'i', all she really wanted was for someone to sprinkle a watering-can's worth of cool water over her head. She tried to imagine the rivulets running down her temples and easing the pain there, how her scalp would eventually stop throbbing. She wondered if she would actually steam in the process.

There was a knock on the open door. As Mr Ellis, frowning, left the room, the murmuring and sighing started automatically.

"Have you finished it, K?"

The question came from a chair to her right, where Shona Syme, continuing to scribble furiously, glanced in her direction.

"What?"

"Have you finished it yet? What d'you get for 3a?"

But Kate could not answer. She was holding her breath, staring at her own words before her, absolutely determined not to look in the direction of the doorway. If she merely sat here, following the loops and slashes that her pen had made in good faith, she would never have to acknowledge what was taking place. She could hear her teacher's footsteps heading in her direction and for the first time ever, hated the man, simply for taking part in this scene. And there was her sister, eyes black and puffy, following his route to her desk. Kate felt herself slowly stand and watched as her own hands began to reload her pencil case with its scattered contents. Silently, she handed over her exercise book, noting his uncomfortable expression.

"I've finished it," she croaked, hauling her ruck-sack onto her shoulder.

"That's fine, Kate," Mr Ellis assured. "I hope ... Well, we'll see you when we see you."

"Let's go," faltered Hazel, taking her sister by the arm. Mr Ellis stood back, unable to say more in front of a class of less than sensitive teenagers, and she was grateful for that. The second they were clear of the stifling room, however, Kate's vision began to swim and she leaned against the corridor wall, clutching her eyes.

"Come on, Kate," sobbed Hazel, her anxiety also suddenly brimming and spilling down her face. "We have to get there yet."

Somehow they made it out to Hazel's ancient Ford Fiesta, encountering only two concerned and knowing nods along the way. As they swung out of the car park and down to the main road junction, Kate saw a few faces staring out from classroom windows. Were they watching them, or were they simply longing for the bell to allow them out into the fresh air? Did it matter either way?

"So, this is it?"

"Everybody seems to think so," sniffed Hazel, wiping her nose with the back of her hand. "There's been a big change since this morning."

Kate wound down her window, allowing the moving air to fan her face. This was not right. In her moments of preparation, her mother would die on a foggy November morning, with the lamps casting golden globes around her head and a fire crackling in the grate. Fiona's sister and daughters would be holding hands, talking gently to each other, reminiscent of when Beth had succumbed in Little Women. It should not be happening on a day like this, when the already turning leaves were blistering and rustling in the hazy heat. It should not be happening at all.

"Kenny phoned the shop," stated Hazel, crunching back into second gear as the road steepened and twisted. At twenty, she had been driving for over two years, but had never really excelled at it.

"What's Beth saying?"

"Well, Mum's been in and out of it all day, but now her breathing is the problem. I think" Hazel stopped until Kate looked in her direction. "I think she doesn't want us to miss the, you know, the chance - "

Kate suddenly flung her rucksack violently over onto the back seat, narrowly missing Hazel's head.

"What the hell?" cried Hazel, swerving in surprise.

"I-am-so-sick-of-this!" Kate punched out the words, beating time with her fist on the dashboard.

"What?" shouted Hazel. Then, "I mean, what *exactly?*"

"Everything!" growled Kate, holding her head which was pounding harder than ever. "This whole saying goodbye rubbish. Too many words! It's all crap. Get all the loose ends tied up, tell Mum for the thousandth time that we love her and that we will be fine, which we won't be. So actually, trying to pull the wool over her eyes, which is something we have never managed yet."

"She's hardly aware of anything," protested Hazel.

"I don't want to do it!"

"Okay, but maybe she does!" Hazel's voice now matched her sister's in volume. It caused Kate to pause for a second.

"Well, it's not right," she mumbled, after a moment. "We're not ready."

It was a meagre argument and Kate knew it. What she really wanted to say was 'Who's going to visit me in Edinburgh when I'm at University? Who's going to arrive, wide-eyed and smiling on the train and marvel at the way I've decorated my room? Who's going to whisper in my ear, while we're doing the dishes, that she thinks my boyfriend is gorgeous?'

"We haven't shared enough yet," Kate's voice had dulled considerably. "Oh, that's pathetic."

"No its not," replied Hazel, softly. And there the conversation stopped.

Kate leaned her elbow on the open window and cupped her chin in her hand. She watched the colours of the day blur past. Kate was a colour person, as her mother had been, and she always made use of what she saw, allowing it to alter her mood. When she was elated or excited, the scenery would provide a pleasant accompaniment to whatever was occurring, but when all optimism had left her, the shades and shapes became a welcome focus for her and she would study her surroundings with fresh eyes. On this Indian summer's day, the heat shimmered above the mossy, olive grasses and indigo larks hovered and swooped. The grey, single-track road wound its way ahead of them, Hazel bumping the car over every pothole and ridge on it. Kate now closed her eyes against the brilliance of it all, wanting only to ease the pressure behind them. Her spinning thoughts settled on her sister for a moment.

Hazel was easy to love. Her face was never guarded or wary and she would talk to strangers in the same manner she addressed old acquaintances, a quality which Kate had sometimes envied, sometimes despaired of. She was perky and easy-going and friends sought her company; her job behind the counter at the baker's suited her sociable nature and Stuart worshipped her. She had seemed genuinely content with life, until the last few weeks, when rather than withdrawing into herself as Kate had done, she had allowed frustration at her own helplessness to drive her forward. She was the oldest child and so had a duty to perform.

As they began their steep descent down to the bay, Hazel's stomach clenched inside her. There were four cars abandoned in front of the cottage. It seemed to make the situation even more definite and unavoidable and she sensed Kate sit upright in her seat.

"It's alright, K," breathed Hazel. "After this, it will get better." This was her job now. To get herself, Beth and Kate through this. If she fell apart, then they all might, and yet she thought that maybe they had every right to do just that.

Fiona was forty years old. She had received the news of the cancer two weeks before her fortieth birthday and had kept it to herself until the celebrations were over. They had held a ceilidh in Portree and all her colleagues from the nursery, as well as Beth's friends from the fish farm had each been instructed to bring as many folk as they liked to it. Stuart and Hazel had spent the entire night trying to get Kate interested in his cousin, but she had spent most of her time watching the band, astounded by the sheer magnetism of the second accordion player. It had been a loud, raucous night and if anybody had noticed how much champagne Fiona had consumed without actually becoming incapacitated, then it was not remarked upon. Guests were still talking about the festivities a week later, when the news broke. Since that time, Fiona had rested only when she had been physically forced to.

Once the final set of tests had proved incontestable, she had positively decided against further treatment in order to concentrate her energies on her 'plan for the future'. Each of them had accepted her decision, because every minute was a precious minute, and it could not be squandered on argument or conflict. The period of time she had been given had appeared oddly acceptable as they had moved through the first numbed hours. Now, it felt as if they were hurtling towards a brick wall, accelerating each day. Hazel saw it as a wall rather than a precipice. There would be no sense of falling when the time came, there would simply be a hard, immovable smack and then nothing. She refused to think about what her mother might be feeling. She could not bear the thought of Fiona being scared, even though she had given no indication that this was the case. But the idea of suffering pain whilst having to walk towards the unknown filled Hazel with iced terror. Something in all of this had managed to keep Fiona sane.

By the time afternoon had crawled into evening, cooler but still bright, Fiona was gone. Kate and Hazel had sat by her bed, dry-eyed for everybody's sake, while Beth had fussed and hovered, coping in her own way. This had included dusting the many photographs on Fiona's dresser and continually rearranging the furniture as officials came and went. Dr Simpson had seemed almost embarrassed to be hanging about, 'intruding' as he had the grace to call it. But he and Jen, the Macmillan nurse, had been such regular visitors in the past week that nobody thought it at all awkward.

When it was over, Kate unfolded her stiff body from her chair and escaped to the bathroom. Locking the door behind her, she perched on the edge of the bath and watched the dust particles dance in the low sunlight. The bathroom was yellow; too yellow. Why would anybody want a pale yellow suite, yellow and orange tiles and bright citrus walls? Didn't they know that even in dying sunlight, it could seriously sting a person's eyes? And when you felt sick to the stomach, all it did was remind you of lemon meringue pie, or thick cloying custard. Kate now recalled the week Fiona had taken off work to decorate the room.

"All hands on deck, mind!" she had cried, depositing tins, brushes and a box of tiles on the kitchen table. "And I don't want any complaints about the choice of colours either, sister. That bath will have to stay and when a room only gets the sun in the evening, I want it bright, bright, *bright!* Are you listening, Beth?"

At twelve and fifteen, the girls had found the painting quite enjoyable, although Beth had designated herself as refreshment provider only. The smell of paint made her dizzy. But Fiona had tiled and stencilled, sewn curtains and hunted the island for a set of deep peach towels, which in the end had arrived by mail order. The finished room had certainly screamed Fiona's personality at all who visited and was at least one contemporary spot in the dated surroundings. They had all loved it. But now, the colours and shades seemed to jar with each other and were just too much. As one salty, hot tear rolled down Kate's nose, she couldn't even begin to compare the young woman who had cheerfully broken four tiles before successfully fitting one, with the cold, wasted creature in the next room.

There was a timid knock at the door.

"Kate? I need a paracetamol. Can you open up?"

It was Hazel. She sounded calm, even composed, but on opening the door, Kate saw that she looked dreadful. Her eyelids remained swollen, the delicate skin stretched and shiny, and pale purple semi-circles had appeared beneath her eyes. She walked straight up to Kate and held open her arms. They stood, silently holding each other upright, both wondering at their continued ability to do so.

"Oh, God," Hazel murmured into Kate's hair, "What do we do without her?"

There really was no answer and instead, Kate settled her head sideways on her sister's shoulder and stared at the shadows on the wall. The shapes sharpened and then blurred as the sun allowed clouds to pass over it unchecked and finally there was a peace to be found in that riotous room. Their bodies shared the warmth of the embrace as only two people who had grown up together could do.

27

No words, no explanations were necessary, just a mutual need for contact. Kate felt Hazel tense as she sniffed and then moaned, "My head really hurts."

As she began to rummage in the cupboard below the sink, Kate resumed her bath-edge seat and frowned.

"What?" asked Hazel, sensing Kate's expression rather than seeing it.

"I didn't get half of what she said," replied Kate, hopelessly. "Did you understand any of it?"

Hazel shrugged. "What I could hear didn't make much sense. It seemed to be mostly for Beth anyway."

Kate nodded. Every time Fiona had spoken, it had exhausted her, but she refused to stop trying. It had resulted in short bursts of individual words, followed by lengthier periods of laboured sleep and nobody knew when the last communication would be. They did not know, even now, if she had said all she needed to, if she was finally at peace with how she had left things. They would never know and there was a danger it may drive them mad wondering. But something else was irritating Kate, cutting its way through the icy numbness to her brain. As she gnawed at her fingernails, Kate knew she would have to start this particular conversation.

"She definitely said his name," Kate's voice was very low. "More than once."

Hazel's shoulders dropped and as she studied Kate's face, she began to nod slowly.

"I know. What do you think it meant?"

Chapter 3

On the morning following Fiona's death, Beth awoke to several realisations. The first was the incredible truth that she would not speak to her sister again. This was surely the most inconceivable and absurd of situations. So unbelievable in fact, that Beth was able to file it away, to visit at a time when she could give it the correct amount of attention. Then there was the acceptance that control was running away from her faster than a receding tide and it made the hollowness within her now ache around the edges. Life was playing with her, dangling many challenges and the occasional solution in front of her, all of which unsettled her systems. Finally, the most pressing of all. Although the girls had seemed to accept sleep as their acquittal at the end of yesterday's trial, she was going to have to wake them soon with some news. News which was not negotiable and which she was sure would bring its own problems and anxieties.

Just after 9am, when she heard the first coughs and mutterings coming from their bedroom, she crept across the threshold and looked at the two heads, still tucked into their sleeping postures, barely free from their slumbers. Gently, she drew back the curtains. The air was stale, but the filthy weather outside dissuaded her from opening a window. Instead she turned and looked at them, trying to memorise what they looked like before she imparted the information. Eventually, Kate sat up.

"You okay?" her voice had not yet found its morning strength and she cleared her throat.

"Yes. Well, I think I am. Thing is, I've got some news. Your Dad has been in touch. He's coming for the funeral."

There was dead silence for just over a second, before Kate started off the two-man onslaught.

"You *are* joking!"

"He's coming *here?* He's actually coming over here?"

"You're having us on!"

"When? I mean, when exactly does he arrive?"

"I can't believe it. You're kidding, right?"

Beth took a deep breath, then "Let me sit down."

Beth seated herself thoughtfully on Kate's bed, while her niece pushed herself further up onto her pillow. At the bombshell, Hazel had thrown off her duvet and was now pacing around the room, hair flying in all directions.

"What gives him the *right?"* spat Kate.

"Look," Beth held up both of her hands, "It's going to take a lot of explaining, but I'm not even attempting to start until you're both prepared to listen."

Hazel cracked her knuckles and continued to pace. Kate bit her lip at the injustice of it all and muttered something about Beth having a long wait. She in turn folded her arms and looked from one girl to another. Eventually, Hazel sat on a pile of clean ironing, got up and moved it to the floor under Beth's exasperated gaze, then pulled her discarded duvet around her and sat once again.

"I can't …" said Hazel, "I mean, this is unbelievable."

"I know," agreed Beth, "But if you'll let me tell you everything, you'll maybe understand why nobody told you before."

Kate let her hand fall away from her hot forehead, then after exchanging a frown with her sister, turned back to Beth. "How long have *you* known?"

Beth had the presence of mind to look uncomfortable and, with the heavy sigh of the condemned, she stood slowly and wandered over to the window. Rain was falling in a steady sheet, giving the room a greyness which Kate's bedside lamp did nothing to alleviate. That was the trouble with Skye, no two days were the same. You could say goodnight to a spectacular sunset, followed by star-encrusted space and silver fingernail of moon, and wake up to wet, drumming rain which nobody –

"Okay, we're listening," Hazel's voice was packed with patient diplomacy. What she really wanted to do was jump up and down in ridiculous excitement, but felt Kate did not share her emotions. Best to let Beth tell them all there was and then react accordingly.

Beth now faced them. Leaning against the windowsill, she pressed her folded arms against her chest, protecting herself from their apprehension.

"It was your Mum's idea. She wanted you all to meet up."

The girls were motionless, compelling Beth to go on.

"She's been planning it for ages, since, well, since the last lot of results. She wanted you to know each other. Wouldn't talk about anything else."

"When was this?" cried Hazel, "*When* did she talk about it?"

"Haze," said Beth, gently. "Your Mum and I did an awful lot of talking. She saw this as a little project, it seemed to give her a kind of purpose - "

"Oh, that's rubbish," sobbed Kate in despair. "Her purpose was to stay alive. For all of us. Why couldn't she have concentrated on that instead of … instead of trying to involve *him* in whatever this is."

"Kate, don't," mumbled Hazel, unfolding herself from her duvet and crawling into Kate's bed. "It's alright. She must have known what she was doing."

Kate wiped her nose with the back of her hand and sniffed loudly.

"Did she Beth?" she accused. "Did she know what she was doing, because I don't get it."

"I didn't at first, babes. But it's all so complicated." Beth hesitated, determined not to say any more than was necessary at this stage. She changed tack. "I just want you to know that speaking to David again - "

"She spoke to him?"

"… speaking to him on the phone, she was a different person. I mean it Kate. She was happier, joking even. She looked great every time. It was worth the gigantic phone bill just for the effect it had on her every week."

"Every week!" Now it was Hazel's turn to look indignant. "She spoke to him every week? She never thought that maybe we might have jumped at the chance to have a word?"

"Not me", scoffed Kate.

"Well, me!" retaliated Hazel. "I'd have said hello. This isn't fair."

"Hold it!" Beth's tone was sharp. "You said you would listen."

"Come on Beth. You expect us to keep quiet while you're laying all this on us?"

"I *expect*," replied Beth, pointing at both girls in turn, "That you'll do your mother the courtesy of trying to understand her point of view. She worried herself sick – literally, more than once – about what you two would think of her when you found out. I said, come on Fiona, give them a bit of credit. They will realise how important you think this is and appreciate what you're trying to do for them. She wanted to let you know sooner, but I persuaded her not to tell you. Do you know why?"

Kate looked at Hazel for guidance who, frowning, could not take her eyes off the ranting Beth.

"Because," she continued, slightly calmer, "you would both have had strong opinions and there would have been a lot of sulking and arguing and slamming of doors." She took a breath. "Frankly, I didn't think your Mum needed the aggravation."

Now Hazel looked at Kate, who made a 'have-we-all-been-transported-to-a-parallel-universe' type of face, but refrained from actually shrugging her shoulders. When Beth spoke next, her voice was mellower and in danger of cracking.

"But the real reason I told her to keep it to herself was so that they could share something again. Just the two of them."

Beth now sat on the windowsill, her heels knocking the crumbling plaster wall below her, which had been softened beneath the wallpaper by years of just such contact.

"I wish you'd seen her," she began again, as Kate lay back against her pillow and closed her aching eyes. "I wish you'd seen her face when she talked to him. And it wasn't all one way. I could hear him blethering at the other end. It seemed so easy for them."

It wasn't that Beth thought this an appropriate place to pause and let the girls think, it was just that she could hear her sister and brother-in-law now, animated and cheerful, rediscovering what they had once marvelled at. Each time they finished a conversation, Fiona would share it all with Beth, more than anything to revisit it herself. The first few discussions between them had been upsetting and guilt-ridden on both sides, but as they both came to terms with the situation, they had slipped into a pattern of easy consolation. He tried to lessen her concerns and she tried to provide him with details of the entire life she had denied him by leaving. It had affected Beth deeply, it still did. Fiona and David had wasted something special and she feared that they had both been very much aware of it.

The silence in the room was broken only by the rhythmic drip of the leaky guttering outside the window. Kate was motionless, eyes shut with her arm flung across them. Hazel stared at the opposite wall, absently picking at the cuticles of her fingernails. Once, the sun lit up the room for a second or two and Beth supposed that there would be a rainbow standing guard in the bay. It was an uncharacteristically tranquil scene. So much so that Beth began to fear that both girls may be going into shock. Genuine shock, the kind medical dramas referred to, the kind that required treatment and the kind that she knew nothing about. She slid off the windowsill.

"I'm going to put the kettle on. Haze, you're starting to shiver."

At her exit, Kate slowly sat up and looked around her. Hazel's side of the room could best be described as cluttered. She had pinned a piece of purple muslin 'artistically' on the wall to hide the marks old posters had left. Her bedside table was overflowing with essentials – hair bobbles, five paperbacks, a glass of flat Coke, an alarm clock and a box of tissues. A plastic tray containing make-up was desperately trying to retreat under the bed to escape the marauding items of clothing which were gathering their forces together and shoes were scattered here and there ready to trip the unwary.

Kate moved her eyes to her own domain. She had at least some idea of where her possessions lived and how to put them back there, but really what was the point of making the effort? Hazel could not change. Their room was a tip; it would always be a tip. It was badly in need of a coat of paint and this thought pulled the knot in her gut even tighter. Who was going to paint it? Her mother had tried to pass on her love of decorating, but apart from the bathroom project, neither Hazel nor Kate had felt the need to pursue the chore any further. Maybe Kenny, Beth's perpetually patient boyfriend, could have a go. She could see only too well the impression it would make on a stranger in its present state.

"Can you take it in?" breathed Hazel, as her sister straightened a picture which hung at eye level next to her bed. "I mean, if I'm going to be honest, I wondered if maybe, you know, later on ..." Hazel paused, anxious not to alienate Kate, who never talked about David or their future. Ever. "But it didn't once occur to me that he'd come here."

"A bit on the late side, isn't it?"

Hazel simply shook her head, her mind following the path her heart had already taken. She was going to see her Dad again. It was incredible. It was scary. It was something she had thought about for years, but it wasn't in any way simple.

When Fiona and Hazel had returned from Canada, her parents and Beth had welcomed them with open arms and immediately David had become superfluous, if not quite irrelevant. Fiona had been a broken, fragile version of the girl that had left five years previously and refused to give an account of her circumstances. 'I'm not going back. Don't make me, *please'*.

So, for years, they had floated along. All were adamant that David would be neither missed nor referred to. There had been a hiccup when Hazel had started school and it was suddenly apparent to her that a Dad was not just a monthly envelope containing a cheque, but that a lot of her friends lived in the same house as 'the Dad'. But they had got through it. When John-Alasdair Mackinnon died suddenly in the summer of 1981, the subject of fatherhood seemed to creep more easily into conversations and in time, Fiona had healed enough to be able to answer most of their questions truthfully.

Kate had been as curious as Hazel in the beginning. They had studied together 'The Wedding Photo', trying to find something of David in their own faces, agreeing that he was at least handsome. Nice smile. And Fiona had always painted an attractive picture in their minds, which her sister and mother had resisted adding their own bitter brushstrokes to. But as the girls grew older, they had reacted to all new information in their own different, blinkered ways.

Hazel saw David as a compatriot, the link with her Canadian family, and the love of her mother's life. His name brought to mind a half-remembered time of giant trees, woolly jumpers and for some reason, bristles on an unshaven face. When she thought back to her earliest memories, there was a sense of someone, a figure she always associated with her mother and she liked to think that it had been him. He was certainly someone she longed to meet.

Kate on the other hand began to regard him as a careless, hard-headed, perhaps cowardly man who could not possibly fit into her mother's mould of him. Nobody who was so 'thoughtful and funny, he always looked out for me ....' would allow his pregnant wife and child to fend for themselves. Had he had a mental breakdown, a personality transplant or was he just a stubborn idiot who had deliberately remained an ocean away from them all of her life? She had never understood Fiona's reluctance to lay any blame at his door.

'Things just changed. People change as well, you know.' Even before Fiona's cancer took hold, at a time when upsetting her was not the cardinal sin it had become lately, there was only so much interrogation she would take before heaving the shutters down. 'You'll understand when you've lived a little,' she would say, tight-lipped, before issuing some order about the tea and the tidying of a certain disgrace of a bedroom.

It was back to this very place that Beth now marched, carrying a tray with three mugs on it and the stainless steel teapot. She was about to comment on how you could hear their brains ticking, when she trod on an old trainer, went over her ankle and literally threw the tray across the bedroom as if it was a Frisbee. The mugs, each with an inch of milk in them, bounced off Kate's bedside table, one disintegrating completely and another losing its handle. The third rolled to a standstill and paired up with the steadily emptying teapot. Kate barely had time to register the stain forming on the green carpet before she and Hazel were up out of bed and at Beth's side.

"Ooww," Beth's wail was one of genuine pain. "Hazel, for God's sake.How many times?"

"I'm sorry, I'm sorry," she squeaked, picking up the trainer and throwing it into the corner.

"Are you alright?" Kate was hauling Beth to her feet, trying with all her might to control the bubbles inside her.

Beth collapsed onto Hazel's bed, rubbing her ankle and knee which had been the first point of contact with the floor, but even she was suffering badly from the family failing at that particular moment.

"Don't you even *dare* think about laughing!" she quivered.

It was too much. Hazel and Kate fell onto the other bed, choking and snorting. They bumped heads which made things ten times worse. What was it about minor accidents that made them laugh more than any sitcom on TV? Beth rolled back on the bed, hugging her knees to her and failing to keep her grin from exploding out loud. None of them – Fiona, Beth, Hazel nor Kate – had ever been able to keep a straight face on such an occasion. Now, it was a Godsend, releasing the majority of the tension between them.

"Look at our carpet," sobbed Kate, gasping for breath. "What have you done, you muckle *elephant?"*

"And that was my favourite mug," wept Hazel, picking up the largest fragment of smashed crockery. "That travelled all the way from Dunoon."

"I'm sorry. But I could have broken my ankle. Look at this place."

"I know, I know. I'll get a cloth."

Kate began to gather together the decimated tea tray. Her laughter had dimmed to a smile, but her eyes were still twinkling when Beth finally managed to make it to her feet.

"I was just wondering what impression this place would make on him," said Kate, amiably. "Not a great one, I don't think."

"It's not the house he's coming to see, honey" replied Beth, then "God, that really smarts. And of course I still have the whole place to clean. Great. It had better be easier by tomorrow ..."

Beth's voice trailed off as she gingerly moved around, testing her injured muscles.

"You really think it's a good idea, him coming now?" Kate continued. "I mean, it really is ridiculous. What the hell are we going to say to each other?"

"Look, pet, it's irrelevant what I think. It's happening and he has a right, you know. They were still married."

Kate's face registered nothing but disdain, "Oh, come on. Don't use that one, Beth. Not with us."

Beth shrugged but did not defend her statement.

"So, when does he get here?"

"Yes, when?" echoed Hazel, appearing with a bucket and cloth. Beth continued to grimace as she hobbled her ankle back into action.

"The day before the funeral," she groaned, then more cautiously, "Monday afternoon."

"My birthday," stated Kate, then shaking her head, she whispered, "No way."

Beth ushered Hazel into the room with an impatient wave, "Hazel, can you mop up that mess before it really soaks in. And Kate," she sighed," he is arriving here on Monday afternoon any time around three. Yes, it's your birthday, and I'm very sorry if that makes it worse for you, although I'm finding it hard to see what could make this situation any more horrendous than it is already. So get used to it, because that is what is happening. I need a pain-killer. It's time both of you were dressed."

As Beth hopped out the door with as much dignity as she could manage, Kate's face burned a dark red, but she could not decide what annoyed her the most – this latest revelation or Beth's support of it.

"What's wrong with her all of a sudden? This is just brilliant." Kate felt more childlike than she had in weeks, but Hazel did not raise her head as she rinsed the cloth and re-dabbed the carpet. "I mean," gulped Kate, now pulling on her dressing gown, "Why is she mad at us? It should be us who are fuming. They kept us in the dark, decided what was best for us and then she wonders why I don't want him to arrive on my birthday."

"Well, what difference does it really make?" asked Hazel. "I won't argue that it's crap timing, but when is a good time at the moment?"

"It's my *birthday*," repeated Kate, "and I don't want him anywhere near. For God's sake, he wasn't there on the *actual* day of my birth; does nobody get what I'm saying? And what I don't understand is why Beth isn't with me on this one. Why is she on his side?"

"And why the hell are you being so bloody negative?" Hazel sighed. "You really cannot see anything good in this at all. What is your biggest problem with it?"

A thousand reasons fought to be number one, as Kate picked her way through the debris to the doorway, but all she could manage was her best 'I-don't-believe-you-sometimes' glare over her shoulder at her naive older sister. The hole she had felt inside for days now felt like a muscular pain, as if she had done one hundred sit-ups, then one hundred more. Food did nothing for her, she drank glass after glass of water to ease her aching head, but still she could not fix her aching body. So, on top of the physical pain, they were now going to pile this incredible mental torture. She was going to have to look at this man and make conversation with him; to watch Hazel fawn over him and giggle at him - it made her nauseous to imagine it. She was going to have to sit there, her insides twisting in agony, while remaining resolutely mute. Worse than all of this put together, she was going to have to do it without the aid of her mother.

Chapter 4

On Kate's birthday, the sun shone like it had been waiting for weeks to show off its brilliance, and Beth had tried to mark the occasion by serving breakfast on the picnic table which perched on the bank facing the bay. Gifts were handed over without much ceremony – a silver thistle for her charm bracelet from Hazel and money from Beth - but Kate thanked Kenny for the ink pen and for coming over to see her. He had accepted her gratitude with his usual waving away of fuss and pulled Beth onto his knee to take the attention away from his red face. For once, Beth did not object and kissed his cheek, settling into his lap. Everything was different now. Priorities had changed.

Fiona had wanted Kate to have her watch and had asked Beth to wrap it in tissue and place it in a box that Kate had once made her as a Mother's Day present. It was not really valuable, but Fiona had adored it because she had never seen another like it. It had a dark green face, the size of a poker chip, and a black leather strap. Fiona had loved the way it sat on her thin wrist and Kate had always wanted to find a similar one for herself. On receiving it, she had merely smiled at everyone and they had returned that smile, feeling that this was one thing that was right in all of this.

By mid-afternoon, Hazel was barely concealing her fevered agitation. She sat on the back door step like a five-year-old, knees bent and chin resting on them. Her hair, still wet from its vigorous washing routine, was pulled into a thick plait which hung down her back. The climate still welcomed her T-shirt and jeans ensemble and her trainers tapped an anxious little rhythm out on the gravel. Occasionally she chewed the end of her plait, then impatiently threw it back over her shoulder. Her eyes never strayed far from the road before her.

"I could have collected him from Glasgow, you know," she shouted into the house, "my driving's not *that* bad."

There was a shuffle and murmur from the kitchen.

"I said," yelled Hazel, "I could have gone -"

"We heard," said Beth, appearing at Hazel's shoulder and handing her a mug of hot water. "But David wanted to meet us all together. And with your hourly throwing up, he might have got straight back on the plane."

There was a definite "humph" from Kate as she stacked dishes.

"I can't help it," whispered Hazel, for Beth's ears only. "I've never been this nervous in my whole life."

"Well, get that down you," instructed Beth, returning indoors, "You'll be dehydrating next."

From her vantage point, Hazel could see the top of the hill road clearly. This was the only way into the village, which spread along the little bay, so she would be the first to know of David's appearance. As she sipped the tasteless drink, she listened to the lapping of the tide against the pebble beach and couldn't help blessing somebody for creating this near perfect day.

"He's seeing it at its best," she murmured, watching a heron pick its way among the sparkling pools. The sea shimmered in the autumn haze and the grass still had its green freshness. In fact, the bay was a whole spectrum of colour, from the red/gold leaves to the purple rocks and Hazel had to shade her eyes against it.

"Maybe I should have washed *my* hair," said Kate, joining her sister on the step. "But I couldn't really find the motivation." She suddenly looked at Hazel. "Do you think I'm being a right cow? I know you're excited, but I don't know what to feel like. I'm scared I'll really hate him and I don't actually want to."

Hazel's eyes softened as she pulled a stray hair from Kate's face.

"We're all in the same boat," she said, "I just think we could maybe make an effort."

Kate picked off a loose piece of rubber from the sole of her trainers and rolled it between her fingers. Her stomach was also churning, but it seemed irrelevant to the violent outbursts her sister was dealing with, so she didn't even mention it. She hated contrived situations like this, hated the fact that all four of them had probably rehearsed it in their heads and would therefore bound to be bitterly disappointed when it all fell apart in front of them. Would she even have a voice when the time came?

"I bet he's gotten really fat," she sighed, then mischievously, "and wheezy."

Hazel hooted. "Wheezy? Where did you think that one up from?"

"And wears a baseball cap," Kate grinned. "Or," she choked, "one of those flat caps, maybe a light blue one. And slacks, I *hate* that word. Yes I bet he wears *slacks*."

They rolled about on the step for a few more minutes, revelling in the sunshine and the shared moment, before the laughter petered out. Hazel put her arm around Kate's shoulder and she in turn leaned against her older sister.

"This is quite a big deal really, don't - " Hazel stopped abruptly and snapped her head in the direction of the hill road. A red car with an unfamiliar of logo on the side was slowly descending towards them. It was not a local car. The stillness between the sisters was tangible, before Hazel was on her feet, pulling Kate up beside her and following the car's painful journey.

"I think it's him, Beth," shouted Hazel. "Nobody around here drives that slowly."

The moment for reassurance had passed and Kate cursed her usual, poor timing. As she stumbled indoors, her stomach did a complete roll.

"I feel sick, Beth. Really."

"Kate," said Beth, facing her squarely and holding her shoulders, "If I have to clean that bathroom one more time today, I may have to retire into a dark corner.

Now come on," she hugged Kate tightly, "He's not a monster. He's probably three times as nervous as you. You only have to meet *one* person."

As aunt and niece emerged together into the glare, it was to find Hazel cracking her knuckles and staring at the stationary car at the foot of the drive. It seemed an eternity before the door opened and David Wilder appeared in front of them.

Their impressions were all so different, but none of them were complex. Kate thought he looked quite cool in his sunglasses, Hazel was surprised at his height and Beth wondered how on earth this man had the strength or will to take this particular step in the first place. She had spoken to him herself recently and there was no animosity between them. Now, her heart appreciated his plight.

From his relative sanctuary behind the car, David stood motionless, his breathing shallow but his gaze never wavering. Above him, were three women.Three individuals with independent features and separate identities, but each one displaying something of his Fiona. He let out a shuddering breath as he realised that the moment was upon him. The moment they had planned for the last six months. Yet what he had longed to experience might turn into his worst nightmare. Just as he was wondering if he would ever be able to move his legs again, the eldest of the three raised her left hand and gave a brisk wave. He closed the car door.

"Come on up, David," called Beth, then as an afterthought, "We're all glad you're here."

As he steadily made his way up the driveway, he faltered for a second to remove his sunglasses, and then continued on his way. He was wearing jeans, boots and a wax waterproof jacket. He must have been sweltering, but his face was quite pale. Beth disengaged herself from Kate and took a few steps towards him. They faced each other.

"I mean it," said Beth, genuinely and offered him her hand. He looked at it for a mere second, eyes crinkled against the sun, and then shook it.

"Beth. It's been a long time."

The effect his voice had on Hazel was immediate. Before Beth had a chance to agree with him, Hazel was at his side. He stepped back slightly, but his face was calm.

"Dad," she choked. "It's me. I mean, Hazel."

'He must have known that already', thought Kate, 'it's obvious you're the oldest. Anyway, he's seen you before.'

Kate was very rarely jealous of her sister, since they craved entirely different things in life, but when David looked at Hazel with that mixture of incredulous pride, and more than anything, *recognition,* she thought she might give up the fight and howl out loud. She took a step back nearer the house. David said nothing but put his hand gingerly on Hazel's head, before thinking he was being too familiar and removing it. She had not flinched.

"You're so tall," he said, loosely folding his arms.

"So are you!" blurted Hazel, "and not fat!" then gave him a quick kiss on the cheek. He followed this by attempting a tentative hug, which Hazel welcomed openly, but he all too quickly let her go before she realised he was shaking. Suddenly, Beth was back beside Kate, her eyes huge and brimming. Her smile was wide and she held her hand out to her niece, but Kate moved independently of her to where the couple stood.

'Do I want him to hug me like that?' She thought anxiously. 'He's never shown any interest, but he seems to care. Be generous, he looks okay.'

She knew what she was doing – she was talking to herself in order to halt the panic and genuine misery inside her. Hazel and he shared something special which she could never be a part of - a past. As if aware of this thought, Hazel reached out and took her sister's arm. For one dreadful moment, Kate thought she was actually going to *introduce* them to each other. But Hazel simply stood, linked to them both, willing them to do something.

Sad, green eyes, thought Kate. Anxious little face, his mind replied, tormented look.

It was not in Kate's nature to ever make the first move; Fiona had warned David of this. But something in his face caused her to try the slightest 'well-here-we-are' half-smile and he nodded his head. Then he took her hand in his.

"Hello, Kathryn."

He looked at her so easily and his hand was so warm, but somehow Kate had to take control of this situation.

"Hi," she replied, taking her hand gently away from him. She was like a child lost at a fairground, too scared to contemplate her circumstances, too intimidated to ask for help. Still, standing there in front of him at least allowed her to commit his three-dimensional face to memory. Until this point, she had only known one, flat, black-and-white version of this man. Young, smiling, but flat. Now she noticed that his hair was dark brown, not black and when it moved in the breeze, tiny strands of grey appeared. There was also a minor growth of stubble on his face, peppered brown and grey. There were lines on his face and a faint scar running from his eye to the centre of his cheek, all of which had been absent on his wedding day twenty-plus years ago.

"Are you okay?" David's voice was low. "All of you?"

"Better," replied Hazel. "Better now that ....well, better."

Something twinged deep inside Kate. Better. Did she mean better now that their Mum was finally gone? Hazel seemed genuinely relieved to see this man, happy even. What was this, National swap-a-parent week? Trade in a sick, spent model for a stronger, eternally sought-after one? Kate looked at all of them in dismay. Hazel was actually glowing, Beth was playing with the locket around her neck and David appeared to be relaxing before her eyes. Kate suddenly wished she could vomit at will and put an end to the atrocity of it all. Her voice stabbed a hole in the eager atmosphere.

"Do you want to see her? She's in the house. I'm pretty sure they haven't nailed the lid shut yet."

It was if she had electrocuted all three of them simultaneously, the air crackling as the smiles blew like fuses.

"*Kate!*" cried Beth, truly appalled. But Kate was already stumbling towards the open doorway. She didn't look back, but was aware of mumbled apologies and reassurances going on behind her. She went straight to her bedroom and slammed the door. Let his admirers deal with him.

She lay on her bed for a long time, watching the odd stray cobweb dancing on the ceiling. The breeze took it and played with it, never quite detaching it from its dance floor. She could hear voices in the kitchen and then the sitting room, but nobody came near her. She was relieved. The duvet beneath her spread heat through her body and her eyes grew heavy. She turned her face to the wall and gave in.

In the sitting room, David sat on the edge of the chair by the window. His long legs, bent at the knee, looked out of place in the compact room, which had always boasted too much furniture. He seemed to take up half of the living space and appeared very aware of it. He had taken off his jacket, revealing a plain open-necked shirt beneath a heavy sweater and was as lean as he was tall. Hazel seated herself on the sofa, watching his every move. Under such scrutiny, he was forced to stand again.

"Do you want a drink? I think maybe Beth…"

"No, no. I'm perfectly fine." He hesitated, looking from his daughter to the dazzling view outside and back again.

"I can't believe she said that," Hazel's voice was genuinely mystified and it seemed to rob her of all further words. Eventually, David swallowed his own dread and sat beside her.

"Hazel," he began nervously, "I want you to listen to me for a second." Pause. "God, you really have the same face after all these years. I had photos of you of course, but it didn't show … Sorry, that's not what I started out wanting to say."

"What is it?"

"Well, you must have wondered, I'm sure Kathryn did ..." he paused, the mention of Kate's name reminding him of her hostility. "It's just that I promised your mother that I wouldn't come here until it was over. She didn't want me to see her and she was adamant. It seems such a … cosmetic ..." words were beginning to fail him and he knew he was messing things up. He stood, frustrated. Hazel was also on her feet in a second.

"Don't worry so much," she said, sincerely, wanting to touch his arm but not quite accomplishing it. "Just say what you need to say. Or don't. We have plenty of time."

David crossed back to the window and Hazel saw his shoulders rise and fall before he turned to face her again.

"She didn't want me to come before. She didn't want to see me nor me to see her when she was ill."

"I know. Beth told me that."

"Oh right," he seemed surprised, but eager to build on her understanding. "She *begged* me not to come. And I know that agreeing to it makes me look spineless and weak -"

"It's okay, honestly," Hazel was beginning to feel out of her depth.

"No, it's anything but okay, Hazel. It stinks. The whole situation is beyond any sense that I can see. I stayed away for years. Years, and yes I could say that physical distance was the cause, or that it hurt less to let things slide, but I think it's because I was stupid and stubborn and proud. I don't even know why I'm trying to justify it, it cannot be done." He rubbed his forehead as Hazel stood helpless. She may be twenty and considered herself a fully matured woman, but this kind of talk was way beyond Hazel's experience and she risked appearing juvenile if she uttered a word. Thankfully for both of them, Beth chose that moment to enter the sitting room, her brow creased in the very definition of the Mackinnon frown.

"I'm just going to leave her," she addressed herself as well as the others. "There's no point in rushing it." Then to David, "I'm sorry if you found that outrageously upsetting, but I'm not surprised. Kate's always been a bit anxious when it comes to you."

Something flickered in David's face, a startled question in his eyes, which Hazel missed altogether and which Beth answered only with a slight shake of her head.

"I'll make us some tea," she continued, "or coffee? Or something a wee bit stronger?"

"Coffee would be great, thanks."

When Kate awoke hours later, her throat was dry and her eyes sticky. 'Wretched' was the word that kept coming to her mind, although only from books she had read, she had never uttered the word in her life. Her head ached where her left hand had been pressed into her sleeping scalp and she rubbed the spot gently as she sat up. It was dusk.

"Some birthday," she muttered. Her day was almost over, but to be fair it was never going to be anything but a date on paper this year. "A date to remember. A date for the diary. Oh yes."

Here she was, lying alone in her dim bedroom, while just along the corridor some lanky foreigner was probably holding forth, relating fondly remembered tales of his earlier life. His life with her mother. Kate was still struggling with the exact reasons behind his arrival. Her mother was no longer here and he was upsetting the dynamics of their group. Yet she didn't want to be the awkward, stroppy antagonist in this. She wanted to be on the same side as the rest of her family. Now he had appeared out of the ether and already she was on the outside. What did he want?

She checked her eyes in the dresser mirror. Not too puffy. But as she stared, she felt the familiar prickly sensation in her nose and her heart sank as the tears welled again. She had no control over this. She was strong, she was sensible; she understood that death was random. Hazel was the scatty one, the one who spoke her feelings before censoring them, the less capable of the two. They all appreciated that. So what was this?

Somewhere inside her, pain was thriving, but pain was a pitifully inadequate name for it. It was malignant, it was impenetrable and every now and again it sent out flashes of ice. Kate saw these as bright turquoise splinters and was aware of the path they cut through her flesh. Sometimes, she could catch her breath and force them back down into the black void that occupied her abdomen, where she kept them trussed up tight. More frequently, however, they were the masters. Now they had wrung tears from her eyes without her permission and as she wiped them gently with her palm, she wondered if she had offended the man by her outburst. She had seen his body flinch and his eyes crease up before she had left them reeling, but had no real clue as to what he was actually feeling. Because he was a *stranger* to her.

"Oh God!" she smashed her fist onto the dresser, knocking over perfume bottles and a photo of Hazel and Stuart. "Just stop. Just stop thinking for two seconds together!"

Kate shook her head wildly, as if to rid it of every endless, annoying, complicated thought. But she only succeeded in feeling dizzy and sick. Finally, she flopped back onto her bed and was caressing her temples when Hazel marched into the room.

"Don't start," warned Kate, noticing the set lines of her sister's mouth and cold expression in her eyes.

"Hey, don't mind me," replied Hazel, rearranging the disturbed dresser items, "I just came in to see if you wanted to join us for a cup of tea. But it's up to you."

"It's us now, is it?" said Kate. "Cosy"

Without hesitating, Hazel stepped back out into the hallway. "Oh, grow up, Kate," she replied, and left the younger girl at a loss for words.

Chapter 5
23rd September – Evening

"Kenny's here!" yelled Kate, as she emptied the washing up bowl of suds and debris, then "and he's got a suit on! Beth?"

"Eh?" cried Hazel, running through from the bedroom, towelling her hair. "He has, as well," she reiterated, pointing through the kitchen window at him. He gave a bow to his audience before entering the house.

"Well, look at you," laughed Kate and Hazel tried and failed miserably to achieve a wolf whistle. She was still trying to adjust her fingers in her mouth, when Beth arrived on the scene.

"That's my man," she grinned, looking him up and down. "And doesn't he brush up nicely?"

"Where you going?" asked Hazel, wiping her fingers.

"Skeabost," said Kenny, smugly. "No reason, before you ask, other than Beth deserves a treat and so do I for dressing like this." He bowed again.

"Okay, nice one," replied Hazel, "Well, I'm going out myself if you want to know."

Kate nearly dropped the plate she was drying at the implication that she would be alone with David, but before any more questions could be asked, the man himself appeared from the hallway. He had met Kenny only once, at the funeral, and felt that his presence in the house might be creating a problem, so he walked up to the local man and shook him by the hand for the second time. Kenny took the gesture in good part and seemed to think nothing of it. Before Hazel could open her mouth to ask why it had been necessary, Beth was in full swing.

"Right, Kenny, you and David go and have a dram while I sort the rest of the house out. Hazel, go and dry your hair or you'll be going nowhere. And remember to put that money in your purse."

As she had not been instructed to do anything, Kate stood by the sink, arms folded, watching the others obey Beth's orders. She looked at her aunt with a mixture of wariness and curiosity, wondering what was expected of her in this scheme. Beth, who was wearing a pair of black cords and a blue satin blouse, paused by the mirror to pull some excess mascara from her eyelashes. Kate waited patiently. Eventually, and with a brisk gesture towards the opposite chair, Beth sat at the kitchen table.

"Sit."

Kate did so, without drama or query.

"Right," said Beth. "This is what's happening – and don't interrupt. Kenny and I are going to Skeabost and we'll be back before midnight. Hazel and Stuart are taking David out for a drink, probably as far as Sligachan but that's up to them, maybe only up to Portree. And you are staying here."

Kate shrugged, not sure if a response was required. There was nothing about this arrangement that upset her or caused a problem, so she pulled at her earlobe and waited.

"Okay then," said Beth, rising from the table. "Good. I think I'll need a jacket."

"And that's it?"

"Yep, that's it. I don't think they will be late either, but you don't have to wait up if you're tired. I've finished that book you wanted to read. It's not too bad, a bit slow in parts. Anyway it's lying on my bed. And there's plenty of water for a bath."

Beth disappeared into the hallway and Kate looked around the tidy kitchen. No more chores to carry out and everyone obviously had plans. The evening was hers to do with as she pleased. A bath sounded appealing and the more she considered it, a night in charge of the TV would go down quite nicely. Yes, this might turn out very well.

Half an hour later, Beth and Kenny having already headed off, Kate found herself saying goodbye to Hazel as she and David climbed into the cab of Stuart's pick-up. It was either that or try to squeeze David into the Fiesta and that idea had been jettisoned early on. As the pick-up did a five-point-turn on the driveway, Hazel shouted that their destination was Portree as the mist was due to come in. Kate gave her the thumbs up and went indoors.

The sitting room was cosy and she noticed that David had filled the log basket, so Kate decided that self-indulgence was the key and that a hot chocolate was called for. By the time she had boiled the milk and failed to scrape the burnt patch from the hob, the fire needed feeding again. While it sparked and spat, Kate flicked through the three channels available and felt her enthusiasm begin to slide. Nothing on and the VCR was broken. She found a Big Country tape, one of Fiona's stalwarts and listened to that instead, sipping the chocolate-flavoured milk. A fishing boat was twinkling out in the bay, but now the house was too still and, eventually, Kate went in search of Beth's recommended novel.

There was no paperback lying on Beth's bed, but there was a shoebox. Kate looked under the bed and on the bedside cabinet, before returning to the shoebox and noticing a piece of A4 paper slid underneath it. It was Beth's writing.

'Kate. I know you are really struggling, so I'm trusting fate and leaving you this little treasure to look at. It's your Mum's diary from when she first went to Canada and I think it might help. If you were meant to see it, then you will now be reading this note and hopefully you will also take a wee peak at what's inside. He is not a bad man. See you later. Love B xx'

Kate was tingling all over, deciding what she felt the most – excited or aggrieved because yet again there were secrets in the household. She had always felt so close to Fiona and guessed she knew her inside out. But this might alter things to a frightening extent and she hesitated. She also shivered and told herself that she was missing the fireside, so she picked up the box and took it through to the warmth.

She sat with the box on her knee, still trembling a little. This was a huge opportunity, a really big deal and she realised that there was no way that Hazel knew about this or it would have been apparent. So, Beth had chosen her to look at it first. Well, there was no harm in opening the lid.

The diary was more of a book of notepaper, like a writing pad, but it had been customised on the front to tell who it belonged to and what it was:

FIONA MACK'S DIARY – DO NOT ENTER!

It also had daisies drawn in biro pen, all different sizes but all of the same design, covering the front cover and entwined through the title. It was dog-eared, but not full. The box smelled of age, it was the only word Kate could think of and the diary was alone in the box, which Kate found a little disappointing. But now her curiosity truly ignited, she threw another log on the fire, turned up the tape and began to read.

3rd August 1971
Well, the letter came today and it's official! I'm going to Canada! Can't really believe it. Some place near Duncan on Vancouver Island. Not much information through yet, but it looks like the Nelson family are quite grand – obviously why they chose me! There's a little boy – James – and she's pregnant again. I can't wait to go. It says I'll fly out at the beginning of October – even that probably won't be enough time for Dad to get used to the idea. What does he think I've been training for? To get a job here on Skye? I want to go somewhere strange, somewhere totally new, where they walk, talk and look different! And now I'm going!!
Weather:Bit muggy, thunder later on.

Kate was completely hooked. This was her mother speaking and she sounded so young. It was definitely the same Fiona though, the same determination and same breathless way of writing, as if she were speaking directly to you. Kate's nose prickled. She missed her so much and she had missed this particular Fiona for months now. She wanted to devour this whole book, so she kept reading.

9th October 1971
I'm writing this on the plane. Didn't like the take-off much at all – am sitting near the engine. Still, it's quite comfy and not too bumpy so far. The 'farewells' were a bit of an ordeal. Mum and Beth were covered in hankies and Dad was in a hell of a mood. For a man of 61, he acts like a complete bairn at times. Anyway,

by the time we said cheerio, he did at least manage a cuddle and to slip me some cola cubes to suck. Daft lad! So that's that. Vancouver here I come!

Later
Well this is my first night under the Nelsons' roof. They will give me the grand tour tomorrow along with the ground rules, which suits me because I really don't want to mess this one up. It was getting dark by the time we got here, but it looks an incredible place. I'm a bit fluttery inside and am sure this isn't really happening to me. The house is HUGE, has a lot of wood inside and out, like you'd imagine a Canadian house to have, but it's also a bit posh. Pillars, a wide staircase. Luckily, the Nelsons themselves seem down-to-earth, so I'm not too nervous. Time will tell!
Weather: Quite cold, but clear. Beautiful moon.

17th November 1971
Jamie is recovering slowly from his cold, but he's still a bit snotty. Mrs N, at seven months gone, was lucky to avoid it. She's starting to talk to me a bit more, and the house and everything is great, as good as I hoped it would be. Got a letter from Beth. She's changed the bedroom around, so she's not missing me as much as I'm missing home. Mum and Dad are still moping however, but not as much. Met a girl called Kathy at the Doctors today. She had heard of me – the Scottish girl! Anyway, she helps out a family in town (the Calders I think) and wants us to go out together when I have some time off. I think she's a bit older than me, but so what? Time I was shown the local talent. Bit of a non-day apart from meeting Kathy.
Weather:Quite a bit colder, but clear and sunny.

3rd December 1971
Took Jamie sledging today – brilliant snow, but c-c-cold! Mr N said we should go up to Lake Cowichan as it's beautiful there, but I didn't fancy driving up with just Jamie, so I borrowed Kathy and her charges and we made a day of it. The scenery was just beyond imagination. Kathy was surprised how much I commented on it, but she's lived here all her life (well, in Victoria) and she's used to big views. The bairns had a great time and Kathy said she would take me out over the Christmas holidays. I'm really looking forward to it because I know I'll be really homesick then. I don't think they put up decorations as early as we do. Hope I get some cards to go in my room. Tired tonight.Must be the fresh air. Mr N offered me a drink to 'warm me up' when I got in. I'm going to keep my distance there and that's all I'm saying.
Weather:Crisp, clear, snowy, sunny. Fantastic!

24th December 1971
Have just had the most brilliant day of my life so far! Mrs N said I could have tonight off if I would stay in on New Year's Eve, so Kathy and I got tickets for the

dance in town – the last two in the shop. I was complaining that I had nothing to wear so Mrs N gave me my Christmas present early – the most fabulous long denim skirt with buttons up the front. Felt pretty good with my orange mohair jumper and boots. Kathy was really jealous! ANYWAY, by the time we got there, it was packed. Didn't know anybody, but Kathy kept introducing me to folk. Can't remember half their names but they were all friendly enough. It was a right good do, and then it got INCREDIBLE! Hell. I'm going to need pages and pages to write this, but I don't want to forget any of it.

Once or twice, I caught this lad's eye, so I smiled at him and he smiled back. Now, we are talking seriously nice-looking bloke here. Most of the lads looked like shaggy dogs, but this one had short, dark hair and was wearing a checked shirt and jeans. He was just GORGEOUS! Really tall!! Of course, Kathy didn't personally know this wonderful person (typical) so I had to introduce myself! After I told him who I was and why I was in Canada, I think we blethered for about 3 hours non-stop. His name is David Wilder, he's twenty-three and he works for his Dad cutting wood. Lives about 5 miles up the road. God, we talked and talked (Kathy got a bit fed up because I wasn't dancing) then we bought each other a drink and had to sit really close together to hear ourselves over the band. He said he had seen me in town before! He's obviously not the pushy type, because I would have remembered if I had seen <u>him</u>.

His eyes are amazing! He has this really deep voice and maybe it was the Canadian accent, but he could have told me he was a mass murderer and I wouldn't have given up my seat for a second. Then we had the last dance together. He must be at least 9 inches taller than me and smelled just, oh I can't think of the word, but I know what I mean. Have honestly never liked anyone so much <u>so quickly</u>. Kathy was very good about the fact that he wanted to run me home, since I had practically ignored her all night and she was dying for the details! Anyway, he did drive me home (in his big truck!!) and I was actually shaking I was so nervous.

I thought I'd better tell him that I was only eighteen, in case his mates gave him a hard time, but he just shrugged and said it would be worth it. I nearly crumpled into a heap right there and then. Of course, I didn't dare invite him into the house, but he didn't seem to mind, and asked if he could see me again sometime soon!!!!!!!! I could hardly answer I was grinning so much. I gave him the Nelson's number and he wrote down his on my hand. Then he kissed me quickly and told me to get going. None of that pawing or pleading or threatening. I felt safe and excited at the same time. I wonder when he'll phone. It's after one o'clock. Can't sleep. MERRY CHRISTMAS!!

Weather: Who cares? Fantastic, brilliant, unbelievable day.

In her engrossed state, Kate had edged herself forward in her seat and was now almost rocking on the balls of her feet. Her back was prickly with perspiration which she only became aware of as she closed the notepad. This was a revelation, she could not deny it, but she was unsure what surprised her the most. The enchanting situation which was unfolding on these pages, the fact that David appeared to be an attractive proposition or that her mother was this young, excited, compelling youth. Kate had never had a serious boyfriend to date. She had been on the verge just before Fiona had first become ill, but then had had no time for anything so superficial. Now, she caught some of the anticipation in her mother's words and wished to read on. But she desperately needed a drink.

Returning from the kitchen, with a brimming glass of apple juice, she noticed that Fiona's bedroom door was ajar. On his first few nights on Skye, David had slept on the sofa bed in the sitting room, while Fiona still lay in the house. But since the funeral, he had occupied her bedroom, and for the first time Kate wondered how he felt about this. Quietly, as if to conceal her actions from herself, she pushed the bedroom door wider and switched on the light. Thanks to the central heating it was warm, but there was still the slightest hint of antiseptic in the air and now there was a suitcase in the corner, some alien accessories on the dressing table and a suit hanging on the wardrobe door. Kate let out a long breath, left the apple juice on the hall table, and walked into the middle of the room.

No essence of Fiona remained, but the wallpaper, bedding and pictures were all comforting in their own way. On the dressing table was a toilet bag, a UK roadmap and some of the photo albums from earlier in the day. She knew each of them by heart and so felt no reason to revisit them, but she picked up the toilet bag, looking for some personal item of David's, anything that marked the type of man he was. There was a possibility that she had judged him too readily, basing it on her own assumptions rather than his actions, and now she needed to find more clues to his character. Was he as genuine as the others thought he was, or even as marvellous as her mother had perceived him? The bag yielded nothing except a brand new razor, still in its wrapper.

A further glance at his suitcase was also fruitless and even though this might be her only chance, she could not bring herself to look in any of the drawers or his suit pockets. She must look only at what she had been given and trust in Beth's 'fate'. Kate re-assembled the room and returned to the haven of the sitting room.

Chapter 6

31st December 1971

So, the day I'd been waiting for all week finally came. I was so nervous I was actually sick after tea. Hope that doesn't happen too often. David arrived about 8.30, so I had time to introduce him to Mr and Mrs N before they left – really weird since I'd only met him once myself. However, Mr N knew David's Dad. It turns out he's quite a big businessman and they're on some committee together. Anyway, they got on alright. It was a wee bit awkward, but David (bless him) had put on a tie. Mrs N seemed quite happy when they left. Jamie never stirred and we just picked up our conversation from the week before. I put some Eagles on, but when the record stopped, I didn't put on another. Didn't need it. Talk, talk, talk!

He is so great. It's that simple. He laughed at my jokes for a start! I'd only really seen him in the half-light before, but now I noticed everything. His hair is dark brown and his eyes are pale green, not blue. He told me all about his family, so I showed him photos of Mum, Dad and Beth. He said Skye looked very impressive – this from a man who lives in BC! We didn't have a drink until later on because I thought I was blethering enough as it was. So then we both had a beer and when the clock struck midnight, we toasted each other. I was going to risk everything and kiss him then, but _he_ did the honours and God, what a feeling! Every time we stopped, I started again and for once, I wasn't worried what that made me look like. I _wanted_ to see what would happen next! In the end, David put another record on and said he wanted to dance with me like the week before, so we danced and held onto each other. It was lovely. I loved being folded up in his arms. Hope this doesn't read like a hospital romance, because it's what I was feeling. He stayed until the Nelsons came back and we all had some coffee together. I think Mrs N was quite impressed. I must write and tell Beth. I want a photo of him first though. He's going to ring at the beginning of next week. I wish it was the beginning of next week now!

Weather: Stormy. Snow and ice. Hope David is a careful driver.

There was an entry for every day, but they varied in length and some of them merely stated what the weather was doing or how long it would be before Fiona next saw David. Kate read every single one of them. The fire now burned low in the grate, but she was oblivious, lying diagonally on the sofa, her stockinged feet resting on an ancient antimacassar.

19th January 1972

Weighed myself this morning and I've lost 10lb in three weeks!

Can't help it, just can't eat a thing. I'm so jittery all the time. Mrs N says its love, she recognises the symptoms! She's just jealous because she looks like a balloon. Only six days to go and then I'll have two wee ones to look after. Must admit, they're the last thing on my mind at the moment. Dave phoned after tea and he wants me to go over to his place on my next day off! God, I feel sick just writing this. I mean, meeting his family. What if they take an instant dislike? What will I wear? Dave says to bring my thick boots and he'll take me up to the Lake again, but that means I can't wear a skirt and if I wear jeans they'll think I'm a scruff. Help! Sent letter and photo to Beth, with strict instructions not to show Dad.Its bad enough Mr N making the odd comment, without Dad getting all worried, writing serious letters. I'm on my own with this one and I like it that way. It's just me and Dave together.

Weather: Stopped snowing, but very cold. Dull.

23rd January 1972

Miriam Jane Nelson born at 10.23am. 9lb 4 oz with black hair on her head and shoulders! It's been complete chaos at the house and I can't have tomorrow off to go to Dave's house. Not happy. This will make a great impression on his folks!! Have postponed it for now and am too annoyed to write any more. When will I see him again?

Weather: Cold. Miserable.

12th February 1972

ONE TO REMEMBER!!!!

Where to start? First of all, got a letter back from Beth saying she thought Dave was lovely looking (good taste) and that Iona Murray was <u>having</u> to get married – to Plug Johnson! What did she see in him? Anyway, finally got to go up to Dave's house and it was a really fabulous day, all sparkly and blue and white. He collected me, cos there's no way I could drive myself up there safely, and I nearly died when I saw him. He jumped out of his truck and looked HUGE! I mean, the biggest pair of boots I'd ever seen, a massive quilted jacket and this hat with ear flaps! I couldn't believe that this great big handsome man was there to pick me up, but then he grinned at me and I was gone!! If he's going to keep smiling at me like that, I'm going to become a complete walk-over. But he's so UNBELIEVABLY CUTE!! Why hasn't he been snapped up long ago?

So, Dave's house is a real home, smaller than the Nelsons but still a fair size. It's wooden-panelled too, with a verandah, and is set in a bit of cleared forest. His Dad's a timber dealer and I met him, his mother and his brother Neil, who looks like he's still at school. He's a right laugh. They were all really friendly, but I only really relaxed when Dave took me up to the Lake. He held my hand! The sun and snow were blinding and my feet were perished, but when Dave kissed me again, I just went crazy. I actually had him pinned against a tree at one point and he looked really startled. So then, like a complete bairn, I burst into tears – told you this was one to remember! He gave me a cuddle and asked me what was wrong.

I tried to explain to him that here he was, doing everything right, how I imagined my ideal man would act, and I was spoiling it by behaving like a rampant maniac. He was busy objecting (he's so lovely) and then I blurted out that I couldn't help it, I loved him so much. Well, that was a show-stopper! He didn't say anything else and I thought I'd really blown it, so just to put the icing on the cake, I started babbling. Told him I realised that the word love was easy for some to say, but that I'd never said it to anyone before which must mean it was a big deal, and that I thought about him all the time and that I couldn't eat. When I finally shut my mouth and looked at him, he was grinning again! Thought he might be making fun of me, so more tears came and I sat down in the snow! Just sat down!

That's when it happened. The anticipation in writing this is killing me. Here goes. David pulled me to my feet and shouted to the sky, "MARRY ME THEN!" Just like that! I think in my high anxiety I made him say it again – and he was serious. So what did I do? Started blubbing <u>again</u>, then jumped on top of him and said yes! Can't even begin to describe how I felt. My chest was actually sore! We kept laughing and whooping and running round in circles like demented folk. Then he sat on this log and I sat on his knee and kissed him and kissed him. He told me how he was feeling, said a lot of private things which I don't want to write down – no need to, I'll never forget them. Did say I was beautiful more than once though! Anyway, we agreed that it was too soon to tell anybody. The Nelsons would think I was leaving and Dave's folks would think we were rushing. As for Mum and Dad, they would completely crack up.

Still, by the time we got back to his place, I'm sure it was obvious something was going on. We tried really hard not to give anything away, but I kept laughing loudly – hope I wasn't too ridiculous. Dave drove me home late, and I was so out of it, I couldn't keep my hands off him. I don't think he minded too much! I wish I could be with him all the time now, but we have to be practical. WHY? Anyway, I've written too much for one day. But maybe this is what a diary is really for, not just for reporting on the post or the weather or who has got the flu. Sitting here in bed, almost bursting with excitement. Just realised I forgot to give him his Valentine's card in the chaos. Won't see him before the 14th now. Will <u>have</u> to tell Beth or I'll go mad. Wish Dave was here.

<u>*10th March 1972*</u>
I'm nineteen today! I'm writing this at lunchtime cos I want to get all the little details out of the way before I report on what happens tonight! Opened the parcel from home – nice presents.Necklace from Mum and Dad, thick scarf and a letter from Beth. She swears she won't tell anyone, but sounds about as excited as I am (wants to be my bridesmaid). She's going to the Scout disco with Iain Richardson – thank God I'm not thirteen again, being groped in the Scout hall.

Yuk! Making a cake this afternoon for tea with the kids. Miriam's colic is a bit better so roll on tonight!

I'm back. Things never happen the way you expect them to and since meeting Dave, they always turn out even better. He picked me up at about seven and instead of taking me out for a meal, took me back to his place where his Mum had made us something to eat. Neil was out at some swimming gala and Mrs W (Rose) was very keen to go to the pictures for some reason, dragging Dave's Dad out of the door. She was smiling a lot!

So, we had our meal, which was lovely but was still not hungry. Then Dave gave me my present. A ring!! A single beautiful ruby with a diamond on either side. He said it was up to me whether I wore it in public or not and admitted that his Mum had guessed what was going on. She was very happy! I could hardly thank him I was so choked. Also laughing, excited, weepy, agitated. All I wanted was for Dave to feel the same, for the pair of us to share it all, so there was only one thing to do. All those months of being frightened just disappeared as soon as I made the decision.

It was fine, quite relaxed. He promised he wouldn't hurt me and he didn't really. It didn't matter anyway because when he was holding me, saying my name, I was the most important thing to him in the world. Knowing I could make him this happy, whenever I wanted to, was worth EVERYTHING. I think it will get better. I love him so much. So, it's behind me now, the big question mark. I wonder what Mum and Dad would make of it all. They'll say I'm too young, but you can do anything when you feel like this.

Kate's face burned red. Surely Beth had not meant her to read this far. Was she really supposed to have this knowledge? These were the feelings of her parents at the beginning of their lives together and it was one thing to share this face to face over a glass of wine on your hen night, but this felt underhand. These were heart-felt words, probably not meant to be viewed. Yet it all made sense. Beth was trying to ease the tension between David and Kate by showing him how Fiona regarded him. It was cheating really – it was underhand on two levels. Still, Kate shifted position on the sofa and read on.

24ʰ May 1972

Mr and Mrs N now refer to Dave as "your David", but don't seem threatened in any way. They would if they knew about the ring!! Miriam has nappy rash and is not letting me get much sleep at nights, but she's still a wee cutie. Kathy dropped by for half an hour with gossip from town. Apparently, Dave and I are a topic of conversation! The gist is that the Wilders think I'm a nice girl (what a title!) and that Neil has been mouthing off, saying David has finally got it together. This got the old brain working a bit and since Kathy never knows anything IMPORTANT, I decided to go early to Dave's and speak to his Mum.

She seemed delighted to see me – I think a houseful of men gets to her after a while. Anyway, we talked about the ring and what our plans might be, and I asked her why there hadn't been a queue of girls after Dave. She said there had been one or two who were keen, but it was all or nothing in everything he did and he was always looking for something different. Got to write down what she said next – "I knew when he stopped eating and started shaving regularly that something huge was going on". We had a good laugh at that. Felt really close to Rose then, hope we never fall out.

Later Dave wanted to know what she'd been saying but I'll keep him guessing a bit longer. Really wanted to stay with him tonight. He's the person I want to be with, not a bad-tempered crying baby. Wish we could get married tomorrow.

29ᵗʰ August 1972

I can't stand this. I just can't face him with it. Pretended I needed an emergency dentist appointment this afternoon and Mrs N let me drive the pick-up. Rose was in on her own and as soon as she saw me, she bundled me into her car and drove up to the Lake. Couldn't stop crying, still can't. But when we got there, and I'd calmed down a bit, it all just came pouring out.

Told her how terrified I was and that I had absolutely no idea what to do next. I said that I loved Dave more than anything in the whole world but I would rather leave than disappoint him. I'm not sure how much sense I was making, although I did say that at least Dave trusted me enough to know that it had been completely accidental. God knows what she was actually thinking, but she was very kind. She cleaned up my face and took me back to the house for some tea. She said she would tell him. Bloody hell!

I left before he came in and went to bed as soon as I got home, saying the dentist had given me a splitting headache. Cried and cried and cried and have just woken up. I'm writing this at 12.15am and I want to see Dave. I miss him.

30ᵗʰ August 1972

Day off. Stayed in bed. I'm so tired! It's now 10.45am and nobody has called. I'm going to have to go home to Skye and face up to it all there. That will be the real challenge, not for me but for them. What will they say, they don't deserve it. How can things change so quickly? And how can it possibly hurt this much? What will I do if I can't see my Dave? He's all I want.

He's been and he loves me!! I don't care about anything now. It doesn't matter what the Nelsons say, or how much Dad rants and raves. Dave loves me and his family are behind us all the way. His Mum only told him at lunchtime and he came straight over, and then forced Mrs N to let him see me! He stayed all day, said a lot of special, private things and made me wear the ring for all to see. I love him.

I won't let one person make us feel ashamed. We'll get married as soon as possible. The biggest cloud is Mum and Dad. It turns my stomach when I imagine their reaction, but it's done now. It's nearly midnight and I can't write any more. Dave says not to worry, so I won't. I'm not scared when he's there.

13ᵗʰ September 1972

Dad isn't coming over, so there's no way Mum and Beth will make it. I'm not going to think about it, it's up to them. To be honest, I'm glad I won't have to face him, the phone was bad enough. But I don't want him hating Dave, this was my choice. Kathy can be my bridesmaid.

I belong to Dave now. Have started thinking about the baby too – it's something else I can give him. I know it'll be different when it's my own, but surely I'll cope? Mrs N was in tears again at tea-time. Can't decide if it's <u>still</u> the baby blues, the fact that they have to look for another nanny or if they will actually miss <u>me</u>. But they're coming to the wedding. Jamie knows something is going on – hope he won't be too upset. Mr N asked me if I would do an overlap with the new girl, which of course I will, then I'll move over to Dave's house. If it wasn't for Mum and Dad, I'd be completely content. Every time I'm with Dave, I love him more and more. He's looking after me already and I know he always will.

Kate carefully put the diary on the floor and turned over on the sofa, staring at the pale orange embers of the fire. The tears which had started a few pages earlier had run silently under her chin and dripped steadily onto the cushion, soaking it through. She made absolutely no sound, but still her eyes leaked hot saline. Her heart was at its lowest and it had been very, very low before.

If she had been asked to clarify her angst, she would have blamed it on the hope that was evident in her mother's words. Fiona had trusted in her future and had loved this man completely. There had been no reason not to. Kate knew she would have followed the same path, because so far he had not done anything wrong. She thought of how they looked on their wedding day, smooth-featured and glowing, and she pulled her knees up to her chest and hid her face in her arms.

Chapter 7

Only when the back door banged, did Kate open her gummy eyes and instantly panic. She prayed that it would be Beth and Kenny, but she heard Hazel's distinctive shriek about needing the loo and her feet fleeing in the direction of the bathroom. Kate had time to wrap the diary in her cardigan and kick the shoebox beneath the sofa before managing to hobble on a dead leg to the door. Without looking back down the corridor, she shouted 'hi' over her shoulder and headed to her bedroom. There, she deposited the diary under her bed, blew her nose on an old tissue and made sure the worst streaks on her face were rubbed off. Then she wrapped her cardigan tighter around her cold body and went out to face them.

David and Stuart were still in the kitchen, the older male leaning against the sink while the other hovered by the kitchen cabinets, probably looking for mugs. So Kate rushed through to the sitting room fire and tried to revive the embers amongst the ash. It was freezing and Kate wondered if she should just cut the night short and go to bed. The previous night she would have done just that, but now she hesitated. In the last three hours or more, she had learned about the man in the kitchen, from the person who had known him the best. Not from Beth's opinions or Hazel's blind acceptance, but from the only real connection she had with him – her Mum. Now, she was curious and perhaps the slightest bit more open-minded. So she threw another log on the fire and unfolded a sheet of newspaper across the front of the fireplace to try to get it to spark back to life.

"Are you having a tough time, there?" David asked. Kate didn't turn at his words, but nodded and cleared her throat.

"Sorry, I fell asleep and it's more or less gone out. Mum always used to do this, something about the draught. Usually it caught fire."

"You want me to try?" It was a bold question on his part, since invariably she snubbed him. But maybe his evening with Hazel had convinced him to give it another go.

"Yes, okay. I'm useless, as you can see." She handed him the double sheet and he got down on his hunkers beside the fireplace. As he manoeuvred himself closer, ensuring the draught only came from below and not the sides of the opening, Kate stood back slightly and looked at the lines of concentration on his face. "Did you have a good night?"

David glanced at her once, his eyes bright, then immediately went back to the task in hand. But he smiled as he spoke.

"Yes. I enjoyed it. And luckily for me, your sister doesn't put up with silence of any kind."

Kate smiled in return. "I never could decide if its awkwardness she hates, or whether she really does have stuff she wants to say *all the time.*"

The fire had begun to roar back to life behind the stretched paper and before it caught alight, he removed it, folded it up and put it back on the pile beside the log basket.

"Whatever it is, it helps."

Now he gave the fire a nudge with his boot and piled two smaller logs onto the one Kate had thrown on.

"Looks like it's worked anyway," he stated.

"Thanks."

Kate suddenly noticed the sodden cushion squashed into the end of the sofa and she made a big deal of plumping it, turning it over in the process. She then sat and was about to make a comment about not having Hazel's flair for conversation, when her sister appeared at the door.

"Oh, you're still up. Great. I'm guessing it'll be tea for you then. Tea for Kate, Stuey!" she yelled down the corridor.

"Right," came the reply.

"I *might* have wanted coffee," Kate said, affably.

"Well did you?"

"No."

Rolling her eyes, Hazel sat on the fireside chair and rubbed her arms. "It's freezing in here."

"I know," apologised Kate, "I fell asleep and let the fire go down, but Dad revived it."

"Good job he's here, really," she said, then cringed slightly and looked at Kate for a reaction. There was none.

"Where did you go?" asked Kate

"Just the Royal. It was okay, bit cramped. They had a singer in, if you can call her a singer. At least nobody had given her a microphone."

"She wasn't that bad, Haze," Stuart entered carrying a tray.

"Stuart, you have no concept of what makes a good singer, and you know that," she replied. "I'll get some biscuits."

"She's so hard on you, Stu," laughed Kate, as Hazel disappeared. "Why do you put up with it?"

"She's only like that when there are other folk about," he said aloofly, then laughed at himself. He shrugged, "Because I'm used to it?"

"And guess what?" Hazel was back. "Mr Ellis was there. He had this ridiculous leather jacket on, and some woman with him. Is he married? Anyway, bet you wish you'd come with us," she teased, throwing Kate a biscuit.

"What's this?" grinned Stu. "He's an arse, Kate. Bloody useless at football."

"Does he still play?" munched Hazel, "Is he not a bit old?"

"How old is too old?" asked David, amused.

Kate's face was scarlet, which Hazel could not ignore.

"Look at her," she said, amiably. "All I'm saying, little one, is that if you'd come with us you'd have realised that outside of school, he's not that impressive."

"For God's sake," cried Kate, "Shut up! I don't fancy him or anything, he's ancient. It's just that out of all them, he's somebody … you know. He's smart enough to make us lot laugh."

"Calm it," conceded Hazel. "I'm just pulling your strings. Hey! Tell you who is worth looking at. That new barman. Not my type obviously," she patted Stuart's knee. "But not half bad."

Kate was seething, but refused to be drawn any further into this. Deliberately, she turned to David who was perched on the arm of the sofa, which he always seemed to favour. Kate wondered if it made him feel less conspicuous, as his legs took up a smaller amount of space.

"Do you hear what I have to listen to? What was it you were saying about her runaway mouth helping?"

Hazel's eyes widened in surprise at her father's apparent betrayal, but Stuart chuckled. David had the grace to look shamefaced for a second then spread his hands and said, "I stand by what I said."

"And what was that exactly?" Hazel accused, tucking the chocolate biscuit into her cheek.

"He said you were completely incapable of keeping your mouth shut – or words to that effect."

David jumped to his feet as Stuart guffawed, spilling his coffee.

"I said no such thing!" he cried, but laughter was playing at his mouth. "I said that you were not afraid to fill in silences, which was a *great help!* I swear those were my words."

Hazel looked from her Dad to Kate to Stuart then back to David, mock indignation stamped on her features. Then she sat back, picked some stray crumbs from her jumper and sipped her tea. "Well, that is a true statement, with which I cannot argue. I am sure it was meant in good faith. I forgive you, Dad."

David made a great show of mopping his brow and retook his seat as Stuart wrapped his arm easily around Hazel's shoulder, their dark hair merging and getting lost in each other. Kate, who was now positioned on top of the damp cushion, relaxed back as far as she could into the sofa's lumpy embrace. The fire crackled as it found a fresh piece of wood to destroy and Hazel threw her biscuit wrapper on as extra fuel.

"Ah, silence," said Kate.

They all laughed, maybe a little too loudly, but they were still in the early stages of familiarity and hopefully it would get better.

David felt almost light-hearted in this company, and he could only put it down to Kate's budding cordiality towards him. Although he could give no reason for it, it was a welcome change and now he began to see her as others did; serious, but capable of wit, and with a very contagious grin. He hoped he would now see more of it. At that very moment, however, Kate yawned audibly and pulled herself up from the sofa, scratching her neck.

"Well, that's me. I'm knackered. See you all in the morning – well, not you Stuart obviously."

"Obviously," tutted Stuart and Hazel punched him.

"Night."

Kate heard them all murmur the word in reply as she exited the room, and for an instant felt almost sad to be leaving. The experience had been reasonable and as much as she had objected to 'the whole situation' from the beginning, it was now easier for her to dismount from her high horse and face it head on. But Fiona's diary was calling and with any luck, she would have a good two hours before Hazel came to bed.

24th December 1972

Exactly one year tonight since I first saw my Dave, and now he's lying sleeping beside me. He's growing a beard but nothing else has changed. All he has to do is grin at me and I am away! I am pathetic. I mean, before I met him, I was quite a strong, sane person. People in love used to drive me up the wall. No wits about them. Now it's happened to me and I babble and giggle and carry on like the rest of the loonies. What I can't believe is that I'm married to Dave, when surely the rest of the world must want him. He's mine. HA HA!

Opened the card from home tonight, not sure what to expect. Beth's letter was typical – concerned but mainly curious. How was sex, pregnancy, marriage – in that order! Does Dave snore? Cheek! There was a letter each from Mum and Dad, which were much better than expected. Season of goodwill must have rubbed off a bit on Dad, because he was <u>nearly</u> apologetic! He's a bit disappointed at how things have turned out, but he misses me and wants to see <u>us</u>. That was a nice surprise, don't know when it will happen though. Mum's letter was more practical. Was I getting enough exercise/rest/healthy food? Tonight, I miss them all. I'll phone tomorrow. Rose is great. Instead of feeling snubbed that they didn't come to the wedding, she wants to invite them over again, so that we can all get to know each other before Dave junior arrives. We'll see.

25th January 1973

Started decorating our room today. Couldn't stand that grey diamond wallpaper any longer and had quite a bit of stripping done before Rose came to see if I was ill. After her initial doubts – 'you're too pregnant' – she agreed to leave me to it as long as I didn't stand on any chairs or anything. The walls look quite good, so I'm just going to paint them. Dave thinks I can't do it – bloody cheek. Yellow or green, haven't decided yet. The room next door can be baby's room eventually. It even has an adjoining door!

Learned today that Neil is adopted – I did wonder at the age gap. Rose wouldn't go into detail (because of the impending birth!) but there were complications after Dave and she lost two other babies before giving up on it. I think they adopted Neil for Dave's sake and he took it to heart. They're very close for being 8 years apart. I wonder if he likes sharing Dave with me. Seems okay. Dave junior is wrestling with somebody tonight – I'm as tight as a drum.

24th March 1973

Miserable, unsettled day. Rose and Pete took Neil to Vancouver to get his spine checked (it's got some slight twist in it) and Dave was out from 7.30 till after 6 – 'Dad left me in charge, Fee'. Then my Dad phoned to say that they had sat down and tried every possible way, but they just can't afford to come over this year. We were both upset, with me crying which was not fair on him. I don't want them to get into debt, but I really want to see them. Was guilty as hell when I came off the phone, and with nobody about, I moped and cried all day. Dave wasn't much help when he eventually did come in, although he tried. I'm such a bairn at times, NOTHING was going to cheer me up. Came to bed early.

27th March 1973

The best news, and it's all settled! Dave, me and the wee one are going to Skye as soon as we've all recovered from Dave junior's arrival. I knew something was going on, Dave and his Mum have been talking quietly to each other since my depression set in three days ago! (I'm SUCH a cow). Anyway, they decided that the three of us should go home and tie up all the loose ends of our situation. I told Dave he was a brave man, showing his face to my Dad and for a split second his smile disappeared! It will be fine. They'll be more interested in Grandchild Number One anyway. Can't wait to see them all and show my Dave off to everybody. Must lose the weight first though.

Suddenly realise how much I depend on Dave and his family now. But I love him totally, so why shouldn't I let him do things for me? I'll always do what I can for him, although it's not much at the moment (!) Don't know how much longer I will write in this diary. Dave is feeling left out since I won't let him read it and I doubt if I will have the energy after the Big Day. We'll see.

Kate paused, adjusting her bedside lamp and looking to see how many more pages were used. Her heart sank slightly as she realised that there were indeed very few left.

19th April 1973

Well, I did it!!! It's 2.25pm and Dave is wandering up and down the ward, cradling his wee daughter. She's exactly seven hours old and Dave can't put her down, God bless. We've decided on Hazel Rose Wilder. Rose after Rose (obviously) and Hazel because it's a tree! She's got brown hair, blue eyes (which apparently might change) and very often a purple, crumpled face. Don't know how I feel apart from sore and very tired (8lb 3oz!) Also relieved, full of love for Dave and therefore his baby. Can't believe she's ours, or that I got through it, but I did and we're all okay. Will phone Mum and Dad in a minute (hope they *weren't dying for a boy) and tell them we're all coming over. Want to see them now!*

It's now 11.30pm. Dave has finally gone home and I've tried to feed Hazel. Don't know how successful it was but she's sleeping now and everything is dark and quiet. Oh, Mum and Dad were so delighted, especially that we are going to visit. Can't wait.

Have decided that this will be my last entry.Seems a grand note to end on. Also, in the short time that Hazel's been here, I've turned into a nervous wreck. I'm trying not to think about how I'm going to keep her safe and I think writing about it could do me more harm than good! Apart from that, keeping a secret diary suddenly seems childish. Still, I'll hold onto it, and maybe Hazel and her brothers and sisters will have a good laugh at it in time. At least they will know how much their Dad and I loved each other.

If you ever read this, Dave, this is for you:

From the very first second I saw you and we spoke, listened and laughed, I knew you were special. You make my life exciting, worthwhile and very, VERY happy. I hope I can always show you how much I love you.

By the time Hazel came creeping into the bedroom, Kate had stashed the diary under her pillow, switched off the light and was facing the wall, feigning sleep. She had heard Beth being dropped at the foot of the driveway and then her chatting with everyone for a moment before retiring. She had listened to David clean his teeth and close the bedroom door behind him. She had even been aware of Hazel and Stuart's murmuring turn to something more urgent before he at last drove home. Yet she was no nearer sleep than she had been an hour ago.

She had been trembling intermittently since coming to the end of her mother's testimony, but she had not cried again. She was devoid of tears, but not emotion. Her whole head was buzzing, the blood whooshing in her ears, but she made herself lie motionless until Hazel finally breathed slowly and regularly, signalling that sleep had overtaken her.

Kate now sat upright and considered her options. There was no way that she was going to drift peacefully into slumber in the near future. A glass of water might help but she dare not risk the chance of meeting David, not now that she had so much more knowledge of him. She needed time to arrange her thoughts and try to separate them from those of her mother before she allowed herself to become more comfortable with him. There was only one thing that she could do tonight. True, Beth was probably sleeping but she had started this. She had unlocked the secret for her and now she might be able to help.

Kate crept into the hallway and listened for any sound whatsoever. Before she could move further, however, Beth's door opened and she saw her aunt standing there, as wide awake as she was. She smiled conspiratorially and beckoned her inside.

"Thank God you're -" whispered Kate.

"Shh!" hissed Beth and pulled her into the middle of the room before closing the door very slowly. She pointed to her bed and Kate crawled beneath the duvet, pulling it up to her chin and adjusting the pillow so that she could sit upright. Beth crept over to join her and indicated that they would have to be very quiet. "He doesn't sleep terribly well," she whispered, "I can hear him wandering about sometimes – and his light is still on."

Kate nodded and then relaxed back into the pillow. She waited until Beth appeared comfortable and then looked at her in despair.

"Did you ..?" asked Beth.

She nodded again, her lip trembling. Then, "Have *you* read it?"

Beth sighed. "I read it a long time ago, when your Mum was at her lowest. You were about three and she was struggling with everything. Then I read it again last night and wondered if it could possibly help us in any way. Do you think it's made a difference?"

"So it was specifically to get me to look at everything in a new light?" Kate's voice was very low. "*Him*, in a new light?"

"I'm not that smart Kate," Beth smiled. "I thought it might show you that she loved him. You never really got a chance to ask her the important things. And I thought it would be nice for you to hear her voice again."

Now the tears rolled again. "It was," sobbed Kate. "It was."

Beth took her in her arms and cradled her, stifling Kate's worst sobs against her shoulder. She let her shake and shudder against her, allowing herself a few tearful moments, glad that Kate had come to her. But there were no more words spoken that night. When Beth woke in the grey light, Kate was still there, their hair tangled together, and she had no feeling whatsoever in her left arm.

Chapter 8
4th October 1993

"How much longer?" Kate enquired.

"What she really wants to ask is 'Are we there yet?'" piped up Hazel. "But if there's one thing Kate can't stand it's a cliché. Needs them like a hole in the head!"

Hazel screeched with laughter at her own joke, while David sort of laughed through his nose without actually snorting. Kate merely shook her head.

"Yes, you're a comedian, sister. Hope this place is ready for your constant wit and banter."

"Oh, they'll be amazed. And full of admiration, I think."

David glanced sceptically at Hazel from the driving seat. "About forty minutes to go, Kate. Roads shouldn't be too bad at this time."

Kate settled herself into the leather of the back seat, marvelling at the size of the gigantic car, which he kept calling a SUV. From what she had seen in the last hour, this was typical of this country. It was scaled up – by a lot.

Skye was home and most certainly worthy of comment in terms of landscape. When Kenny's family had driven up from the Borders the previous summer, they had toured the island with them, out of courtesy as much as anything. Kenny, Beth, Hazel, herself and a fit, active Fiona. Out of seventeen days, only one had been wet, two misty and the remainder had put the rest of the UK to shame.

They had camped at Glenbrittle, ascended minimal amounts of Cuillin, both red and black, and of course climbed Ben Tianavaig more than once. The highlight had been the Sunday they had parked at Sligachan and trekked over to the Fairy Pools. Hazel had dragged along a protesting Stuart who, within minutes of exiting the car, had developed vast amounts of enthusiasm for the whole trip and dismissed Hazel's moans about synthetic socks and blisters with the words, 'If you knew they're bad for blisters, why did you wear them?'

Fiona had taken photos of every view from every angle, trying to include people for scale. By the time they had walked the last few steps up to the clear, aquamarine pools, the whole company had been a little browner and a little more in awe of the island, even the islanders themselves.

Skye was home. It could be black and jagged, it could be white and dome-like or it could be green and rocky. Some days you couldn't see your hand in front of your face, but it was always both familiar and remarkable. Canada appeared to have similar features but it was magnified. The roads, the cars, the views. From her seat, Kate was unable to see the tips of the hills unless she leaned forward. Were they hills or were they mountains? Either way, you needed to see the summits to appreciate them, the shape of them against the sky and the contrast of colours there, otherwise you may as well be looking at a wall. She sighed and wondered at the logistics of this whole trip and how it was going to work out.

Hazel had practically bounced her way across the North Atlantic. Since David's arrival she had made no languid movements whatsoever. She ran, she fidgeted in her chair, she talked faster than was humanly possible and she fell out with Stuart because he 'wasn't keeping up.' She had shown no sign to date of running out of fuel.

Kate had watched this from as close as she allowed herself to be, without commenting much at all. Beth had initially pleaded then demanded that Hazel calm down, that she was exhausting everybody and finally in desperation had shouted, 'you're making yourself look like a major nut-case in front of your dad.' All had achieved nothing.

David meanwhile had taken part in this pantomime with a mixture of congenial disbelief and paternal awe. Since reading the diary, Kate had scrutinised him continuously, albeit from behind a paperback or amongst groups of well-wishers. To her critical eye, he had been frequently surprised, troubled, amused, intrigued and grateful. He wore all of his feelings on his face, which provoked her a little. She was also mystified that this stranger showed every emotion so openly with people he had only just met. He rarely followed up his facial expressions with words and the assumption that a laugh or a wince was enough had irked Kate more than she had known why.

Conversations had settled into a pattern of sorts, where Hazel or Beth would spin a yarn, and David would react accordingly, throwing in the odd acknowledgement or whistle or superlative. More often than not the others would answer him with 'I know! But it's true.' Kate had joined in after a while, deciding that it was easier than trying to maintain a significant distance; easier on herself as well as him.

Two days after Kate had consumed the diary, Hazel had gone into the kitchen to make coffee, followed by Beth who had suggested that possibly something with less caffeine was a better option. Kate had dropped her magazine at her feet at once.

"How come," she had started, as David looked as if he might be rising to look out at the sun on the water, "your face shows so much of your feelings?"

He had regarded her for a moment, and then thoughtfully sat back in his chair.

"Do you mean my face in particular, or are you talking about the human race in general?"

His lack of confusion had thrown her off course for a second. She had expected an 'excuse me?' or similar. But he had heard her clearly and clearly had not been afraid of a discussion.

"Yours specifically," she said firmly. "You show how you're feeling all the time. Have you always done that? I mean, I don't know you well, if at all, but your face keeps telling me what you're thinking."

David had continued to look at her, his eyes showing more amusement than his mouth, which was a straight line.

"I hadn't realised I was being watched so closely. Looks like I'll have to be more careful." He had paused and scratched the back of his ear. Kate had waited patiently, still wanting an answer. "I was aware of my, em 'habit'," he had eventually continued. "Your mother pointed it out to me time and again. Although interestingly, she didn't see it as a fault."

Panic had set in then and Kate had jumped up, her face turning pink. She had felt compelled to leave, even if it was rude, because it had been far, *far* too soon for them to discuss Fiona. She had hesitated, trying to think of an excuse but had failed and had headed for the door anyway.

"Kate!" he had called after her, hoping she would stop, if not turn back.

She had indeed turned around, if only to see what his expression had said. For once, his face had been a complete blank and she had feared he might be making fun of her. But she had remained there, peering at him from behind her fringe. He had sat forward in his chair, his long legs bent at an unearthly angle at the knee, and had cleared his throat.

"God knows, I've got little right to talk to you about anything. I'm sorry if you don't like what you find here but I can't start playing games just to win your favour."

"I don't want you to," Kate had cried, upset. "Maybe I just wish you said more. This is the most I've heard you speak, I think. You just make faces most of the time."

"It's not easy," he had frowned, pain fleeting across his face but staying in his eyes. Again, this had been left to Kate to interpret.

"But remember," he had continued, his voice strong again although he had not been able to look at her, "Letting people see a reaction doesn't mean you are telling them what you're thinking. I've got tight reins on that one."

At that point, Kate had thrown her hands in the air. "I have no idea what you mean! I can't see the difference. You're not making any sense to me."

"Well, I - "

Kate had bulldozed over his words. "How can you sit there and say you shouldn't play games with people and in the next minute tell me that what your reactions show isn't the same as what you're thinking. That's complete rubbish!"

David's face had not altered from the impassive expression it had adopted since the start of her tirade but now he shook his head.

"That's not what I said."

"That's *exactly* what you said," Kate had spluttered, but had sat down at last, ready to talk, "and don't look at me like I'm a child and can't understand. Or talk to me like I don't matter. Don't do that."

64

At that point, the sitting room door had opened slightly, but had been pulled back shut abruptly, amid whispered enquiries and chinking crockery. Both David and Kate had held their breath, but nobody had appeared. When Kate had turned back to him, David had looked mortified, his eyes wide from her last pronouncement. Before he had been able to address her concerns, she had thrust a finger towards him.

"Do you feel as horrified as you look, or is it just a game? See that face you have on now? Tell me what it means. Tell me what you're thinking."

"I'm wishing that we had never started this," he had muttered, then, "Kate, I'll explain exactly what I mean in a moment. First, what's with the 'you don't matter' comment? I need to know what would make you say that. Is that the way I come across?"

Kate had sighed and leaned back on the sofa. "No, not really," her voice had been weary. "I wouldn't blame you anyway; I've been a right cow. Sorry. It's just that I always feel crap when I'm feeling left out. It's my own fault."

There had been a few moments silence then, each of them waiting for the other to comment. When it had not happened, Kate had raised her head to find a look of anticipation on his face, which had made her smile a little.

"Thing is," she had admitted, "I didn't really want you to come over here. I mean, I *really* wasn't keen at all. Sorry if that offends you and don't be all understanding and say it's to be expected or anything because that doesn't change the fact that Hazel was desperate to meet you and for some reason even Beth was in agreement. But I didn't want it."

Kate had watched him carefully as she explained all her doubts and grievances which had set her apart from the people she had needed the most. He had accepted with empathy that he had made her feel worse than was fair and that being at loggerheads with the others had compounded it.

"But did I ever imply that you didn't matter?" David had repeated, again looking disturbed.

"Okay, no, you didn't really. It was everybody else. I kept asking them why after all this time you had to be brought over and nobody would give me a proper answer. Hazel could never understand what my problem was and Beth kept saying it was what Mum wanted. Of course, she wasn't there to ask, so I just had to accept it."

Kate had looked him straight in the eye then.

"But you must know the reason, Dad."

He had bitten his lip and the bleakness she had seen as he had scanned the photo albums returned.

"I - " he had croaked and immediately cleared his throat, moving once again to his favoured retreat by the window. She had waited until he composed himself.

"Look Kate," he had said finally, his face still safely hidden from her. "There are so many reasons, but if I told you all of them now, together, it would make them all less significant. They are all individually important. If you can let me away with feeding them to you over time, you will realise what your mum was thinking and why she orchestrated this. I know you're not a child and *of course* you matter. Just believe me, it should all make sense eventually."

Kate had sighed, "But I would like to understand it while you are still here! I mean, that way I might get to ....like you better, while I can still see you and talk to you."

David had then turned to face her.

"But we'll have all the time we need."

"Why? How long are you staying?"

David's face had become instantly still, apart from the creases around his eyes. He had held up his finger in a 'just-a-minute' gesture and had walked over to the sitting room door.

"Beth!" he had called down the corridor. "A minute of your time, please."

There had been a frantic screech of kitchen chairs on tiles before Beth and Hazel had both bumbled into the room. Hazel had rushed over to Kate, fearing the worst and had been batted away. David had collared Beth at the door.

"She doesn't know yet. Does Hazel?"

"Know what?"

"Know what?

"Oh Lordy, what have you said?"

And so Hazel and Kate had learned of the Grand Master Plan.

Fiona, in her lifetime, had been the creator of many a 'Master Plan'. She had thrived on them - decorating the bathroom, creating the raised veggie beds in the back garden, the Photo Wall, all with home-made frames. Now, just days after they had laid her to rest, her *Grand* Master Plan had been unveiled to its final two participants. If any of them had come across a copy of the GMP written in Fiona's right-sloping scrawl, they would have seen the following:

The Grand Master Plan (GMP)

1. David to arrive on Skye for the funeral and to get to know Hazel and Kate.
2. After introductory period, David to return to Vancouver with Hazel and Kate for a holiday – to last as long as they want.
3. This to allow the following to happen:-

    a) Relationship to develop between H & K and David.
    b) Change of scene for girls following last morbid few weeks.
    c) Beth to have some quality time with Kenny and to decide which steps she wants to take next (wish I could be here for that one!!!)
    d) H & K to meet the Canadian side of the family and fill in the gaps.
    e) Let David enjoy company of H & K. He deserves it.

As it was, this had to be explained to the girls by Beth, with David chipping in occasionally. The pair of them had dealt out the questions equally, sometimes calm, mostly loud, until the subject had been done to death. Tea had been drunk, sandwiches made and consumed and yet it was dark by the time all four of them were on the same track. Beyond surprisingly, there had been no tears or accusations. It had ultimately appeared a reasonable idea to all, perhaps even a GMP worthy of its name.

Kate's main concern, apart from Beth's ability to cope without them and her forthcoming Higher exams, had been the fact that they would be leaving Fiona behind. She had been visiting her daily and felt it was just a bit early to stop. Hazel had had a minor blip in consideration of Stuart, but it had passed. Beth had appeared to be relieved to have it out in the open. David on the other hand, had looked drained of life itself at the very prospect. If the convoluted and misunderstood conversation he had just had with Kate was anything to go by, he did not stand a chance of surviving it.

So here all three of them were, in the country that only two of them had been born in, in the midst of Autumn – or Fall, depending on your inclination – driving through a spectacular palette of shades. Kate's eyes however were growing gritty from watching the great outdoors and she settled herself, before closing them altogether.

Hazel's continuous chatter could not prevent the sensation of her mind slipping and, having negotiated the sea of pink prawns, Kate had arrived at the top of a large electricity pylon, looking down on the toy landscape of green and gold. She grasped at the metal upright for support and it morphed into Fiona's upper arm.

'I've got you,' cried her Mum, reaching for her hand. 'But now we're up here, what can you see baby? Look how huge it is, how colossal. Those trees go on for miles, Katy.'

'Where's Hazel?'

'Oh, she couldn't come,' her mother laughed, 'But we don't need her. Let's see what we can find.'

The air was citrus clear as they flew over the trees, but Kate wanted to feel the mossy earth under her feet. Below them, between the vast turquoise lake and the Christmas tree forest, she could see a replica of their cottage. It was on fire, yellow flames bursting out of the roof and dark smoke polluting the air from every broken window. However, before Kate could point it out to a seemingly unconcerned Fiona, it had sparked into the trees and roared up the side of the mountain like a cartoon.

Kate immediately opened her eyes, swallowed and tried to slow her breathing before anybody commented on it. However, Hazel's voice had not altered in intensity or flow, so she had gone unnoticed. After a moment, she sat forward, leaning between the two front seats.

"Three miles," said David, his eyes not leaving the road. "You can catch a glimpse of it before we go into the wood, but you'll have to be quick. I'll tell you when."

"You mean the house, Dad?" asked Hazel, wiping her passenger window.

"The house and the river. You can see that already down to the left. River Cowichan."

"I'm on the wrong side," moaned Hazel. "What's it like Kate?"

"Can't really see it, think I might need glasses ..."

Five minutes later, David slowed the truck down as they approached a ninety-degree bend in the road. "There," he pointed, checking his mirror and easing down another gear.

As he slowly negotiated the bend, a clearing appeared in the thick conifers to their left, across the deep ravine caused by the river. Both girls strained to look and were awarded with a two-second glimpse of the square, white-painted building that was known as The Edge. There seemed to be an incredibly steep conduit, adjacent to some dilapidated steps, leading down from the back of the house to a platform on the riverside, but other than that, it was entirely surrounded by trees. Kate barely had time to register some square windows near the eaves before it was once again engulfed by the wood. Both girls were still craning their necks when David's voice broke the silence.

"Remember, that's the back of the house. There's a lot more to see at the front."

"It's huge."

"It's massive."

They spoke together, Kate in honest awe and Hazel wanting to assure David about the appeal of the family estate.

"Yes, well, it's big enough for *us*."

"No, really Dad, it looked fantastic. Can't wait to see the rest."

"Actually," continued David, reassured, "The only reason you get to see it at all from the road is that we needed access to the river at one point. Plus, I suppose it lets a bit more light into the back rooms."

Still facing the rear of the car, Hazel made a 'bloody hell, did you see the size of the place?' expression to which her sister's face replied, 'I know. Didn't realise.' She then rubbed her hands together excitedly and turned back.

"What?" laughed David.

"Absolutely nothing at all.Brrr, it's getting colder I'm sure."

"Well, this is the main entrance now," announced David, and swung the SUV through the gates.

Chapter 9

"Stop! Stop! Look," cried Hazel, pointing back at the gateposts through which they had just driven. "Oh, Dad, slow down a bit, we're missing important bits of this."

"What?" he smiled, "It's not as if you won't be going through those gates a hundred times a week." But he slowed down anyway, and reversed back along the hard standing of the driveway. Kate opened her window, letting in a blast of frosty air and leaned out to survey the source of the excitement.

The two gateposts, which bore no actual gate, were of rough, red-brown timber, approximately two foot by two foot and stood at least eight foot tall. The central portion of each post had been intricately carved into Celtic knots on all sides and made them appear almost like totem poles.

"Blimey," breathed Kate, "bet that took ages. Must have been really complicated getting all the sides to match up."

"Not that I would know," said David, easily. "Give me a fence to erect or a hen-coup to build at a push, but that kind of work we leave to Neil. The man with the hands."

"Well, they're amazing. We'll need to take some photos of them."

"Can we go now? Your Grandma will have seen the truck from the top of the house and will be about to call out the search party."

"Sure," said Hazel, as they continued along the driveway. "Who's Neil?"

"Neil. Your uncle Neil."

"But I thought you said he lived over at Port ....Albert."

"Alberni. He does. The posts went up years ago."

"Did Mum see them?" Kate's voice was nothing but curious.

"No, she didn't."

"Pity," added Hazel. "They would have been right up her street."

Before any more could be said on any matter, the house side-stepped into view and simultaneously the girls leaned forward and said, "Mercy on us!"

"I thought the back was impressive ...."

"Look, the verandah must go all the way around ...."

"It's amazingly clean for being painted white ...."

"Is that Gran? Is that her?"

"That's her," grinned David, breathing a mental sigh of relief of gargantuan proportions. Now, he had an ally.

Rose Wilder was standing at the head of the wooden verandah steps, one hand on the railing, the other holding an ancient wooden stick, which appeared to be the only things keeping her upright. As the truck pulled up in front of her and the girls tried to ease their way out of it without taking their eyes from her, Rose painfully negotiated one step at a time. Her face crinkled in degrees of agony and her breathing was ragged. She wore a floral apron and a straw hat.

Kate felt embarrassment creeping up her throat and moved closer to Hazel, who watched in dismay before turning to David.

"Dad?" she faltered, when she took in his folded arms and the fact that he was now leaning against the SUV, watching the scene unfold. He shaded his eyes against the low sun to take in the full performance and shook his head slightly at the marvel of it all.

"Dad!" Hazel's voice was now a sharp half-whisper. But he stayed her with his hand, and then refolded his arms, smiling.

As she put her weight onto the final step, Rose suddenly leaned forward and guffawed into her knees. Her straw hat fell to the ground, something which seemed to add to her inability to stop laughing. "I'm sorry," she choked, literally jumping down onto the gravel and throwing her stick into the shrubbery. "I tried to resist the urge, but it was too great. Your face, Davey boy!" Again she hooted and held her hands to her hips, allowing herself another few seconds of breath-catching and eye-wiping, before she composed herself and tore off her apron. She was wearing a T-shirt which read 'I Love Scotland'. It looked new.

"Oh, girls, you'll have to excuse me. But I've had a long time to think of this moment and I got to wondering what you might be expecting. It was just too much of an opportunity to appear like a dottery old matriarch, gathering her family to her side." She turned to David. "And your face. Do you like the apron? I found it at the back of the laundry cupboard. Ugh, mothballs. So," she turned to the dumbfounded females, "you going to introduce me or what?"

"I may just do that very thing, Rose," said David, "if you give me a chance to get the words out."

She pooh-poohed him with her hand and walked over to Hazel.

"Well, I know you, Hazel Rose Wilder. Still got that look in your eye. The one that made us all very nervous! Remember me?"

"I might, you know," Hazel acknowledged, delighted by the lady in front of her. "I remember that hat anyway. Will that do?"

"Good enough," beamed Rose. She immediately turned to Kate. "And if I didn't know any better, I would still place you as Fiona's girl. Kate isn't it? Or Katy?"

"Kate," replied Kate, and offered to shake her hand.

"Don't need to shake your hand, missy. I'm your Grandma, not some maiden aunt, in spite of first impressions!"

Rose allowed herself one last chuckle before she pulled both girls into a tight embrace.

"Well, here we all are," kissing the head of both in turn. Then, releasing them, "There's only one rule. Do not call me Grandma, or any derivative thereof. I haven't been called Grandma for seventeen years and I can't face it now! So, just call me Rose – he does, don't you boy?"

Rose and David embraced quickly.

"Welcome home, son."

"Always great to be back, Rose – quite a show you put on there."

"Wasn't it?" she agreed, happily. "Let's get in. The coffee's on already and we can unload later. Okay, ladies?"

*　*　*　*

"Here, let me," Rose reached over and took Kate's watch from her, "you're all fingers and thumbs."

"I think it might be jet lag ...."

David had left the girls in his mother's capable hands while he had gone to retrieve the suitcases and 'make a few calls.' Hazel was wandering around the large sitting room, looking at every photograph on display. She would take her time over some and skim over others. There seemed to be an inordinate number of them on show, and Hazel shoved her hands into her cardigan pockets as she took in more and more of them, her head drooping gradually as she toured the room. Kate meanwhile had tried and failed to adjust the time on her watch. When Rose handed it back, Kate looked at it.

"Rose, do you think we could phone home and let Beth know we've got here?"

The older lady pushed the plate of biscuits across the coffee table to Kate and said, "Sure honey. Although I think that's one of the calls David was thinking of making, I'm sure he'll call you to the phone when he gets through."

"That's fine," accepted Kate.

Having completed the circuit, Hazel now stood in front of the fireplace, warming her hands. "I suppose you have to have huge fireplaces. It must get really cold. Ours is tiny."

Rose smiled and refilled the mugs. "Why don't you sit for a while, Hazel? I like to look at your faces."

Hazel obliged, picking up her coffee again and reaching for a biscuit. When Rose smiled, her eyebrows tended to go up slightly, and suddenly Kate noticed the resemblance between her and David. She however had sandy hair, grey blended with mid brown, which was pulled defiantly into the tiniest ponytail Kate had ever seen, while remaining still thick and shiny. The lines on her face were soft, like folds rather than crevices and she had a surprisingly lithe figure for a woman in her early seventies. Kate supposed running this house kept her active.

"So," began Rose, sitting forward in her chair opposite the two girls. "How are you both doing? Really?"

"Fine," answered Kate, far too hastily, then giving Rose a little leeway said, "Well, okay. I think."

"I don't need to tell you how desperately sorry I was at the news. Apart from the fact that your Mum was so young ..." Rose seemed to stop herself, then

"Well, you two shouldn't have to experience something this big at your age. There's time enough for that."

Hazel's eyes were now huge, hiding behind her coffee mug. She had yet to acknowledge the initial question and now looked utterly desolate. Kate was about to offer her a word when Rose spoke again.

"Hazel. Don't fight it, honey."

"I'm not. I don't. Honestly, it comes and goes and sometimes I *can't* cry. But looking at the photos. That one of Mum ...."

Kate got up and followed the direction of Hazel's gaze. The photograph was in a ring of six, all with identical frames and it showed Fiona sitting on an overturned log, the dazzling snow making her screw up her eyes. To Kate, she looked incredibly young, younger than either Hazel or herself. She appeared to be pointing her finger at the camera and laughing.

"Pete took that one," nodded Rose, "and the reason she is laughing is that David had just tripped and fallen his length. Twisted his knee, if I remember rightly."

"She looks really happy," murmured Kate, noticing that the photo was of the same quality and age as the rest of them, and seemed always to have been there, not just positioned for their sakes. She felt an odd mixture of satisfaction and sadness at this. Perhaps they had missed her; perhaps they had looked at that image regularly and wondered how she was.

As Hazel tried to explain how her emotions were a law unto themselves, Kate quickly scanned the rest of the room. The wallpaper was flock, but not overwhelming, and of a light rust colour. There was a shelf of some sort which ran the whole perimeter of the walls, about a foot below the ceiling. On this were a few small trophies, a number of china figurines and a collection of glass paperweights. Kate noted that there was no actual colour scheme to the room, and that it housed a diversity of fabrics and styles which did not particularly suit each other or any of the knick-knacks. Still, it was homely and warm and Kate had never been a stranger to old-fashioned furniture. But nowhere were there photographs of babies or toddlers.

"... so even now it just doesn't seem like it's done and dusted. I mean, when Dad was there, that sort of took over from everything else. And now Kate and I are over here. But it feels like we didn't finish anything properly at home."

"At last," breathed Kate.

Hazel looked at her selflessly. "I know. You kept trying to explain that's how you felt, but I wasn't listening. Now I see her again, in a different place, and I'm more heart-broken than I've ever been. We can talk about her to you, Rose, but we can't all have a conversation together, you, us and her, and I would have liked that."

"Oh, honey," sighed Rose, "I would have liked that too."

"What have I missed?" asked David, strolling into the room as Kate was about to ask Rose if *she* had spoken to Fiona in the last few months. It went unsaid, and David grew aware that the atmosphere had altered since he had left them an hour ago. If he felt uncomfortable, he did not show it, and Kate wondered if he would be much better at hiding his feelings now that he was back at home. "Rose?"

"Well now, David," stated Rose, "I think that maybe there is still a lot of grieving and talking to be done here. But nobody is going to force it or ignore it or walk away from it. These two deserve all the attention they can stand from us while they are here, and they are in charge."

Although his expression had sobered, he did not even hesitate to confirm this. "Absolutely. This is all about healing."

"For all of us," added Rose, as she got up from her chair. "Now, did you get through to Beth?"

Both girls looked at him expectantly but he shook his head. "No answer. I'll try again in an hour."

"Okay, boy." She headed to the door. "Now stay here and warm those hands. The radiator up in that office is not what it should be."

Kate smiled to herself as Rose retreated. David may be more at ease in these surroundings, but it didn't mean he ruled the house. Before any of them spoke again, he did indeed make a point of trying to revive his hands in front of the fire. Hazel rose and stood next to him, shivering as if to show the reason behind the action. She too put her hands out to the flames. They stood with their backs to Kate for a moment or two.

"You cold, Hazel?" he enquired.

"Just a bit weepy, really. Always feel cold when I'm miserable."

After a week in each other's company, he felt able to put an arm around her shoulder, and she leaned into him as they turned back to face the room. Kate smiled faintly in their direction, picking at the brown moquette of the sofa. But now that there was a lull in the proceedings, she wanted some answers.

"When did granddad die?" she asked.

David thought for a moment then, "Nearly six years ago. Yep, the winter of 1987.Doesn't seem as long as that," then he dropped his arm and spoke as if to himself, "Wow, Pete's been gone six years."

Hazel scowled at Kate and she shrugged apologetically. But she continued along the path she had started.

"I just wondered how you start to make changes. You know, what you do first. Do you try to remember everything, every detail, for as long as you can, or do you just do what you always do and hope that the memories come along in their own time?"

Hazel was now re-seated, glaring at her sister, but Kate was having none of it.

"Stop looking at me like that, Haze. Dad just said it's all about healing, so I'm just wondering how we start. God, you never give me the chance to have one thought of my own."

"It just came a bit out of the blue, that's all," explained Hazel and looked up at David. He appeared to be waiting for them to sort out the issue, looking from one to the other with his clear, green eyes. But now Kate sat with her head down, defeated.

"Kate's right. I've been through it. What do you want to know?" encouraged David, now moving away from the fire slightly as the heat seeped through the back of his jeans to his skin.

"I just wondered," she repeated firmly, frowning at her sister, "How it works. What did you do when Granddad died? I suppose you had work to take your mind off it, but Rose must have been lost without him."

"I missed him at work and at home. Your Dad is such a big part ..." he began then halted, startling himself at the implication of his own words.

Kate stared at him whilst he rubbed his forehead, her heart seeming to fold itself up like a piece of origami. She could feel the creases in it being sharpened as she fought off all manner of reproach. Days ago she would have launched herself verbally at him, but now all she felt was bitter disappointment that he had voiced such a statement. It felt like a huge step in the wrong direction, and they had all been trying so hard. But to his credit, he did not leave and he did not attempt to diminish the effect of his words by covering them up or excusing himself. He stood exactly where he was, looking down at his feet, chewing his bottom lip. After a moment, he looked straight back at her.

"Well, ok, if you say so," Kate's voice was non-committal.

"Aw shit," murmured Hazel, then to the room, "Look, I'm sure we've all got a load to say on the subject. Me, I'm cold and tired and to be honest, if you both think this is the time to open negotiations, then I'll have to leave you to it. I need to sleep and you ..." she pointed at Kate "...are as white as a sheet."

"Yes," agreed Kate, surprisingly, "that's how I feel. Maybe we can phone late on tonight, Beth won't mind what time it is over there and I'll probably be chattier by then."

"Sure," said David. He looked and sounded broken, but still did not turn away from them or sit. He appeared to have more backbone than Kate had first imagined.

Hazel touched his arm as she crossed over to the hallway, "I'm going to tell Rose we're going for a nap. See you later, Dad."

"See you," he replied.

Kate stood and faced him. If he could show courage then she could match it at least. His eyes never left hers as she approached him, but they did crease slightly as if in preparation for something unwanted.

"This is hard on you," she stated.

"Yes," he breathed. "but not just for me, Kate."

"It shouldn't be so hard. I'm sorry."

She hugged him then and realised that it was for the first time. He smelled of smoke from when he had lit the fire on arrival and she remembered the night he had rescued her pitiful fire on Skye. Well, there was their first memory to share.

"See you later, Dad," she said, moving away from him and telling herself that if everybody was open-minded and listened, then maybe something could be achieved from this trip. There had to be very good reasons behind the whole separation catastrophe. They just needed to thrash it all out together.

"Get some sleep," David said at her departure, hoping that their last exchange signalled another positive step forward.

Chapter 10

The first two days at The Edge seemed a bit out of focus for the youngest two generations of Wilder, due to lack of sleep and desperately trying to adjust to each other's company in yet another setting. David, who had already missed a fortnight from work, seemed torn between accompanying the sisters everywhere and dealing with phone-calls and mail. Eventually, on day three, Hazel sensed his agitation.

"Look Dad, we don't mind if you have to go to work. Seems ridiculous – and lazy, actually – that you're still taking time off. It's our holiday, not yours and somebody has to keep this place going."

"My sentiments exactly," agreed Rose, clearing the breakfast dishes. "Do what you need to do. We promise not to talk about you …much."

"There are just one or two things that *can't* wait," he explained, reaching into the hallway for a padded jacket which hung there. "Once I get those sorted, it will just be a matter of dealing with anything urgent and letting Rob take on the rest. His shoulders are broad enough."

"Whatever you think," Rose replied. "Out you go and earn us a living. Out!"

"I'll see you later, you two," he paused just long enough to ensure that both girls were reasonably happy with the morning's turn of events, then headed out the kitchen door, yelling, "Don't let her boss you about. She thinks she rules the world."

"Thinks?" she laughed, watching the brimming sink, "thinks!"

Kate wandered over to the kitchen window to watch David leave. He walked differently on his home turf, taller and with a definite purpose. She surprised herself when her nose prickled and her eyes filled up a little. How had this man coped with the task of two weeks in a strange place, under the worst circumstances, trying to ignite such a fundamental flame? He had appeared capable at the time and so she had never considered the magnitude of the mission. But he was so much stronger here. As she watched him check the security of the tarp on the old truck, she felt herself expand inside. She did not love this man, but she thought that perhaps she could admire him. Fiona would not see admiration as a betrayal, she was sure of that. Hazel appeared by her side.

"What you watching?"

"Just him going."

Hazel suddenly hammered on the window and they both saw his startled face break into a wide grin as she waved her farewell. He gave an open-handed salute and climbed behind the wheel of the truck. Kate moved back to the table, wondering if she would allow this man to affect her in any further way or whether this holiday would change very little.

Rose was an expert at being inconspicuous. Or maybe she just wasn't used to having company during the day. Either way, she was humming to herself, engrossed in drying dishes.

"Do you have a cloth, Rose?" Kate asked, shyly. "I'll wipe the table."

"Thanks dear," smiled Rose, wringing out the dishcloth and handing it over, then, "Hazel, go and scrape that lot onto the mound for me, please, honey."

The mound was the name bestowed upon the collection of organic materials heaped into a wooden pallet behind the garage, next to the converted outhouse. Converted implied that the oversized shed had been refurbished and put to contemporary use, whereas in fact it consisted of the removal of the WC unit and the storage of every piece of rusty or obsolete equipment from the household or barn. Next to these buildings stood the garage, its doors permanently open. It was used to house the vehicles in the winter and was relatively free from clutter, a situation Hazel marvelled at as she passed by, balancing the breakfast leftovers on the plate.

The garage at home was so infrequently used that the adjacent clematis had climbed over the metal door and settled itself there. No car, in Hazel's memory, had ever crossed its threshold. The side window was so thick with dust, cobwebs and other unmentionable excretions that you could not actually see inside and it was an unwritten rule that only items which you had *absolutely* outgrown, but could not be thrown out, were stored there. Once goods had been deposited in that vault guarded by creatures of varying numbers of legs, they did not come back into the house. When Kenny's niece had visited, mention had been made of a pair of pink roller-skates to be found there, but not one person had had the inclination to scavenge for them. In the end, they had taken her along the shore, where she had looked at shells and prodded crabs, an altogether more pleasant option.

Having carried out her task, Hazel rinsed the plate under the external tap, but instead of returning to the kitchen, she made a tour of the exterior of the house, wandering along the lawn below the verandah. This was the third time since her arrival that she had done this and she knew that she would do it again and again. Hazel loved this house, but not from a nostalgic coming home aspect, although she thought she might recognise the front steps and the bathroom seemed familiar. Rather, she loved it because somebody had kept the white clapboard blemish-free, had left the hardwood floors inside to darken with age and had not stripped them back to a fashionably lighter colour and had planted shrubs and flower borders exactly where she would have put them herself.

The house was so private but the air still circulated freely around it. It was protected by the surrounding woods but was so open to the sky above. Hazel wished she was more poetic so that she could explain how the place made her feel. It was a mixture of thickening memories and now, almost unbearably exciting possibilities. She found herself embarrassed at how little she had thought of Stuart in this nerve-tingling new world.

Back in the kitchen, Kate finished re-housing the dishes and then asked if she could take a good look around the house. Rose had regarded her genially over the top of her glasses, as she read the previous day's paper.

"I know we've seen a lot of it already," Kate blushed, "but if you don't mind, I like to look at things slowly."

Rose now leaned back in her chair, the paper folding in half, and waited for Kate to talk some more.

"I mean," the girl continued, her speech gathering speed as she tried to explain herself, "it's such a big place, and of course, I wouldn't go near any rooms you told me to steer clear of." Pause, then, "Our house is so tiny; it would probably fit into this kitchen."

"Kate," smiled Rose, "There's nowhere in this house that is out of bounds. But here," Rose pointed to a pile of the girls' clean laundry, "take that lot up with you, then feel free to roam the plains of our existence."

Kate grinned at this lady of unexpected phrases and hoped that they might grow really fond of each other in the short time they had together.

The top drawer of the oak dresser in their bedroom was a little sticky, giving off a tinge of mustiness when disturbed, but with some persuasion Kate was able to close it on the clean underwear. It was a huge, heavy piece of furniture which still managed to look at home in the floral room. Because of its dual aspect, the sun, even at this time of year, illuminated the space and made it look fresher than it actually was. Kate guessed by the grey outline of absent pictures and the odd corner of wallpaper peeling away from the wall, that the decoration was aged. It had been well tended nevertheless and the repeated posies were still a vivid yellow, faded only in the window recesses.

From the outset, Kate had wondered who the previous occupant or occupants had been, the room being at the front of the house and therefore in quite an enviable position, but felt that it was too contentious an enquiry. Surely it would come up in conversation further down the line. There were two single beds against the wall facing the door, with a window between them and the oak dresser skulked behind the doorway. The beds, although adorned with twin duvet covers, did not match. One was very obviously brand new and had been recently situated. Kate smiled to herself, wondering if David and Rose had 'disagreed' about the allocation of rooms and also who had emerged the victor. Whatever the case, she was glad that Hazel was still her room-mate. Too many changes at once could unsettle a person.

So, this had not always been a twin room and the realisation awakened Kate's curiosity once more. On exiting the room, Kate was faced with the choice of turning left towards the front of the house and arriving at Rose's bedroom door and the stairs to the third floor, or moving right towards the rear, where the bathroom, a further bedroom and the stairs to the ground floor were located. She knew from the sounds of the retiring household that David occupied the floor above, but the bedroom at the rear of this landing was a mystery and so she purposefully headed straight to it. The door was unlocked.

Kate smirked to herself as she entered the room. Well, of course the door was unlocked. She wasn't part of some Victorian novel, where dusty tea crates and chattels hid beneath grey sheets. There were no broken tennis rackets or ancient rolled-up rugs. Instead, there was a clean but sparse bedroom, housing a huge wardrobe, a double bed minus its headboard and a chest of drawers displaying a stereo system and pile of LPs. Only one of the windows had curtains, as if the other pair had been required elsewhere. Otherwise, the room was plain and functional – and a bit disappointing.

The wallpaper was a pale blue, with a thin, red, vertical stripe every six inches or so. The remaining pair of curtains was chocolate brown, which echoed the shade of the carpet. Kate grimaced at the choice of colours but supposed that at some stage it may have been fashionable. Maybe this had been Neil or David's room when they were boys. The records gave little away and the wardrobes now housed overcoats, presumably the winter attire of the whole household. The chest of drawers looked a little more hopeful.

In front of its oval mirror, next to the stereo, there lay a brush and comb set which looked like it had been used very rarely. A pair of carved, wooden bookends held three paperbacks between them. And that was it.

Carved wood.The man with the hands.

"Neil's room?" Kate murmured, tracing the delicate carvings with her finger. Or perhaps he had made them for his older brother. But then, they would have been in David's present room, surely. "Neil's room," she confirmed to herself, and opened the top drawer to find some old hankies and an unpaired sock, another couple of combs and an empty packet of Marlboro cigarettes. No photos, no stories to tell. The remaining drawers held only some folded linens and a broken pen.

Sighing, Kate rose from her squatting position and then remonstrated with herself. It stood to reason that Neil would have taken anything of interest with him and used this room only when visiting. Anything of real value would adorn the walls or hide within the confines of Rose's or David's room, neither of which she felt comfortable invading without their knowledge, in spite of Rose's permission to do so.

"Kate?" Hazel came thumping up the stairs and her sister met her at the top.

"What's in there?"

"I think it's Neil's old room. There's no sign of life anyway. Nothing to see."

"Oh," replied Hazel, glancing into the room momentarily, and then fixing her twinkling eyes back on Kate. "Well, come with me then. Rose wants me to empty Dad's laundry bag into this," she held aloft a plastic basket, "and says we can look around upstairs at the same time, as long as we don't disturb his desk. Apparently, he has a particular system."

"Excellent," replied Kate and they both ran along the corridor and up the final flight of stairs, to the top of the house.

"Oh, wow. Now I'd give my right arm to have this as a bedroom."

"It goes right from the front to the back."

Both girls stopped at the top of the stairs and gazed around David's 'office'. It did indeed cover the whole of the depth of the house, with only a shower and toilet space occupying the rear corner above the main bathroom. Behind them lay two further bedrooms, identical in shape and position to Rose and Neil's rooms on the floor below.

"First things first," said Hazel, firmly and emptied the laundry bag suspended from the shower door into the basket with a flourish, then "Right, let's get to it."

The office walls were adorned with enormous maps of the area, containing shaded forest plantations and highlighted routes which meant absolutely nothing to either girl, but impressed them nevertheless. There was a fireplace on the external side wall, but a table had been placed in front of it, on top of which were box files and a coffee-maker, so it appeared obsolete. In the centre sat a large desk with a chair on either side and a lot of paperwork sprawled around a phone and a word processor. Apart from one other easy chair and a row of metal filing cabinets, this made up the entire furnishings of the room.

"That's a system?" asked Kate, looking at the mess of forms and letters, one pile held down by a paperweight, another clipped together with a bulldog clip, the rest lying freely for a passing draught to disturb.

"Forget that. Let's go through here."

Grinning, Hazel opened the door to David's bedroom and it was if she had been struck in the face. Kate actually walked into the back of her, as she stopped abruptly just inside the doorway.

"Ow," Kate rubbed her nose, "Haze?"

"Oh ..." breathed Hazel, her hand still on the door handle. "Oh wow."

"What?" asked Kate, gazing around the completely non-descript room. "Wow what?"

Slowly, Hazel walked into the room and immediately looked to her right. She noticed the curtained door in the centre of the far wall and crossed over to it at once. Kate on the other hand was taking in the remainder of the room. Dark green walls, big wooden framed bed, same heavy dark furniture as the rest of the house. There was a large double wardrobe and a thick patterned rug which covered almost the entire floor, leaving dark wood showing only at the periphery. Below the windowsill, on this strip of wood, were lined several pairs of boots, all of varying ages and conditions. Very, very ordinary thought Kate. She was about to voice this heresy to her sister, when she noticed that Hazel was behind the curtain on the wall, rattling the door handle she had found there.

"Locked," she sniffed, and re-appeared, her face shiny with tears.

"What is it?" asked Kate, aghast.

"That's my bedroom behind there," explained Hazel, "and it's locked away."

Kate was at a loss for words and knew better than to offer advice which she was unsure of, so she simply followed Hazel around as she touched furniture and renewed her acquaintance with the view from the window. The atmosphere in the room was now subdued and Kate remained uncertain of how to correct this.

"I mean," continued Hazel eventually, "I think I understand why he wouldn't go in there very often. But to lock the door and hang a curtain? It's a bit ...well, it's not like I died or anything."

Kate was about to agree when Hazel suddenly marched back through the office, heading for the alternative door to the room.

"You won't get upset, Haze? You don't have to go in, you know. It's not essential."

"I want to see if I can remember it, that's all."

The door to the bedroom was not locked, but had to be persuaded to open and even then it protested noisily as Hazel scraped it inwards against the wooden boards. Hazel hesitated for just a second, recalling her reaction to David's room, then pushed herself across the threshold. This room really was from a different era, and Kate found herself dismayed at it. The sadness she felt as she surveyed the surroundings could only have been a fraction of what Hazel was experiencing and instantly, she put her arm around her sister's shoulder. Hazel said nothing, but neither did she move.

The curtains were open and there was plenty of light streaming in, but all it illuminated was the greyness of the place. The colours seemed to have seeped away into the dusty floorboards and it was the barest of all the rooms they had visited. There was a single bed against one wall, which surprisingly still wore bedclothes and a cot against another, which had boxes sitting on top of its bare mattress. Hazel still stared, slowly moving her eyes around the room, trying to catch some of the feelings she had experienced next door. In her father's room, she felt the life and sensations of the past, but in here, all she felt was her throat tighten against the dust in the air.

Simultaneously, Kate began to feel bitterly disappointed. Not because it was obvious that Hazel had slept in both the cot and the bed and she had done neither, but rather that Rose had allowed Hazel to find the room in this state. Yes, the room was no longer used, but it *had* been, and it would have been nice for Hazel to see it as more than a box-room behind a curtained door. Hazel now let out a slow breath, but there were no tears. She tried to sound upbeat and falsely offended, but it came out more honestly and she just sounded gloomy.

"That's great, not even a photo."

"It used to be a great colour though," Kate tried her best.

Hazel humphed a reply and picked at the cardboard of one of the boxes.

"You know," she said, "I'm not even going to look in these. Some things are better off left well alone."

"I agree. Let's get some tea."

As Kate followed her sister out of the disheartening room, she made a mental note to come back and look at the boxes at a later date. Maybe she could find something that would really cheer Hazel up.

Chapter 11

The journey to Duncan was glorious, the autumn colours displayed to their maximum effect in the still robust sunlight. As they travelled along in the SUV, the spruce trees guarded the roadside like sentries, while the gold and copper foliage of the smaller bushes seemed to glow, presenting their blushing shades like crinoline dresses. Kate wished she had brought along the camera. For once, Hazel had allowed her to sit up front with David and she could not help but remark on the passing scene.

"Look at those leaves. Just incredible."

David said nothing, but smiled across at her, proud to show off his homeland. Almost immediately, he glanced in the mirror at Hazel, who was slouched into the corner of the back seat. She was not frowning, but was biting her nails and watching as the same countryside passed her by, strangely not commenting on it.

"Okay, Hazel?" he enquired.

She held his gaze and allowed him a smile, "Yeah, fine."

Kate also looked back in her direction and her heart sank. She had not shared her life with this almost transparent person without knowing exactly why or when her mood had altered. It was mid afternoon and since discovering Hazel's now abandoned old room that morning, her vivacity had bled from her in one slow, steady stream. Kate had witnessed it, trying desperately to steer her away from that path so that Rose and David would not detect too much. When Hazel went downhill like this, she could not contain her emotions and Kate knew that before the day was out, her sister would have started talks which might prove to be less than fun. Kate watched her now, as her blank eyes stared outside and her nails were savaged to the quick.

"Hey, Haze. We'd better see if we can get a postcard for Beth today, or we might be back home before it gets there."

"Yeah, okay."

Turning back, Kate answered David's questioning look with a simple shrug, but before she could think of how to fill the growing silence, Hazel sat forward.

"Hey Dad, what are the chances of you ever letting me drive this *ridiculously* big car?"

"You, drive?"

"Of course. I'm twenty, I live in the middle of nowhere and I need to get to work every day. Did you think I biked?"

"I meant, you want to drive this? Your mom said something ....." He slowed down to let a timber wagon pass on the other side of the road and lifted his hand to the driver, his face flushed. In all the time the three of them had been together, their conversations had either been fairly superficial or deeply intense and it seemed that there was no middle ground. They seemed incapable of accepting the fact that Fiona was going to surface in discussions unexpectedly and they had to deal with it as it happened. Kate now felt it was the time to mention this, when he was safely engaged in the act of driving and Hazel was physically separated from her by the seating arrangements.

"You know, we're going to have to stop tripping each other up when we talk. Mum is never going to be far away – at least, *I'm* not going to avoid talking about her. She's still with me as far as I'm concerned. So, why don't we just agree that we can bring her into conversations any time we want, and we won't be all awkward or sorry or sad? Well, we can still be sad."

She had delivered this entire speech whilst looking out of the passenger window. She couldn't risk Hazel cutting her off with a glare and she didn't wish to see David's face at all while she spoke. She waited for some sort of response.

"Okay," said Hazel, one of her nails now bloody and raw.

"Deal," said David, eventually, and when Kate finally risked a look in his direction, he was staring straight ahead. His face was a mask of concentration and he frowned at the road, which to Kate's mind, did not appear to deserve such attention. Was he angry at her for voicing what they had all been aware of? Confused, she looked back out of her window, and was vexed that her pronouncement seemed to have killed dead any further dialogue. It was at times like this, that Kate missed Fiona more than she physically thought possible. Fiona would have covered any misdemeanour shown by her daughter and would have instantly made her feel better. Now Kate was on her own and baffled. Had she done something wrong, had she seriously misjudged their burgeoning relationship and overstepped the mark? But then, she had a right to speak. She was part of this whole scenario and she mattered. He had told her that very thing.

"Anyway," Hazel broke the tension, "If you were going to say that Mum was less than impressed with my driving, that is only one person's opinion."

"Oh God, Dad. Please don't risk it. You have no idea what her driving is like," Kate pleaded.

"Hey!"

"Hazel, you know it's true. Apart from the week the car spent in the garage because the suspension was completely shot, what about when you took the fence out on the top road because you couldn't keep your eyes off the full moon?"

"Once," cried Hazel, but a smile was twitching at her mouth. "That happened one time and there was a frost that night. Could have happened to anyone."

"Yes, anybody who thought the moon was more important than staying on the road, you ... lunatic."

"And proud to be one."

With the conversation lightened by a degree, Kate glanced again at David whose frown had disappeared, but who had paled slightly. Kate couldn't decide if it was the thought of Hazel's near demise that caused this or the fact that she may seriously want to get behind the wheel of his truck, and that she could be very persuasive.

"Anyway," Hazel, somewhat revitalised, now sat forward, her face between the two bodies in the front. "I think it's only right I should learn to drive a Canadian vehicle, being half Canadian myself."

He hesitated then took a deep breath in. His eyes were wary but he was smiling, a sort of resigned, cagey, half-grin. He then breathed out quickly and shrugged his shoulders, apparently re-assessing what he was going to say.

"Our driveway might be the place to start. There's the weight of this thing and the gears to consider. The public road may - "

"Yes okay. That will do. Just want a photo to show Stu when we get home. Then maybe he'll let me drive his truck without any of the usual carry on about why 'somebody like you will never drive this baby.'"

Kate smirked at the outside world and David actually laughed. "Oh, right, so you want to cut your teeth on my vehicle? Well, that fills me with confidence."

"You could always just take a photo of you sitting in the driving seat," piped up Kate.

"Absolutely not. Anyway, he's agreed now, so that's that."

With her mood remarkably improved, the remainder of the journey was amiably dotted with opinions, Kate continuing to point out things which caught her eye.

When the girls had arrived in Canada, David had given them some currency to spend as they liked. It was not an excessive amount, little more than pocket money, but it was enough to persuade them that a shopping trip was required. Now, on a day when Hazel's sparkle was apparently waning, an outing to the shops had been suggested and Kate had jumped at the proposal. From what she had seen on their first day, Duncan was not huge although still bigger than Portree. It looked as though it might be visitor friendly, with a seemingly endless variety of totem poles on show, and so Kate looked forward to finding postcards and keepsakes and spending a bit of money. David had suggested maybe going as far as Victoria, but they had left it too late in the day, so that was booked for the following week. Now on this sunny Thursday, David was heading along the wide road into the centre of town, when Hazel jumped forward in her seat.

"Wait, wait, wait! I know that place!"

David quickly scanned the immediate area, trying to fathom out what she was looking at.

"That building there. What is it? I'm sure I know it."

David's face cleared at last, as he slowed down slightly, causing the driver behind him to sound his horn and overtake him in an angry flourish. He ignored this and pulled into the side of the road.

"I'm sure you do remember it. It used to be your second home."

"The Library!" shouted Hazel, seemingly back to her usual level of enthusiasm. "Can we go in?"

"Not the Library any more, I'm afraid. That moved to the Community Centre years ago. Still, it's great that you recognised it."

The three of them sat in silence for a moment. Hazel was looking at the building and surroundings, the totem poles, the tall trees and cherished the feelings growing inside her. She felt goose-pimples on her skin as she remembered the smell of the books and the furniture polish and slowly smiled to herself. David's heart, on the other hand, sank a little as he recalled a time when this place had been part of his life. Not directly, he had never taken his daughter there, but he had relived every visit with her, as she sat snuggled against him, head tucked under his chin. Kate studied the road ahead of them, not allowing herself to wish that she had been part of it. She needed to see this town, this whole area, as somewhere completely original. She was a visitor and she wanted to visit.

"Where are we going to park?" she asked, brightly and David finally pulled away from the kerb.

The centre of town was not particularly busy in the low sunlight, but it held plenty of interest for the girls, and they were in no hurry as they checked their money and tried to work out the equivalent cost of items in pounds. They continually remarked on how wide the streets were and that nobody was in a hurry to develop every possible inch of space like they were in Portree. They talked and pointed and exclaimed and David happily listened rather than taking part. He was dressed in his usual jeans and timber boots but had been persuaded by Hazel to don a black sports jacket rather than his waterproof windcheater. She had found it in his wardrobe and decided that if he was spending the day with them, then he should definitely smarten up – 'what happened to the well-groomed gentleman we met on Skye?' He conceded, but insisted on wearing a sweater over his shirt, rather than a tie. Now he felt conspicuous, as if strolling through the town with two babbling Scots females did not draw quite enough attention.

"You're kidding me," David breathed, halting in his tracks. Kate had already paused by the window of a shop called Equator, which seemed to be overflowing with highly coloured bracelets and beads, scarves and miniature totem poles. At his strangely unguarded proclamation, she looked to where Hazel had walked on a few steps, but could see nothing of interest. David now joined Kate in front of the window, his eyes ironically unreadable, but his mouth set in a tight, narrow line. He seemed instantly engrossed in the goods on show.

"Dad?" questioned Kate.

"Hey," he said, then cleared his throat and pointed to the window. "You're bound to be able to find something in here for Beth, don't you think?"

Hazel had wandered back to their side and immediately spied a shoulder bag, multi-coloured and covered in metallic buttons.

"Wow," she pointed, "She would love that bag. *I* love that bag."

"Let's go in then," he instructed and led the way. Kate frowned at Hazel, who seemed oblivious to everything as usual, but again glanced quickly at the pavement ahead of them. Nothing.

Later, as they assessed their purchases over a coffee, Hazel began to look more and more pensive and her contributions became less animated. Kate braced herself for what might be coming.

"Shall I buy us all another coffee, Dad." Hazel stated rather than asked, waving her purse in the air. "I have the means." She did not wait for a reply but was up out of her seat and crossing to the counter as David was glancing at his watch. He pointed at it and looked as if he might call after her, but then turned back to Kate with a resigned look. She wondered if he would ever try to assert his authority, and what would happen if he did.

"So," he said. "Today was a good day."

"Yes," she agreed, bemused by the statement.

"Great."

He picked up a sugar-cube which had spilled onto the tablecloth and placed it on his plate. Kate waited until he looked in her direction once more and she threw him what she hoped was an encouraging expression - there were still two people waiting in line at the counter in front of Hazel, and it looked as if this may turn into a very protracted silence. He cracked his knuckles.

"Hazel does that *all* the time," she grinned, "especially when she's nervous."

"Just one more thing I didn't really know," he shrugged.

Kate watched his face as he tapped his fingers on the table, then stopped himself, trying to hide his state of mind. He rubbed his jaw-line instead. She had not seen him this agitated since Skye. Something had to be said.

"Dad, I think I should tell you, Hazel is a bit out of sorts."

"That I had gathered. What's going on?"

"Well, we were in her old bedroom this morning and I think she was a bit surprised at the ... well, the condition it was in. She's been quiet since and I know what she's like. She's going to ask you about it, so I'm giving you some warning."

Immediately, fresh concern showed on his face, but some of the other tension seemed to seep away.

"Really," he sounded dismayed, whether at Hazel's disappointment or the imminent discussions Kate was not sure, although she recognised genuine regret when she saw it. "Damn," he said, staring down at his hands resting on the table. "I never thought. To be honest, I never really thought either of you would actually come over, even after all the plans," he stopped talking and sat in solitary silence, his jaw muscle twitching, then swallowed and looked up.

"Hey," he said, looking directly at her. "We do whatever we have to do to get this sorted. Your mom did the most selfless thing I have ever known by letting me in, and if she can do that, then I can do this."

Kate studied his expression. His face was so earnest and she knew he believed what he was saying. She thought back to the diary entries she had read and now began to understand why her mother had trusted this man so completely. It was because he made solutions sound plausible, and had faith in them himself.

Her heart constricted in her chest, as she wondered what on earth had happened to obliterate that trust.

"Well," she replied, "there are certainly things that need to be talked about. I don't know if you will, though, because Mum never did. Unless the pair of you came up with a Master Plan for *that* one."

He acknowledged the reference with a weak smile, but only said, "You know your mom."

Hazel was at last making her way back to the table with three coffees and a giant chocolate chip cookie.

"Look at the size of this thing," she said, "we must be talking at least 600 calories."

"None for me then," he replied, patting his completely flat stomach as he cleared a space for the cups.

"Get away!" cried Hazel, lowering her voice as heads turned, "I mean, you're carrying no extra weight, considering your age."

He sighed. "I'm barely forty-five. I'm not antiquated."

The girls smirked as he looked from one to the other and then broke into a grin.

"Does anyone here think Clint Eastwood is particularly old? And he's in his sixties by now!"

"Are you comparing yourself to the fittest-looking spaghetti westerner on the planet, Dad? Are you?" asked Hazel.

"And why would you know how old he is anyway?" added Kate, "Unless this argument has had to be used before."

David threw up his hands in mock despair. "I'm just saying, forty-five is not old. Although I will admit that since meeting you two, I have aged by at least ten years."

"It is you, David," said a voice to his right, "I was almost positive it was."

Both girls instantly looked up at the owner of the voice, completely missing the way David's face altered and body stiffened simultaneously. He stood and turned away from them before he spoke.

"Hi, Kathy," he said, putting his hand on her arm and placing a quick peck on her cheek.

"I can't believe it," the small brunette's voice was genuinely surprised. "You're so rarely in town – how long has it been?"

David spread his hands in a 'who-really-knows' gesture and shrugged. There was a dampness to his face and now he put one hand in his pocket and held his brow momentarily with the other, just managing to refrain from wiping it. The girls were frozen in their seats, awaiting some kind of revelation, good or bad, but when the stranger turned her eyes to them, they saw a slow dawning of understanding. Unexpectedly, they also witnessed a look of real pleasure appear. She glanced back at David, not sure what to say, so he turned towards them and said, "Kathy, this is Hazel and Kate. Girls, Kathy. She was one of your mom's best friends."

"Oh, my goodness," Kathy cried. "Hazel. Of course it's you. I can see it now. And you're Kate? Did you know that you're my namesake, Kate? Your mom stayed with me for – oh," she broke off blushing. "Well."

"Are you back living here, Kathy?" David asked, putting his body between this intruder and the girls, who looked at each other warily, daring themselves not to read too much into the situation.

"It's Johnnie's weekend for the boys, so I brought them down a day early. I'm still up at Ladysmith for my sins."

Now she made a determined step towards the table, her face sympathetic. Kate's gut tightened at the sight of it.

"I am so sorry about your mom."

"How did you find out?" David's voice was gruff as he glanced to see the girls' reaction and then studied his own folded arms.

"Oh," Kathy sounded startled. "Well, Fiona and I kept in touch."

Apparently this was all the explanation that was forthcoming and suddenly Kate's face lit up.

"Kathy." she stated. "We always got a Christmas card from Kathy, remember Haze? It was always a snow scene with a big tree, and one year it was a musical one."

"Yes!" laughed Hazel. "'From Kathy and co'.Same every year."

The relief felt at the table was almost worthy of comment. David, however, seemed to be less than impressed and stood perfectly still, never taking his eyes from the lady who was now shaking both by the hand and complimenting them on their looks and apparent ability to grow. When eventually the commentary began to peter out, Kathy made some reference to the long drive back and the encroaching dusk.

"But, I have to say," she concluded. "This has made my day. I am so glad to have met the pair of you, you are an absolute credit to her. There, I've said it and now I'm going before I get upset. David, nice to see you."

She shook his hand this time and tried to avoid his deathly serious face. She turned towards the door, waving at the three of them in general, but before she began to fight her way through the tables, she suddenly reached into her shoulder bag and handed a card straight to Hazel.

"Hey, give me a call sometime if you're bored. We can have a good gossip about anything you fancy. Oh, and don't look at the picture, it's the worst one of me *ever*. Bye."

Kate immediately leaned in to share the information on the card with her sister and Kathy walked straight out the door, head held high and not bothering to look again in David's direction. He sat slowly, biting his lip.

"What's a Realtor?" asked Kate.

"Sells houses," replied Hazel. "Like an Estate Agent. I saw it on 'Dynasty' once."

"She's right about the picture mind. Look at her hair!"

"Do you think we could get on the road, Hazel? I'm sure you could take that biscuit with you."

Hazel looked up at David as he now rose decisively to his feet, his demeanour much more resolute than previously, and replaced his chair under the table. Her reason behind ordering the coffee now re-entered her head.

"But I've just - "

"We're going. I need to get on the road before dark."

Hazel looked astounded. She did not move, not recognising his unyielding features and Kate held her breath, cringing against this new shift in government. David now folded his arms and stood absolutely still, holding Hazel's stare, until finally, without flounce or drama, she did stand and start to wrap the biscuit in a napkin. Kate half-expected him to make for the door and leave them to it, but he did not. He watched as Hazel gathered her shopping, glancing once at Kate to indicate that she should perhaps do the same, and within ten seconds, they were ready to leave.

"Okay?" he asked and waited for them to speak.

"Yes, let's go," said Hazel and followed his lead. Kate brought up the rear, marvelling at the events of the afternoon.

Chapter 12

The sitting room was dimly lit, neither of the Wilders ever resorting to the main overhead light, unless it was to look for a lost needle or to read a specific article of importance in the local paper. It was after 8.30pm and inky black outside. Only two lamps were alight, but the fire gave off enough heat and glow to make it a comfortable place to hole up in. David was seated in the armchair by the fire, or rather he was slouched in it. His bootless feet were stretched out in front of him, knees bent slightly, his head supported by the hand resting on the arm of the chair. His other hand embraced a glass of whisky, but it had not touched his lips in the last twenty minutes or so. He was aware at one point of a set of soft footfalls appearing at the door, then retreating, accompanied by the whispered statement that he was asleep. He had never been asleep, but sat staring at the worn hearth rug, motionless.

He could hear the sounds coming from the kitchen, as the three women in the house discussed the various items bought in Duncan, who the recipients would be and the re-housing of the famous Library. He also had the impression that Rose was keeping them occupied for his benefit. He had seen her reaction to his face on their return, but she had asked no questions, and steered the three of them through a subdued dinner like an expert. His gratitude for this hour or so of solitude was more than he knew how to express.

What had made him imagine in his wildest dreams that he could deal with all of this? His stomach was continuously knotted up; he ached with guilt every time either one of the girls even spoke to him. He had missed so much of them, years of their experiences, what had shaped them into who they were now. Kate had told him that he wore his heart on his sleeve but if she knew what it took to simply remain articulate in their presence she would see that it was all an act. Meeting Kathy had been a trial, but worse than that was the realisation that Fiona had kept up correspondence with her. She probably knew more about them than he did, and that was just plain wrong. Thank God it had been a mercifully short encounter.

Daily he felt as if he was vetting every sentence he spoke, but to what end he was not sure. The discussions, the questions, the probable accusations were all sitting on his shoulders, waiting to jump down and turn on him. It was going to be very soon now, he knew that. He stretched one leg straight, his only acknowledgement that he still owned a body which occasionally needed movement to subsist. He had spent the last hour inside his head. Fiona was there and they were re-running every conversation as he desperately tried to remember why this had made such perfect sense at the time.

'They are very close,' she had said. 'Nothing is going to change that. But they will have a lot of questions.'

'They never asked you?'

'They did. And I palmed them off with the usual. You know, what people say every time, to try and justify what can't be justified. I know it will be *really* difficult, but you must see that it's so much better this way, because they won't have to consider me. They won't have to think about me at all when they react to you. They can ask about me and you will know what to say, but they won't have to bring me into it, or let me cloud it. Because I won't be there.'

That part had almost killed him.

They had been talking for so long, not just about the plan, but about everything. When he had received the first cautious phone-call from his estranged wife, he was so surprised that he forgot to be defensive and it meant that she had taken her time and explained as gently as possible what was happening. He had disintegrated in seconds, not comprehending the words she was using, and was unable to speak for any length of time. He had asked her to let him call her back and she had agreed without debate. He was almost ashamed to recall that, in the time between the first and second conversation, it had dawned on him that perhaps this would result in an alternative future for him. As horrendous as her news had been, it had meant that he was once again needed.

They had put hours into those discussions, and at some point the Grand Master Plan appeared to be the best solution. The only fair thing to do.The only right thing. David wanted them in his life more than anything and they needed some answers and some connection with their roots. It meant that a lot of soul searching would take place and he was sure there would be tears by the bucketful. But what could he do? The events of the last year had put paid to any schemes or deceptions. All they could do now was be truthful. When people had visited and accepted their worst fears, there was no room for anything other than frankness and sincerity. He hoped the phrase 'brutally' honest would not apply.

Then, as he always did at the end of these spells of painful analysis, he remembered other things Fiona had said to him. He recalled the sound of her voice, so sure of herself, so accepting of his opinions but adamant of her own feelings. He thought of the particular way she phrased her words and her habit of answering her own questions. It was a trait he had rarely come across since, but then how much company had he actually sought after she left? They had gradually begun to relax into each other, the telephone becoming their intimate friend, and agonisingly, he wondered how he could possibly have lived for so long without that crucial contact. He *required* it to live.

It had broken his heart into shards of glass when she had implored him not to come over to see her. She had appealed to everything that was decent and wise about him – his ability to see what was best for everybody, his good nature, his duties as a parent, but most of all, the love that they had once shared. Someone with less to lose may have appeared manipulative and harsh in this respect, but

Fiona had only one goal in this and that was to 'start to make amends. These are *their* lives and they need to know how it was.'

So he had agreed. He would grant her wish and not visit. He remembered the conversation that had brought him to that point.

'Are you in a lot of pain, Fee?'

'I can't decide what is hurting any more. People have told me what to expect, but truly, physical pain doesn't scare me.'

'What *are* you scared of?'

'I'm selfish, I can't bear the thought of not being with them. They are everything. Not seeing them scares me and – please forgive me – I realise now what I took away from you. It seemed to be the only answer back then, but look how it hurt you. I can only say sorry.'

'Let me see you. Please.'

'Dave,' she had whispered, 'You have to let me do my penance, but it's not just that. If you see me like I am now, it will taint the way you speak to the girls. You'll think of me as some poor creature, and I don't need you to do that. They can see that every day, but I want you to tell them what we were like back then.' Pause. 'And if *I* see *you*, it will break me in two. Do you understand?'

Of course he had understood. The luxury of choice had been taken from them.

"Dad?"

He flinched from his trance, his whisky swilling wildly for a second. He looked up in the dim light to see Kate gazing at him; the concerned look on her face all Fiona. He shook his head against the image.

"Sorry, were you actually sleeping? I didn't want you to drop your glass."

Now David hauled himself up into the seat, every muscle in his body screaming against the injustice of having to work. He grimaced against the pain then put down his glass and smiled weakly up at her.

"I'm fine, Kate. How are things going tonight?"

"Oh, okay," she replied, sitting on the sofa opposite him. "I've persuaded Hazel to go to bed. She wanted to come in and chat, but I said we were all too tired. So, it looks like you owe me one."

She smiled brightly at him, hoping that he would see this move as the beginnings of an alliance. But he did not reply. Instead, she watched his eyes stare into the distance, and was suddenly aghast as his head dropped onto his chest. He placed one hand on his brow and rested it there, concealing his eyes from her. But he could not hide what was happening and he could not stop it.

"Dad?" Kate's voice was a thin croak.

He held his free hand up, a signal for her to give him a moment, and so she sat there, perched on the edge of the sofa, anxiety carved into her face. She was at a complete loss as to what to do. In all the time they had shared on Skye, amongst all the chaos of feelings he had been thrown into, he had never been brought to this present state. He had appeared shaken, grief-stricken and humble but had never fallen apart in front of them and now Kate was horrified that his collapse had been at her hand.

Her every instinct was to go over to him and apologise for somehow causing this descent into grief, but she didn't know what his reaction would be. Perhaps he did not even want this situation to be acknowledged. She stood up, unable to sit any longer, then hesitantly moved over to the chair. His shoulders were hunched and she watched for a moment more as he silently wiped a tear from his jaw. She was aware that she was hovering and finally, she knelt at the side of his chair.

"I'm so sorry," she whispered, silently imploring him to say anything in return. "I didn't mean to -"

"It's fine," he stated, sitting further upright and shaking his head. He managed to wipe his entire face in one speedy movement and then put his hand on Kate's shoulder. She covered his hand with hers, very close to tears herself.

"You've never ... before. I can't believe it was me," Kate stammered, tears now beginning to teem down her own cheeks. "Sorry."

"It's okay," he stood at last and helped her to her feet. "We'll get through this, Kate. It was a tough day and it's only the beginning, but we *can* do it." He tilted her chin up, "Do you trust me?"

She nodded and wiped her face on her sleeve. When it was dry and clean, she gave him a quick hug then walked away, passing a motionless Rose who stood observing in the doorway. David met his mother's stare and shrugged. There were no words to say.

The following morning, after breakfast had been cleared away and David and Hazel were occupied in the SUV, going over the basics of keeping the vehicle on the road and intact, Kate joined Rose in the Dining Room. She was seated at the big table, surrounded by paper patterns and all the sundry items required for making curtains. Rose smiled at Kate but her eyes never left the sewing machine, where she was trying to insert the spool of thread.

"Need any help, Rose?" she asked, picking up a stray triangle of material from the carpet.

"Well, you could come and sit by an old woman and keep her company, unless you want to go and witness Davey's hair turn grey and listen to Hazel's attempts to activate the gears. It's not pleasant."

"No thanks," laughed Kate, then "Mum used to sew. Granny knitted but never sewed – did you teach her, maybe?"

Rose sat back in her chair, thinking. "She was a quick learner. I think she wanted to make all their curtains and furnishings herself so that it felt more like their house, you know?"

Kate wandered around the room as Rose continued reminiscing, talking about Fiona with affection and warmth. Was that for her benefit, or did she really think of her mother fondly? When Rose paused to hunt for her reading glasses, Kate sat at the table and studied her hands. She picked at the cuticles of her thumb.

"Something on your mind, Kate?"

She shrugged but added, "Yes. Loads."

Rose leaned over and picked up the heavy scissors lying next to Kate, saying, "Well, I've got all day. And don't be fooled, it may look as if I'm not listening, but I will hear every word. I do my best listening when I'm sewing."

Kate gave her an indulgent smile, then frowned once more. She tore one of her fingernails off with her teeth and sighed. "You saw what happened last night, right? I can't believe I was so stupid. I mean, we all knew he needed some time alone. He was in there for hours. And he's not made of stone, I should have known that he might have been thinking about her. Maybe I've been a bit selfish, assuming it was all about Haze and me. He was married to her for God's sake. That's supposed to be as close as you can get. It's just that it's really difficult to share this amount of sadness with somebody you've never had any contact with."

In spite of Rose's earlier words, she found herself quietly sitting back in her chair, her sewing neglected, as she let Kate continue to speak. For the most part, her speech was unstinted and continuous. She was not quite babbling but took few breaths and Rose recognised that she was not holding back or even organising her opinions. Rose heard them as Kate thought them. It was illuminating and endearing in the same measure.

"I thought I was getting to know him a bit, although he's not the same person as he was in Skye. I think he was trying so hard to not make things worse over there and I misjudged him altogether. Here, he looks much more touched by it all." She paused. "You can tell me all about him, if you want to."

Rose smiled, the kind of smile that a mother cannot contain when thinking about her own offspring. "I can indeed. But it's better if you ask me specific questions. Fire away."

The back door slammed and Kate heard the kettle being filled. There was an agitated ring to the sound and she frowned an apology at Rose as she heard Hazel mumbling crossly to herself. A moment later, she came thumping through from the kitchen.

"He *said*," she addressed them both, hands on her hips, "that he would be patient. He *promised* he wouldn't get frustrated. I mean, Kate, you did warn him about the driving. I'm not technically minded and there's the possibility that my hand, eye, feet co-ordination is underdeveloped. But I was *trying* to do it right."

"Did he shout at you?" Rose grinned from her seat. "I can't believe he did that."

"No, he didn't shout …" admitted Hazel, "… as such. But when a person starts repeating the same word over and over and not allowing you the time to 'get it', then you might as well shout. Then," she paused for dramatic effect, "he rolled his eyes."

"Oh no," laughed Kate, "how dare he!"

"I know!" she cried in reply but said nothing more as they heard the back door close again. Hazel now folded her arms, deliberately keeping her eyes on her female allies and refusing to acknowledge his presence at her side.

David in turn looked from one person to another, his face an image of bewilderment. Rose's expression gave him no clue what to do next, regarding the whole situation with interest. Kate's expectant gaze on him was worrying, as it meant he was supposed to make the move. Hazel determinedly kept looking straight ahead of her, an air of pure indifference about her.

He sighed. "Hazel. In Scotland, what does the word 'forward' mean?"

"It means forward," she snipped, then, "going ahead. Like I was *doing*."

He threw up his hands and his voice was incredulous. "No, you were not. I say forward with the gearstick and you push it away!"

"Yes!" she finally faced him, "Forward", and her hand made a motion of pushing forward from her body.

"I meant forward!" he countered, miming a pulling towards him movement.

They each paused for breath, unaware that Kate was shaking, hiding her mirth behind her hands. Rose slowly picked up a piece of material and was started to pin the fold in it. She made a supreme effort not to catch Kate's eye.

"Okay," he now conceded, "I can see our problem. Well, I suppose that makes sense."

"Hah!" Hazel thrust a finger to his chest, then she too submitted, her triumphant grin changing into a softer smile. "Yeah okay," she punched his arm instead, "But next time, you really *have* to be more patient."

David opened his eyes wider at the implication that there would be a next time, but kept his thoughts to himself.

"Anybody want a cuppa?" enquired Hazel, already heading back to the kitchen.

David leaned against the door frame, his boots untied but not removed in his attempt to rectify the situation as soon as possible. His woollen jumper had a dead leaf sticking to one of his sleeves, which he removed and stuffed into the back pocket of his jeans.

"Okay?" he specifically asked Kate.

"Fine," she replied, finally conquering her bubbling laughter, although she began to feel a little cheated when Rose got up from the table, patted her hand and muttered, "another time." Sighing, she also got to her feet. David lingered in the doorway.

"I wanted to apologise - " he began.

"No, don't," she cut in. "Please don't say sorry for showing me what you were actually feeling. No games, remember?"

He accepted this argument and followed her through to the kitchen.

Chapter 13

"So, what's all happening then? Has Kenny proposed yet?"

Kate was seated on the hall chair, the phone cradled between her ear and shoulder as she tried to pull on a pair of socks. She had just come out of the shower when Beth had called, but had had plenty of time to dress, as Hazel had hogged the phone for at least ten minutes. Apparently Stuart had been invited to take part in the call and she had giggled and chatted at a million miles an hour to him before finally allowing Kate to speak to their aunt. They had been in Canada for just over a week, and the plan was to stay for another, but Stuart had been anxious to reconnect with his girlfriend and Beth had taken pity on him.

"Oh he has, has he?" Kate announced, her eyes growing wide, then to Hazel, "Kenny's moved in at last."

"Not before time," shouted Hazel, for Beth's benefit, "I assume he's sleeping in our room?" She laughed out loud as she ran upstairs.

Beth and Kenny had been together for as long as the girls had been aware of relationships, which in their particular case was about fourteen years. When their granddad had still been alive, John-Alasdair had been the only man they had ever really known, apart from Aeneas, who kept the hill free from foxes and who would sometimes drop in for a cup of tea and blether with the old man. After his passing, Aeneas had not felt it was his place to call on a household of five females, although he continued to wave at them as he wound his way up the side of the Ben. Fiona's job as a nursery nurse meant she rarely saw anyone but young mothers and this suited her outlook fine. But Beth had been young and pretty, running the fish farm office single-handedly and confidently. She had been a very attractive prospect for any of the men who crossed her path and Kenny had been the one to catch her eye.

Beth however had been in no hurry to get married. Fiona had assured her time and again that her own circumstances were not to be held up as an example, but that was not the reason behind her decision. She simply did not want the ceremony, the cost or the fuss. Kenny was of a similar frame of mind, never being the type of man to court attention, but they had come to an agreement in their first six months together that they were in it for the long haul and that they would consult each other on all major decisions. This had caused many a discussion between the sisters, with Fiona questioning the level of commitment being made by both and Beth sending out the message 'this-is-my-life' without actually using the words. But time had been kind to Beth's relationship and even Fiona had had to admit that there had been no lack of passion, the pair of them merely approached life from a different angle. Even when their mother Mary was alive, he had never been far from the door and in the last year or two, had spent every Sunday with them. He was an easy companion and a loyal friend.

Now, with the worst months of their lives hopefully behind them, he and Beth had decided to finally take a step forward. Although it was yet another change, Kate viewed it as both unsurprising and constructive. It was exactly the time to do it, after everyone had been blown up in the air. The new establishment would be different, yet still familiar enough. She went in search of someone to tell.

The kitchen was empty. David's truck was gone so that answered a question, but Rose was so frequently to be found on the ground floor, that Kate stalled for a second. A quick look showed that her boots were still at the back door, and indeed as she wandered back through the house, she could hear mumblings somewhere above her head.

"Hello?" she called at the foot of the stairs, but there was no reply, so she took them two at a time in her stocking feet. A floorboard creaked overhead and she knew instantly where they would be.

As Kate entered Hazel's old bedroom, Rose was standing on a chair, gently unhooking the last of the curtains, gingerly, so as not to be completely consumed by dust. Hazel had moved the small amount of furniture into the centre of the room, her conversation every so often interrupted by a dry cough, as she tried not to inhale the thick air.

"... and then when Kate came along, there were six of us all squashed in there. Don't remember it being horrendous, but it was always easier when it was just the four of us. Or maybe it just seemed that way because that's what I remember the most. *This* room is the only one I ever had to myself."

"Sorry for cramping your style," smiled Kate, walking over to Rose and taking the heavy material from her. She dropped it on top of the other three lying on the floor. "What are you doing, anyway?"

"I thought I'd give it a spring clean and Rose reckoned it would be okay, right?" Hazel enquired in her direction.

Rose stepped down from the chair and rubbed her hands on the front of her trousers. Her face was strangely blank. "Sure, why not?" she agreed, continuing to rub her hands together. "Maybe I could turn it into a sewing room."

Kate could not read her expression at all, but when she turned to Hazel to clarify what was going on, her sister had her back to her, trying to dislodge cobwebs from the far corner. She tried a different tack.

"Did Hazel tell you that we are having an addition to the family?" Kate asked Rose, grinning. When she did not respond, Kate added, "Kenny is going to live with us, not before time."

"Oh, yes," Rose's face cleared. "David said he was a very decent man."

"Yes," replied Kate. What on earth was happening? Rose was not known to be reticent or awkward in their company, and yet she looked positively ill-at-ease in this room, with the pair of them. Kate walked over to the adjoining door and turned the handle. It remained locked and a thought suddenly occurred to her.

"Does Dad know we're in here?" she asked, almost shyly. As she spoke, Hazel also turned towards Rose to gauge the response. Rose now sighed audibly and sank onto the chair. She looked at Kate, surprised by her intuition and then to Hazel, whose enthusiasm to clean the room had made her oblivious to the signals Kate had picked up on. They both now regarded her with growing discomfort.

"Do you think he'll mind?" asked Hazel, now drawing nearer to take an actual look at Rose's face. "Is it, I mean, I just thought I could clean it up. He doesn't even need to know if you think it's better that way."

Rose looked at their alert faces. They stood before her, both tall, both young and yet less fragile than she ever thought they would be. Hazel had been such a little gem as a toddler, nothing ever appearing to worry or upset her too much because she had a ring of adults watching and nurturing her. She had obviously remained generous with her love and Rose's heart was grateful for this. Kate also seemed very accommodating and Rose knew she was a good person. Yet she had naively imagined that they would fit into the life here without bringing their own agendas, when surely that was the reasoning behind all of this, to let them see who they were and to allow them to ask and enquire and learn. Now that they were here, their eyes searching her face for clues, Rose suddenly felt her legs and her resolve both weaken. For the first time ever, Rose Wilder felt her age.

"Would it be better if we just left it?" Kate asked. She had propped herself against the edge of the bed, and Rose could see genuine anxiety on her face. She had folded her arms, awaiting a reply. Still Rose did not speak and it was if the sudden expanding silence told them that perhaps this situation was a much, much bigger deal than they had realised. Hazel put down the brush she had been holding and sat on the bed amidst the old, battered boxes. Finally, Rose found her voice.

"When your mom left, it was a dark, horrible time for everybody. David was a wreck, it goes without saying, but your grampa Pete, Neil and I, we were all lost. You don't live with a personality like your mom's without feeling bereaved when they go. And you," she looked at Hazel, "you were the whole point to our day. You had all of us, every one, just marvelling at what you were. Then you were gone."

Kate glanced at her sister, who sat with her arms loose by her sides and her face the colour of ivory. Hazel chewed her lip and looked at the floor, unable to acknowledge the level of pain Rose was relating to them, without thinking of her mother. Then, the tears fell.

Kate put one hand on her shoulder and returned her gaze to Rose. "Did nobody try to sort it out?" her voice was the smallest, weakest she had ever heard come from her own mouth.

"Oh God, Kate, you have not one clue what it was like. I can't remember much about the first year. David was still recovering from the accident and never went out of the house."

"Accident?" sobbed Hazel.

"You probably don't remember - "

The back door banged and for some reason, all of them froze. Hazel looked bleakly up, wiping snot from her face, Kate glanced at Rose requiring instructions on what to do next and Rose merely looked resigned to what was coming. No point in prolonging it any longer.

"Hello the girls!" the voice below was heartbreakingly cheerful and Rose for one brief second, took a little gasp of air into her lungs, before standing and holding her arms open.

"I need a hug," she stated and the three of them held each other, briefly before she shook herself visibly and said, "Please just wait up here for two seconds. Then, I think we should all have a chat."

As Rose left them, looking back once directly at Kate, the girls adjusted their stance to hold each other in a firm embrace. Whatever it was that was coming, whatever knowledge they felt they needed, was soon to be upon them. Kate felt her sister keening against her, amazed that it had taken one reference to her past life to burst the dam inside her. But she let her sob against her shoulder, soaking the material there and crying mutely for a moment or two further.

"Here, Haze," she said eventually, leading her back to the bed. "Please don't. We're going to be fine, remember? It's going to be fine."

While Hazel tried to gather herself together, Kate stood at the open door, straining to hear what was being discussed downstairs, but she could perceive nothing.

"Oh God," sniffed Hazel. "Where did all that come from?"

"Better?" asked Kate, with a concerned rather than warm smile. Hazel did not reply, but wiped her face again then began to crack her knuckles.

Kate tried to imagine what was happening downstairs, how Rose was explaining to her son that things had reached a critical point and that what they had been skirting around for days would now have to be addressed. She imagined his eyes growing larger and him rubbing the bristles on his chin, thoughtfully. She wondered if she had enough regard for him to take his words and make sense of them. She had been attached to her mother her entire life, she had seen her perspective and appreciated it. She was perhaps going to hear more than one upsetting thing from this man, but what she wanted more than anything was to be impartial. She wasn't sure if she could be that yet. She turned to Hazel.

"How do you feel about him, Haze?"

Her sister looked blankly at her, not in the same mental place at all. She sniffed one last time and frowned.

"Do you think you can listen to what he says and still feel okay about him?" continued Kate. "Are we going to give him that chance? He could criticise her, you know. Hell, he's almost *bound* to criticise her. What do we do about that?"

Hazel shrugged. At least she was being honest and not spinning a yarn about loving him regardless. Words failing her, Hazel shrugged again. "I'll listen. See what happens after that."

"I think I like him enough to try," supplied Kate. "He seems to ... well, he's not obnoxious or stupid or even over-confident. He sometimes looks like the whole world is his responsibility."

"I remember him." said Hazel, dry-eyed at last. "I remember him from back then, and back then he loved me. I want to love him again. I think I probably do already."

Kate wandered over to the window and looked out at the bright world. Rose had obviously worshipped Hazel, and yet she treated them both equally. She wondered if David had ever ached for her as he had ached for Hazel. Resigned to waiting until they were summoned, Kate opened one of the brown boxes on the bed. It was a risky move, given Hazel's fragile state, but maybe she could find something to bring her back on board. Maybe a crayon drawing or a stuffed toy.

The first box contained a scrap book stuffed with newspaper cuttings and what looked like letters from Skye, which had been glued to the pages still inside their envelopes. How Kate longed to read those, but they were not going to help Hazel at this particular moment. There was a bunch of knitted items for the tiniest of people and a miniature plastic clock with a gnome on it, which looked more than a bit creepy to Kate. Near the bottom there was a pair of black patent shoes with red rose buckles. She handed them to Hazel who immediately smelled them and laughed. Well, that was a start. Still Rose did not call them.

At the top of the second box, Kate found a cardboard folder, plain brown and dog-eared and was about to place it on the bed when she noticed an old photograph protruding through the unglued fold at the bottom. She pulled open the folder and grinned instantly as she recognised a tiny Hazel in front of the cottage at Camastianavaig. She had one hand wrapped in her hair and was holding up a brown stuffed moose in the other. She stood almost shyly on one foot and her dark hair was in two long bunches. She wore a grey pinafore and white socks and Kate guessed she was in her first year at school.

"Hazel! " she cried. "Look at these."

They spent a minute or two, sitting with their heads together, crowing or laughing or exclaiming at the changes apparent in Hazel. Some of the photos had dates on the back, one had a hand-written message to David in his daughter's awful spidery scrawl, and Hazel began to try to arrange them chronologically. As she handed her the final one from the emptied folder, Kate began to feel a little light-headed. Her neck was now blotchy with her nervous rash and the skin of her arms seemed slippery inside her shirt sleeves. She waited for Hazel to cotton on to the change in atmosphere. Her sister looked up at her once, embarrassed and Kate smiled an odd smile and shook her head, one tear forming at the corner of her eye. Hazel was on her feet in a second.

"Hey, hey! I bet there's another folder. I bet you have a folder all to yourself too. We just have to find it."

"But," stammered Kate, not comprehending what was happening, but frantically searching the box for another folder. "There isn't even a photo of us *both*. I know they never met me, knew me, but that's no reason –"

Without another word, she was out of the room and marching downstairs. Hazel, took off after her, slid on the pile of photographs and went down painfully onto one knee. Cursing, she hobbled after Kate.

In the kitchen, Rose was seated at the table. David leaned against the range, deep in thought, listening to his mother. It was true, it was time they all brought their feelings to the table – God knows, he was familiar with the bleak reality of not communicating. He was strong enough, he had drawn on Fiona's own strength whilst she had been coaching him, but now even his mother was providing no real answers. However, there was no room for debate on this, he had to be completely honest with them or risk losing them completely. He could not lose anybody else.

"But how?" he asked simply, following Rose's thoughts on the matter. "How can I be honest without destroying them? Fiona said they would handle it; she said it would be okay."

"Then trust her. You can't really do anything else."

There was sudden movement overhead and David stood upright, eyes alert and face serious. Rose slowly rose from her chair and, as if to try to inject some normality into the situation, reached for the kettle to fill. First on the scene was Kate. Any words that David had thought might start the conversation were obliterated from his mind when he saw her face. Her neck was a livid red and her eyes were as hard as diamonds, her turmoil glinting within them. She slowed down slightly when she saw the pair of them, skulking in front of her, then sat heavily in the chair, eyes fixed on the man before her.

"Were you not interested enough to keep them? Or did she never send any?" her voice had a tremor which was not anger or grief; it was far more desperate than that. David stared at her. Never in all her earlier hostilities had she shown this level of panic and he had no clue what she was referring to.

"What is it?" he asked, as Rose made an impulsive move towards Kate then stopped herself. David alone had to manage this situation, she did not need to steer Kate away from it. She glanced at Hazel as she limped into the room, out of breath and her features still streaked with dried tears. Her expression was as heartsick as Kate's voice had been. David now moved towards the pair of them, but Kate was already standing again, behind the table, not wanting any space between them that he may try to fill. Her breathing was shallow.

"I don't know what you're talking about, Kate. Tell me." David's voice was now gentler but did not waver for a second. His moment had come.

"Why are there no photos of me? In this whole house, there is not one photo of me. Not even in an old, worn-out folder. Not one."

Rose involuntarily put her hand over her mouth and turned away. Hazel joined her beside the sink, feeling her own stomach begin to cave in on itself, but could not take her eyes off the couple facing each other across the kitchen table. David swallowed, hesitant to reply, but whatever this predicament was, it was too dreadful to be endured in silence. Kate felt the same.

101

"Why?" she now asked. The space she occupied seemed to be insulated in thick cotton, and she wanted to burn her way through to the clearer air beyond. She looked at him, no smile accompanying her stare, trying to fathom his mind and why this man was not coming up with a million simple, harmless explanations for her betrayal. His face was verging on desperation as he fought to bring her to a place where she would understand. There was only one way to do this, but as he swallowed once more and looked as if he had the answer, Kate's shoulders suddenly drooped and she took one step back from this hideous situation.

She looked at Hazel, who was completely frozen to the spot, and she knew at once that she had come to the same staggering conclusion. But was it the correct one? Maybe it was a ridiculous assumption based on utter terror, which had entered their heads – and this was the unbelievable aspect of the whole thing – *only* at that very moment in time. Could they really be so completely naive, both of them? Kate, to her further horror, felt her face contort in pain. Somebody needed to speak, and yet they were determined that she remain in this silent torture chamber. She did not deserve it.

"Is that why?" she whimpered, taking another step away from all of them. "Is that what all of this is about? Please, please just tell me."

Finally unable to watch her agony any longer, David strode over to her, about to take her shoulders when she grabbed him by the elbows and pushed him back against the nearest wall. "No. No, you don't get to touch me," she choked. Startled, he did not move. Hazel was now crying openly, clinging to Rose. Her grandmother. Kate grabbed the edge of the nearest chair and closed her eyes as the room swayed, yet she stayed upright and asked through gritted teeth. "Tell me who he was."

She did not open her eyes again until the room stopped spinning, when she looked straight at David, willing him to laugh and dismiss her fears as ridiculous. But his eyes were pained and he said simply. "She never told me."

Kate now saw David as if for the first time. She recognised the face, she had studied it for three weeks now and she had grown used to his expressions and the way his eyes lit up when he engaged them in conversation. She knew that she liked what he was, that he was decent and honest with them and that when that face was in the room, she felt at ease. She had allowed him into her life, even into her heart a little and it had been strange, but not that difficult. Now, it was like looking at him through a piece of misshapen glass. He stood there, leaning against the wall, his face grey and shining with sweat. His features seemed to have doubled in size, his eyes black and his jaw square. For one fleeting moment she saw the 'wedding photo Dad', but that was ripped from her mind as quickly as it had entered it, and now even that term was obsolete. She tilted her head to the side slightly, her eyes never leaving his, and wondered what he saw when he looked at her.

Hazel was now shouting in her face, but the words were incomprehensible and she pushed her away with a frown. Her sister tried to take her arm, tears spilling down her cheeks, and to pull her into an embrace, but she twisted herself out of it with a grunt.

"Leave me alone," she snarled. Rose moved Hazel away from her and out of the room, talking gently to her, but Kate heard nothing of it. There was no sound except for the high-pitched whine in her ears and still her eyes never left David's face. She could see his lips moving, as he slowly walked over to where she stood shaking, but no words reached her brain. She was appalled that he had sat on this knowledge all of this time. She wanted to punch him in the face, she wanted to scream until her throat burned raw, she wanted to run and run for one thousand miles if necessary, anything to rid her of the twisting knife inside her chest. But all she did was clench her hands into fists, hard enough for her fingers to cramp up, so that she did not lose her mind completely.

David now stood immediately in front of her but his arms stayed securely by his sides and he made no further attempt to speak to her. She looked up at his face which still appeared like somebody had taken apart the features she had known and put them back together slightly differently. She could read nothing in his present expression. His lips were slightly parted, his eyebrows met in the middle and a muscle twitched in his cheek. None of it meant anything to her. She looked at every part of his face, sorrow suddenly cutting one more deep fissure inside her as she realised that she had inherited none of his looks. She had been sure that they had shared a chin. This thought almost choked her as did the fact that there were so many others out there waiting to invade her mind. They were going to come and she could not stop them.

Apparently also helpless, he made no move. Maybe they could just stand there for the rest of their lives, not thinking, not speaking, not asking questions, not sharing information. Kate felt the tiniest spark of hope that perhaps she could just die there, on her feet, and never have to face anything again. She would just become inanimate and all would be peaceful and quiet and dark. Dark seemed appealing. As her eyes began to glaze over, David took a small step nearer, willing her to tell him what to do, and immediately she felt reality's ruthless light blind her. Finally, she fell into the chair and sat with her head down.

David knelt by her side, but was careful not to lay a finger on her. She moved her eyes towards him once and whispered, "I want my Mum."

103

PART II
December 1975

Chapter 14
December 1975

"Do they even make snow shoes this small?"

It was a thought voiced out loud and Fiona smiled as she pictured a miniature pair of tennis racquets bound to Hazel's feet and her subsequent attempt to walk in them. Now, as she picked through the mountain of tiny footwear that was Hazel's shoe collection, her daughter sat beside her, squealing delightedly every time she picked up an old favourite. Her eyes were shining as brightly as they had been when visiting Santa the week before.

Fiona sighed. With the winter clothing and boots all now bought and in full use, Hazel's feet had suddenly sprouted and she complained daily about the discomfort. Fiona had been hunting in vain for a pair that may have some spare growing room, but now that Hazel had joined her, it had turned into an entirely different activity.

"What about *this* pair? Remember these?" Fiona held up a pair of black patent leather pumps which sported a similar scarlet flower on the buckles.

"My rose shoes!" Hazel laughed, her hair immediately getting caught in one of the buckles as she hugged them to her cheek.

"Here. Don't move, dafty."

As Fiona carefully unthreaded Hazel's brown strands from the buckle, pulling her onto her lap for a better look, she sighed again. It was two days before Christmas, how was she going to get outdoor shoes before the holiday?

"There you go, missy. Now, I know what to do. You sit by the heater – not too close – and you can sort the shoes for me. You see how there are two of these rose shoes? Well, there should be two of *all* these shoes. See?"

Under Hazel's inquisitive gaze, Fiona extricated two ancient blue boots and laid them side by side in front of her daughter. "See, Haze? One, two blue boots."

Hazel nodded, grinning. "One, two," she repeated.

"That's my girl. See if you can find two of everything. Look, I'll start you off with this one."

As Hazel threw herself into the task, kneeling on shoes and toppling over occasionally, Fiona got up to stretch her legs. They were in Hazel's room at the rear of the house, bathed in the false, cold light that the snow had created. As she headed through the adjoining door to her and David's room, Fiona pressed the play button on the child's cassette player and grinned as she heard her daughter agree, in her squeaky almost-perfectly formed English, that it was indeed the most wonderful time of the year.

Fiona took a quick glance at the weather as she carried on through to the living area which they had created next door. Previously the top floor of the house had been used mainly for storage, although it had never been as lowly as a roof-space or loft. The windows up here were no smaller or less frequent than the floor below and there was a working fireplace. David and she now had their own little place.

There was a three-seater sofa and one armchair. They did not quite match, but between them Hazel and Rose had crocheted multi-coloured blankets to drape over both so they looked like a suite. There were toys kept in an old trunk which had lost its lid, but the majority of Hazel's playthings were down in the kitchen. They did not alienate themselves up here, there was no bathroom or kitchenette and everybody was perfectly at ease sharing and occupying the whole house. But it was a place to retire to when it was needed and the fire made it into a cosy haven. Although there was no TV, there was a radio and record player, a bureau and a coffee table, which Neil had made for them the previous Christmas. Now, as Fiona stirred and refuelled the fire, inhaling the spruce garlands she had placed on top of the mantelpiece, there was a shout from below.

"Hello, the girls!"

Fiona's heart jumped, then she checked her watch. He was early and she was delighted.

"Hey, you!" she cried, replacing the fire guard and securing it to its hooks. "This is a nice surprise," then, "just tell me you left your boots at the back door."

David appeared in the doorway, peeling off his inner jacket and removing his hat. He was grinning.

"Do you really think, Fee, that Rose would have let me get this far?" His hair stood up in short tufts where it had been released from its buckskin prison and his face was pink and chilled.

"Just keeping up the standards of the house," she explained. "Come here by the fire."

As he joined her, she put her arms under his and rubbed his back, briskly.

"You're frozen," she sympathised, her lips brushing against the prickly wool of his jumper, "but mmmm you smell all fresh and icy. I like it."

He encircled her inside his embrace and leaned his chin on top of her head.

"And I like that you like it," he murmured.

She linked her hands behind his back at waist level and leaned back, looking at him. A razor had not touched his face for three days due to the fact that all outstanding log orders had to be met by Christmas and he barely had time to sleep let alone shave. With one hand still resting on his waist, Fiona smoothed out the tufts in his hair and ran her finger across the bristles on his upper lip and chin. She said nothing for a moment, long enough for him to catch the mood, then as he closed his eyes to her touch, she put her fingers on his lips.

"And I *love* this face."

Her arms went up around his neck as he pulled her soft warm frame forward to his wiry, cold one. She knew however that his kiss would be neither cold nor chaste and she sought it out, moulding her mouth to his. It was so familiar an action, but she was continually surprised at her body's reaction to it, whatever the duration of the kiss. David now pulled his face away, his eyes burning.

"You are ... incredible." he whispered.

"You are the lord and master," she smiled back, her eyes now twinkling.

He grinned in reply, then, "You're the devil in disguise."

She nodded in resigned agreement. "I am indeed the devil and you are at my command. I need some more logs."

"Logs," he groaned.

"Indeed logs," she repeated, pushing her hands into the back pockets of his jeans and pulling him against her once more, "if you know what's good for you." She completed the sentence by pinching him hard.

"Ow," he yelped loudly.

"Daddy!" The rapturous call was accompanied by small feet shuffling hastily towards them, before Hazel came to an unsteady halt in the doorway. Her face developed an extra layer of pleasure when she saw that it was indeed the man himself. Fiona chuckled as she noticed the four different shoes she was wearing, one stuffed awkwardly onto each foot and one on each hand.

"Look," she held both hands and one foot in the air, "Old shoes!"

David knew better than to laugh directly at his excited daughter, but Fiona could feel him shaking to control it.

"What have you been up to then, Miss Priss?" smiling broadly instead, as he crossed to where she stood, still balancing on one foot. He knelt at her side, his long legs as always a hindrance to a direct hug, and lowered her foot.

"Shoes," she repeated, and shook them all off for his inspection.

"Well, I certainly know who these belong to. But," his voice was full of awe "don't tell me these are too small for you. Your feet can't be as big as this already?"

Still smiling, Hazel wrapped her arm around David's neck and allowed him to lift her up. "Yes they are. They don't fit."

"Really mom?" he enquired of Fiona, his voice thick with mock disbelief. Before Fiona could join in, Hazel turned his face back to hers and looked him straight in the eye, her voice a serious half-whisper. "They're baby shoes."

"Oh, I see," David's face cleared. "That explains it."

Hazel struggled back and forth in his arms and when he released her, she grabbed his hand. "Come and look."

Fiona followed them through to Hazel's bedroom and was genuinely pleased at what she saw. Apart from the four odd shoes which Hazel had been sporting, the remainder of the items were now all paired up, sitting in a large circle around the box they had once occupied.

"Hazel," she cried, "You have done such a good job!" Her daughter beamed from one parent to the other, but settled on David's face.

"What does Daddy think?" prompted Fiona.

"I think," he said, shaking his head, "that I have never seen so many shoes in my whole life. And I also think that the person who tidied them all up like this deserves some hot chocolate."

Hazel jumped up and down and squealed at Fiona, "That's me! Me!"

As David grabbed Hazel and swung her, giggling, onto his back, Fiona found her daughter's discarded slippers and followed them downstairs.

"Actually, Dave," she began, as they entered the empty kitchen, "We do have a wee bit of a problem."

"We do?" he asked, sitting at the table and hauling Hazel around onto his lap. She immediately stuck her third and fourth finger in her mouth and twirled her hair with her free hand. Fiona handed him the slippers and reached for the milk pan.

"Well, it's nothing major, just a matter of our usual poor timing."

"I always thought our timing was immaculate," he stated, innocently, finally fitting Hazel's foot into the reluctant second slipper.

"Hurts," muttered Hazel, her eyelids drooping.

"That's the problem," Fiona sighed, stirring the milk with one hand whilst watching David trying to settle his mildly squirming daughter.

"Her feet have grown since we bought those last boots. She says *everything* hurts her feet now and I think they've gone up at least two sizes."

"Really?" his face did now show honest dismay. "Wow," then into Hazel's silken hair, "Who knew you'd be so expensive?"

"Hmm," Fiona addressed the boiling milk. "Is she still awake?"

"No, she's gone."

Fiona shared the milk between two of the three mugs and brought them to the table. "You want me to ...?" she indicated to Hazel, whose hands now both swung at David's sides.

"No, she's fine. Where's Rose?"

"I've no idea. Wrapping presents maybe. It's just that I can't see us being able to get anything for outdoors before Christmas."

David blew on his hot chocolate, protecting Hazel's head with his other hand. "If I tell you something, can you keep it under your hat?"

"Well what do you think? I am the mistress of secret-keeping."

He raised his eyebrows but continued, leaning forward slightly to check that Hazel was still out of it.

"I'm only telling you this so that you will stop worrying. And you have to look genuinely surprised when -"

"Oh, just tell me," hissed Fiona.

David's face became instantly aloof and he raised his mug to his lips unnecessarily slowly. She waited as he wiped some hot milk from his infant moustache and finally looked back at her. His green eyes regarded her steadily.

"You going to listen?"

Tight-lipped but smiling, Fiona nodded meekly.

"Okay. Well, Rose thought that she should get some extra footwear in because she wasn't sure if the ones we bought would last the whole winter, especially if we got snowed in. Plus, I think she's knitting her some sort of slipper sock combination ....what?"

Fiona's initial relief at his words had dissolved a little and now she felt her face fall. She sat back in her chair, trying not to show the extent of her dismay.

"What is it?" David repeated, although he had an inkling.

"Why didn't we think of that? I should have thought of that one, Dave."

"Does it matter, Fee.Really?"

"She's so much better than me at this whole thing."

"Hold it," his voice was sharper than he intended, but it served its purpose. "You're going to stop this right now. No more of this."

Hazel stirred slightly and he lowered his voice.

"Listen to me. You've got to realise something. Rose brought up babies, yes, but there's no way she could be any better than you are. The only thing she has which is helpful – and you should see it as such – is experience. Not just experience of children but also of winters out here."

Fiona had indeed listened to him, feeling no resentment and tried to reconcile his words. He was deadly earnest and she wondered how long he had been so aware of her self-doubt.

"Do you have a problem with Rose? Does she but in too much?"

Fiona was instantly appalled. "No, no, not at all. It's me. I can't - "

"Please stop that," he now implored, his voice slower and gentler. "You are such a great mom. I love watching you with this one. Rose compliments you all the time."

"Really?"

"Yes," he adjusted Hazel slightly so that she was propped against his arm, and then folded her onto Fiona's lap. Hazel turned over, her fingers again in her mouth and nestled against her mother's shoulder. David knelt down beside them. He now smelled of chocolate and Hazel's shampoo.

"You're the most important to her, the best thing she has in her life."

"Well," Fiona leaned her forehead against his. "I think you might be ahead of me on that one."

David shook his head and stood. Fiona wrapped her arm around his leg to show her gratitude at this words and he kissed the top of her head before moving back to his seat.

"She wasn't going to tell you about the boots, she was just going to substitute them if the time came, that's why she bought the exact same ones."

Fiona smiled, eternally grateful for Rose's sensitivity. "And that," said Fiona, "is why I love your mother."

"Just don't tell her you know," he reiterated, finishing his drink and picking up Fiona's still brimming mug. "You want me to reheat that?"

"No, I'll do it later when Hazel wants hers. She'll remember she hasn't had it. Anyway, not that I'm complaining, but why are you early?"

"Because," he sat once more, his legs now stretched out in front of him and his fingers laced behind his head, "I am now officially ..." he yawned "...finished work for the holidays."

"Hurrah!" Fiona clapped her hands and Hazel sat up, bleary-eyed.

"Where's my chocolate, Daddy?"

"I'll get you some chocolate, Hazel Rose Wilder," Rose answered, entering the kitchen with a pile of cardboard boxes in her arms. In spite of his fatigue, David took them from her immediately and simply asked, "Where?"

"Oh, the pantry will do for the moment. Now, who wants chocolate again?"

"Me, Gramma. They said I could have some, but I haven't."

"Hey, missy," Fiona tickled her mercilessly, "You fell asleep."

"Did not," shrieked Hazel, crying with mirth. Then she stopped suddenly and slid from Hazel's grasp.

"Toilet," she said and ran out of the kitchen.

"Are those boxes the Christmas decorations, Rose?" Fiona asked, hopefully.

"Yes, I thought we could have a go at them tonight."

"Ooh yes please," laughed Fiona. "Can't come soon enough for me."

David wandered back through from the pantry, and positioned himself against the range. His jeans were crumpled and wet where they had been tucked into his boots and his knitted socks seemed to have stretched and grown. He yawned again and gave an involuntary shudder. Fiona doubted she had ever loved him as much as she did at that moment, when he caught her eye and winked at her.

"That you finished now, Davy boy?" Rose moved him gently aside as she began to heat some fresh milk.

"Oh, yes," he breathed. "No more logs for the next four days." Pause. "Apart from the ones my wife insists we need upstairs."

Rose chuckled. "Well, that's one order you do need to fill."

If she was aware of the loaded look David threw in Fiona's direction, Rose made no reference to it, but scooped Hazel up as she ran up to her and fastened her into her high chair. Fiona turned away, her face burning, and busied herself with washing the dishes.

"Two more minutes, Hazel," Rose instructed her grand-daughter, then returned to the range.

"Looks to me like you could catch a chill from those damp jeans," Rose's voice was businesslike. "Why don't you take some logs from the sitting room and I can get Pete to bring some more in when he comes home."

David's protest evolved into an incomprehensible yawn and Rose physically pushed him out of the way.

"Go. You need some sleep, boy."

"Well, I could maybe do with a couple of hours," he accepted.

"And maybe a shave," added Rose.

As he passed Fiona at the sink, his hand rested on the back of her neck and he leaned over to kiss her. She kissed him back, then murmured, "You don't *have* to shave."

She watched him pad across to Hazel and ruffle her hair, which made his daughter giggle and then ignore him as her hot chocolate was placed in front of her. He stretched his arms high in the air as he exited the kitchen and they could hear him trudge up the stairs. He very rarely trudged.

Rose now sat beside Hazel, tying a bib around her neck against spillage.

"So, shall we have a look at those decorations before supper?" asked Fiona.

"I think," replied Rose, "that you should go and spend some time with your husband before either, or both of you spontaneously combust."

"Wha–at?" began Fiona, colouring immediately, then, "I mean, what about supper, or Madam there?"

Rose finally looked at her daughter-in-law.

"He works hard and this one ..." she tapped Hazel's head, "... can be hard work too. You've barely seen each other this week and I haven't seen Hazel Rose all day, have I sweetness?"

Hazel gave Rose a toothy, chocolaty grin but said nothing. There seemed so little point in opposing something which would be to everyone's benefit that Fiona gave in.

"Thanks, Rose," she said, quietly, then "I'll take the logs up with me."

"Do that," she replied. "Sweetness and I are going to make cupcakes."

Fiona could hear David moving around their bedroom as she restocked the log basket, the noise of which brought him to the doorway. He stood, pulling off his remaining sock, his shirt off but his jeans still clinging loosely to his lean waist.

"Dammit," he said, eyeing the fresh logs, "I knew there was something I'd forgotten."

"Don't worry about it," Fiona threw a couple of logs onto the embers, then marched up to him, laying her head against his bare chest.

"Hello you," he said, putting his arms around her.

"Are my hands too cold?" she asked, tucking them into the back of his jeans.

He shook his head, pulling her tight into him. She raised her face to his and as he found her mouth, she began to stroke his back beneath his waistband. Instantly, she felt the sweat gather beneath her fingertips and heard the gasp catch in his throat.

"What about ...?" he croaked.

"She's with Rose," Fiona whispered urgently, leading him to the bed. It took David less than fifteen seconds to remove his jeans and shorts, but in that time Fiona had discarded everything and dived under the covers. Undressing each other was a summer activity. As he joined her, David marvelled again at the capacity of their love. It was always a mutual longing and, tired though he was, he wanted her now above anything and everything.

"Come here," he said, pulling her head against his shoulder, holding her body to his.

"You're not too tired?" she asked, dreading that the answer may be yes.

"Never, for you," he whispered and pulled her on top of him. He lay perfectly supine; her body mirrored his. Fiona tasted salt as her lips and tongue traced the curve of his smooth chest, his hands cupping her buttocks, then caressing the tops of her thighs in response. He could almost span her waist with his hands and she liked him to hold her there, guiding and teaching her. They had learned their art together, but felt there were still discoveries to be made. Finally, whilst Fiona's mouth was latched onto his, he placed her where she needed to be and slid inside her.

Fiona always relished the control he allowed her to have when she looked down at his face and within seconds she had sought and found what gave them both the most pleasure. He was so familiar to her but that was what excited her the most. She knew what he was capable of just as she knew when they both wanted a quick, intense release. He grabbed her hair as it fell across his face and held it aloft, almost triumphantly, as she moved astride him, fitting her fingers into the grooves in his rib-cage and drawing the skin away from the bones. David's other hand still held her by the waist, recognising and acting upon every expression on her damp face. In turn, she studied him. David's eyes were growing black before her, his pupils so enlarged with the intensity of it all that his beloved green irises had almost disappeared.

"Oh, Fee," he gasped, "Fee."

She felt herself lose sense of reality, as if the world was rushing away from her and knew that the time was near. As if to prove this, she suddenly felt David grab both her hands, lacing their fingers together and pull her down to him, so that their faces were inches apart.

"I ... love you," he groaned and screwed his eyes tight in the ecstasy of the moment. Fiona felt her insides dissolve to liquid and she shuddered twice before sliding her arms beneath his shoulders and lying with her cheek next to his. She could feel his bristles tickle her face, as his breathing gradually calmed and his hands rested at the base of her spine, their work complete. He did not speak – he was indeed tired.

Before he drifted away completely, Fiona climbed from his body and lay snuggled into his side instead. In the gathering gloom of the late afternoon, she ran her finger once more along his rough chin and whispered, with some regret, "*Now* you can shave."

Chapter 15

When Christmas morning arrived, it was to find the previous night's snow frozen solid and the accompanying silence almost supernatural. Fiona opened her eyes to the beginnings of a paling blue dawn, which had no sun as yet to make it sparkle. The house was quiet and David slept soundly, his left arm thrown high above his head. Perfect, she thought and edged her way from the bed. Her husband merely rubbed his nose at the movement and inclined his head further under the covers. Fiona felt around with her feet for her slippers and pulled a thick jumper over her pyjamas.

In Hazel's room, a tiny toy-sized lamp gave off a pink glow but it was still as black as night at the rear of the house. However, at the first sense of her mother's entrance, Hazel sat up in bed, and stuck her fingers in her mouth.

"It's okay, baby. It's just me."

"Mommy?"

"Ssh, honey. Are you ready for an adventure?"

"Venture?" she repeated, as Fiona lifted her flannelette-wrapped body from its snug burrow. Hazel reached automatically for her little blanket as she was lifted into her mother's arms.

"Can 'Byes' come?" she enquired, holding the blanket aloft

"Byes can come," whispered Fiona, "but you have to be very quiet, because Daddy is still asleep. Here, put your dressing gown on."

"Slippers hurt," she reminded Fiona in her own attempt at a whisper.

"Your bed-socks will be enough."

The pair of them crept across the bedroom, avoiding the known creaky floorboard, and headed out to the top of the stairs. David watched them go, smiling at their poor efforts at secrecy, then turned over in bed. This was obviously important to his wife and he wanted her to love every second of it.

As children, Fiona and Beth had always been the first to rise on Christmas morning and were allowed to light a candle each on the mantelpiece and switch on the tree lights, if they promised to be very, very careful. They would then sit and shiver in the relative dark, their teeth chattering with excitement, as they waited for their parents to join them. The multi-coloured bulbs would create circles of light around themselves, making them look bigger than they actually were and the candles would flicker in some draught, weird shapes dancing on the ceiling. Fiona and Beth would sit huddled, not wishing for the moment to pass, even though it meant they could then open their presents. It was just too special to hurry - and personal only to them. Fiona could smell the anticipation of those mornings now.

The generator had kicked in about an hour earlier, and Fiona was grateful for the warmth which had begun to creep through the house, but she switched on no lights. Hazel sat upright in her arms, hugging Byes close to her face, eyes as big as they had ever been.

"Are we going outside?"

"No, no, it's far too cold. Anyway, I think there's something much more special inside today."

Fiona now deposited Hazel on the hall seat and asked her to sit there quietly for a few moments. Hazel accepted this with no argument, but wondered what on earth her mother was busy with in the sitting room. A few seconds later, Fiona emerged from the room, carrying a thick candle in the shape of a conifer, its wick alight and sputtering in the draught.

"Oooh," whispered Hazel, watching the wavering flame and reaching her hand towards it.

"No, no, you can't touch it baby, it's very hot. But, if you promise not to squirm too much, I can carry both you and our tree candle into the sitting room. Can you do that?"

Hazel nodded immediately, wrapping Byes safely around one wrist and putting her arm behind her back, out of harm's way.

"Okay then," smiled Fiona, helping Hazel to stand on the hall seat and then settle onto her hip. "Do you know what happened last night, Hazel?"

"Did Uncle Neil sleep on the sofa again?"

"Something *much* better than that," Fiona chuckled, pausing at the sitting room door. "Santa paid a visit and left something behind."

"Santa? He's been *here?*"

"Let's take a look," nodded Fiona, and swung the sitting room door gently open.

In the far corner, between the front and side windows, the Christmas tree stood, displaying its jewelled beams of colour which twinkled from floor to ceiling. They had dressed it the night before, after Hazel was in bed, because Fiona had wanted her to get the full effect on the day that it mattered. David had not argued, as he had feared Hazel might have exploded with excitement at the sight of all the tinsel and trimmings, and that more than one glass bauble would have suffered a similar fate at his daughter's hands. Now, the toddler was speechless, leaning further into her mother's shoulder, the nearer to the tree they became. Fiona sensed her confusion.

"Do you like it Hazel? Aren't the lights pretty colours?"

Hazel's voice was a quiver, but her eyes never left the spectacle, "It's a tree – and it's in the house. Did Santa leave it here?"

Fiona put the candle down carefully on the coffee table and brought Hazel round to face her, the girl's legs wrapping around her mother's waist tightly.

"No, honey," she hugged her close and then said softly, "Daddy brought the tree in from outside. It's a special tree for Christmas, that's why it's got lights on it."

Now Hazel turned back to face it and slid down from Fiona's arms. She looked closely at the lights, noticing that they were in fact tiny plastic lanterns.

"What's your favourite colour?"

"That one," said Hazel.

"Red. Well, that's a fine colour to have as a favourite. Mine is green."

Hazel was about to touch one of the bulbs, when she stopped herself and let out a little gasp.

"Mommy, there are lots of boxes under the tree."

"Are there, Haze? Are they brown boxes?"

"No, they are all different ones. Snowmen on one."

Fiona now took Hazel's hand and knelt beside her. "Well, that's what Santa left. Lots of presents for all of us."

Hazel's open-mouthed joy was something to behold as she held onto both of her mother's hands, Byes now crumpled at her feet. "For all of us?"

Fiona nodded slowly, enjoying her daughter's sheer glee at the morning. Hazel dropped onto the floor, sitting cross-legged in front of the tree, staring up at the vision before her, and Fiona knew it was one of those influential moments, like the first time she saw the moon on the river or tasted hot chocolate. The previous year, Hazel had been choked with cold and slept through most of Christmas, leaving Fiona bereft of her usual yuletide enjoyment. But this had far surpassed her expectations and, elated, she turned towards the banked down fire to revive it. Neil was standing at the door, arms folded, but moved back into the hall at being noticed. Fiona crept over to the doorway and beckoned him closer.

"Did you see her face?"

He laughed quietly, nodding, then looking past his sister-in-law, he pointed to Hazel. "She isn't even going near the presents. If that had been Davey and me, we would have had them shredded open by now."

"Oh, I must go and get him. He should see this. Could you just make sure she doesn't touch the candle."

"Sure," he agreed. "I won't disturb her though."

As Fiona headed up the first flight, she heard a tiny voice behind her, "Uncle Neil, look what happened in the night ..."

* * * *

It was Fiona's fifth Christmas in Canada and she was finally accepting that although they did things to a different schedule, this was not the crime that she had thought at first. Breakfast and chores were essential before presents were even considered and she gradually found that the anticipation was a welcome addition. Hazel's initial excitement had grown steadily as she had shown everyone in the whole household, including an enchanted Pete, that Santa had been and had 'left something behind'. She had prattled incessantly as the three men dressed for outdoors then left, gave both Rose and Fiona her thoughts and feelings on the day so far whilst attempting to set the table, then talked through

117

mouthfuls of cereal until David pointed out that even on Christmas Day, you shouldn't chew and chatter at the same time. She had accepted this with good grace and remained silent for about three minutes.

The remainder of the day had been spent preparing, eating and dozing. Rose was never off her feet, but preferred it that way and Neil left to visit his girlfriend in the middle of the afternoon. Otherwise the entire family enjoyed the novelty of each other's company with no pressing matters to attend to. Hazel lasted until just after 4 o'clock, delighting in being the centre of attention, before cuddling up on Pete's chest and falling instantly asleep. It wasn't long before his gentle snores accompanied her deep breathing.

The only cloud on the horizon had been when Fiona had felt the customary cramping in her lower belly and had unwrapped herself from David's arm and retreated, disappointed, to the toilet. She had really hoped that this month would see the beginning of another little Wilder, but again it was not to be. She wasn't entirely surprised, given the lack of opportunities that had arisen during the build-up to the season, but it would have been a nice extra gift for her husband as they headed into another year, and Hazel was nearly three.

She felt at this moment that a phone-call home would be beneficial, but of course it was the early hours of the following morning, and they would worry about two phone-calls in one day. The first had been made when Hazel was at her loudest and chattiest and it made little difference that she had met these people only once as an infant. Fiona, ever mindful of phone bills, had had to cut her short and then try to get in all the latest news and good tidings in half the time. Sometimes, she missed them all so much and now, after a disappointment, it seemed like she would never have that precious connection with them again. She wandered through to the kitchen and picked at some roasted vegetables. Rose appeared as if from nowhere.

"All okay, sweetheart?"

At the maternal care infused in that one sentence, Fiona slowly drew out a kitchen chair and sat, her lip quivering slightly. She nodded, not trusting her voice.

"You miss them, I know. You're always restless on Christmas Day. Want some soup?"

"Yes please," she said, ever gratefully. Then, "it's not just that Rose."

She waited until her mother-in-law turned to assess her, and then said, resignedly, "I thought I might be pregnant, but I'm not."

Rose smiled in empathy, "Well, I know all about that one, honey. Your body can be your best friend sometimes, other times it doesn't want to play."

Fiona nodded, not wanting to think about or compare herself to what Rose had gone through. As if sensing this, Rose came over from the range.

"Things are way different now, Fiona. Remember, I was older than you are for a start, and conception was never the problem, I just couldn't seem to carry. How long have you been trying, if you don't mind the question?"

118

"It's not that straightforward. I'm the only one who knows that we have been. David is happily ignorant - which really is 'happily' if it's not working."

Rose placed some soup in front of Fiona and handed her a clean spoon.

"My advice?" Rose sat beside her and patted her shoulder. "Concentrate on enjoying Hazel, the other will sort itself out. I was so consumed with my problem that I barely remember Davey's early years, and that's a crime. Besides, you never see him at the moment. The odds are against you."

"Thanks, Rose," Fiona sipped some of the thick liquid and enjoyed the feeling of it warming her thought-chilled bones. "You're right about Hazel. She's a Godsend, pulls me out of myself every time I slip."

"She's that alright," laughed Rose. "Do you want one of your pain-killers?"

"I'll get one once I've eaten this, thanks, Rose. Then I think I'll just go and snuggle up to my man and wait for the light of our lives to wake up. I think there's still some of this day that she needs to explore."

The next day, Fiona did not get up until nearly lunch-time. When she made it down to the kitchen, she found that David and Pete had taken Hazel out to sledge in her new boots, and Neil was sitting at the kitchen table, the blackest of looks evident on his face. She knew that she had interrupted something, as Rose's calming words ceased as soon as she appeared.

"Oh, sorry," she apologised, embarrassed. "Let me just get some coffee and I'll be right out - "

"It doesn't matter," he scowled. "You'll find out soon enough."

Fiona looked helplessly in Rose's direction, who pulled a face in reply and said simply, "Cindy."

"Oh?" it was all she could think of to say, hoping that it would convey whatever meaning Neil wanted it to.

"It's finished."

"Aw, that's ... a thing that you were not expecting?"

"You could say that," his eyes never left the table, as he bit his nails one after the other. Rose poured her a coffee and pulled a chair out for her.

"Oh, I don't want to interrupt -"

"I'm not worried," he replied and Rose made motions behind his back to get her to stay.

"What happened?"

He shrugged. "She has plans and I'm not part of them. Took her long enough to tell me."

"I'm sorry. Was this yesterday?"

"Oh, yeah," he sneered, his young face still racked with regret, but his voice taking on a bitter tone. "She waited until I tried to give her..." he looked away momentarily, then shrugged again, "well I asked her to marry me."

"Oh shit," Fiona breathed, then made an apologetic face to Rose, who waved it away. "But Neil, you're so young, maybe she –"

"You were married at nineteen and had a kid by twenty. Don't preach age to me."

Fiona opened her mouth to reply then closed it. She had absolutely no argument and was busy trying to catch Rose's eye when Neil put his hand on hers.

"Sorry, that was harsh."

"No," she submitted, "it was absolutely true. Did she say what her plans are?"

"Basically, not to get married at the moment."

"Oh, well that is a shame, if that's what *you* wanted."

"I wanted her," he murmured. "I wanted what you two have."

Now Fiona really was lost, but as she turned to Rose for assistance, her mother-in-law was signalling that she was going to leave them to it. Fiona gave her a panicked shake of the head, but Rose nodded as if she knew best. Fiona sipped her coffee and floundered for words.

"It doesn't work if you're not in exactly the same place, Neil. In life, I mean, not geography, obviously," she cursed her inadequacies. "But with us, we both wanted exactly the same thing, so that was where we started from. I could say that we were really lucky, but that would suggest that you were unlucky. You weren't, you were just in different places."

She squeezed his hand then let it go. His blond head looked so dejected, however, that she could not leave it quite yet.

"Was she, I mean, did she make you feel stupid?"

"No," he was genuinely surprised. "She was crying, which just about killed me altogether. She was really upset, but at the same time, she wouldn't take the ring. Said it wasn't what she had planned on."

Fiona's face cleared at an idea. "Maybe you could give her a few days and then tell her that you understand completely."

"What?" he cried, frowning up at her.

"No, listen. If you don't want to kill it here and now, you tell her that you understand and that you hope - "

"Don't say it! Don't use those words! We were 'friends' before and it led to this situation. Is she going to keep saying no each time we get back to here?"

"I was going to say," Fiona's patience was endless, "you tell her you hope you didn't upset her too much and that you're there if she wants to discuss it."

"She won't," he said hopelessly, at which point Hazel came stomping through the back door, her face smeared with tears and her coat ripped at the front.

"I – fell – off – the – sledge," she sobbed and held up her arms to her mother. Pete followed her through the door, apologising unconditionally for being the cause of the misfortune, but Fiona simply smiled her forgiveness over Hazel's head as she peeled off her filthy coat. When she had calmed sufficiently, Fiona placed her onto Neil's knee.

"You two need each other," she stated, and to Pete, "and you need some coffee, I think."

120

When Rose returned to the warm room, she found Hazel and Neil playing snap at the table and Pete watching them from his favourite chair, pulled up to the range. Fiona was gazing out into the falling snow. Her family seemed relatively contented and as Rose crossed to where Fiona stood, she brushed the top of Neil's head. It was a simple gesture, but they both knew what it meant.

"Where is he?" Rose asked Fiona.

"Pete left him by the shed, trying to fix the sledge. Madam there was involved in a *major* drama and the sledge is now in two pieces. You know what he's like, won't stop until it's fixed. I think I'll take him a drink, see how he's getting on."

"Good idea."

Fiona loved the complete silence created by falling snow. She loved to stand in the dark watching flakes drift past the outdoor lights. They were endless, they had all the time in the world and they disturbed nothing as they made contact with the earth. Now, on this calm morning, they turned the woods black and grey behind their moving veil and only Fiona's footfalls could be heard. At once, this struck Fiona as odd, as there was no sound of hammering, or even cursing, travelling from the rear of the shed.

"David?" she cried, arriving on the scene. There was the sledge and she was instantly horrified at the extent of the damage to it. She had barely acknowledged Hazel's fright, writing off her daughter's reaction as excessive. Now it looked as if she'd been very lucky to escape injury. On closer inspection, however, Fiona noticed that the sledge had been systematically dismantled, the metal runners put safely aside to re-attach later. One of the wooden runners was split in two and David would obviously have to replace this. But he was nowhere around.

"Dave," she called again, placing the hot coffee on the shed windowsill. Nothing. Perhaps he had made his way back to the house by the other route, but there could be no earthly reason for him to use the front door in this weather.

Looking around, Fiona noticed the imprints of his boots had at some point headed off in the direction of the old river steps and she wandered there now, blowing on her un-gloved hands. Near the top of the steps, she found one of David's axes, but still could see nothing of him.

"David!" she now yelled, not caring how much she shattered the silence she loved. "You down there?"

Because the tread on her own boots had seen better days, she dared not step any closer to the edge, but as she leaned forward for a better look, she heard her name being spoken, calmly and sedately. It was the most disturbing sound she had ever encountered.

"Dave?" she repeated, sweat gathering under the collar of her jacket.

"Fiona," the voice repeated, softly, "Don't move any closer, honey."

"I can't see you," she whimpered, fear and vertigo now making her legs weak.

"Just please, move away from the edge, Fee."

121

As slowly as she could manage, she moved backwards, one measured step at a time. When she felt more clear-headed and less likely to slip, she hurried along to her left, where the trees once more walled her in. Grabbing a branch, she leaned out over the drop, desperately searching for her love.

"Oh, God in heaven," she breathed, as she caught sight of him. Her chest tightened with a pain she could not quantify and the vision in front of her swam crazily before she could control it. Even then, what she saw did not make sense to her. David was suspended against the near vertical drop, one hand gripping a rotten hand rail, the other thrust into the snowy earth for support. Beside him, the set of steps he had obviously tried to negotiate had crumbled and were still intermittently shifting. The handrail itself had moved; somehow remaining nailed to the treads in one place, but surely not securely enough to support his weight. As she stared in horror, she could see in his face the effort it was taking to avoid the wood disintegrating further.

Saying nothing more to him, Fiona turned and sprinted back to the house, ignoring all fear of slipping. "Pete! Neil! Help, please!"

She was vaguely aware of Rose's face appearing at the window, before Neil was out of the back door, hauling on his boots, Pete not far behind him.

"He's going to fall," she screamed, pointing back to the clearing, "Quickly!"

Now all three of them were running towards the ravine, but Fiona managed to catch Neil as he flew towards the edge.

"Slow down! Slowly, please!"

"Neil!" barked Pete, "the rope."

In an agony of wasted time, Neil retraced his steps to the shed as Pete used the same vantage point that Fiona had done to assess the situation. Fiona lay flat on her stomach near the edge, unable to see David, but addressing him through chattering teeth.

"I'm here, babe. Hold on. Can you hear me?"

"Yes," he stated, gently. "It's not as bad as it looks. I'm just ....losing the feeling in my hands."

"Neil's bringing the rope, son," cried Pete, his voice strong despite his anguished face. "We'll make a loop and you can grab that."

"Not sure I can grab anything, Dad."

David so rarely called Pete by that name that Fiona began to sob wildly into the snow, terror not allowing her to stay strong. At that moment, Neil appeared, hauling coils of rope, first in front of him and then behind him as they began to unravel. He cursed like a madman, despair etched on his face.

"Calm down," Pete spoke to him steadily, as he hauled Fiona up and out of the way. She stood holding the trunk of a tree, gasping for air and trying to stop the tears which were as pointless as she was helpless.

Panic now made her turn to watch them, as Pete and Neil hastily tried to create a loop from the thick hemp. They worked as a team and she loved them for it. But she needed to see David. She could not bear the thought that he was struggling alone, out of sight, so once more she leaned out from the trees. He was fighting to keep his legs motionless, willing the rail to stay attached to the treads for a few seconds more. She could see that his eyes were screwed tight shut, as effort and concentration isolated him from the rest of them, but she needed him to be part of her world again.

"They're nearly ready," she called.

David opened his eyes, inclined his head to her in acknowledgement, and felt the hand-rail finally snap free.

Chapter 16

"Broken," repeated Fiona, "in three places, but the ankle is the worst one."

Impatiently she waited for the time delay to send her an acknowledgement from her father. When it came it was full of concerned intimations of how luck had definitely been on their side etc and although she agreed with this, she desperately wished to end the conversation and return to the people who were physically present for her. In a matter of moments, thankfully, she was back in the ward where David lay.

Pete got up from the window seat as soon as she entered and looked surreptitiously at his watch. "Fiona, I really think we should be getting on home."

"I want to stay." It was such a plain and simple statement, not said with any drama or irritation that Pete was not sure what to do next. David had been brought to hospital conscious, but bleeding and broken and it had taken hours for them to clean him up, X-ray him and set him in traction. Now he was sleeping and Rose had told Pete to bring Fiona home when he was settled, worried that Hazel would become restless and scared. Now it was late and dark and there seemed little more to accomplish. Neil, standing at the back of the room, stepped forward.

"You go, Pete, I can bring her home in my truck when she's ready."

Pete remained hesitant, scratching his left ear.

"You may as well go Pete," Fiona agreed, "because I'm staying. I haven't talked to him nearly enough yet." She turned to Neil. "I don't mind if you go or stay, but I'm staying."

This seemed to satisfy Pete. "Okay, I'll go. Neil?"

"I'll stay."

As Pete made his way to the door, Fiona caught him and hugged him hard. "I'm so sorry Pete. If I hadn't spoken to him ...."

"That's enough," he silenced her kindly. "I'll see you soon."

He touched David's hand once before leaving the room. Neil smiled sympathetically as Fiona brought her chair closer to where he lay.

"It's true, you know Neil, and we all know it," she stated.

"It just happened. And he's going to live."

Fiona looked at her husband's features. His left eye was swollen shut and was a hideous yellow shade. There was a deep cut from the edge of the eye socket down across his cheekbone, which although stitched up, was a livid red-purple. Her heart sank as she counted the ugly black stitches and realised that she had caused this damage to his perfect face. She shook her head again.

124

"So stupid," she murmured, then to Neil, "Why Neil? You and Pete were nearly ready. Why did I have to speak to him?"

Neil moved forward, bringing another chair up to the bedside.

"He's fine, Fiona. Okay, so he's not as pretty as he was this morning, but there's no permanent damage. He's going to be alright."

As if to support this statement, David let out a slow deep breath and opened his one good eye. He blinked once, then smiled up at Fiona who was on her feet in an instant.

"Hi babe," he said, stretching his right leg under the bedclothes. His left leg was in plaster, raised slightly off the bed and both hands were bandaged for cuts and grazes, but he still managed to haul himself upright. Fiona took his face gently in her hands and kissed him softly on his uninjured cheek.

"David, I'm so, so sorry," she wept.

"You're sorry?" he questioned, his eyes bemused. "Why? You found me."

Neil also stood now and David turned his perplexed face to him. "Why is she sorry?"

"She's being Fiona. She's always sorry." This explanation seemed to suffice and Fiona did not protest, but sat again, caressing his bandaged right hand. "So, how do you feel?" Neil continued.

David seemed to consider this for a moment or two, during which time he screwed up his eyes in some degree of pain, then let out his breath quickly and relaxed further back into his pillow. He managed a grin at his wife, who seemed to have stopped breathing altogether in anticipation of his answer. "Lucky to be here," was all he said. He had tried to lighten the mood, but Fiona, suddenly overcome with fatigue and fright, burst into fresh tears at the significance of the words.

"Oh, God," she sobbed, bending over and keening into her own chest. "Don't."

The two men looked at each other helplessly, David because he could not get near her to comfort her and Neil because it was not his place to do such a thing. At the third failed attempt to even reach for her hand, David, sweating with pain and anguish, implored his brother, "Please, Neil."

Embarrassed for himself as well as for her, Neil put his arm around Fiona's shoulder and held her while she dealt with her inner anguish alone. David lay back, trying to control the pain his exertions had caused, until he could speak again. "Fee, come on now."

She desperately wanted to stop crying for his sake, but she was so cold and beyond exhausted that she found it difficult to do anything other than what her body commanded. She gazed down at the stripes on her woollen jumper, winking out the last of the scalding tears, breathing as deeply as she was able. As she felt Neil's arm grow a little tighter around her she finally managed to draw a breath that did not catch in the middle and wiped her face with the heel of her hands.

"Sorry," she whispered, to both of them. "But every time I close my eyes, I see you falling, then crashing and sliding. I can hear it all, like it's just happened;

Pete shouting and you moaning at the bottom. I didn't know how it was going to end."

Fiona hoped that this would at least explain her reaction, and now, gradually, she managed to stop the involuntary shuddering and reach for David's hand again. She smiled apologetically at Neil and he finally released his grip on her.

"We all had a shock," Neil's words were designed to make her feel less isolated and David nodded his agreement.

"I'm probably the only one here who can't remember what happened," he said. They sat for another few moments in amiable silence, until David looked around him. "Hey. What time is it? It's dark."

"About one-thirty," replied Neil and immediately failed to stifle a yawn.

"One-thirty? Hey Fiona, you need to go home and sleep. Do you hear, honey?"

"Why? I don't want to close my eyes, I told you."

David patted her hand with his swathed mitt. "You need to go and look after the little one. She must know something's up and she needs you to tell her I'm okay."

This revelation caused Fiona to hang her head momentarily and peer at him through another watery film. She was on the point of decrying her mothering skills yet again, when she noticed David close his eyes wearily against this, guessing what she was going to say. So for his sake, she stood and pulled Neil to his feet. He was almost as surprised as David was at the lack of argument from her.

"Neil, could you just give me two minutes?" she appealed to his unremitting good nature and he came through as ever.

"I'll go and warm up the truck. Take it easy, Dave."

David nodded his gratitude and the expression in his one good eye was heart-breakingly earnest. "Thank you."

Left alone, Fiona sat down for a moment longer and studied him as if she could siphon off all his injuries and pain with that one look. He was gazing at her with tired concern and that was not right. She was not the one who needed looking after here; she was neither the one in pain nor the one who would be away from their daughter for however long this took. Suddenly Fiona saw what she could do to help. She could take away his angst by becoming what he was to her. A mender, a fixer and a strong support for whatever he had to face. She leaned over and put her face against his forehead. It was cool but damp.

"Do you need any pain-killers?" her voice was firm.

"I will soon, I think. My ankle is starting to ache."

"Well, I'll see the nurse as I go out. David, you don't have to worry about me, okay? I'm going to go home and look after Hazel. And I'm going to come and see you whenever this place and the weather allows. When your eye gets better, I'll bring her in to see you. And she'll be fine. She'll talk you to the point of insanity and all will be well. Do you believe I can do it?"

"You can do whatever you want, babe. I love you."

126

"Oh God, David. I love you so much. I feel like I've been ripped into pieces today, yet you're the one who's covered in wounds. It's not fair. Just think of me trying to get to sleep in that big, cold bed. That's my punishment for this."

He raised his head to be kissed, but she noticed the pain that crossed his face before she managed to gently touch his lips. He needed medication, and although it took all of her strength to walk away from him, she could arrange that for him. At the door, she looked back once and he briefly raised his hand in farewell.

"See you tomorrow, babe."

"You will indeed, my love."

Outside, Neil sat in the ancient truck he had inherited from the business the previous year and which he now regarded as his pride and joy. The cab was tidy and free from the usual jettisoned cans and newspapers found in vehicles used by young, male owners, but then Cindy had made him keep it like this. She had never been adverse to 'truck action', as long as the truck in question did not swill with garbage. The engine was now rumbling nicely, kicking robust fumes out into the frosty night air, as Fiona climbed into the passenger seat. Her face was flushed, but there appeared to be no more tears. In fact, her look was surprisingly resolute and Neil breathed a sigh of relief. The drive home may be endurable after all.

"Let's go," she instructed, then in a softer voice, "please."

He did not argue, but pulled the truck tentatively out of the hospital car park onto the public road beyond. The snowploughs had been along the road twice since David's arrival but there had been no more snow since nightfall. Now the highway was more icy than slushy and Neil was careful to keep his speed to a minimum, yet bearable pace. Though relatively short, neither of them was particularly keen to make the journey, as the level of concentration needed was formidable, especially when tired. Neil switched on the radio, but allowed Fiona to search for a better reception. When none was forthcoming, she gave up and switched it off.

"I've been a spoilt little child, Neil. Sorry."

He never took his eyes from the road, but he frowned, at a loss as he tried to pick up her point. "Oh?"

"Oh, yes, you mean. The more I think about it, the more embarrassed I get."

"Not really sure what you're getting at ..." he admitted, slowing slightly to avoid a clump of snow obviously dropped from the back of an earlier vehicle.

Fiona sighed, irritated that her brother-in-law's nineteen year old brain was not mature enough to receive the messages she was sending. Then she closed her eyes and relented. Of course he didn't know what she was saying. He wasn't David and he didn't know her inside out. In spite of this horrible lacking, he was here and he had cared enough to wait for her and make this awful trip with her.

"I'm embarrassed because I always seem to need to bring everybody's attention back to me. Look at tonight. David is the one in pain, on his own, wondering what will happen if his leg doesn't mend, missing his daughter. Do you see? Yet everybody has to make sure that Fiona is okay, that she can cope,

127

that she's not blaming herself for something which was *undoubtedly* her fault. I don't know why you all put up with it. I *am* a bloody child."

Neil's frown cleared at last. He smiled at the road, then glanced quickly at her as she rubbed her window clear and lay her face against the freezing pane. Her expression was not of self-pity, it was harder than that, more of disbelief at what she had become - in her own eyes and therefore, obviously, in theirs as well.

"You're not that bad. I've met worse."

She seemed to accept this without voicing it, then looked over at his focussed face. He looked younger than ever, the dark circles under his eyes visible in the passing of the street-lights. She marvelled at his contemplation of marriage – he should have been out there, treating loads of thin little blondes to a spin in his pristine passion wagon - then smiled at her ridiculous naming of the truck.

"I'm sorry about Cindy."

"Yeah, well. Seemed much more important earlier."

"It will again, I'm sure. It's not every day, well, you know. Talk to me about it if you need to. I still think there's hope."

"Okay," his voice was both unimpressed and pessimistic. "Maybe I don't need to chase somebody who doesn't want what I want. Maybe I'll just forget the whole thing."

"Well," yawned Fiona, audibly, "You don't have to decide tonight, that's one thing for sure."

He nodded, then prodded her shoulder with his hand. "Hey, don't go to sleep on me. I'll never stay awake on my own."

Immediately she sat up and rolled down the window three or four inches, lifting her face to the arctic blast and shook her body back to full consciousness.

"You're right. Well, what shall we talk about? Not what happened today and not Cindy. What else is there?"

"I don't know," he grinned, but looked up for the challenge. "Do you miss Scotland?"

"Wow, that came out of nowhere," she said, taken aback. "I'm impressed. Okay then, yes I really miss my family. Especially when something like this happens – bugger we weren't going to talk about that. But I do miss their opinions on things, we used to do a lot of talking. My Mum never really left the house much, so it meant she was always ready to help and Beth was always so nosy that most stuff was thrashed out by all of us together. That's what I miss, being able to ask their opinion at the drop of a hat. Oh, God, does that make me sound ungrateful? I didn't mean that at all, I can talk to Rose about *anything* and I do, she's been the best thing ..."

Although Neil did not contribute much to the conversation in any way, the Scottish lilt to Fiona's voice and her ability to apparently argue with herself at varying pitches ensured that he did not drift off at the wheel. When they finally pulled up at the back of the house, which was still illuminated for their expected return, they had moved on to the subject of a possible visit to Skye by Neil to 'bring him out of himself.' He had nodded, allowing her to organise the whole trip in her head, as they stomped and hurried themselves into the kitchen.

"I'm telling you," Fiona had now lowered her voice to an excited whisper, "you would have an absolute whale of a time. Beth's friends would not be able to keep their hands off you with your blond hair and your Canadian accent ...oh."

"What?"

"No. Maybe not. Thinking on, Beth would be completely enchanted by that same blond hair and Canadian accent and my Dad might have to kill you. He knows what the Wilder men are capable of."

"I'm going to bed," he grinned, "before you manage to get me hitched after all."

"Good idea," she smiled back, but before he moved off, she gave him a grateful hug. He bore it with good grace, although his face was scarlet when she pulled away from him.

"Thanks for being there, Neil. You're a good man."

He shrugged and moved off, exhaustion now affecting his ability to walk in a straight line. "Boots," she called after him and watched his shoulders sag at the inevitability of his having to remove them. "Okay," she whispered, "I won't tell if you won't."

Gratefully, he continued on his journey, but not without altering his gait to conceal from the whole household that he was climbing the stairs still clad in his outdoor footwear. Fiona, however, did seat herself at the kitchen table and begin the theatre of trying to undo knotted laces with frozen fingers, whilst having zero energy and patience. In the end, she switched off most of the lights apart from the one above the range, and slumped into Pete's chair, laces still intact. She noticed that the odd flake was making its way past the window once more and could not believe the interminably long day they had just put in. One which had started with a broken sledge and had ended with her David miles away, strapped up and damaged. The snow seemed to be the only constant to the scene.

She had no desire to go to bed, although she felt that Hazel should find her there in the morning. The range had lost the ability to send forth the pounding heat that it did during the day and Fiona now shuddered, still not wanting to go upstairs. Besides which, one person breaking the boots rule could be tolerated, two could not. So, slowly as if she had been asleep on a solid board for twelve hours, she negotiated her way through to the sitting room. Once there, she stirred the banked down fire and switched on the Christmas tree lights. Then she sat on the floor, leaning back against the wires of the downstairs fireguard, the wool of her jumper immediately heating up and warming her through. Her boot-clad feet were there in front of her, turned in to meet and support each other. Her jeans were damp and she heard Rose's voice of a few days previous, commenting on how such a thing could cause a chill. That had been a good day.

She looked at the lights which continued to glow, unaware of how the household had changed since they had first captured Hazel's thrilled devotion. They were still vivid and captivating, they were still trying to brighten everyone's mood, but Fiona could not catch that spark of anticipation any more. Now they were too static.

"And you are too tired," she murmured to herself, allowing her eyes to droop.

Immediately, she felt herself fall against rushing, burning ice, heard a cry and jerked herself upright away from the fireguard.

The cry had been her own and she stood immediately. Yes, this would be her punishment alright for the next few days, but if she was going to be the strong, independent type that she wished herself to be, then she must face it and deal with it. She crossed over to the bureau drawer and took out a pair of scissors. Without hesitating, or giving any thought to what she would wear on her feet the following day, she deftly cut the laces of her boots and shook them off. She then climbed two flights of stairs, breathing against her fatigue and slowly thawing hands, and made her way straight to where Hazel was wrapped up in Byes, her silken hair hiding her angelic face from the person who needed to see it the most. Removing only her jeans, Fiona then climbed into the tiny single bed and put her arms around her daughter. She smelled like bliss.

Chapter 17

Over the next few days, the roads improved significantly. The mercifully few bursts of snowfall were cleared as they fell and although everything still froze by sundown, there was enough grit and traffic present to ensure that the roads remained passable.

By New Year's Eve, David's face was almost back to normal, with only a faint discolouration around his eye and the swelling on his cheek was down to an acceptable level. On her last visit, one of the nursing staff had assured Fiona that his stitches would be removed the following day and so plans were discussed to bring Hazel in to see him. Their daughter had been awaiting this confirmation since the morning following the accident.

When Hazel had awoken to find her mother in bed with her, half-dressed and sleeping soundly, she had been thrilled and anxious in equal measures. She had always considered Fiona's rare presence in her bed as a real treat, almost as good as she being wedged between her parents in their big bed on birthday mornings. Her mother was always warm and she always held her just tight enough without crushing her. But on that morning, Hazel had found herself out of sorts and uneasy. She had tried to sit up, but Fiona had her in a desperate grip and had not stirred. Byes had been tucked somewhere out of sight and as she had tried to locate the ancient strip of blanket, she had begun to remember events from the previous day.

Neil had been sitting with her at the kitchen table, making faces every time she shouted 'snap' in error and poking her in the ribs, causing her to shriek in painful glee. Then suddenly her mother was screaming, the men were up and out of their chairs in noisy single movements and the cards were sent flying in all directions, some landing in her lap. She remembered Rose glancing out of the window, her face pure fright and it had been that, rather than the hasty exits, which had brought on her tears. Rose had been on the point of pulling on her own boots, when Hazel's wailing had reached her ears. She remembered Rose had looked at her, frantically, glanced out of the back door one more time, then closed it. She had lifted Hazel from her seat and cradled her, trying to assure her that everything was going to be fine and to stop crying.

But everything had not been fine. She and Rose had stayed in that kitchen alone for what seemed like an age, trying to find something to occupy themselves. They had begun a 'new game' with the cards, but Hazel had not been able to follow it and it had been constantly interrupted by Rose rising and peering out of the window. However, they had both stood at the sound of feet hammering towards them and when Pete had entered the kitchen, wheezing and white-faced, Hazel had held her breath against the complete awfulness of the situation, then let it out in one huge, terrified bawl. She remembered Pete on the phone and Rose's arms around her, but little else apart from the gnawing pain inside her tummy.

By the time the ambulance had arrived, slowly reversing up to the back of the house, its coloured lights mesmerising her, Hazel had stopped crying and was sitting on Rose's knee, fingers in her mouth and hair. Her mother had not re-appeared, her Daddy was nowhere to be seen and Pete and Neil were still somewhere outside. It was absolutely not fine.

And then she had awoken with her mother taking up most of her bed and lying on top of Byes. It had been light outside and her Daddy had still not appeared. The discomfort in her stomach had returned in an instant.

"Mommy?" she had poked Fiona, looking at her face which was dry and dirty-looking. "Wake up."

Fiona had opened her eyes immediately, but had not moved at all. She had stared into Hazel's pillow for too long a time and only taken a breath when Hazel's crumpling face had appeared in her eye-line.

"Mo-o-o-m?" her voice had been a scared question.

"Hello baby. Give me a kiss."

Hazel had done as requested, relieved to see that her mother was at least smiling.

"Why are you here?"

Fiona had finally sat up and released her daughter from her grip. She had rubbed her face and groaned slightly at the headache which had taken root in her brain.

"Well, let's see," she had begun, "Daddy's still in hospital and when I *finally* got home last night, I was so cold that I needed my favourite little hot water bottle to keep me snug." She had rubbed Hazel's nose with her own until her little girl had smiled and relaxed a little.

"Hopstital?" she had enquired.

"Hospital," Fiona had corrected, then re-arranged the pair of them in the bed so that they were both comfortable and warm. "Remember that story about the kite? The book you borrowed from the Library? Jodie's little brother had to go to hospital when he fell off the swing?"

"Yes!"

"Well, that's where Daddy is. He's gone to the hospital to get better."

"He fell off my swing?"

"No, baby. He fell down those terrible steps at the back of the house and he's hurt his leg. It's broken."

"Like my sledge."

"Yes indeed, just like your sledge. But, the good news is, that they can both be fixed. It might just take a while."

132

Hazel had seemed to accept all of this information with no great bewilderment and had begun to wipe Fiona's gritty face with the edge of Byes. "You need to wash your face," she had stated, "and I need to go to the toilet."

As she had clambered over her mother and out of bed, she suddenly turned back. "When can we go to the Library again? I like it."

"We can go as soon as you are allowed to visit your Dad. We can make a day of it."

"Goodie! I'm going to tell Gramma."

And so here they were, Fiona, Hazel and Rose on their way to Duncan, on the morning of New Year's Eve. A phone-call ahead had confirmed that David's face was stitch-free and also that the Library was open from 10am for a couple of hours, so they headed in that direction first. Rose had come along on this her second visit, hoping to see a marked improvement in her son. His ankle had had to be re-set a couple of days previously and that had taken its toll, but now the surgeon was much happier with the way it was lying, and every day was now a day nearer his release. Rehabilitation would be slow, but it had to be better at home, where Hazel would keep him amused and he could at least be part of the family again.

Once inside the heated haven that was the Library, Hazel bounced over to the corner reserved for children's books and immediately started whispering very loudly "Granma, look, this is the one."

Rose was instantly at her side, pulling her onto one of the seats to assess the merits of the one book which Hazel had rabbited on about for the whole journey. Fiona stood by the radiator, trying to reheat her hands. For at least the fourth time that week, she wondered how on earth David had managed to hold onto that rail and the side of the sheer drop for so long in the freezing cold. She hated the aching throb of the cold in her hands, and worse was the feeling when the blood flowed back into them.

"Hi Fiona."

Startled from her thoughts, Fiona turned towards the voice behind the counter.

"Oh, hi, James. How was your Christmas?"

James Benton's delight at seeing one of his more regular customers transformed itself into a 'oh-well-you-know' expression utilised by those people who preferred being at work to participating in public holidays. "My brother's brood arrived on Christmas Eve and stayed until yesterday. The house has not yet recovered. But hey, nothing to what you've been going through."

"You heard then," Fiona crossed over to where he had begun to handle returns, and leaned on the counter.

"Monica came back with the news a couple of days ago. How's he doing?"

Fiona, exhausted from the past week, could not summon enough energy to relate the story in its entirety and so settled for, "Well, they've removed the stitches from his face, so we're taking Hazel in to see him for the first time.

Making a day of it. I'm so tired ......" the words were out before she could stop them.

"Hey, why don't you sit? I can make Rose and you a coffee, if you're staying?"

"Oh, that's okay," replied Fiona, mildly surprised. There was a water dispenser inside the door, but she had never seen a coffee machine in all the visits she had made over the years. "I didn't know you could get coffee ..."

He winked at her, "I have my own kettle."

Fiona had never been entirely sure of James' sexual orientation. In all the time she had been coming to the Library, first on her and Rose's behalf, then latterly to satisfy Hazel's fascination with stories, she had talked to him many, many times about all aspects of life. He had been enthusiastic to the point of obsession about all things Scottish, being a Mackay from Wester Ross somewhere on his grandmother's side, and she had been glad to regale him with facts and opinions. She knew also that there was only he and his brother still living, which she found a bit disturbing since he was barely in his thirties, but he had been a 'happy mistake' and seemed perfectly content to be almost a generation younger than his sibling. In addition it was apparent that he got on very well with Monica, his colleague, but that could have merely been the way he accepted her doe-eyed adoration with patient good grace. He was actually very good-looking, short dark hair and a slim body, his youth and vanity not allowing him to carry any extra weight and Fiona had heard many a tale of weekend mayhem that he and Monica had experienced.

But there was still something which stopped her asking him outright if they were together, and really it was irrelevant. He was friendly and charismatic and this took away the necessity of knowing his every past mistake or triumph. All Fiona knew for certain was that he had once been a delivery driver for Canada Post and that he had moved to Duncan because it was the first place that had agreed to take him on after he got his Degree. And he 'was here to stay.'

"I would really like a coffee, James," Fiona finally agreed and went off to ask Rose if she was in similar need.

James watched her wander over to the children's corner, speak to Rose and at the mention of his own name, Hazel's head snapped up from the book. She waved at him, grinning madly. He saw her take a deep breath in, but Rose's hand went over her mouth before she could shout to him. Hazel immediately realised her mistake and her eyes opened wide. When Rose took her hand away, Hazel replaced it with her own mittened hand, and laughed silently behind it. James waved back, totally in love with the child.

"Rose is okay, thanks," Fiona advised on her return. "My hands are freezing!"

"Soon sort that out. How do you take your coffee?"

Over the next ten minutes, Fiona's hands did indeed thaw out and by the time Hazel had analysed the book for Rose's benefit, the pair of them agreeing that Daddy would be sure to love it too, she was relaxing in a seat by the radiator.

134

The steady stream of warm air wafting over her was so unexpectedly comforting, that her eyes almost began to droop and she was unable to conceal a yawn as James strode over to her.

"I saw that," he grinned. "I imagine you've not slept much lately."

"The bed's too big," she replied, and then sat up, amazed at her own words. "James, I can't believe I just said that. What on earth do I sound like?"

He leaned against the wall by her chair and smiled, not in the least bit uncomfortable at her words. "You sound like somebody who is too tired to be anything but honest. That's not a fault, Fiona. So, how is he actually doing? What's the word from the Doctor?"

"His ankle is the worst thing," Fiona sighed. She drained her cup and handed it back to him gratefully. "But there are two other breaks, so they're saying maybe a month off his feet? He's very positive, especially now that he's going to see her Ladyship, but I just want him home. You know," she stated, sighing once more. "I used to love the snow when I was little. Now I just see it as a dangerous game. Something that causes problems and even keeps people apart." She eventually smiled up at him. "Ignore me. I'm just so *tired.*"

"James!" Hazel came running towards them, tripped over her untied bootlace and landed in a sprawl of coloured snowsuit at the foot of her mother's chair. Before she could summon the energy to pick her up, James had stepped in and set her on her feet in such a speedy, fluid movement, that Hazel had no time to be embarrassed or hurt.

"Steady, Little Miss Wilder. Where are you hurrying to?"

Hazel now handed her precious book out to him, her eyes alight with happiness.

"Can I get this one? Please?"

"Now it's definitely got to be this one?" he asked, looking down at her seriously, then studying the blurb on the back of the book. "I'm not sure if this is the best book in the Library, and special customers like you, Miss Wilder, deserve only the very best."

Hazel's eyes looked like huge shining marbles in her face as she looked back up at him.

"But this one *is* the best one, James," she replied solemnly, "I think it's the best one in the whole place."

"Well, in that case, you can most certainly borrow it. Come on, let's get it stamped for you."

Hazel stood on her side of the counter, watching James' every move, whilst transferring her weight from one foot to another. Rose glanced down at Fiona, who was yawning again.

"Shall we get going, honey? You might be asleep if we wait much longer."

"Not a chance," smiled Fiona, hauling herself onto her feet. "I've been waiting to witness this reunion for days. Yes, let's get her and the best book in the Library over to see him. Knowing our luck, there will have been a blizzard in the last half hour and we'll be stuck here."

135

She tried to sound jovial, but fatigue cut into her words and they came out jaded. Rose touched her arm.

"He'll be out soon, you know."

"I know," smiled Fiona. "I really can't wait."

As Fiona gathered Hazel into her arms and rested her on her hip, Rose studied her daughter-in-law. She stood at the counter, juggling Hazel who was already flicking through the storybook, whilst saying goodbye to James and she seemed cheery enough. She had been so determined in the last few days to be strong and independent, that her smile had not been so much in evidence. Hazel had been her prime concern, but when she was napping or playing happily by herself, Fiona had wanted to help Pete and Neil. She felt that there must be something she could do, aware that David was not able to fulfil his duties at work.

Pete's lumber business was extensive and county-wide, but during the winter months, David and Neil had developed the domestic aspect and had weekly log orders to contend with. Fiona was not physically capable of cutting or delivering these orders, but had suggested that she could man the phones etc, allowing Pete to take on some of the workload. The slack was being taken up by one of Neil's friends and so far it was working out. But Fiona was tiring herself out, Rose could see it happening, her fatigue and worry showing on her face. She needed some good news and a bit of a boost.

Hazel had squirmed her way out of her mother's arms and now Fiona was bringing her conversation with James to a conclusion, smiling wanly at his obvious words of encouragement and reassurance. Eventually, she patted his arm in gratitude and wandered over to Rose and her daughter. His eyes never left Fiona. Rose waved her farewell and only then did he look away.

As soon as she entered the hospital, Hazel wrinkled her nose and grabbed Fiona's hand. The corridors were dazzlingly bright and this seemed to intensify the aroma of disinfectant, but Fiona barely noticed it, although it did lighten her heart somewhat as she now associated it with visiting David. Hazel had never been in a lift before and gave a small squeal as it moved upwards, defying gravity. She was now incapable of standing still, much to the amusement of the two orderlies also taking the journey. Rose smiled down at her as she hung onto Fiona's arm, her mother patiently withstanding the constant movement. When at last the doors glided open, Hazel was out in a second, dragging Fiona after her. However, on recognising nothing and seeing two nurses in starched white uniforms, she now put herself in Fiona's care, and stood behind her.

As the three of them wandered along the ward, one of the nurses saw Fiona and came over to her.

"Hi, Fiona," she greeted her, and without being asked, said, "He's doing great." Then, bending to address Hazel, who had her free hand wrapped in her hair, she said, "So this is Hazel. How are you, sweetheart?"

"Fine," Hazel replied, becoming more sure of her surroundings. "I'm here to see my Daddy. He hurt his leg. It's broken."

"Well, he is a lot better now, you'll be glad to hear. And he has been talking about you all morning."

Hazel's grin now broke into a chuckle and she started again to jump at Fiona's side.

"We'd better go," smiled Fiona.

The three of them walked quickly along the ward, the anticipation now taking hold, but just as they reached the door of David's room, Fiona slowed down and knelt beside her daughter. "Right, Hazel," she whispered, conspiratorially. "I want you to stay here with Gramma for a wee minute, because I want to check that Daddy is awake and ready for this great big moment. Okay?"

Hazel nodded and solemnly took Rose's hand. Fiona crept through the open door to find David craning his neck to look in her direction. She put her finger to her lips and grinned at him. His face was now merely discoloured, his stitch-less scar far less prominent and his eyes matched once again. She looked at him and put her hand to her mouth, trying to press away any tears that may be near. He was so handsome and alert, his smile genuine and eager. He reached out his hands to her face as she leaned over to him and he kissed her keenly on the mouth. There was a wealth of promise in that kiss, and she could sense that he was finally looking forward again, planning his recovery, instead of stagnating in his pain.

"I just wanted to see if you, you know, if you looked ...." she indicated her head at the door.

"And what do you think?" he grinned up at her.

"I think you never looked more *gorgeous!*"

They laughed together for a second, their foreheads touching, but she could wait no longer. She moved off towards the door, asking, "Are you ready for this?"

"Oh, yes."

Hazel stepped over the threshold, stopped, looked around the room in wonder and settled on David's bed. She hesitated only for a second, and then she was scurrying up to where he lay, her hair flying and arms flailing. Fiona saw her intention and took one step forward to try to stop the catastrophe, but astoundingly, she herself halted instead of jumping onto him. Her eyes scanned the plaster on his leg and then his face. He smiled his most doting smile and said, "Hey, Miss Priss. You're here. I thought I would have to wait *forever* to see you again."

She was almost dumbstruck by the oddity of the whole situation. Almost.

"Your leg is so *big*! Why is it so big and white?

"My leg's inside the big, white ...blanket, keeping it safe, making it better."

"Oh. Your leg's broken, like my sledge."

As David and Hazel got reacquainted, Fiona drew up a chair for her daughter to sit on, but before a minute had elapsed, Hazel had climbed carefully onto the edge of his bed, knocking on the plaster, touching his face and kissing his eye better. He had his arms around her, talking directly to her and laughing at her opinions. She divided her time by looking at the healing cuts on his hands, telling him how snow was still good fun even if your sledge was broken and rubbing the bristles on his face with her own. Rose joined in the chatter, confirming or correcting Hazel's tales, but Fiona took a step back and simply watched the scene. It looked as if the best book in the Library would prove surplus to requirements.

Chapter 18

Two days after the beginning of the New Year, Fiona came down with a head cold. Nobody was surprised and if the truth be known, Rose was delighted because it meant that she *had* to stay in bed and rest. She developed a temperature and lay sweating rather than sleeping for two days solid, but at least she was off her feet and was forced to eat at regular intervals.

"You're far too thin," stated Rose, refusing to leave the room until Fiona had eaten her soup. "If you want to visit him again, you need to get your strength up and get yourself germ-free. So you might as well do as I tell you and eat that."

"What's she up to?" Fiona asked, obeying the orders.

"She's fine. Neil took her down to the yard and I can take her in to see David tonight if you like. I'm going anyway."

"Well, if you don't mind, that would cheer him up I'm sure. Wish I was going," she moaned, following this with three sneezes one after the other. The soup slopped onto the bedclothes and Fiona gave Rose her most despairing look yet. "Oh, Rose."

Rose recognised the blues when she saw them and, cheerfully reassuring Fiona that nothing was as bad as it looked through a germ-ridden haze, went to fetch a cloth. Fiona in turn, sipped the remaining spoonfuls and laid her head back against the pillow, closing her eyes against her throbbing sinuses. What she wanted more than anything else at that very moment was David's arms around her, kissing her forehead so softly with his cool lips that the pain and pressure would simply evaporate. He would soothe her with his words, smiling as he retold her some work-related tale that meant absolutely nothing to her except that he was sharing his world with her. She really missed his presence in the house and yet it had been only just over a week. Was it advisable to be so completely dependent on another person to fulfil basic needs? She ached just to see his face.

"Oh get a grip," she told herself, easing her way down the pillow and stopping the flow of snot by sniffing loudly.

"You need a hankie!" Hazel's voice was heading towards the room and Fiona smiled at last.

"Hey, baby, I thought you were out with Uncle Neil." Fiona cried, as the squirming body tried to climb onto the lofty bed.

"I was. We're back."

"I'm glad," sniffed Fiona, putting her arm around Hazel's shoulder as she fussed to settle herself on David's side. Initially, they had tried to keep her away from Fiona but Hazel, bereft of her Dad, was having none of it. Now she sat on David's pillow, tugging off her socks and shoving her freezing feet under the covers. It took her a few seconds more to get herself completely comfortable and then just as she relaxed into Fiona's hug, she immediately sat up again.

"You're too hot," she cried, wrinkling her nose to emphasise her words. "How can you be hot when you have a cold?"

"That's a *great* question, Haze. It's a bit of a mystery really."

"I'll get you a hankie."

Her mother watched patiently as Hazel began the untucking and re-dressing actions required for her to go and locate what she needed. "Won't be long!"

Fiona, guiltily grateful for the return of peace, waved to her retreating figure and closed her eyes with a yawn. When she opened them again, it was to find the shadows in the room less defined and a gentle murmuring coming from Hazel's room. Listening intently, she realised that the calm, single narrative was coming from Neil, his voice typical of any story-teller, but with the volume purposely subdued. What was not typical was the lack of participation from Hazel and as if to clarify this, the voice slowed to a near-still whisper and a moment later, he tip-toed back into view. When he saw Fiona was awake, his face was instantly apologetic.

She shook her head to excuse him. "Sleeping?"

"Just," he replied.

"Thank you," she smiled, weakly. "She's the light of my life, but ..." she shrugged and saw that he completely understood. He hovered between the two bedroom doors, more self-conscious than usual, so she hauled herself upright in the hope that it would make him less so. "Are you coping, at work?"

He nodded, wandering over to the window and glancing at the position of the sun.

"Sure, I'm going back there now. Nic is great, you know, but he's not ... well, he works the hours we pay him for and that's it. It's fair enough," he finished, with the acceptance of someone indebted to a friend.

Fiona had met Nic only once and he had appeared a pleasant and willing enough addition to the workforce. On Christmas break from University, he had been itching to make some extra money to set up the next semester's social activities and was a hard worker during his agreed hours. He was also ridiculously good-looking, as fair as Neil, and Fiona prayed that he did not take a shine to Cindy before Neil had decided what his own plans were. There was no need for any further drama in their lives at the moment.

"Well, I think I can come back shortly," said Fiona, "Two days in bed is plenty for anybody."

He made a doubtful face, flicking the hair out of his eyes. "Depends on what the boss says." They both knew he did not mean Pete, or even Hazel. "You don't look all that hot."

She laughed. "I'll take that the way it was intended, don't worry."

Now he was retreating and gave a quick nod to Hazel's door. "I think she'll be okay for an hour. I'll let Rose know what's happening."

Without waiting for an acknowledgement, he was out of the door and away. Post sleep, Fiona did indeed feel a bit less lethargic, or that may have been the soup. Whatever the reason, she pulled back the heavy bedclothes and dragged her pyjama-clad body over to the window. The day was still bright, the trees were dripping and she dared to hope that things were improving. David had started physiotherapy, maybe he could be home this time next week and she was feeling less sorry for herself. Not only that, but she had managed to carve herself the smallest niche in the business which she wished to exploit further, Hazel had not succumbed to her cold and she herself had not cried at their big, empty bed in the last twenty-four hours. There was so *much* to be positive about.

The following day, without Rose's permission and secure in the knowledge that she could withstand any admonishment that was headed her way, Fiona was dressed and downstairs as the others still sat at the table.

"How's my girl?" she cried to Hazel, who sat in her high chair, arms outstretched and squealing at the sight of her mother. "No, no, sit still, I'll come to you."

She kissed both of Hazel's cheeks and put her spoon back into her hand. "Eat up."

"How are you feeling?" enquired Pete, rising from the table as he always did when someone came into the room. She hugged him as she made her way around the table to her own seat.

"A bit better," she replied, ignoring Rose's sceptical look. "So I thought I'd stop being a lazy besom and get myself down here for a change. Want to know everything I've missed."

Surprisingly, Rose did not make any pointed or weighted remarks about the wisdom of being out of bed. Instead, she placed a plate of scrambled eggs and bacon in front of her daughter-in-law, allowing herself the tiniest twinge of satisfaction at the expression which fleeted across Fiona's face. She may have been determined to appear strong and independent, but she could not conceal the fact that her stomach was nowhere near ready for one of Rose's breakfasts. Yet, she smiled bravely and picked up her fork. "Thanks Rose."

While Fiona chewed slowly, the hot food tasting better than she imagined it would, her thoughts returned to David.

"How was he then?" she asked Rose, as the coffee made swallowing the food more acceptable.

Glancing quickly at Hazel, Rose hesitated before pulling out her chair and sitting down to her own food. Fiona was instantly alarmed. Rose never sat at breakfast time.

"Fine."

It was so non-committal and abrupt an answer that Fiona's mouth turned to water. She put down her fork and was about to interrogate her, when she noticed the eye signals Rose was throwing her and the gestures she was making towards Hazel. She made her own desperate 'what?' face back at her.

"Hey, Hazel, honey-bee," Neil called, as the youngster scraped the last cornflake from her bowl, "Wanna come and tie the tarps with me?"

She nodded eagerly, hauling herself to a position where he could easily lift her from her chair. "Is that the same as sledging?" her voice was pitched somewhere between hope and joy.

"Not quite," laughed Neil, "but I'll try to make it fun. Trust me?"

"Yes!" She jumped into his arms and Rose handed him her coat and boots. Fiona remained seated at the table, glancing from one adult to another, her appetite destroyed as quickly as it had been formed. It seemed to take Neil an eternity to clothe himself and Hazel for the outdoors and if she had possessed enough strength, she would have stomped up to him, cursing, and taken over. All she could do was watch and wait. As Hazel, disappeared, giggling through the back door, Rose sat back down beside her.

"What?" Fiona's voice appeared to belong to someone else.

"There is absolutely *nothing* to panic about. I just didn't want Hazel to see you upset."

"Okay. But tell me now."

"It looks like he has developed a chest infection and it *may* be bordering on Pleurisy."

"Pleurisy?" Fiona immediately put her head in her hands. "Isn't that like pneumonia? Oh for the love of God!"

Pete having finished his breakfast, knew he was superfluous to the scene and so patted Rose on the shoulder and hauled on his winter jacket. While he pulled on his boots, his wife talked calmly to Fiona who looked ready to explode and he was grateful to breathe clear morning air into his lungs as he exited the house. His spirits were lifted further at the sight of Hazel trying to bounce on the taut tarpaulin stretched across the back of the pickup.

There was no real elasticity to the material, but it was expansive and slippery and his granddaughter's face was creased in pain from the laughter inside her. She shrieked every time Neil pulled it a bit tighter and she went flailing back into the safety of the centre. Pete grinned as she tried to crawl towards where Neil was standing controlling her every move.

"What's that?" Neil cried, "You want to fall over *again*?"

"No-o-ooo," she howled, reaching for him and throwing herself in his direction. This time, he caught her and she clung onto his neck until he lowered her to the ground.

"Granddad!" she cried. "Uncle Neil is being mean."

Hazel's voice however implied the exact opposite and as she wobbled over to where Pete stood pulling on his gloves, she was still giggling. She held his hand to steady her and Neil firmly tied the tarp in place at last. He looked questioningly at his father.

"You coming?" asked Neil, heading towards the cab.

"I'll follow you down," Pete replied, then gesturing back towards the house, said, "I'll keep this one company for a little while longer. Time enough for her to go back in there."

Nodding his understanding, Neil set off in the truck, waving at Hazel as he drove past them. Although the threat of more snow hung in the air, Pete felt that the best place for he and his granddaughter at that moment in time was to retreat to the shed and assess the state of the broken sledge. Hazel was delighted at the hint that sledging might recommence in the near future.

At the timber yard, Neil was met by Nic who wore far too prominent a scowl for a Tuesday morning. He had promised Neil that he could manage another two weeks before he absolutely had to return to UBC and was more than happy to rake in the cash for this length of time. Now he watched Neil jump down from the cab, shaking his head and anger dancing in his brown eyes.

"What's up buddy?" Neil enquired.

"Jeez, Neil, I am so sorry – and so pissed off." Nic's resentment was evident; there was no real need for any such clarification. "I've been hauled back to Vancouver because I didn't get enough credits before winter break. Can you believe that? What is the rush with these people?"

"When?" Neil asked, his business brain speaking before he could stop it, but added for Nic's sake, "That's tough, I'm sorry."

"Hey, I'm the one letting you down, Neil, don't you be sorry. It's a pain, I know you could do without it."

Neil waved this away, then, trying not to make his High School friend feel any worse, repeated, "When do you go?"

"I can give you until Friday morning, then I need to get there Friday night. God, it's annoying."

They walked towards the small office at the far end of the yard, Neil aware that the rest of the crew had left a good half hour earlier. Now, time was of the essence once more, and as Nic continued to bemoan his situation, Neil was trying to work out the most efficient use of the remaining time he had left with his friend at his disposal. So far, 1976 had been less than a happy new year.

When Pete walked into the office later in the day, it was to find Nic out with the chainsaw and Neil leafing through the latest batch of orders. He sensed Neil's frustration as soon as he removed his coat, but had no time to enquire before Fiona came stomping in after him, rubbing her hands and heading for the kettle.

"It is *freezing!*" she announced.

"I can't believe she let you out," Neil's voice was incredulous, as he looked from Fiona to Pete. "How did you manage that one?"

"Sometimes, Neil, I can be strong and determined."

"Or," Pete replied, with not a hint of accusation or malice, "maybe Rose just didn't want to argue any more. Maybe she needed a rest from it all for a while."

"Well, whatever the reason," Fiona replied, accepting the point Pete was gently trying to make, "I'm here and I am ready to *work*. So, give me the heads up and be on your merry ways, the pair of you." She moved him firmly away from the desk.

"Actually you couldn't have appeared at a better time."

As Neil explained the latest development and what needed to be done on the admin front, Fiona made coffee, restoked the stove and picked up some crumpled papers which had died on their way to the wastepaper basket. The office had missed her tidying influence and she sighed as she tried to bring it back up to her standard. When she was satisfied, she pulled on her fingerless gloves and looked at the paperwork before her. Pete rubbed his chin thoughtfully.

"I'll be sorry to see the back of Nic," he said, not having had very much to do with him at all. "He seemed to fit in."

"I know!" Fiona suddenly looked up. "We should take him out for a drink, just to thank him for all his hard work. When does he finish?"

"Friday morning."

"Well, we should go out Thursday night then. What do you say?"

Pete and Neil looked at each other blankly, then back at Fiona without commenting. She suddenly felt very prickly under the collar of her flannel shirt and it was nothing to do with her receding cold. She held their looks, and then laid the papers back on the desk.

"What? You think I don't deserve to go out? You think I should be at his bedside all day every day?"

"Hey, Fiona - " Pete's voice was gentle.

"No, Pete. I'm sorry but I really, really need a change of scene, or I may actually go insane. Nothing, and I mean *nothing* is going right. Dave's more ill than he ever was, Neil, you're going to be rushed off your feet again, everybody's worried about everything, I feel like my head is the weight of a diving helmet. Since the day after Christmas, the world has turned to shit – sorry for swearing. Hellfire, Hazel can't even go sledging and it looks like there's more snow on the way, so she's going to want to. I need David at home and I can't have him. I just want five minutes of not missing him. That's all I want."

If two men had ever looked more uncomfortable, Fiona had never witnessed it, but she was so caught up in her feelings that she couldn't even put them at their ease. Eventually, Pete's face cleared.

"You know what," he said, "I think that's a great idea. Where's a good place to go on a Thursday night? Neil can drive."

Neil, still stunned by the speech, nodded without thinking. It was the first time he could recall that Fiona had made any sort of demand or request which was so geared towards her own needs, and it suggested that she was indeed close to the end of her rope. "Sure, I'll try to set it up. I'm going over to join Nic now. Let's see what we can do."

"Great," said Fiona, although she seemed more satisfied that she had finally managed to control something rather than delighted to be going out on the town. "Will you be able to make it, Pete?"

"Think I'll give that one a miss, thank you."

"Okay then. We can go and see David first, if they'll let my snotty nose through the door, and then we'll go somewhere loud and ridiculously riotous. And I *will* enjoy myself. And so will you"

"Yes, sir," replied Neil, his face genuinely serious.

Pete glanced at his watch and declared that time was marching on. As he exited the office, Neil stood also, wondering if he was to be issued with any more instructions, but now Fiona seemed to have shrunk slightly in her chair. She looked up at him, less sure of herself but smiling. He grinned back.

"I know," she laughed, "where the hell did that come from? Well, anyway, it's a date. You don't really mind, do you?"

"No," he replied simply.

"You might even see Cindy."

"Depends on where we go. Anyway, I'd better get going. Got a lot to do if we're keeping Thursday night free."

He had almost closed the office door behind him, when Fiona spoke again.

"Neil?" her voice was back to its normal level of assertion, somewhere between submission and complete acceptance. He looked at her questioningly. "What do you think Rose will say about it?"

Chapter 19

Fiona blew her nose for the umpteenth time and cleared her throat of all thickness. She then shook her hair about her shoulders and opened her eyes wide.

"What do you think?" she asked Neil, smiling her most confident smile.

"Fit as a fiddle," he mocked her with one of her own phrases, as they hurried across the threshold of the hospital, out of the windswept car park. Fiona was wrapped in a huge woollen coat, which showed only her shoes and stockings, and she now hid most of her face inside her scarf. Her brown hair, however, shone around her flushed cheeks and highlighted her looks, as was evident by the number of heads which turned as they marched towards the lifts. Neil kept up the frantic pace of her walk. He had donned a clean pair of jeans and a brown leather jacket which emphasised his height and lean, labourer's body. Using a chainsaw all day resulted in muscles that any weight-lifter might envy and his hair, more of a dirty blond than a white blond, did him no harm either. Just as many women watched the pair of them hurry on their way as did men. They noticed neither.

"Hey babe!" cried David, then immediately caught his breath at the image of her. She was literally a breath of fresh air breezing into the room, all cold and unpolluted and exquisite, the impression only shattered by the one sneeze which escaped her before she could catch it.

"Dammit," she hissed, looking around to see if she had been found out, then hurrying over to him, removing her scarf and sniffing wildly. "Hi honey. I wasn't sure they would let me see you. I'm only going to kiss you once, because I've had a cold and I don't - "

David cut off the flow of words by taking her face in his hands and kissing her so warmly and deeply, that Neil actually retreated back into the corridor. There, he caught the eye of the only nurse at the station and gave her a half-hearted wave. She smiled in return, recognising his face, and went back to her notes. He stayed there, hovering, until David called him in.

Fiona was now seated on the bed, her eyes shining brighter than they had in days and her hands wrapped in those of her husband. She had the grace to look bashful when Neil came back in, but not in the slightest bit sorry for losing herself in her husband's desire. For his part, David could not take his eyes off the transformed woman before him.

"So," her voice was breathless, "how are you feeling?"

"Stunned," he laughed. "Look at you. Hey Neil, how's it going?"

"Good, Dave, good. How's the chest?"

"I'll live. It looks like I'll be in here another week at least though, and that's the highly optimistic view." He turned his head back to Fiona, still slightly shaking it in awe of the sight of her. She touched his lip and wiped a smear of lipstick from it. It was something she rarely had to do, since make-up hardly ever touched her face. But she had tried every trick in the book to make her look that little bit healthier than she actually was. It was of paramount importance that she saw him tonight. Now, she felt slightly overdressed and showy. At the same time, the looks he was giving her made her ache to be in his arms and she grieved at how long it had been and how long it might be. Neil went over to the window and busied himself with watching the ambulances arrive and leave. "So, how is everybody?"

"Well, Hazel is … as ever. Pete is being the rock, Rose is looking after everybody and Neil here is completely rushed off his feet. That's about right isn't it?"

Fiona looked over her shoulder at her brother-in-law who had turned back to face them and was trying to pull a loose thread from his jacket without unravelling anything.

"That about sums it up. Nic has to go back to Vancouver tomorrow."

"Sooooo," drawled Fiona, before David could comment negatively on the situation, "We're taking him out for a drink tonight to thank him for his time."

David nodded his head and smiled widely. "Now it all becomes clear. And I thought this ..." he waved his hand up and down in Fiona's direction, " ... was for my benefit."

Fiona sat back and folded her arms. "And have you not benefitted from it? Not one tiny bit?"

"Guys, please," groaned Neil. "Tell you what, I'm going to get some coffee, does anybody want anything?"

They both shook their heads, laughing, as he left the room. David reached for her hand again. "So, do I get to see what else you're wearing? Or is that exclusively for the patrons of wherever you are going"

Before she could answer, he began to cough. He struggled to sit up, hampered by his plastered leg and Fiona was at a loss as to what to do to help, unsure if she should call someone. Once he was more upright, however, he managed to bring the hacking, choking cough back to a more manageable level, and eventually brought some gunge up from his lungs. Fiona handed him the roll of tissues which had obviously been placed at his disposal for this purpose and waited until he had wiped the perspiration from his red face. "Sorry," he croaked.

"Babe, I really shouldn't have come, you have to get better. And you're going to be skin and bone before you get out of here."

He was wearing a pyjama top, something which Fiona knew did not belong to him, but she could see that his face was thinner and his left collar bone was jutting out from the material as he shifted back in bed. He shook his head, wheezing slightly from the attack, but could not yet speak. She waited patiently for him to settle. Finally, he took a deep breath and said, "You're the best thing to happen to me all week. Don't be sorry for being here."

"Oh, babe," she felt tears come out of nowhere, "I want you home so much."

He held her hand until she swallowed her longing and finally managed a smile of resignation. Before he could reassure her in any way, she continued, "But I've been really strong. I even went to work when Rose told me she didn't think it was a good idea."

"You are, and always will be, my hero."

"And for that, young man, you get to view the rest." Fiona started to try to unbutton her coat suggestively, but could not keep her face straight and in the end fumbled with the final two buttons, cursing softly, and threw the coat on the chair. "Ta –daaa!"

It was not the yellow silk shirt or the short denim skirt, both of which were items he had seen before, that made David grin from ear to ear and attempt a whistle in appreciation. It was the way she wore it with confidence, after the weeks of jeans and jumpers, scarves and hats. Her hair hung loose down her back and her ankle boots had a heel on them, lengthening her slim legs. She sneezed twice and immediately looked at him in desperation.

"You look gorgeous. Now all you have to do is to drug the nurses, find me some smart clothes that can accommodate a plastered leg and I'll be ready to date you in style."

"Hold that thought, my man, for when I am not streaming from my nose and you are able to walk me to the dance floor in one smooth move."

In the corridor, Neil was leaning on the reception desk of the nurses' station, waiting for one of the staff to return. He hoped it would be Melanie, the nurse he had waved at, whom he had spoken to at length on the night of David's arrival. She had been very professional and extremely efficient, but there had still been enough of a spark between them for him to seek her out on the couple of times he had visited since. As he sipped the bitter coffee, he thought of the night ahead.

Since Cindy's temporary or permanent departure from his life (the decision was still hers to make), Neil had had little time to pursue any social activities whatsoever. The accident and subsequent fallout had drained him of all of his spare time and most of his energy. But tonight he had made an effort. Fiona's enthusiasm to escape the house and the entire situation had rubbed off on him and he had sorted out the mess that was his hair and dressed in his least faded jeans and a plain white shirt under his jacket. He was almost nervous at the possibilities. Melanie appeared at his side.

"Hi," he smiled, easily. "Busy night?"

"Very quiet," she replied and sat at the desk. She did not, however, pick up her pen, but leaned back in her chair and scratched behind her ear. "I can't wait to finish tonight. I've been on two-till-ten shift since Christmas Eve, but tonight is my last one. Four days off, here I come!"

Neil watched a tiny nerve twitch in the side of her throat and for a moment marvelled at what she was saying and the manner in which she was saying it. Melanie was a qualified nurse, she must be Fiona's age at least, and yet surely she was making a move in his direction. Neil was perfectly happy in the company of girls. He had none of David's initial reserve. But at still a few months short of twenty, neither had he sufficient self-confidence to assume that he could pick them up without some effort. He needed a little sign.

"This is the first time I've been out since David's accident," he offered. "Fiona and I are going to Beverley's after this. There's a band playing."

He left it at that. The information had been shared, but there had been no obvious implication made that could embarrass either of them. He gulped the remainder of his coffee down, not quite able to stop himself grimacing at the taste.

Melanie laughed, then, "Beverley's? Does it stay open past eleven?"

"I think so. If there's a band on."

Melanie said nothing more, but looked at Neil. True, he was young, but where did age come into it when there was enough attraction? And there was certainly enough attraction, the fluttering in her stomach when he had waved at her was testament to that. She looked from his straight hair, down past his clear eyes to his Adam's apple. He swallowed at that instant and she raised an eyebrow as his charm went up a further notch. But even more engaging was his ability to keep looking at her as she appraised him. When she returned her eyes to his, he merely grinned at her and stood back from the station. A connection of some sort had been made and he was happy with that.

"Well, I'd better see how he's doing. Just wanted to give them a moment alone." As he walked away, he tossed the empty coffee cup into a bin. He looked back one and called, "Enjoy your time off."

Melanie acknowledged him with a wave of her hand, her eyes never leaving his retreating figure and allowed herself a little shiver of pleasure at the way his jacket dressed his body to perfection.

Back in the truck, Fiona's bright mood had dwindled a little. She had had to be persuaded to leave David, by both of them, and now the prospect of an evening without his company was not in the slightest bit appealing. Sitting at home, with the distraction that was Hazel and talking about the business or the weather or his expected return home was not the same as sitting in a crowded bar, shouting over the music and never having that one person to turn to when you noticed something funny or outrageous. At her suggestion that she 'just go home', David had made noises about how she had appeared on arrival, excited and ready for a change of scene and that he thought a night out would suit her well. Neil had managed to stop himself rolling his eyes or protesting that the whole night had been her idea. Instead, he had helped her into her coat and pointed out that David was growing weary and needed to rest. Now, as the truck idled and the windscreen slowly cleared, she rubbed her hands together and tried to look enthusiastic.

"I *do* appreciate this, you know. I'll be fine once we're there."

"Good," replied Neil, turning to look at her, "because Nic is really up for it and this band is supposed to be good. But," he hesitated, then decided to carry on, "I'm not taking you if you are going to sit with a miserable face. It won't be worth it."

Although there was no malice in his words, Fiona raised her eyebrows at the comment, before realising that he was making a very good point.

"Fair enough," she conceded, then, "And will Cindy be gracing the scene?"

"Who knows?"

The car park at Beverley's was only half full when they arrived, but there was a steady stream of pedestrians making their way through the front door and Neil, not for the first time, wondered if agreeing to drive had been the best option for him. Fiona deserved a drink, but he could not help thinking that a bit of alcohol might smooth out any sharp corners to the evening. Fiona looked out at the scene, and gave Neil a 'well-here-goes' grin.

When she and David had first been dating, they had come here fairly regularly, and although it had not changed significantly in the last four years, it felt more than a bit strange to be stepping over its threshold once again. However, the atmosphere inside was instantly friendly and Fiona even led the way to one of the few remaining free booths. Neil offered to hang up her coat, but she preferred to keep it beside her. It still smelled slightly of David's embrace and if the worst came to the worst, she could pathetically hold it to her face when Neil was not looking.

"Can you see Nic?" yelled Neil. Although the band was still at the setting up stage, a jukebox in the corner was playing loudly enough for shouting to be necessary. She glanced around, peering through the smoky light into every nearby booth. Neil made signals that he was going to the bar and she waved him happily away whilst scanning the immediate area. Nic's face did not appear, but in front of her, waiting for her eyes to land on him, was a grinning James Benton. Fiona squealed in delight at seeing her friend out of context and immediately jumped out of her seat.

"James! Hi."

He came over to where she stood and gave her a quick hug. "I can honestly say," he grinned, "that you are the very last person I imagined seeing in this place. Tonight.Or *ever* actually!"

"I'm here with Neil. David's brother. Och, it's a long story. Are you with anybody or do you want to sit here?"

He looked around for a second, "Well, as it happens I'm waiting for a date. I know, it's ridiculous. If I was out on a date, why would I meet them here and not pick them up. But it was her choice, so who am I to argue?"

"Ooooh" cried Fiona, clapping her hands together. "A date. Well, you can just sit here and tell me all about it. This will be my only night out for a while so I deserve to know *everything*."

At the bar, Neil stood flicking through his wallet when Nic appeared at his side.

"Well, if you're sure," he grinned, "Make mine a Scotch."

Neil could smell whisky on his breath already, but his eyes were clear and his words perfectly formed. He was not drunk, but was apparently not pacing himself either. Neil shook his head at him slightly and laying a note on the bar, ordered three beers. Nic shrugged and leaned back, surveying the scene. He lit a cigarette, offered one to Neil and adopted his best 'come-and-get-me-girls' stance. This did not last long however as he straightened immediately and peered into the thick air before him.

"Is that Fiona?" he asked, pure incomprehension written on his face.

"Sure," replied Neil, reaching into his jacket pocket for some matches.

"Wow. Who would have reckoned?"

Neil, settling himself back on the bar, looked at Nic, whose eyes were obviously very much appreciating what he saw. He continued to watch him, his face passively wondering how much Nic would say before he himself found it inappropriate. Instead, Nic asked, "Who's she with?"

Neil looked over to the booth to find Fiona deep in hilarious conversation with a fit stranger, their foreheads almost touching intimately. He frowned through his own cigarette smoke and, shrugging, moved over towards them. Nic followed him, swigging his beer.

"But her sister? Oh, James, that's just cruel."

"She was the one who introduced us! Hey, she's gorgeous and blond *and* only here for another week."

Neil placed a bottle of beer in front of Fiona, who finally stopped giggling and looked in his direction.

"Oh, thanks Neil. Here, James move over a bit, there's plenty of room. Hi Nic! You look smart."

The four of them eventually managed to squeeze into the booth, Fiona next to James, Neil and Nic perched on the opposite seat. Nic could not take his eyes off Fiona who was once again almost bubbling with enthusiasm, which her beer did nothing but add to. Neil was less relaxed at the situation, however, and after a moment, he leaned forward and said something which Fiona did not hear. When she leaned further towards him, he placed his hand on her shoulder and shouted in her ear, "Are you going to introduce us?"

Half an hour later, when the band had begun their first set, the four of them were contentedly onto their next beer and trying to make conversation, although Nic and Neil were finding it increasingly difficult to find anything in common with James and were quite relieved when his date appeared and the lack of space made it necessary for him to move. Fiona shouted something about a dance later and when James turned back to look at her, she gave him a thumbs up at the calibre of his date. He clandestinely returned the gesture, before placing his hand gently on the girl's back and moving her forward to a space at the bar. Now Fiona sat back against the seat, grinning as she sipped her beer from the bottle. Only when she realised that both men were gazing at her did she sit forward and frown. "What is it? Is there something on my face?"

Neil shook his head, "You're fine. But listen, if I'm going to drive, I can only have one more drink. What do you think of the idea of booking a cab for later? I can come back for the truck tomorrow, if Nic will bring me in."

"Sure," agreed Nic.

"Good idea," stated Fiona then jumped up. "In that case, this round's on me. Anybody fancy a short? I think a small whisky might be just the thing for my cold. Only the one, mind, we all still have to work tomorrow."

At the bar, James had at last found a seat for himself and Monica's sibling and was talking intently to her. Fiona smiled to herself, remembering that when you had a conversation with James, you were the only person in the room and indeed the lady in question was obviously not immune to this level of attention. Her eyes rarely left his face and Fiona hoped that the next time she took Hazel to the Library, she might find time to glean all the details of the evening from him. Returning to the booth with a tray containing three beers and three shot glasses of Macallan, Fiona found only Nic in situ.

"Neil thought he spotted somebody," shouted Nic, as she sat. They clinked glasses and downed the fiery, golden liquid without waiting for him.

Fiona began to relax as the heat in the alcohol soothed her throat and the company around her became more animated. The soft leather of the seat warmed her back as she pressed herself into it and when Neil and Nic were not up mingling, smoking at the bar or dancing, they shared with her tales of youthful woe and triumph alike. She only held her coat to her face once, and it caused her no regret, but instead made her heart lighter. David was getting better; she was having a great time. She wondered if perhaps they could get back into the way of socialising when he was fully recovered.

Fiona looked at Nic and wondered how his life at University compared to this, a Thursday night with two local guitarists and a drummer. His face was completely relaxed in this company, and he was charming and funny, so perhaps his post-degree plan was to return here and settle down. She smiled at her own naivety. He was relaxed because of the flow of the 'ambrosia in a glass', as her father would say, and because the band played a contemporary selection. A man of his looks and confidence did not sit in his room, head in a textbook, planning his life and longing for the old country. She imagined either one slim, red-head who dropped by with candles and red wine whenever the mood suited, or a string of shy brunettes who constantly tried to think of ways of standing in his eye-line. He saw her smiling at him and raised his glass.

Neil had returned and was kneeling on his seat, chatting to the female in the adjoining booth. Although he was always sociable, alcohol tended to make him smile more readily and he had a very engaging face. Fiona could hear the girl giggling, even above the band, and silently wished him all the luck in the world. Cindy had not appeared and at this stage was unlikely to, so he was fair game. His white shirt was untucked and exposed his lean waist and stomach as he reached over to light his conquest's cigarette. Without thinking, she reached out and tucked it swiftly back into his waistband. He looked down at her, not even surprised - she was the most maternal person he knew, next to Rose – and made a big show of tidying himself up. She grinned her approval as he eased himself out of their booth and slid into the one next door, his arm resting along the top of the seat between them.

As Nic got up to replenish the drinks, Fiona noticed James on the dance floor and sniggered into her beer. He had absolutely no natural rhythm. Yet he was so lovely. As he danced with Monica, her sister now seated and watching them from the safety of the bar area, Fiona remembered her own promise of a dance and took another long sip of beer for Dutch courage. It would be entertaining if nothing else, and she found her face slackening into a further grin. For one final time, she inhaled the fragrance lingering on her coat, and found that disappointingly, she could only smell smoke.

PART III

October 1993

Chapter 20
October 1993

When Kate opened her eyes, the sun was squinting through the slats in the wooden blind and she immediately began to count the shadowy stripes on the wall. She had done this for the past two mornings and the simple action prevented her from thinking about anything much for a moment or two. She was lying on a couch of black faux leather, her head protruding from the mess of sheets and blankets that were unable to stay tucked in for an entire night of unsettled rest. If the sun was this strong, then she had overslept again, but nobody ever seemed to mind. She could hear voices now coming towards the room they called the den, and she lay there, awaiting the quiet knock on the door.

"Kate, honey, are you awake?"

"Mmm, "she murmured, her throat objecting to the effort involved.

Kathy opened the door and came in carrying a mug. As the door swung slowly closed again, Kate caught sight of Joey, Kathy's youngest, staring into the room, but he turned on his heel when she glanced at him. He was seven years old and as shy as she had ever known a boy to be.

"Sorry to wake you, but I have to take Joey to the medical centre this morning. He can't seem to shift that cough and we're heading into the cold weather again." Kathy handed Kate the mug and sat on the seat opposite where she lay. "His asthma. Well, he needs it checked every fall."

Kate nodded. She had not spoken much since her arrival and she hoped that today David would keep his distance, so that she could lie under the blankets where it was breathless; as black and silent as the grave.

"I was wondering," began Kathy again, "If you should come with me and maybe see someone? You seem to be retreating from us a bit."

It was true. As Kate sat there and looked around yet another strange place, she felt no compulsion whatsoever to open her mouth. She sat cradling her mug in her hands, feeling the heat transferring across to her palms, but there was no desire to drink anything and nothing really to be gained by speaking to anybody. Words. There were no words which could possibly make this sickening situation disappear. She looked at Kathy, and marvelled at her caring for her at all. Everybody in this country seemed unnaturally hospitable. Had the connection to Fiona been so strong that it was second nature to help out her kin? She continued to watch her mother's friend through sad eyes but could not make her lips move.

"Look, you would be doing me a favour. I *have* to take Joey, but I can't possibly leave you here like this."

"Mom?" the closed door muffled the little voice. "We have to go."

"One minute honey," Kathy replied, her heart lifting as she watched Kate finally put the mug down. But Kate simply turned over on the couch and pulled the pillow over her head, leaving Kathy with no choice. She would have to get a doctor to come to the house, and she would have to trust Kate to stay where she was.

"Okay, Kate. You know where everything is. I may be an hour or two, depending on the appointments, and then I have to drop him off at school, if he's okay." Kathy neither expected nor needed an acknowledgement and quietly closed the door behind her again.

One, two, three, four, five. Kate couldn't decide if she was counting sheep, or seconds, or the number of hours she would have to wait until she felt like something other than a cold lump of lead.

Back at The Edge, Rose had decided that today was the day that normality would revisit them. She had forced herself out of bed at just after five-thirty and had begun work in the kitchen. The house was a disgrace, but since nobody had done anything but talk or cry or sleep for the past three days, it had not even been noticed. Now, she needed things back in some semblance of order and would insist that the three of them ate breakfast together, whether they were hungry or not.

As she began to assemble bacon and pancake batter on the worktop before her, she thought again about how they could have handled the situation differently. Yes, they could have instigated discussions the very first day the girls had arrived in the country. But David had wanted to understand them better, and to gain more of their trust before he had to speak of Fiona in any terms at all. He was partly responsible for their estrangement, even if it had not been he who had created the untenable set of circumstances. But it had fallen to him to ease them forward into their current position and he had accepted his fate, because he was a decent man. Rose found herself continually surprised at his level of commitment to this, when he had so few of the actual facts to fall back on.

David now wandered into the kitchen, sockless, dragging an old woollen jumper over his head. His hair stood on end after this abuse but he seemed unaware and his face was rough and unattended. As if to emphasise this, he now rubbed his jaw with the heel of his hand and frowned.

"You know, son," began Rose. "It's time to do something positive. If Beth can't come over, then you don't have a choice. We knew it might be like this."

"We knew it would be hard," he agreed and appeared to be leaving it at that. He filled a glass with orange juice and stood by the sink, gulping it down. She had not seen his smile in days and she missed it. It was too reminiscent of the bad days. Had she really thought that they would never have to revisit them?

"I'm going over there," he announced, looking straight at Rose, "but I'm going alone. Hazel isn't up to it and I just cannot stand the thought of what is going through Kate's mind at this moment. I know she's complicated, but she's also young and she's in so much pain."

"I know," accepted Rose. "I can't believe we were so ill-prepared. I know it was ridiculous to hope that it would go well, but - "

"We can't keep going over the same ground," David stated. "I screwed it up and I've got to make it right. I just wanted to know, are you okay being with Hazel today? She's going to be so angry I left her behind."

"We'll be fine."

In the days since Kate's elected absence, David had spent hours with Hazel and such concentrated conversation and opinion sharing had allowed them both to ease into each other's way of thinking. They were, after all, two adults with a single goal and an equal sense of priority. It appeared as if, between them, they might have enough information to help the worst injured of the little group, and so began to seek out each other's company at the beginning of every new day. There had also been more than one frustrated, sharp comment made in defence of previous actions, but Hazel's temperament and David's desperation to keep a positive outlook had soon put a stop to them. He now wondered if she would see his leaving her behind as a lack of trust, but he was also sure that another fruitless day would not do her any good.

As David was about to butter some toast, the telephone rang in the hallway and he padded across the kitchen, his face resigned to there being only bad news on the way. Rose poured pancake batter into the hot fat, whose sizzling and spitting prevented her from hearing any of the conversation coming through from the hall. By the time the pancakes were ready, David was walking back at a quicker pace. Rose handed him a plate, ignoring his impatient frown and said, "I don't care if the Queen has died, you're eating this before you do anything."

As he sat, consuming without tasting, she found him a clean pair of socks in the laundry basket. "Well?"

"Kathy has had to take her son to an appointment and Kate won't get up, so I'm going to have to get there as quick as I can."

"Okay. Well, call if you need me. I'm taking Hazel out this afternoon but we'll be here all morning. Oh, and son," she continued, as he finished the remaining pancake in one mouthful and began to pull on his socks, "You know I'm very proud of you. Just please don't feel you're alone in this one."

He was on the point of condemning her misguided respect because he had so little faith in it himself, but instead allowed her to have positive feelings where she found them, and looked at her with gratitude.

"Thanks, ma," he said simply and they both allowed themselves a smile at the title.

An hour later, Rose crept into the girls' bedroom, determined not to spill a drop of the hot chocolate she had made for Hazel. She had put an extra sugar cube into the mug at the last moment, but resisted adding cream. This was a medicinal drink, not a celebratory one.

Hazel was in bed, huddled up against the wallpaper, her duvet bunched around her upper torso. Her feet were uncovered, unless you counted the pair of tartan bed-socks she wore and her head remained buried until Rose actually sat on the end of her bed. She unwrapped her face from her arms and shifted slowly to look at her grandmother.

"It's morning again, then," she stated, rubbing one eye free from sleep, "Great."

"Today's going to be different," replied Rose and handed her the mug. "For a start, I'm cleaning this house from top to bottom and I could do with some help, but that's up to you."

Hazel looked unimpressed and totally disinterested, but Rose had expected as much.

"Then, after we have *eaten lunch,*" she emphasised, "You and I are going for a walk. A long one, even if it's raining."

"We're not going to try and talk to her today, then?"

"Your Dad has already gone," Rose sighed, dreading the reaction to the news, but Hazel merely considered this for a second, and then replied, "Oh well, I suppose we've tried everything else."

As her grandmother rose to leave, mumbling something about mess not clearing itself away, Hazel sat up as quickly as the mug of frothy liquid would allow.

"Rose, I would still like to clean up the top room, if that's okay. I mean, now that I've started I would like to finish it."

If Rose was surprised at the request, she did not show it. The room remained as they had left it that dreadful day, curtains piled on the floor, boxes half-emptied and photographs strewn everywhere. Nobody had even closed the door, which meant David must have seen the evidence himself from the landing when he went to bed. It was incidental now however and had not figured at all in the past three days, where their time had been spent travelling between home and Ladysmith and, ironically, getting nowhere at all.

"I just want to look at everything once, pack it away and leave the place clean and tidy and looked after. That wasn't a criticism," she added, sheepishly looking up at Rose.

"That sounds fair," agreed Rose, standing by the door. "In return, you promise to call me if you feel the need for company. Do you understand?"

"Deal," smiled Hazel, then followed it with a grin. "Wow, my face wasn't expecting that. It was easier than I imagined."

Rose smiled in return and left the room.

As he neared Ladysmith yet again, David was absolutely determined that this trip would make the difference. For a start, the concerned phone-call he had received from Kathy explaining her dilemma meant that it would be just Kate and he present in the house, which *must* alter things. Kathy had been very patient, allowing her house to be commandeered whilst trying to avoid being drawn into any discussions. But her very presence meant that she was nearly always being called upon to comment, especially by Hazel who needed more than David's perspective on things. Now, he could speak to Kate and have a captive audience. The last coherent thing she had said to him had been a pitifully childish request to see her mother and he had not been able grant it. As far as he could see, he had not been able to do anything for her at all.

In the beginning, when the plan was just a bare outline, David had always expressed doubt at his ability to give anything to Kate, but Fiona would not accept this. She pointed out to him again and again how fair he was, how strong and level-headed and that these qualities were exactly what was required. God knows, when the time had come for Fiona to physically get on the plane back to Skye all those years ago, he had been prepared to do anything, *anything* to stop her. He had begged her to stay, assured her that they could make it work, that the baby would be theirs. In truth, he had said everything that any man in his position would say, when they were panicking and sweating and fighting hopelessly to retain some form of the life they had enjoyed. He had honestly and sincerely promised Fiona whatever she needed and she had known he would do this, which made it all the more unbearable for her to leave.

If she had stayed, he liked to think that he would have tried daily to ensure they built a normal life around this thing and that Kate would have fitted in somehow. But now, when her entire life was a mystery to him and her origins still a mass of black, twisted wiring in his head, he could not even imagine how he could give her what she needed. Why would she listen to him? They had *almost* developed a relationship, he had almost been ready to trust her ability to withstand the news, but it had not worked out that way and now he had to rescue her from her own assumptions.

Kathy's driveway was empty, confirming that she was still out of the house. Her real estate business must have been reasonably successful, as her house was situated in one of the prettier cul-de-sacs on the western edge of the town, the back yards of the individual houses protected by tall woodland. She had told him where to find the spare key and he was not afraid to let himself in, as her neighbours had witnessed the recent activity from behind their curtains and from their back yards, and his face and vehicle must be familiar to them. As he turned the key in the lock, what struck him was the silence in the house. No television, no washing machine whirring or even the pages of a magazine turning. He stooped to untie and remove his boots, then took a breath of courage before heading towards the front sitting room.

Somewhere in her brain, Kate was aware of a door being closed, but was so cocooned under her blankets that moving seemed an effort too far. However, when she did not hear Kathy speaking to Joey, or the fridge door banging or the radio being switched on, she began to emerge from her stupor and pulled the covers away from her face. Her hair was wild with static and she could feel how flushed her face was now that it was free from its confinement. Somebody was definitely moving around the ground floor and now she felt her skin begin to prickle. She eased herself off the couch, and cautiously moved towards the door, listening desperately for a sign that things were okay. What she did hear were footfalls in the hallway and she took a step backward, grabbing a blanket and wrapping it around her like a battle cloak.

161

When the door was gently opened inwards, she looked upon David's face and uttered a desperate sound, like a cornered animal. She was newly awake, scared and now trapped. There was no end to this. David stalled in the doorway, unprepared to see Kate so incredibly exposed and defenceless and immediately stepped backwards. If she had slammed the door in his face, he would not have been surprised, but she seemed incapable of any movement and he realised with horror that she had descended even further into isolation since the previous day. Yet, she was looking at him, her eyes almost hidden beneath her dark eyebrows, with complete compliance. Perhaps she did need him; still, he hesitated. Her face suddenly crumpled and she started to fold herself up, sinking to the ground as if melting, the sound coming from her a high-pitched, grief-stricken wail. He caught her before she collapsed completely, and this time she did not flinch, nor try to extract herself from his arms.

"Here, sweetheart, here," he coaxed her limp body back to the couch and sat her upright. But her arms were clamped onto his, clutching his elbows as if she were about to lose her grip on reality. She looked at him through her glassy eyes, her face a mask of sheer terror that he could not understand. "Kate, Kate!" he clasped her face and forced her to focus on him. Tears made his grip less effective and now there was saliva hanging from her open mouth as she wailed unrestrainedly. Finally, he held her face against his, trying to calm her madness by introducing another human body to her terrorised world. He began to rock her, like a baby, one hand on her head and the other around her back. She was coiled into a hard knot, sweat and tears pouring from her, but he held her and he would hold her for as long as it took.

"Shhh, honey," he soothed. "Sshh. It's okay. It's okay. Come on, baby." He spoke to her in gentle monotone, over and over repeating the same message, hoping that eventually it would pierce her consciousness and bring her back to him. After a few moments, the noise began to diminish and he felt the grip on his elbows release to an acceptable level. She did not move her face from his, and instead, rested against it, sobbing and sniffing and eventually, closing her eyes to the world. He felt her relax, bit by bit and only then began to wonder where to go next. It was such a relief for her to be calm, that he dared not move until she did, but if she fell asleep it would present its own problems. As this thought entered his head, Kate now peeled her face away from his and looked straight at him. She appeared more focussed and aware.

"Kate? Honey, what can I do?"

She licked her lips and looked around the room for inspiration. She cleared her throat and shook herself back into the present, yet still she did not speak. Now, she moved out of his embrace and sat upright against the back of the couch. In turn, he settled into a more comfortable position without moving too much. He could not risk her receding again. He waited.

"My Mum loved me." Kate's voice was slow and languid. "She never ever hated me. But she was completely in love with you, so I don't understand ..." She was stating facts, accepting them as such and trying to explain what she was feeling. David had never felt so *essential* to another person for many a long year; still, he dared not interrupt her to voice his understanding, and so let her speak.

"My throat hurts," she croaked, reaching for the cold mug of tea still sitting at their feet.

"Here, let me get you some water instead," he said, but she shook her head and reached for his hand.

"Don't leave me. Please. I need to talk to you while I can, while it makes sense."

He sat there, holding her hand as if it was something they did every day, while she tried to sort her thoughts in her head, the whole time her face showing nothing but pained confusion. She was still flushed and was radiating an unnatural heat, but David held her small hand in his large one as she sipped the cool liquid, and braced himself for her words.

"I don't care who, not at the moment. I might at some point," she paused, holding her head with her free hand, as an incredible shooting pain pierced her forehead and rummaged around for a place to settle. After a moment, it had eased into position and she could continue. "I just need to know why you would agree to do this. I don't understand why you would."

"Your mom asked me to." It was a simple, and completely truthful answer.

Kate shook her head. "That's not like her though. She was always really fair, not always right, but always fair. That's not fair, asking you to do that."

"I think her hand was forced," he offered.

Again, Kate's face was the very essence of pain. "I read her diary you know. The one she used to write when you first got together. Beth showed it to me."

David drew air in through his teeth, memories coming flooding back in a torrent. The diary. How many nights had he patiently waited for Fiona to complete an entry, sitting up in bed in one of his old shirts, biting her pen as she decided what to include for posterity. He had only asked to see it once, but had been informed that he might be able to do that when they were old and grey and needed a good laugh, and not before. When Hazel had arrived, she appeared to have little time to think of anything but sleep, and so the diary had disappeared out of their lives. Now, he remembered the little notepad covered in daisies and wondered if he qualified at last to view it.

"She was completely in love with you," Kate repeated, so sure of herself.

"I know she was. And she was my life."

Her hand still lay in his and now she tightened her grip as she felt herself falling again. She grew white before his eyes and he held her against him as she swayed forward.

"Kate, stay here with me, honey. Come on, sweetheart." He had no other words and could only hold her until she steadied herself and breathed again.

"The thing is," she wept and caught her own tears in the palm of her hand, "I only had you for a little while."

Chapter 21

The first thing Hazel had done on entering her childhood room was to release and open both windows wide to the air. She had worked hard in the chilled atmosphere, sweeping, dusting and washing every surface – floorboards, skirtings, windowsills and doors. The curtains had been hung outside and beaten until her arms protested, but now they were pressed and back in situ. The shade on the ceiling light had been wiped dust-free.

She had repacked the contents of the boxes, with the exception of two framed cross-stitched ballerina pictures, whose colours matched the faded lilac of the room. Rose had patiently stitched them during Hazel's second year, when the only shoes she had ever wanted on her feet were a pair of satin pumps. She would spend hours twirling and dancing in them until, when they had become tight then stretched beyond use, she had turned her attention to adventure stories and wished to wear boots only. Now the pictures were back on their original tacks in the wall.

Carefully, Hazel had placed the photographs back in the folder and shoved it in the bottom drawer of David's wardrobe. She had to have faith that one day there would be a resolution to this horrendous time and that then, David might want to view them again. They had to be within his reach. She was doing the right thing.

The bare cot had looked so depressing that Hazel had taken it apart and slid it under the single bed. On top of this she had spread a crocheted blanket she had found in the airing cupboard and a couple of cushions from her own room. When Rose had finally climbed the two flights to see if any progress had been made, she had been in time to see Hazel close the second window and place the one chair back against the wall. Her grand-daughter had then picked up the brush and mop and moved them to the landing to give the best impression possible.

"Basic," Hazel had sighed, "but clean."

Rose had put her arm around Hazel's shoulder as they both stood just inside the room.

"Fresher," Rose had agreed, her eyes lingering on the ballerina pictures just long enough for them to well up a little. "Lunch is ready. Come and eat."

Now, Hazel stood gazing up at the sun winking through the tips of the trees. She tried to imagine the scene when it was snow-covered, sparkling and dripping in the solar rays, the air making her gasp in cold delight. She wondered at the possibility of a snowfall before their return home. She doubted it, and for the moment, there was just the rustling as the breeze beckoned herself and Rose onto the muddy path. Finally, she lowered her head and regained her bearings before continuing on her way.

"There were some letters in a scrapbook," she informed Rose. They were strolling, not striding and the leisurely pace set the tone for discussion. There was nothing to be gained by rushing forward with thoughts and opinions, they had time at their disposal and calmness settled between them that David's presence never really permitted. Hazel carried a stick which she absent-mindedly trailed through the scrub, beating the odd bush which appeared along the way.

"Oh," replied Rose.

"They were from Mum. But you must have read them."

"Hazel, I would no more read a letter addressed to someone else than I would willingly climb that conifer bare naked. I knew they were there, but I never read them."

Hazel picked up a large cone, brushed off some mud and needles, held it to her nose and pocketed it. She shrugged. "Well, they were not exactly love letters, more commentaries on my life. Like they had been written for a newspaper or something. They never did mention Kate though, although to be honest, it looked like the first letter came well after she was born. Almost like," she thought of how to explain it, "like Mum had waited until she could get away with *not* mentioningher. Like enough time had passed for her to ignore the whole thing." Hazel stopped, shaking her head in disbelief. "You know, for the first time ever, I have no idea how to talk to my own sister."

When the shell had fallen on them three days ago and splattered their minds to the four corners of the room, Kate had transformed into a hard, alien outsider in a matter of seconds. Hazel had seen the horror dawning on her face, her features twisting as the implications of the discovery had piled themselves onto her, layer after layer after layer. Her mother was not what they had assumed her to be, David was suddenly a more innocent party, Kate's conception had resulted in the dissolution of a unit, neither David nor Rose were related to Kate and so on. Realisation had come so fast and it had been witnessed and felt by all of them. Hazel herself had been gripped with nausea as she realised, as Kate must, that their own relationship was being compromised. It was unimaginable that any of this had happened.

Kate's subsequent meltdown had been excruciating to watch. She had not let Hazel anywhere near her and remarkably, only David could be in the same room as her, as long as he kept his distance. Any attempt at comforting her had either been brusquely shaken off or had resulted in her screaming obscenities at anyone who was there to take it. Rose had been on the point of calling the doctor when Kate had finally grabbed Hazel's rucksack and tipped its contents onto the floor. In the strained silence that followed, she had fished out the card that Kathy had left with them and blindly headed to the telephone. David had followed her at a safe distance, his jaw set and his eyes black, but he had not tried to stop her. When it came to dial the number, however, her fingers had not co-operated and she had been in danger of smashing the piece of equipment against the wall, when

David had gently taken the receiver from her hand and replaced it in the cradle. She had looked at him through the eyes of a convict and had sunk onto the hall chair.

Carefully, he had prised the card from her clenched hand and knelt beside her so that she was aware that he was still there. He had held the card in front of her. "If this is what you need, I will do it." He had spoken so softly and evenly that she had dared to look in his direction and all she had seen was the opportunity he was offering her. She had not seen an acquaintance, or a betrayer or an enemy. She had seen someone with a solid solution, no matter how temporary it might prove to be. She had closed her eyes and lowered her head.

"Please," she had whispered. "Please."

"David, what will it achieve?" Rose's voice had wavered with emotion. He had looked at his mother once, then back at Kate.

"Kate," he had said, "If you can look at me and tell me that this is what you want, I will call Kathy for you. We will find the best way for all of us."

Kate's trembling had seemed to come from deep within and it had remained consistent and visible as she had finally looked him in the eye.

"Please do it."

And so, Kathy had been come to The Edge and taken Kate back to Ladysmith. It had been necessary at the time, but Hazel had not understood why Kate had not wanted her to accompany her. She had forced Kate to look at her pleading face, but she had met with blank eyes in a mask of misery. Kate had never disregarded her before. They had always been able to communicate.

Hazel now looked at Rose. "I've never seen Kate like that. I don't understand why she didn't want me, or even what Mum was thinking. Why would she put her in this position?"

Rose was now walking ahead of her granddaughter. That morning, she had mapped out the route of this conversation in her head. They would have a quiet time together, no shouting or crying, just straightforward answers to ridiculously complicated questions. Now, she was at a loss as to where to merge Hazel's thoughts with the plan she had made. Worse than that, every hesitation seemed to give the appearance that Rose had more to hide, which was the last thing she wanted to imply. She had lived with this situation for as long as the rest of them. More than that, she had lived *inside* it, had breathed it every day whilst trying to hold her remaining family together. In all the years she had spent steering and guiding and trying to console, Rose had never envisaged anything like this.

"Do you think he'll bring her back today?" Hazel asked.

"I think he'll try his best."

* * * *

Kate stood under the shower and slowly massaged her hair until the water ran clear of suds. It felt odd to be doing something so mundane and she wondered when she had last had a simple thought. As she slid a bar of soap across her

166

abdomen, she was suddenly alarmed by how prominent her pelvic bones had become. She looked at her wrists and arms, then down at her ankles. As if her brain had magically clicked back into gear after days of freewheeling from one burning wreck to the next, she acknowledged that perhaps the gnawing in her gut was hunger as much as it was anxiety. Later as she wiped the mirror clear of condensation, she finally saw what others did. Startled grey eyes in a peaky face.

Back in the den, Kate found the clothes she had not seen in days, still packed in her rucksack, and pulled them on. Her jeans were indeed a little looser at the waist, but her jumper concealed this. She knew herself that her body needed nourishment; she did not need people commenting to that effect. When her hair had been towelled as dry as possible and brushed so that she could tie it back without difficulty, Kate began to try to tidy up around her. Kathy had been so great. She had let Kate set the pace, crying or sleeping when she needed to, whilst trying to encourage her to speak to David and Hazel. In return, Kate had robbed the family of their cosiest, most informal room and probably disturbed the boys into the bargain.

The whole space seemed to smell sour, not so much of sweat as of distress and now Kate opened a window and folded up the scattered bedclothes. Carrying these and her pyjamas, she crept through to the utility, glancing once into the kitchen where David thankfully had his back to her. She could smell food. She should try to eat something.

David looked at the table he had set. There had to be something amongst the fruit, toast and porridge that Kate could eat. Being in a foreign kitchen, he had deliberately not hurried, tidying up as he went along, but he was now aware that Kate's shower had taken a considerably long time. His heart sank slightly. To go looking for her was so full of potentially awkward moments that he gave her another minute. But the food was cooling down and he reminded himself that he was the strong one in this drama.

"Kate?" his voice echoed in the empty hallway.

"In here," the sound reached him from the small utility room near the back door. As he stood in its doorway, he was momentarily confused as to what was going on. Before him, Kate was standing in front of the washing machine. She had piled the dirty items on top of the huge washer and was staring at it, her hands resting on either side of the crumpled bedding. She was completely stationary and failed to move even when she sensed his presence.

"What is it?" he asked, keeping his distance until he understood the situation.

She turned slowly, then held out her hands and shrugged her shoulders. "I have no idea how it works."

"What?"

"I don't know ... where you put the washing. It just looks like a metal box."

David was so relieved by the simplicity of her problem, that he could not stop himself from smiling. She did not smile in return, but neither did she object as he moved to where she stood and eased her aside.

"It's a top-loader," he explained. Within half a minute, he had filled the machine, added soap and switched it on. Kate had watched him blankly, her arms loose at her sides, grateful that he had not tried to show her what to do but had just completed the task instead. When the noise of water gushing through the pipes confirmed that all was well, David indicated to the doorway.

"Time to eat."

Kate had always preferred chewy toast to crunchy toast and so she buttered it and mashed a banana on top. David took a seat at the table to show solidarity, but did not touch any food, glancing at the mush on her plate with an intrigued face. Instead he sipped coffee and looked around the ultra-modern room.

Kathy kept a comfortable house and, not for the first time, he thought about the dated furniture and large, chilly rooms at The Edge. Neil's place had been decorated by his long-term girlfriend, who was an interior designer. His brother had been more than willing to let her 'creative juices' loose on the property and the last time he and Rose had visited, David had looked at it properly, recognising its full potential, and had come away feeling unsettled and out-of-date. He and Rose were existing, at best, in a house that had seen no major changes in twenty years. That visit had been over a year ago, before the current crisis was even on the horizon, and after a couple of quite depressing days of self-analysis and frustration, he had decided that a change was overdue. The business was steady, he was respected by colleagues and peers and could even have been described as eligible, so perhaps the effort involved would not be as gargantuan as he imagined. He would start slowly, improving his surroundings and then *possibly* moving on to his own person. He had almost re-invented a social life in his mind when the phone-call had come from Skye.

"This is a nice place," he said.

Kate looked at him curiously for a second then nodded. "Yes."

"I should make some alterations to The Edge. It could be brighter. Some of the furniture is older than I am."

"I like it."

"So do I, who am I kidding?" he grinned.

Kate looked down at her food, trying to hide her face. The lump in her throat felt like a walnut, gnarled and inflexible, and she wasn't sure if she could even force words past it. But this whole scenario had to be faced.

"David," she whispered, but could go no further. The word itself said so much. She looked at him, as he sat squarely at the table, coffee mug in hand. His features were back to what they had always been, before the horror of the past few days had distorted them. His eyebrows were knitted in a frown, but his eyes were clear. She marvelled at his ability to even look at her. She took in a breath.

"I need to go home, I think," she held his gaze, wondering at the actual thoughts going through his head. He had become quite adept at hiding his feelings from her.

"Then let's go," he spoke as if it was the simplest solution in the world.

"Thank you," she smiled for the first time, before it wobbled into something more emotional. "Thank you for not thinking I meant Skye."

He shook his head slightly, confused at the point she was trying to make.

"I don't have any right to call your home my home. I have no right to be anywhere near any of you."

David's eyes now grew black, but Kate was unaware of the change as she could not continue to look at him. He rubbed his chin, and then stood, not caring at the harsh sound of the chair against the cushioned vinyl. He strode over to the kitchen window and leaned his hands on the sink, head down and breathing heavily. Now Kate dared to look up. At that moment, when words and actions could change lives, she had never felt so scared. She watched his back, his hunched shoulders and felt his discomfort. Her mother had loved him, which made the burden she had given him seem extraordinary.

She twisted her hands together as he finally straightened his back and turned to face her. His eyes were calm and his face clear. She got the impression that he was also aware of the importance of the moment and was searching for the words. But when they came, he spoke without doubt or reservation.

"When this idea of your mother's was planted in our heads, I had absolutely no idea how it was going to be, how I was going to feel or how I was physically going to communicate with you. *Either* of you," he paused, then, "You should eat."

So compelled was Kate by his honesty and willingness to finally tell her the actual details of the charade, that she brought the banana toast to her mouth blindly, never taking her eyes off him.

"You probably think I thought of you separately, because of what happened, but I didn't really. I didn't know how Hazel would feel about me and I didn't know how I would feel about you, so the two of you became one single challenge." He paused to see if he was making sense to her. She did nothing to suggest he was not. "Plus, you were both strangers. I could kid myself that I knew what Hazel would be like. But really, it's sheer luck that she still has that same spark. We're talking about seventeen years apart and I did nothing to shape her. Her photos showed me how she looked, not who she was. I'm fortunate that she's so open-minded and accepting."

Kate chewed slowly, wishing to tell him that if he was to travel the world over, he would never find another so accepting of him as Hazel, and she had always been that way. But she did not speak, and instead listened to his voice. Everything he was saying, whether he was filtering it or not, made sense – his doubts, Fiona's assurance that she and Hazel's relationship would ultimately survive the hammering it would take, his willingness to spend time and try to begin the healing – except for one huge flaw. Why not explain all this on Skye?

Kate had been taken away from Beth's support and her mother's ghost; she had been brought here and put on show, for no obvious reason. Rose had been amazing, warm and receptive from the first day. Kathy had welcomed her into her world without question and David had been nothing but patient and attentive.

169

But this did not alter the fact that they had known she was on the outside and she had not. It was this which chilled her as much as anything else.

She thought of the night she had found him slumped in his chair and how she was so pleased with herself for persuading Hazel to give him some breathing space. She almost baulked at the recollection, because possibly it was she he had been trying to escape. Her stomach did a little roll and it must have registered on her face, because David stopped in mid sentence.

"What is it?"

"I don't understand why I was brought over here when it surely could have been sorted when you were on Skye. Why did she want this?" She had begun to sweat and felt the fingers of a nervous rash tickle her throat.

David finally sat back at the table. For all he must have been tired, and his unshaved face spoke of untold compromises with his time, he did not sigh or cave in. Instead, he handed her another piece of toast and indicated with his eyes that she should keep eating. Only when she complied did he continue.

"I don't know how much Beth told you, I understand they kept the fact that we were in contact pretty quiet." When Kate nodded a reply, he went on. "Well, in all that time, I learned to listen a bit more. You know, people argue and fight because they want to believe that what they are saying is right and they can't quite understand when no-one else can see it. But when you really listen to someone, especially someone with nothing to lose, there's no need to even disagree. You just accept it."

Kate was following his words and when she connected it to her mother, she knew exactly what he meant. A person with a given amount of time was allowed the luxury of free speech. And no-one had ever questioned Fiona or her ways of dealing with her burden. That was the way it was.

"Remember I told you on Skye that she had more than one reason for all of this? Well, one of them was that she felt she had deprived me of something truly basic, and that was the relationship with my daughter. She hooked me with that one, as if I needed to be persuaded."

Kate's face was bleak as she once more felt bereft of something, something she had barely had time to adapt to in the first place. But David reached out and squeezed her hand quickly.

"But she insisted that you come too, because the most important thing in all of this is that you and Hazel stay as close and as intimate as you have always been. *Nothing* else in this mattered to her. The truth was always on the horizon, it's just that you pair didn't know about it. And, she trusted me to guide you both through it, if I was willing to do it. Do you know how good it felt to be needed and trusted by Fiona again?"

A tear slid down Kate's cheek, no longer for herself but for the memory of her mother and how it felt to be loved by her. She imagined that to be needed and trusted by her fell into the same category.

"And that was all it took for you to do this?"

His animated face faltered for one second and he then cleared his throat and looked down at his hands folded on the table. There was something more.

"Well?" Kate's voice was almost a whisper.

"One other thing. Your mother thought that maybe, if you needed to know anything more about what happened, there might be people over here who could help you. And, for what it's worth, I'll support you whatever you want to do. We'll find out, or we'll leave it be. You're in charge now, Kate."

And there it was. Whatever was coming could mean enlightenment for both of them. It felt like an alliance after all.

Chapter 22

As Hazel was scraping the mud from her boots at the back door, she heard the sound of a vehicle on the driveway and immediately yelled to her grandmother that she thought they might be returning. Without waiting for a reply, she ran around to the front of the house, but was disappointed at the old Dodge Caravan, caked in filth, which was pulling to a halt before her. She hesitated for a second, not recognising the driver, before she walked a bit more sedately back to where Rose was exiting the doorway.

"It's not them. A brown jeep thing with some sort of wood panelling along the side. It's not Kathy either."

Rose nodded, taking Hazel's arm as she guided her back to the parked vehicle. The driver had not yet emerged, but Hazel saw a white hand raise a greeting to Rose, who in spite of everything, managed a genuinely warm smile and strode over to the truck. Now the door opened and down stepped a tall individual, whose facial features were as good as obscured by the brim of the hat he was wearing. Hazel screwed up her eyes, not knowing exactly the significance of this stranger's arrival, but sensing that perhaps she should. Without hesitation, the man picked Rose up like she was a five-year old and held her tightly until she beat him to let her down, knocking off his hat in the process. Hazel found herself smiling ever so slightly at the scene and almost instantly saw something she had seen before in photographs and in real life. Fair hair and a grin which split open the entire face and crinkled the eyes. Neil.

Rose now stood beside him, dusting the brim of his hat while he tried to pull his hair back to some reasonable shape. It lay resting on his shirt collar and was still a mid-blond shade, just a little lighter than the thin beard he wore. He also had on an ancient padded jacket which bulked him up and might have proved intimidating if it wasn't for the ridiculously happy look he was sporting. Hazel guessed he was an inch or two shorter than David, but only that and he still dwarfed his mother.

"Looking younger than ever, Rose," he grinned, pulling her ponytail, which instantly unravelled in his hand. For a moment he looked contrite, and then smiled as soon as she touched his face.

"And you look like you need a good wash. Ever heard of the word razor?"

"You love me," he teased, then finally looked over to where Hazel stood. She may not have recognised her old playmate instantly, but his eyes opened wide on contact with her face and immediately she felt herself blush. He stared for a moment or two, allowing Rose to place the hat in his hands, and then he took a couple of steps nearer. Hazel had never felt so scrutinized, but it did not even bother her now, for she knew that face and those eyes and she knew that they spelled safety.

"You're kidding me," he laughed, almost beside her. "This is honey-bee? This tall, pretty thing?"

"Hi, Uncle Neil" she said, and smiled self-consciously at him.

"Wow," he stammered, glancing back at Rose, "Haven't been called that in a long, long time."

"You look just the same," It was all Hazel could think of to say.

"You, on the other hand, look and sound a little bit different. What happened to your squeaky Canadian twang?"

"My …?"

"Neil, reign it in," sighed Rose, still smiling. "Hazel is much too sophisticated these days for you to be teasing her. She'll see right through you, make no mistake."

He tilted his head and looked at her with some regret. "Well, that's a crying shame. Come here, you."

Hazel found herself folded against his jacket involuntarily, but returned his brief hug with genuine affection. She must have been well known to him at some time and she hoped that maybe a little further down the line there might be a trigger that would let memories come pouring down on her. But at that particular moment she viewed him as an added complication. He was not who she wanted to see right there and then, and she was not sure if her brain would cope with the niceties and the questions and the recollections. When she stepped back from him, Rose immediately recognised the confusion and distraction on her face, but before she could intervene, Neil saw it too.

"My God," he cried, "That frown. You're Davy's double."

Hazel took another step back and started to crack her knuckles. She tried to keep smiling, looking from Neil's interested expression to Rose's concerned one, but eventually she turned her back on them, unable to keep up the act. As her grandmother made a move in her direction, she began to run. "I'm just putting the kettle on," she shouted over her shoulder, and to their credit, they did not follow her immediately.

In the warm kitchen, Hazel sat at the table, listening to the kettle as it rose in volume and pitch. It marked the passing of time and she knew that at any minute, Rose and Neil would join her in the house. Worse than the threat of company, her knuckles were finally beginning to object to their continuous abuse and Hazel felt the sickening lurch as the last of her optimism left her. She folded her arms onto the table, mimicking her sister, and sank her head onto them. There was an element of comfort in their dark confines, but she could no longer resist the pull of her grief. She was overwhelmed by it.

She had come here with so much hope. Her mother's generosity had initially amazed her, not because she had given her blessing to this passion play, but because she had actually planned and negotiated the whole trip. Hazel had felt a connection with her Dad immediately and had even watched Kate slowly lose her animosity and start to share in their new experiences. It had eased the pain of Fiona's passing by providing a quick burst of excitement, followed by the prospect of a more long-term relationship. But that had been before, when literally only half the story had been told.

Now, Hazel felt cut off from her closest kin, with only half-acquaintances to reach out to. She ached for Fiona, for her arms to go around her, the heat from her to ease away the ball of fear and sorrow which had been growing since that horrendous day when Kate had refused to look at her. It was all too awful to comprehend. And here she was, in a comfortable yet alien room, where she had spent her first years of life amongst people who had adored her. And these people were here now, but she didn't want them. They were filling a gap for a short time; they were distracting her and loving her, trying to help her. But they were not enough. Not even her Dad was enough and he had gone through God knew what pain since she had last lived here.

Hazel did not even try to stem the flow of tears. Instead, she shuddered into her locked arms, eyes squeezed tight. She was sobbing for her mother, who was not here to explain it until it appeared somehow acceptable. She was sobbing for her father, who was trying his best to salvage their newborn association and could not, even now, bring himself to denounce his dead wife. She did love him for that, and for who he was. But mostly she was sobbing for her sister. She wanted to see that dark-haired, grey-eyed girl standing in front of her, smiling again. The girl who had shared her whole life and had been there through all the stilted conversations and half-truths concerning their history. Kate was the only other person who could connect what their mother had told them over the years to what was happening now and she needed to see if her conclusions were the same as her own. More importantly, she wanted to hug her close and be reassured that nothing would ever change them. Apart from Beth, Kate was the only true constant in her life.

The keening tears continued but she did not fight them. It had been days since she had let herself go and in a way it seemed to be removing a burden. Fiona had not been allocated nearly enough thought in this; she had been pushed aside time and again, as each day had passed. Now the truth had brought her to the fore in a way which was shocking and felt like the most monstrous betrayal of her. In front of all of them, Fiona had been revealed as the keeper of secrets and she had had no voice. Now Hazel wanted to give her time and empathy and consolation. She wanted to revisit her love and give it back to her, if only in her mind and her heart. She wanted to do it with Kate and nobody else.

"Hazel, my dear girl," Rose's voice was soft as she gently laid a hand on her shoulder.

The sleeves of Hazel's sweatshirt were soaked as she raised her head and quickly wiped a trail of saliva from her chin. She could see Neil's figure in the corner of her eye, but she would not look at him, not yet. That would be like saying 'Look at me. Look at what this is doing to me' and she did not want him to acknowledge it. Rose's face looked on the brink of collapse as she pulled a chair to sit close, but she overcame the notion and took one of Hazel's hands in hers. Hazel did not try to justify her misery; there was absolutely no need to explain anything. But she gripped her grandmother's hand and let out a deep juddering breath.

Neil stood against the range, hat laid to one side and jacket now lying across the back of a chair. His arms were folded and the only movement he made was to occasionally rub his thumb under his chin before relocking his arms. It looked to him as if this scene had been played before, his niece obviously trusting his mother in spite of their relatively short re-acquaintance. His face took on a tired look, showing off his thirty-seven years and adding to them. There was no support he could offer here, not for the time being, but he did not wish to diminish Hazel's reaction by leaving, so he stood silently, waiting for some other person to steer the boat. Rose took up the challenge.

"Tea please, Neil?" She instructed, not letting go of Hazel's hand.

He moved instantly over to the sink where mugs had been draining all day, but then he hesitated, apparently thrown off course by the request. He switched the kettle on to reheat, and then turned, frowning in their general direction. "Tea?" his voice was genuinely mystified.

"Tea," repeated Rose, with infinite patience. "The pot is on the windowsill, you'll need to use two bags."

Hazel, through the blur of her final few tears, saw Neil's completely blank expression before he turned to carry out the task. She noticed that his jumper had a hole in the elbow through which his cotton shirt poked and that without his bulky jacket he was a bit on the skinny side. His jeans were loose and dark, probably new for the occasion. Hazel's eyes brightened at the thought, wondering if his girlfriend had picked them out for him, or whether he had taken the initiative himself in honour of their visit. Rose stroked her hand.

"Okay?" she whispered, to which Hazel nodded.

Neil ran his hands through his hair again, as the tea stewed. Without thinking, Hazel now got up and retrieved the milk from the fridge. He watched her tentatively, possibly dreading her next breakdown, but she handed the carton to him with an apologetic smile. He took it from her and grinned in return, before he pulled an ancient crumpled hankie from his back pocket and offered it to her. Amazingly, she did not take a step back from the uninspiring item.

"Thanks but I've got my own."

As they sat around the table, drinking tea with sugar, Hazel tried to put her face back together. Rose had provided a damp flannel and she had rooted out her own hankie. A minute or two more of sniffing and blowing, wiping and drying had brought about a puffy but healthier looking sight and she sipped her tea with the rest of them. It was very sweet and she could see the struggle Neil had with each unfamiliar mouthful.

"Don't drink that on my account," she said, massaging her aching fingers. "Maybe I could make you a coffee?"

"Actually, that would be really great."

"I'll do it," Rose interjected.

"No, it's fine," replied Hazel. "I want to do it."

Hazel had become an expert with the coffee maker and had grown to love the bitter smell of it percolating. While she busied herself with the emptying and the measuring, Rose and Neil seemed to be discussing everything under the sun except her recent embarrassing show of emotion. He and his girlfriend Andie had been on a tour of craft fairs and specialist furniture stores in and around Vancouver itself, trying to procure markets for his carved bespoke items and wooden artefacts. Hazel listened intently, without obviously showing any interest, as she did not wish to halt the flow of information.

So, apparently he was a craftsman, no longer in partnership with David in forestry, but still pursuing some wood-related vocation. It made a sort of sense. He was obviously a very skilled artist, judging by the gateposts. By his own account, he had made the trip here as soon as he could and in a way Hazel was grateful that they had got this far without him. She had no doubt that he would have been sympathetic and may have been an additional support for her Dad, but really would he have been anything other than a laid-back observer in the background, standing around with folded arms and an impassive look on his rugged face? Kate, she was sure, would have resented the added audience.

"So, we were a bit tied up. But I'm here now," he concluded. "Thanks, honey-bee, erm Hazel," he looked slightly flustered, as he took the mug of steaming liquid from her. "Sorry, that name sounds a bit weird, now. Sorry."

"It doesn't matter."

Hazel sat beside Rose once more, and allowed mother and son to catch up with each other's news. They talked fluently enough but when the subject came around to the last few days, she braced herself by holding her almost empty mug to her face and hiding behind it. However, by the time Rose had explained the current situation, she had joined in and felt grateful for the opportunity to explain her initial reaction to his appearance. He accepted it all with the same genial face and refused to let her apologise for it. He seemed truly unflappable and yet something was off kilter.

As she watched him talk and drink and lean forward in his chair, Hazel tried to figure out what it was about him that was, at this moment, keeping him apart from herself and Rose. He seemed to be making all the right noises, but did not actually dig deep during any part of the conversation and if Hazel had learned anything from the past two days, it was that the Wilders were not superficial. Neil was different. Hazel had known that he was adopted from stories of old, and therefore was not surprised that there was no family resemblance between her Dad and him. But he had grown from an infant in this house, so why did it feel like he was more of a visitor than she was? His eyes were soft and friendly, his tone was full of empathy and he perpetually rubbed his thumb under his chin when there was a lull in the proceedings. Yet something about his character irritated her.

He was trying to appear so relaxed, but his bent knee could not stop moving; Stuart's knee only did that when he was nervous or excited. This man was putting on some act, she was surer of this than anything else and she felt suddenly defensive. There was no place for duplicity in this house any longer, and she was surprised that Rose was not pulling him up on this. She looked at her grandmother for some help, but at that moment she excused herself and headed out into the hallway. Hazel felt herself frown, to which Neil once again likened to David's expression. She did not acknowledge this and after one or two seconds of silent scrutiny on her part, his easy smile at last faltered and he looked down at the table.

"Are you up to all of this?" she asked.

"What do you mean?" It was now his turn to hide behind his mug.

"Do you know what you've turned up in the middle of? It's not pleasant. Are you as strong as your brother?"

Slowly he put down his mug, his face at last showing some genuine feeling. His eyes had hardened slightly and it made him appear more sincere. His knee was suddenly still. He bit his lip and tilted his head to the side.

"Am I as strong as my brother?" he repeated his voice more incredulous than angry. It fortified Hazel even more.

"He's taken everything onto his shoulders. Kate's gone off it a bit and he's trying to save her. It's been pure chaos for days and I just need to know that you're aware of it, because when they come back, you need to help him."

For the first time in years, Neil was completely dumbfounded. He was looking at a face he had known when it was rounder and less defined and happier; when it had either been lit up with squealing laughter, shining with total awe or crumpled in childish angst. He did not associate that child with the person across the table from him. She was serious and strong and loyal, worried that he would be unable to maintain the same level of support that the three others had apparently been developing. He was not angry. Instead, he felt left out.

Long before this girl had been born, even before her mother had squeezed her way into the mould, he had been a central part of this world and now it was being unceremoniously pointed out to him that he was currently on the outside. He would have to find his place again and quickly or he was going to cause more harm than good. The most surprising element of these thoughts was that he was ready to do this. He had not lived in this house for years, but it was still his most cherished place, even if he rarely allowed himself to think of it as such. He looked at his niece, with her eyes that matched her name and her Dad's frown, and wanted to help. She mistook his gaze for offence.

"I'm sorry," she sighed. "You might think I'm totally out of order, speaking to you like this. But if my sister ever makes it back here, there won't be any room for spectators. I can't let you sit on the side, watching, being the nice guy with the smiles. She needs people to explain this to her, not to sit and watch her suffer."

Neil seemed to have frozen in his seat. The only animated parts of him were his mouth and his eyes, the former which had grown slack and the latter which grew wider and more concerned by the second. Hazel's face burned red. She had been completely confident that the words had needed to be said, but was now mortified that she had caused a grown man to look so dazed. However, when he spoke again, his voice was composed.

"And what about you?"

Hazel shook her head. "Me?"

"You," he repeated. He seemed intent on being ambiguous.

"Well," Hazel spread her hands. "So far, I've lost my mother. As far as I'm concerned that's the worst loss there is. I'm *not* going to lose my sister and I need lots of help with that one. So, I'm not really very happy at the moment. But," the tears which had been threatening were abruptly retracted as Hazel's tone hardened. "Kate has lost a Mum, Dad, grandmother and uncle, just like that. So I think she's dealing with a lot more. And the worst thing, the very, very worst thing is that she needs to be told she's blameless in this, and to do that, we need to talk about our Mum. Maybe in a way that will hurt us.And everybody. Oh shit."

Hazel felt herself running out of steam and put her face in her hands for support. The whole idea was just too awful and in truth, if she could be at home now, watching the post van bumping down the road to the bay, she would go without a qualm. Her mind seemed to enjoy the silence and so she sat still for a few moments more. Little gold stars were appearing behind her closed eyelids when eventually she felt a warm hand gently prise one of hers away from her face. Through her blurred vision, she saw Neil's hand envelop hers and rest them both on the table in front of them. She wiped her face with her remaining hand and finally looked at him.

"Okay, Hazel," his eyes was alert and resolute. "I'm here to help."

Rose was now hovering by the range. Hazel was not sure at which point she had come back into the room, but her face was flushed. Had she been listening in the hallway; had she witnessed the dressing down her granddaughter had given her son? Her eyes were brighter and her cheeks pinker.

"Hazel," said Rose, "You might have been away from us for way too long a time, but that backbone of yours. That's all Wilder."

Hazel allowed herself a smile at last which she shared between the other two adults in the room.

"Am I allowed to smile back?" asked Neil, squeezing her hand before letting it go.

Hazel blushed one final time. "Yes, sorry. I can be a right cow."

Neil winked at her, and then turned to his mother. "I'm the nice guy with the smiles. That's pure gold, isn't it?"

"Oh, don't," cringed Hazel. "Sorry."

She could hear the kettle once again, and marvelled at the way time could deceive when it wanted to. The thirty minutes or so since the last time the kettle had boiled seemed hours ago, yet it was still light outside and the clock had not yet reached four o'clock.

Rose tapped Neil's shoulders as she passed him. "Boots!" she stated.

Now he grinned spontaneously and made a huge show of looking at his watch. "But Rose, seven more minutes and I would have broken the record. Come on now, would you deny me that?"

"Now," she cried, rinsing out their mugs.

Shaking his head, he began to unlace his boots, muttering to himself about injustice and free will and age. Hazel watched his nimble fingers deal with the cracked laces and wondered at which point he had decided that those hands were better suited to carving and whittling than tuning a chainsaw. "The man with the hands," she murmured, more to herself than anybody.

As Rose put another tea in front of her, Hazel got up to use the toilet.

"Hazel?" Rose called after her. "I just spoke to your Dad. They're on their way home."

179

Chapter 23

Kate could not get the thought of hot chocolate made with milk out of her head. In this oil-spill of a situation, where every word spoken produced pain of some degree on at least one person's face, a warm, sugary drink seemed a beautifully simple thing.

She had always prided herself in her ability to lie completely motionless in bed, a trick she had learned at a very early age when the cottage had been without central heating and any slight movement beneath the covers would break the seal on the parcel of warmth you had created. So, she lay as a corpse, a thinking breathing corpse whose thoughts kept returning to how that drink would taste in her mouth and how, for a few minutes, it would make her insides seem full and relaxed.

Two things were preventing her from moving. Since her return, as one of two prodigals it seemed, Rose had been devoid of her usual sparkle and was obviously feeling the strain. She needed to rest, and if she was sleeping now, Kate did not want to be the one to disturb her. More than this however, she could not bear the thought of anyone joining her in the kitchen and any tiny noise she made on the journey would almost certainly result in that very thing. And it had only been an hour or so since the house had grown silent.

Hazel, at least, was sound asleep, breathing steadily through her nose - 'I do *not* snore!' - and Kate could feel herself on the verge of making a move. She remembered the endurance shown by the madman in 'The Tell-Tale Heart'. Mr Ellis had loved gothic literature, Edgar Allan Poe in particular, and had insisted on reading it aloud to them in class, slowing down to emphasise the man's persistent patience and stealth. And Kate had all the time in the world. Surely, she could get there silently if she went very slowly and was very careful.

By the time Kate had reached the top of the landing, she had perfected the art of gliding along the floorboards in her stocking feet. Spreading the weight seemed to cut down on the creaking and as long as she did not walk with a rhythm, then people would assume it was just the house settling around them. The stairs looked decidedly more complicated and she hesitated, but she could almost taste that sweetness on her tongue and in one quick, mindless movement, she swung her leg over the banister and slid from the top to the bottom. Silently.

The hallway was dark, but wide and obstacle-free and Kate knew that once she was on the other side of the kitchen door, she was safe. She was in luck, the loudest sound that she made was switching on the light after she had painstakingly eased the door shut, and she leaned against it. For a moment, she delighted in her successful attempt at secrecy, but a shiver took her by surprise and it left her teeth chattering in her mouth. Neil's jacket was still slung over a chair near the range, and she huddled herself into it. It smelled of wood and chemicals, but it was quilted and would soon warm her up. As would hot chocolate.

The suction of the fridge door alarmed her for a second, its sound amplified in the silence, but she decided to ignore it. She noticed the clean pans on the range, as if they were perpetually anxious to start the routine of cooking at any given moment, and Kate's lips turned up at the corner slightly when she thought of the obstacle course that was the pan cupboard back home. You had to fight with the door knob for a start. The cupboard sat underneath the inbuilt grill, which loaned itself to airborne grease descending on it, and you almost always had to use a tea towel to get enough grip to release the handle. Once the door was open, pans never seemed to sit and wait to be chosen; they either fell like the leaning tower of Pisa onto the tiles or refused to budge at all. She could not remember a time when opening the pan cupboard did not result in a cacophony of spilled metal and oaths. Perhaps she would suggest they just wash the pans and leave them on the cooker from now on.

As the milk started to simmer, Kate tried to zip up the jacket she was wearing but found that some of the teeth were missing a couple of inches into the task. Irritated, she left it partially attached and held it clasped at her throat instead, trying to trap as much warm air as possible. As she debated what use a jacket which did not fasten was, she saw the milk rise to the rim of the pan and started to view her goal as achievable. But, stirring the milk into the chocolate mixture was an art form, you had to make a paste first otherwise little islands of powder floated on the top, and suddenly, it was an effort too far. Kate pushed the pan to the back of the range and let out a whimper of sheer frustration. She tore the jacket from around her and threw it against the wall. She did not care how much noise she made, and, dramatic though the gesture had been, it made her feel a little bit better. Sighing, she bit her lip. She would give it a minute and then try again with the hot chocolate.

As she slid down the front of the range to the floor, Kate noticed the crumpled hankie and chewed pencil which had been flung from Neil's jacket, but could summon no energy to retrieve them. They belonged to another member of the family, Hazel's family not hers, and she viewed them as irrelevant. Her arms were now rough with goose-pimples and, forcing herself to her feet, she pulled one of David's thick jumpers from the clothes horse and hauled it over her head. She felt better, and now, chocolate forgotten, she allowed herself to think again of the events of the newly ended day.

She would always remember the complete elation written on Kathy's face when she had cautiously returned to her own home. She had been delighted at the clean, calm person in front of her and insisted on making them lunch, even though they had barely had time to clear away the breakfast things.

"God, David," Kathy had marvelled. "Don't know how you did it, but I'm glad you did."

181

Kate remembered David's relieved smile at her words and then a long conversation between the pair of them to the tune of his gratitude and her happiness at being able to lend a hand. At one point, she had felt the absolute need to stand and hug this woman, who was more than willing to reciprocate, as Kate had not welcomed any contact at all in the days she had been there and Kathy was a very tactile person. They had stood, chins on shoulders, thanking and acknowledging each other for as long as it had taken and when Kate had glanced back at David, he had been sitting, head down but back straight.

Over lunch, Kathy had decided that the safest topic of discussion, this soon after Kate had emerged from her broken state, was her life on Skye. She had wanted to know all about the cottage, Hazel's boyfriend and the life and times of a Scottish upbringing, which Kate had been willing enough to share as it had not appeared to upset David. He had joined in the discussion more than once, agreeing that Fiona had always talked of it lovingly and even his few extreme days on the island had been breath-taking and welcoming. When the subject turned to Kate's future plans, she had hesitated, and then shrugged amiably at the two intrigued faces.

"Well," Kathy had dismissed her vagueness. "I never knew what I wanted to do. Still not sure if I'm there yet."

"It's not that," Kate had replied. "I always wanted to go to Moray House. It's a teaching University in Edinburgh, and I love Edinburgh. But even the thought of going back to the High School now seems just ridiculous."

"Ridiculous?" Kathy had repeated.

"The thought of sitting with those people in a classroom.Even the thought of revising for exams. What on earth does it matter? Anybody can write answers on a piece of paper, and it would be just the same at University. Pointless."

Kate had seen the look they had exchanged then, and had wondered if they would dare try to persuade her away from this opinion, but they had not. Whether they had agreed with her or whether they had simply chosen not to address it there and then, she had not known and cared even less. On the journey home, after Kathy had been assured that she would be kept abreast of developments and welcomed at The Edge whenever she was passing, Kate had turned to David in the driving seat and waited until he had acknowledged her look.

"Tell me how Hazel is feeling," Kate's voice had sounded scared, even to herself.

"She just wants to see you. And she's terrified."

"That's because I lost it. I'm okay now. I need to make it up to her because she's my best friend and I really hurt her."

Kate closed her eyes at the memory of those words. She had never meant to cut Hazel out; she would never have done such a thing in her right mind. But all she had seen was her sister's shocked face and with each desperate reassurance that was screamed at her, Kate had felt the separation between them stretch and stretch. Hazel had tried so hard to let her know of her support for her, that Kate had seen it as an instant acceptance of the situation and somehow therefore a betrayal.

But that had been back then. Later, when she had jumped from the truck and sprinted to the back of the house, Hazel had been waiting on the doorstep. They had flung themselves at each other, both unable to get enough apologies out because of the crying and the hugging. To Kate, at that moment, there had never been anything as lovely as the shining, bright-eyed face that was her sister's. Every line on her brow, every expression, even her crooked front tooth spoke of home and family and her Mum.

"Don't you *ever* run away from me again, Wilder," Hazel had yelled in her face. "Do you hear me?" Her words had sounded like a melody.

Later still, the five of them had sat by the fire in the sitting room. Hazel had settled herself beside Kate and taken her hand in hers. She had not let go until the second cup of tea had forced her to go to the toilet, at which point, David had poured himself a whisky and stood with his back to the fire. The conversation had seemingly stalled. Kate remembered the scene well.

Neil had been picking at the bobbles of wool on his old socks. He had barely had a chance to address Kate directly, as Hazel had monopolised every minute of her return. But now he looked at her in the growing stillness and gave her a smile, the sort of smile that could be used with a shrug, but could also say 'hey, we're all here together and maybe it's not so bad.' Rose had cleared her throat and left the room, mumbling something about making up Neil's bed. With five reduced to three in an instant, Kate had fought off the threat of the monkey in a zoo sensation by asking David if she too could have a drink. His face had been one of wide-eyed surprise, but even more unexpectedly he had poured her a small measure without comment. Neil had grinned at her grimace, the peaty liquid burning its way to her stomach in a way that prevented her from hiding her disgust. David had also laughed softly.

"I thought I was being sophisticated," she had choked, "but that is not in any way nice."

She had offered the remainder to Neil, who had shaken his head slowly.

"Never touch the stuff," he had said and in that moment, Kate had seen the first sign of the man behind the beard and the worn clothes. His eyes had grown so forlorn that his whole face had not been able to compete with the emotion and he had looked away, into the fire, where the flames had reflected his misery back at him. Hazel had reappeared at that very moment, but Kate could not concentrate on a word she was saying. She had wanted to ask this stranger what had caused this reaction to his own inoffensive words and had looked at David for help, but he had been staring out of the window, his glass empty. No more had been said.

Kate no longer could stomach the thought of a hot drink, feeling more comfort by snuggling inside David's large jumper. The sleeves reached her knuckles, and she instantly pictured Neil's isolated figure marooned in the fireside chair, his own jumper loose on his lean arms. David and he had been quite chatty at first. Manly chat of course - trees and snow tyres and the price of fuel – but it had petered out quickly. Rose had shared her attention between them, at the same time continually touching Kate's arm or Hazel's head. She had looked so tired. They had eaten a huge dinner, and the only mention of the bigger picture had been when Rose had suggested that Kate phone Beth later that night to let her know that she was back with them.

It had seemed to Kate that since the moment they had met David, those in charge had been continually waiting for the 'best time' to let she and Hazel know what they needed to know. Just after the funeral on Skye, they had all been cautiously getting to know each other – 'too soon to tell them about the GMP.' Here in Canada - 'let's build some sort of relationship and cushion them against it'. And now – 'maybe when Kate is stronger, when she is less likely to break down'. She was sick of it. The time was now.

So, there they had sat in the sitting room, testing out the family dynamics. Considering an entirely new personality had been thrown into the mix, it had been a reasonable success. Rose had settled herself in the window seat, nursing her own small brandy while she tried to sort through the dry laundry. Hazel had lounged next to Kate on the sofa, her legs tucked under her, asking about Kathy and if she had spoken about their Mum at all. David and Neil had sat on opposite sides of the fire, David slowly sinking further down the chair as he consumed more whisky and Neil alternately answering Rose's questions about Andie and rubbing his chin. Kate had wondered why someone who was so obviously irritated by his own facial hair did not just shave it off.

The atmosphere had not been overly intense, but Kate had begun to feel a pressure on her chest, as if someone was tightening screws on a breastplate. In this room of adults, it was apparent that she, the youngest of all of them, had been allocated control over what they did or did not discuss. If she asked a question, they would all look at her and have to answer in one way or the other. It had given her a power of sorts and she had commended herself for not wading straight in. She could have blown the room to smithereens if she had wanted to, but she had far too much regard for them and the fact that they were showing her respect in dancing around the subject had endeared them further to her. When Neil had gone to get a drink of water and David had finally stopped his body from sliding off the chair, rubbing his eyes vigorously back into the present, Kate had sat forward.

"Sorry I went running off," she had said, looking straight at Rose. "I didn't want you all looking at me like that. Especially you Hazel. But we're okay, aren't we?"

Hazel's face had fallen, desperate for Kate to believe her words. "Of *course* we're okay. And we always will be."

David had looked straight at her. His eyes had been a little puffy from his abuse of them and possibly the whisky, but his face had seemed completely alert and even anxious for her to continue down this road at last. She had seen so many expressions on his face since their first meeting. Pain, hope, desperation, amusement.She had criticised him for it, he had assured her that not everything was as apparent as she had insisted. But tonight, when he had sat straight-backed in that chair, his hands resting on his knees, she had seen something else entirely. He had held her gaze, his eyes clearing in front of her. Eventually, the corners of his closed mouth had turned up and his eyebrows had risen ever so slightly. He had nodded his head enough for her to be aware of it and she thought that maybe there had been some affection in that look. Certainly there had been encouragement. It had been enough. She had glanced back at Hazel's patient expression before speaking.

"Don't hate me."

"Kate, you know - "

"I mean, don't hate me when I do this," she had explained, then, "The pair of us have just travelled a long way to meet you Rose - and now Neil. It turns out that only Haze is related to you, so there must have been another reason why Mum wanted me to come. She never did things without a reason, we all know that. She wanted something put to rest."

Hazel's face had paled slightly and she had started to wriggle on the sofa, needing to speak, but Kate had carried on, making eye contact with all three of them, like a professional speaker.

"So, I need you to tell me, us, what happened. As much as you know. And that, Haze, means talking about her. Talking about what she was like back then and all the rest. Please. Please will you all do that for us?"

She had noticed Neil then, leaning against the door jamb, arms folded as ever. As soon as she had caught his eye, he had moved his gaze to his brother. Rose had wilted in her chair, the laundry forgotten at her feet, but she had not looked away when Kate had sought her agreement. Hazel had looked scared to death. Nobody seemed able to answer her immediately, but it had made her feel even stronger. She had noticed Neil shrug once at David, who finally had been the first to speak.

"Just try to understand, that we haven't talked about it in years," his voice had still had strength, in spite of his painfully strained face. "It might be ...... disjointed."

"We don't know anything," Kate had replied. "So everything will be a bonus."

"It won't make you bad again?" Hazel had looked so anxious, but already the constriction in Kate's chest was easing.

"If I can't be part of this..." Kate faltered, trying to get the words out before emotion took hold. "Look, you're all still important to me. It would be great if we all knew the same, don't you think? All in the same boat.All reading from the same book.Whatever other cliché you want to use. That's what I would like anyway."

Thankfully, they had not made any half-hearted promises to do their best, but had sat thinking it through. It had proved that they were taking her seriously, and while they mulled it over, she had left the room. She had needed to phone Beth, a phone-call which had inadvertantly crushed her ability to continue the discussion she had asked them to participate in. The conversation with her Aunt had made her eyelids sting and her throat ache, and on returning to the sitting room, she had simply told them of her intentions and left them to form their opinions without her.

Now she sat shivering in the kitchen, unable to sleep. She thought of Beth who had not understood anything, she thought of Neil who was somehow involved enough to want to stay and help and she thought of Rose, who seemed to be as tired as she herself was. She pictured Hazel, fearful and uneasy at what might be revealed and she saw David, resigned but willing to do what was necessary.

What on earth had Fiona been thinking? Kate had no doubt that her mother had wanted to sort something out, to close some chapter somewhere and all she could do was to trust her judgement. Fiona was not malicious or cruel. What she had done and what Kate was doing now were both essential to somebody. She just wasn't sure who that was yet.

Chapter 24

Beth lay on her side, staring through the thin curtains. She was watching the branches outside swaying in the moonlight, the wind bouncing them at random as the fancy took it. It had been her favourite way of falling asleep until Kenny had moved in, but now it was reserved for those hours through the night when sleep packed its bags and left for sunnier climes. She did not hear the wind; the only sound in the whole house was her own heart and the steady breathing of Kenny beside her. His arm was lying across his middle, resting on her hip and she was glad of his body heat, as a deep shiver ran through her. It seemed to start in her lungs and radiate out, the kind of shiver that would have been pleasurable if it was not caused by the knot in her stomach and the pain in her head.

'Three more days,' she thought to herself, and as if he had heard her, Kenny shifted across the tiny void between them and put his arm fully around her waist.

"Can't sleep?" he mumbled, pulling her closer still.

"Three more days," she repeated, this time out loud, interlacing her fingers in his across her stomach. "Then they'll be back where they belong."

The bed was snug but Kenny felt that he had crossed into the area of waking rather than dozing and so stretched out beside Beth, glancing at the clock. It read just after five am, too early to get up, but not too early to talk. He silently switched on the bedside lamp and watched as Beth curled up against the harshness of the light. He pushed himself up onto his pillow and gathered her folded body to his, stroking her hair until she was ready to speak some more.

This had more or less been the pattern since he had moved in over a week ago and he too wished that things were on a bit more of an even keel. He alone had taken on the task of sorting and distributing the "goods and chattels" he had brought with him, whilst trying to find a suitable tenant for his own house. Beth seemed incapable of concentrating on any one task for more than half an hour at a time, although she had made sure that on his first night, they had sat down to a three course celebration and talked deliberately about their personal plans for as long as possible. Since the girls had got on the plane, she had spent all of her free time wondering, assuming, surmising and baking. Kenny, not a man of many words at the best of times, absorbed it all with the growing understanding that this was the definition of sharing a life and helped her out by consuming cakes, scones and biscuits. He was not a bit worried or overawed by any of it. Beth was his and he was hers. This was their existence.

"Shall I make some tea, Beth-lamb?" he asked her, happy for her hair to be tickling his chest, in spite of her anxiety.

"Can you really be bothered, Ken? I don't mind just lying here."

"I'll bring it back to bed, don't worry."

Beth watched him hunt for a pair of socks to protect his feet from the freezing kitchen tiles, and then touched his back as he sat on the bed to pull them on. He turned his face to smile in her direction, his tongue touching the tip of his lip as he concentrated on the task in hand and she sat up, encircling his waist and leaning her face against his warm skin.

"I love you, Kenneth Andrew Elliot."

"Well, there's a lot to love," he joked. "Although I'm fast fading away. I don't think you are making nearly enough sugar and fat-filled baked goods. Back in a minute." He kissed her forehead gently.

As he padded out into the dark hallway, she touched the spot he had kissed. Even that ached and she reached for the paracetamol which permanently resided on her bedside table. She watched it fizz up the sides of her water glass and wondered if it would spill over the top or whether the glass would magically halt the effervescence as it reached the rim. She bit her lip as she realised, not for the first time, that she did far, *far* too much thinking. Even when she was talking to others, actually forming words and communicating about mundane or work-related tasks, her mind was pondering some query or happening that she had no part in and even less control over. Why did every single scenario have to be looked at from every imaginable angle, when ultimately she would have to choose only one opinion to stick to if she was even given the chance to contribute? It was little wonder that her head ached and sleep had given her up as a lost cause.

This was not a new concept to Beth however. She had always envied people who took less interest in second guessing what was to come. She, on the other hand, had to explore absolutely every avenue, working out what her reaction to each circumstance would be, how others would respond and then trying to envisage the best outcome for all concerned. How relaxing it must be to wake up each morning, look out at the day and accept that whatever happened might be incredibly boring or completely unexpectedly exciting, either of which was acceptable.

More than anything else, she marvelled at people who could sip coffee in an airport lounge whilst reading a newspaper. People who could actually look forward to their forthcoming trip without worrying about the last time the plane had had a maintenance check or whether the pilot's marriage was on the rocks, causing him to drink to excess. Or even if the rising wind and hail would be enough to cancel the flight, or if it would be at the optimum limit just below cancellation status, which was even worse. Beth had consequently been on a plane twice – once to visit Fiona, when Hazel had had her first birthday, and once to make the return journey. She never intended to go down that road again.

Even now, when the worst had happened, she could only pray that Hazel and Kate would brave this state of affairs without her. Financially, if she was superbly creative, she could manage the cost of the trip and the fish farm had promised her whatever time she required. But she could not contemplate putting her 'life at risk' as she saw it, because it would not be fair to the girls. Kenny had been incredulous and it had caused the only major disagreement of their short cohabitation.

"Beth, honey, you are being completely ridiculous – "

"Please don't start with the statistics, Kenny. I've heard every argument, countless times, and every quote to do with car crashes or lightning or winning the pools. Well, no statistic can alter the fact that if I don't get on a plane, I will never be in a plane crash."

"You will also never see anything further than the mainland!"

"I don't want to."

"That doesn't mean that maybe you shouldn't think - " he had hesitated then and cleared his throat, aware that, when Beth's eyes lost their sparkle, there was no way on earth she would be open to any further persuasion. He had not wished to be heavy-handed, Beth was still grieving, not only for her sister but for the nieces she had never been apart from for seventeen years. And it would have been cruel to suggest that their needs were greater than her fears, but he had wished to do that more than anything. In the end, he had tried to be supportive and cunningly manipulative, "You have to do what you think is right. I can't decide for you."

She had been adamant. "Well, I think the right thing is to stay here, *safe*, at the end of the phone when they need me, and welcome them home as soon as possible. When they are back here, I'll take time off and we won't stop talking until everybody is okay again."

She had believed this, a few days ago, when she had said it. Now this plan seemed as likely to succeed as the paracetamol was to cure her headache. Should she have gone over there, where the world was crumbling around them, and tried to lend some sort of normality or continuity? She liked to think that it would have simply complicated matters further, but it was impossible to tell. The questions were endless, the answers completely obscure.

On the day they had flown to Canada, Beth had managed to keep most of her agitation under wraps and what did show itself, she felt could be explained by her well-documented terror of airports themselves. The worst part for her had been knowing that when they returned, the girls would be different people. The extent of the change would depend only on how it was handled by a man who barely knew them and how much they wanted to pursue the facts. She had wanted to tell them to be safe, to be open-minded and to trust each other. As Kate had hoisted her little ruck-sack onto one shoulder, she had given her aunt a hopeful 'well-here-goes' grin which had nearly broken Beth's already cracked heart. In the end, as she had hugged them close, all she had managed was the firm reassurance that she would always be at the end of the phone, at any time of day. It had been an innocuous enough statement, so bland it was almost meaningless, but David had acknowledged it for its actual worth.

As they had inched forward in the queue for the departure lounge, Beth had touched his arm. He had turned to her, his face calm and his brow clear and she had looked him straight in the eye, trying desperately to convey her unspoken support, gratitude and best wishes. He had picked up on her meaning immediately and leaned down to hug her.

"I'm so sorry," she had whispered. "But remember, just ring me if it goes really badly. Don't feel you need to do this by yourself. You never did anything wrong."

As he had pulled away, his eyes had shone at her words, at her vindication of him and he had taken hope from that as much as anything.

"You're generous," he had stated, touching her shoulder. "But this is the very least I can do."

"Dad?" Hazel had shouted from six feet away "We need you!"

He had turned at her words to find Hazel and Kate both standing at the gate, awaiting himself and, equally importantly, their travel documents. Facing Beth one last time, he had worn a jagged smile and shrugged. "They need me."

"Phone me," Beth had replied, then over his shoulder to the girls, "Phone me!"

They had indeed phoned her. Once to pass on excited details of the flight, the house, the planned trips and the scenery and then again to assure her that they were fine and having an enjoyable time in spite of the fact that they were missing her. Only two upbeat and hopeful calls to her and one in return, before the fourth containing nothing but tears and disbelief and baffled questions. She had not spoken to Kate at all since the truth had been acknowledged and this had driven her almost to distraction. Apparently, she had gone to stay with an old friend of Fiona's. She could not comprehend that this had been a solution and dreaded to think of the scene which had caused it. Hazel had tried to convey to her that it had indeed been necessary, but had been so full of her own non-comprehension, that her niece's questions had taken over every conversation.

David had been able to reassure her that Kate was safe and better off removed from himself and the house, even from Hazel, for the time being. His voice had sounded shattered, and although he insisted that he had the situation in hand, the defeat that was present could not be hidden, even over the phone. He had, in his defence, called her every day since to report the state of play. She in turn, had tried her best to explain why she could not make the journey and, in fact, he had begged her not to even think about it.

"If you take this over," he had tried to explain gently, but firmly, "You will cut me out completely. Do you understand that? I need you to let me do this."

And so, due to her own phobia and his earnest plea, Beth had been forced to take a step back and let him try to find a way of communicating and helping. It seemed to her an almost insurmountable challenge. But Fiona had wanted it this way and nobody had argued with Fiona. There were times when Beth feared she might start to resent her sister and her wishes.

Kenny appeared with the steaming tea, yawning widely enough to threaten jaw dislocation. She took the mug from him gratefully, desperate to rid her mouth of the grainy bitterness of the painkiller. When he was settled beside her once more, she placed her hand squarely over where his heart beat steadily and looked up at his face.

"I know," he mused, "How did you ever live before I moved in? How did you even get out of bed in the morning without my booster cup of tea?"

"You can joke all you want, Elliot. But if you weren't here, I'd still be wrapped up in Fee's quilt, watching the world go past the front window. I wouldn't even be back at work yet."

"Well, I'm not complaining. You can thank me all you want in whatever way takes your fancy. However," he lifted her chin to kiss her, then "You really need to cut back on the baking. The last thing I want to come between us is my spare tyre, which I swear was not there two weeks ago!"

Beth planted a quick kiss on said stomach, just above his navel, then patted it affectionately. "Oh, okay then, if you insist."

As Kenny tried to pull her back into the crook of his arm, the telephone began its shrill call to attention in the silent house. Beth was instantly alert. She was used to morning calls from Canada, but calling at this time meant only one thing. This crisis was more urgent. For once, she could not move, but stared at the hallway, eyes wide and mouth slightly open. Kenny was out of bed a second later, lending only a moment's thought as to why Beth was not. First things first.

Beth could hear his voice, acknowledging and reassuring, but not laughing. She also, for the seventy-fifth time cursed the fact that they had not yet purchased a cordless phone and finally forced herself out of the sanctuary of the bed, pulling her dressing gown around herself tightly as she walked. In the hallway, Kenny was shivering slightly in his boxers and one remaining sock. He turned as soon as he heard Beth's footfalls behind him, but continued to listen and pulled back from her slightly as she held out her hand for the receiver. The longer he held onto it, gazing at her with a non-descript expression, the worse she felt and she gave him her best, most practised anxious look. He held up his finger for one more second, then he placed his hand over the mouthpiece and whispered, "It's Kate."

"Oh God, at last."

Silently he handed her the phone, then put his arm around her shoulders as she leaned against the wall.

"Hi baby."

She listened carefully for a few moments and nodded to herself. Two 'yes, of courses' and an 'oh okay' followed before, about thirty seconds later, she suddenly put her hand over her eyes and began to silently weep. She could not seem to catch her breath and slowly released her grip on the phone. Kenny grabbed it before it fell and slammed down the receiver, holding Beth upright against the wall.

"What? Tell me."

She finally took a breath, but had to inhale slowly twice more before she could even raise her face to his. Instantly she saw that he feared the very worst and grabbed both his hands, shaking her head.

"Oh Ken. What do I do now? What on earth do we do?"

"What is it?" his voice was fantastically patient.

"Kate. She's back with them. But," she bit her lip in disbelief, "She's refusing to come home."

"You just said she was -" he began.

"She says she's not coming home to us. To Skye."

He caught her under the arms as she began to slide down the wall, but manoeuvred her to the safety of the bed before she collapsed completely. He could not credit her words, what she actually meant by them, and knelt in front of her, holding her face in his hands.

"*Now* will you go?" he implored.

He saw the pain crinkle her eyes and the complete and utter hopelessness of her situation.

"I can't," she wailed. "Don't ask me to. I can't do it."

"It's not for me, Beth."

"I know," she cried, "But Fiona knew that I couldn't do it. Why do you think I didn't go over there with them? I promised I would do anything she asked, as long as she kept that out of the equation, and she took pity on me. Do you know how it feels to be terrified beyond reason, and at the same time so completely and totally useless?"

Kenny climbed onto the bed beside her, his arm around her shoulders in an instant. Her pain was clear, but now she was breathing more steadily, her frown suggesting that her brain had latched onto an option. He allowed her the time to assess and organise, rubbing her shoulder and upper arm, before kissing the lines on her head to show his support.

"Okay," she said. "Okay. I need to get in touch with Kathy."

He nodded his understanding. "You think it's time for that?"

"Fiona left the timing up to me. She gave me that much, even though I let her down. I think there will never be a more desperate time than this. I'll phone her later today. When I can string words together better."

They sat, breathing through the latest crisis, and waited. Waited for Beth to gather her strength and waited for the sun to rise.

Chapter 25

"But I thought you said we were fine." Hazel was sitting on Kate's bed, carefully trying to dislodge her brush from her newly showered hair.

"Bloody hell, Haze, how many times? We are *completely* fine. In fact," Kate sat up quickly, the most animated she had been in days, and grasped her sister's hands, "we are way better than fine. We are the strongest we have ever been!"

"Well you can joke all you want, missy," Hazel frowned, pushing Kate back onto her pillow, "But just tell me why – one more time - before I smother you."

"No, I'm not going to. It's your fault if you weren't listening the first nineteen times."

Kate now rolled out of bed and tried to find her towel amongst the muddle of clothes on the floor.

"I was listening well and good. I just didn't *understand* it. In fact, a lot of the things you say are beyond me. How old are you again?"

"Old enough to know I'm right," replied Kate, pointing her finger at her sister as she left for the bathroom.

Sighing, Hazel plaited her untangled hair and, glancing out at the near horizontal rain, picked up an extra cardigan to pull over her sweater. She found the kitchen warm and full of people. David was by the door, untying his boots, Neil was drying dishes, the most non-masculine thing Hazel had seen him do to date and Rose was making griddle scones.

"So," said Hazel brightly. "Here we all are. Again. What will we talk about *today?*"

David looked at her sharply and immediately she felt ashamed. Neil however, looked around at her with an amused look and she merely raised her shoulders in apology. She walked over to David and gave him a quick hug. "Sorry. Just to trying to be a smart-arse . Worked well, didn't it?"

"Here, Hazel," Rose handed her a plate of scones and indicated that she should sit. "Where's Kate?"

"In the shower. By the way, she seems a lot more with it today. Like she's not going to take any shit from – oh sorry. Mum didn't like us swearing. My God, if she could have heard them at the school, she'd have been delighted with our lack of imagination."

Neil, having dried his hands, poured some coffee and joined her at the table. He reached for one of her scones, intrigued to see how she would react. Hazel watched him take a huge bite in front of her, looked down at the reduced pile and then back at him. She could see his eyes daring her to say something and suddenly, she wanted to take him on. Slowly she folded her arms. It was his signature attitude and she put as much into it as he usually did. She leaned back in her seat, rolled her tongue in her cheek and, just once, rubbed her thumb under her chin, letting it rest there. Neil stared back at her, grinning now, and glancing around to see who else was witnessing the piece of theatre. Rose had not really cottoned on and absently began to clear the worktop of flour and other debris. David, on the other hand, was leaning against the range, laughing silently. When he laughed his shoulders almost always moved, but he very rarely made any noise. Hazel didn't care. She was just overjoyed that at last he looked happier and without a word of acknowledgement, she picked up a scone and stuffed it in her mouth.

"By the way," she addressed the room, her mouth still full of food, "Is anybody going to help me persuade her to come home with me, or are you all on her side?"

Hazel saw David sigh through his fading smile.

"Well, it's tomorrow afternoon you know," she continued, "we don't have much time to think about it. And apart from the obvious, I'm not sure I can sit that length of time alone on a plane, even if there is a film showing."

"What's Kate saying this morning?" Neil asked.

"The same as last night and I hope you were listening, because apparently she explained it *nineteen* times."

Rose brushed her hand over Hazel's head as she headed off upstairs.

"So," Hazel continued, "What are we going to do? I'll tell you this for nothing; Beth will be heading for outer space at this moment. She likes things to go according to plan. There was this one time when Mum was supposed to be taking us over to Lewis for a music festival. Well, the ferry company - "

"If she wants to stay, she can." David's voice was firm and Hazel looked straight at him, dismayed. "She said she needs to understand everything and she can only do it here. That was the gist of it, I think."

"I know what she *said.* But it's ridiculous!"

"Why?"

"Because," Hazel spluttered, "Because she needs to get back to Beth and school and ... back to normal." As she uttered the last phrase, she caught the futility of it and it seemed to make her instantly livid. Her brow was nothing but black lines and she screwed her eyes up in furious frustration. "Shit, shit, shit! That's what all of this is. Complete crap! You know, this time last year, the most I had to worry about was whether the car was going to survive the winter. Then all this junk got dumped on us."

Pausing to catch her breath, Hazel glanced at David to find his body stiff and his mouth set in a hard, straight line. Instantly she was on the point of justifying herself, when Neil moved in the corner of her eye and his passive face ignited her anger once more. His features were wax-like and she found herself beyond the point of self-censorship.

"And why are *you* here?" she asked, her voice businesslike. "You don't seem to have an opinion on anything."

"Hazel," David snapped, moving to the table. "That's enough. Watch what you're saying."

Her mouth fell open as she stood, resting her hands on the table, surprised but not put off by his tone. Neil again said nothing, but looked at his brother, alarm now shining in his eyes. "You see?" she cried, "Why don't you speak? You came here for a reason, apparently. So far I've seen no reason. You're a bloody spectator after all!"

"What's going on?" Rose enquired. She was followed into the kitchen by Kate, fresh and dressed and clearly confused by the atmosphere. Hazel's irritation had finally spilled over into the room and Neil was now on his feet. But moments after beginning her second rant of criticism, demanding that he explain his presence, his timing and his worth, her words were halted at the sight of him backing away from the table. His face was blotchy, his cheekbones coloured pink just below his eyes, the rest white, and his hands fisted at his sides. David took one step towards him but he held up both hands to keep him at a distance. He could not have spoken now, even to appease Hazel, because his jaw was so tightly clenched the tendons were visible on his throat.

Rose moved swiftly to where Neil was backed against the sink and painstakingly began to unfold his sweaty hands, murmuring to him the entire time. As she managed to release his clamped fingers, he gradually relaxed his jaw and his head which had been inclined upwards, came back to its normal angle. Slowly, his eyes began to move from sheer terror to alarm, and then seemed to settle on humiliation. Hazel, now silent, felt her own face burn with shame. Surely that had not solely been due to her sharpness. She could have given a lot worse, the frame of mind she had been in, but now she was mortified; and completely mystified.

Kate found herself standing next to David, having no memory of moving across the room to him. He had also witnessed the scene in silence, although now that Rose was working her magic, he stood one hand rubbing his jaw, the other propping himself against the range. She tried to catch his eye for reassurance, but he was completely immersed in Neil's dilemma, whatever it was, and she saw for the first time, the depth of their relationship. It had never been even slightly apparent until that moment. Now his face was damp and his eyes were crinkled with worry. From the way that Rose was speaking and easing Neil back from where he had been, this was something they had all been through before.

"I'm sorry," whispered Hazel, to anybody that would listen, and Kate took her by the arm and led her out into the hallway. When they were safely by the front window of the sitting room, as far as they could get from the kitchen, she dropped her arm gently and lifted both of her hands in the air.

"What the hell?" Kate almost mimed.

Hazel shook her head vigorously and tried to speak as quietly as her puzzled brain would allow.

"Not a clue," she hissed. "He was okay. You know, not really saying much and then he was in that state. What would you call that; I've never seen the like."

Kate was equally intrigued. In her short acquaintance with the man, she had thought him the least complex or intimidating person she had ever shared a room with. She had assumed that the artist in him allowed situations to unfold around him without feeling the necessity to contribute. He probably spent most of his day in a silent bubble, focussed on the material in his hands and thinking, not speaking. So this episode was bewildering.

"Did somebody say something?" Kate continued.

Hazel failed to hide her guilt as she rolled her eyes and sighed. "Okay. I did get a bit short with him, but it was nothing. Nothing like when we get going anyway."

David had appeared in the doorway, one hand in his pocket and the other resting on the door frame above his head. He wiped his face with the sleeve of his shirt before looking back at them. He seemed weary. Hazel, vexed at his expression, moved silently over to him, pulled him gently into the room and closed the door. He looked down at her, his eyes so much more forgiving than his mouth.

"I am so sorry, Dad. Is he okay? What happened? I wasn't even really shouting ..."

During her plea for forgiveness, David had laid his hand on her shoulder. Now he shook his head to halt her words.

"He's okay. He'll be fine. We'll give them a bit of time, I think. Rose is all he needs."

For a moment more they stood quietly. Hazel's face was shame combined with sorrow, a marriage which made her look about eight years old, and like an eight-year old, her chin gave a dangerous wobble before she sucked in a breath and bit her bottom lip. Kate remained by the window, thinking it the safest place to be, and asked nothing further. Instead, she watched David. He pulled Hazel into a hug, resting his chin on her head, and she saw her arms embrace him quickly before letting them fall to her sides.

"I don't deserve that," Hazel murmured, "I'm a horrible person."

"You didn't know," he offered her this simple absolution and moved away from her.

More than anything at that moment, Kate wished that they could all just sit down in each other's company and not speak. That they could relax into a chair each and take a few deep breaths together. In that silent hope, she turned her face to the window and began to watch the rain.

She knew this weather well. The sound of water droplets being thrown against glass was as familiar to her as the mist which occupied the top of the Ben. If she closed her eyes, the dim light could be that which draped the bay and she could be in a tiny cramped room, too full of furniture for its own good. Maybe she could be waiting for the sun to suddenly emerge and warm her face and she could open her eyes to find a startling shard of rainbow in front of her. And the fire could smoke at each gust of wind and Beth could curse from the kitchen that she had not brought in the washing earlier. So she kept her eyes open. She did

196

not trust herself to be able to return from there. Instead, she sank into the window seat, welcoming the peace.

Hazel took a seat on the sofa and stared absently at the grey embers in the fireplace. What had been so vibrant the previous night, golden flames and fizzing sparks, now lay lifeless and cold. There was nothing so bleak as a burnt-out fire. Her eyes remained on the pile of wood remnants and ashes, as she tried to remember how to feel optimistic. She had always had so many tricks to help her do this, something Fiona had nurtured in her, years before her illness. Had her mother recognised a trait in her that she had stood beside her in times of stress or fear and pulled her back from the edge? 'Find something to look forward to, Haze. Anything. London's Burning on the telly. Fish and chips tomorrow night. It doesn't have to be big, it just has to be good.' It had worked for a huge percentage of the times she had needed it and, as a few drops of heavy rain created dust clouds in the fireplace and black spots on the hearth, Hazel tried to think of Stuart and his strong grip. Her heart did a little jolt as she saw his face in her mind and reminded herself that she had a life outside all of this.

Shifting slightly in her seat, she leaned forward and rested her chin in her hands, beginning to let her boyfriend take possession of her again. She thought of the way he came stomping into the kitchen, shaking rain onto the floor and apologising to Beth for the inconvenience. Or the way he would sound his horn from the bottom of the drive and wait there until her tardiness drove him insane enough to come jogging up to the door. She was in love with the way his scowl would immediately split into a grin as soon as he saw her, no matter how long she had kept him waiting. He was two years older than she was and she remembered him playing football for the school team, but she would never tell him that she had noticed him even then, let alone fancied him. It would make him a different person. She wanted him to think that he had done all the chasing and won her over, by insisting on trying every cake in the baker's until he found his favourite. The day he had announced his decision was the day he had asked her out.

Now, she wanted to be sitting beside him in his truck, eating Fab ice lollies and watching tourists flying kites on Glenbrittle beach. He might even let her drive back, now that she was a 'truck driver', but she didn't even care if he refused. Oh, she missed him. What a strange time to have that revelation. Something to look forward to, she thought and got up from her seat. "I'm going to pack," she announced and did not wait for a response.

David, sitting in one of the fireside chairs, left it too late to ask after her or follow her, and so placed his hands on the arms of the chair and remained in situ instead. He was facing the window, but did not raise his eyes to Kate, who was content to let the room settle around them for another few minutes. It seemed to her that people never allowed silence to be a part of things. Peace and quiet. They were forever being spoken of as a couple. But everybody was always in such a hurry to explain themselves and understand everything that they forgot how therapeutic stillness and individual thought were. Kate knew all about it. She healed best when the only person she could hear was her mother in her head and knew that nobody could interfere with the practice or put an end to it, because they were ignorant of its existence.

However, in this house today, nobody was comfortable or at ease and perhaps only spoken assurances of support and care would help. She watched David scratch his knee, wondering how much more of this he could tolerate. He must wonder himself when there would be an end to it all. She had seen so many impediments thrown at him and yet had seen for herself that he was only human. He had shown her his pain, his despair and his awe at what was happening and still he got up in the morning and faced it all again. That was surely a sign of strength. Strength and commitment. He was a strong, committed man and her mother had known it. Perhaps the reason he kept going was because he too trusted Fiona's judgement, even now.

"That was upsetting," Kate's voice was unduly loud in the silence. "What was it?"

"Short version?" replied David, "He has problems with anxiety, has done for years and sometimes it can get the better of him. That was mild."

Kate frowned. It made no sense to her. "But David, what on earth could Hazel say that would cause that? She's completely harmless."

David now pursed his lips in resignation and, pushing himself from his seat, he made his way to her side. But standing beside her still seated figure, he seemed more occupied with the raging elements than responding to her question. She remembered the first time they had stood by a window and how he had kept his distance because of the signals she had shot at him like arrows. Now, his presence was nothing but essential to her. He had the only thing resembling answers that were available and he was prepared to share them. Finally he looked down at her and she hoped her smile was one of encouragement.

"Neil is a great guy."

When nothing more was forthcoming, Kate widened her eyes and nodded her head. "He seems it."

"Look I'm just going to say it. Remember, you weren't born so there is no way on earth that this was your fault, okay? You accept that now don't you?"

Kate's stomach contracted but she sat up straighter and nodded.

"He was nineteen, that's younger than Hazel is now, and he wouldn't listen to any of us. We told him time and again that it was not his fault. Hell, I couldn't think straight for months but even I kept telling him to let it go. Rose went to his appointments with him, but it was a long, long time before he would talk about it. It certainly was *not* his responsibility, but of course, he couldn't accept that. I think he was getting there, but since I saw him again yesterday, I've known he was struggling."

Kate was completely baffled, but it did not stop David pulling her to her feet, his face pleading for her understanding. "He was my brother and he promised to look after your mom. All he has ever acknowledged from that night to this is that he failed me and he failed her. And, he still has no idea what happened."

"What?" Kate was aghast. "What are you talking about?"

"I was in hospital and Neil took your mom out for a drink. They were going to see a band, meet friends, whatever. It was so ordinary."

"Hospital?" whispered Kate. She tried to recall the last time an accident had been mentioned, and remembered that it had taken place in Hazel's old room; when they had been discussing the separation. Kate's mouth dried in an instant. "You're telling me that that's when it happened? That's what you're saying. That it happened that night. And Neil knows. He knows what happened?"

"Not as such. He was out of his head. They all were."

"Drunk?" Kate could no longer keep her voice down.

"He was *nineteen*. He's never had a drink since."

"But he knows who was there. He can at least tell me that much?"

David nodded, looking out at the windswept puddles, before turning back to the girl at his side. There were no tears on her face, but the grey eyes were flitting back and forth as realisation of some sort began to show itself there. "Are you sure it was then?"

"It would make sense, the time seems about right and your mom never really went out."

"Then that's why I'm here."

"Sorry?"

"Mum doesn't just want me to find out who I am. She wants me to help him find some peace in all of this. You didn't blame him, she didn't blame him. Maybe when the truth is out, he'll stop blaming himself."

David was reminded for the first time since Skye just how young Kate was. Did every intricate problem, woven tight over time, appear so loose and simplistic when you were seventeen? But Kate was through the door before David could utter another word and he could only follow her quick stride to the kitchen. Neil, having regained his colour, now rose from his seat next to his mother, his lips already forming an apology. With an expanding heart, David watched Kate take his arm and shush him with her eyes. Neil swallowed as she spoke.

"I think I might be able to help. Will you let me try?"

Chapter 26

Kate did not kid herself that the morning was going to be easy. It was the day of Hazel's departure and her sister had been very subdued before breakfast and positively morose during it. The plan was to leave for the airport just before mid-day and although she had talked of nothing else but getting 'back to normality' in a very pointed tone and was dying to see Stuart, Beth and Kenny, her face kept clouding over. She picked at her food, in spite of Kate's reminder of how awful the meals on the plane would be and tutted and sighed until Neil beat a retreat outdoors, followed by David.

"Wonder what they're talking about," she muttered into her cereal, then pushing the bowl away "Oh, you make me so *mad* sometimes, Kate. You get these things into your head and nobody can ever talk you out of them. You're so like Mum it's untrue."

"Thank you. That does not bother me at all."

"What do you think Beth's going to be like? It's not fair to let me face it on my own."

"Kenny will protect you."

"Oh, yes, it's hilarious. And what about the journey? It's bad enough that Dad won't be there this time, but I'll be completely on my own. Please, *please* come home with me."

Rose, who had been drying dishes, picked up some old papers and the cinder bucket and headed through to the sitting room. She always seemed to know when to stay and when to leave and Kate wondered if that skill came to everybody with age. Hazel did not even seem to notice her departure, pinning Kate to her seat with her scowl, who had seen it all before. There was nothing scary or worrying about arguing with Hazel.

"Do you want to spend the rest of the morning fighting or would you like to do something nicer, like going for a walk?" Kate spoke as nonchalantly as she could, trying to impress on her sister that more attempts at persuasion were futile. "Come on. Let's go for a last look around together."

"Why should I do what *you* want? You're not exactly playing that game."

Kate shrugged in reply and cleared the rest of the table, while Hazel sat picking the sides of her fingernails, head down and bottom lip tucked in. She took as long as possible with the remainder of the dishes, scrubbing the insides of the mugs until they were spotless, because years of disagreements had taught her to be patient. Hazel hated silence, it had been acknowledged many times by countless people and it was a fact. Silence following arguments almost killed her.

So Kate bided her time, knowing that in a moment or two, there would be a figure standing beside her, drying the mugs.

"And don't think I'm going to help you dry those either, missy."

At Hazel's tone, Kate now smiled into the emptying sink and dried her hands. She grabbed their boots from the door and handed a pair to her sister.

"Let's tour the grounds of your family estate, Duchess."

The rain from the previous day had just stopped, the sun making the puddles on the hard standing steam as they hopped over them. There were voices coming from the big shed and so they wandered over there to find David and Neil bent over paper plans, apparently in total agreement that 'the time had come'.

"What're you doing?" asked Hazel, scraping the worst of the mud from her boots onto the garage siding. "It looks suspicious."

Kate smiled to herself, as the two men indeed looked conspiratorial, lifting their heads at precisely the same time, concentration on their faces. David ushered Hazel in with his arm and placed her between the pair of them. As he began to explain the plans to her, Kate kept her distance and watched her beloved sister delighting in what he was saying. Neil also watched her move and point and laugh. Perhaps he was remembering the child he had known and marvelling at the way she had turned out. Kate felt the familiar prickling in her nose and was appalled that she was about to cry, but she could not prevent it. Before her was yet another reminder of what Hazel should have had; a Dad strong enough and compassionate enough to protect her, love her and share her living hours and an uncle interested enough to provide a shoulder to cry on or a sanctuary when her parents irritated her too much. She had missed far too much and now she was leaving again.

Pursing her lips against her sorrow, Kate had time to wipe one tear quickly from her face before she noticed that Neil was now staring in her direction. Hastily she turned away and wiped her face properly. She had said she would help him. Well, he needed to know she was strong and could handle anything, so crying in front of him was not allowed. A moment later she felt him at her shoulder and, assured that her face was now dry, she turned to him.

"I was just thinking," she made herself smile up at him. "They haven't had much of a good time together. Not since it all came out, anyway."

"Well," his voice was steady and his features the most aware she had seen them, "Let's give them a minute then."

He walked at her pace, his hands safely tucked in the pockets of his padded jacket, which he apparently had been able to zip up. She thought about asking him how he had managed it, but it would mean too big an explanation on her part and instead just pointed at the gap left by the missing teeth and said, "I think you need a new zip."

"Oh, yeah," he grinned, "It's a pain. But you know, this jacket is really warm and it fits. I like it. The one I wear in winter is better."

"It suits you."

They walked past the back door and ended up on the front verandah, where one of the many wooden tubs around the door was overflowing with water. Neil frowned at it, dragging it away from the still dripping hole in the overhanging roof. Kate watched him trying to assess the extent of the damage and his ability to fix it, before he shrugged back at her and leaned on the railing.

"So, you're definitely staying a bit longer?"

"I am. If I can just get through this morning without Hazel knocking me out and shoving me in the back of the car, I should be okay. But I was thinking, I should let David take her to the airport alone. They need to have each other to themselves." She sighed. "I wish it wasn't so far away. What do you think?"

He turned to lean on the railing, arms folded. "I think if you can get her to agree to that, you're more of a miracle-worker than you think you are."

She frowned but said pleasantly, "I'm no miracle-worker."

He did not reply immediately, and it gave her time to really look at him as she tried to fathom his meaning. His words had not sounded critical, but it was still an odd thing to say and she struggled to find the significance of it on his face. She thought for a second of all the men she had come into contact with – her grandfather, Kenny, Stuart, David, this man – and of all of them, he seemed the most detached, the most solitary and, apparently, the most damaged. She had met him two days ago and already she had been witness to his most personal demons. Had he thought her offer of help childishly naïve? This unspoken question must have registered on her face, because his eyes widened and he stood upright, clearing his throat to break the tension.

"It's a very generous offer, you'll know better than anybody if she will go for it."

"Who knows?" she replied, then for want of something else to say, she pointed down at his vehicle abandoned on the drive. "That's a monster. I'm surprised Hazel hasn't asked you to let her drive it; she thinks she's capable of anything now. Just don't let her. It's really not a good idea."

He looked down at the Dodge and smiled. "A classic. You want to give it a go?"

Kate for the first time in his company, burst out laughing, and it allowed him to grin in return. "Em," she laughed, "I don't even have a provisional licence. If I turn out to be as rubbish at it as my sister, I think it might end our relationship here and now!"

"Okay," he seemed relieved and before the conversation had time to start and stall again, they heard the sound of another vehicle bumping up the driveway and Kathy's silver Honda Accord swung into view. Neil winced as he thought about her suspension on the uneven driveway, but it did not appear to make her drive any slower. If they had not been high up on the verandah steps, they would have been showered in day-old puddled water. Kate shyly waved at her before she exited the car.

"Who is it?" Neil enquired.

Kate was already halfway down the steps before she said Kathy's name and did not see that it meant nothing to him. At the sound of the vehicle, David and Hazel had also appeared on the scene and Kathy looked a little intimidated at being met by the whole family. But Kate was the first to reach her and the woman was so delighted at her obvious continuing recovery, that she could only grin and hug her warmly.

"Hello," cried Kate. "Did you come to see us off?"

"You *are* going then?" Kathy's voice faltered.

"I am," confirmed Hazel. "But Kate is being unnecessarily cruel and unhelpful and is making me go all that way on my own."

Her attempt at levity was lost on Kathy, who made eye contact with all four of them before settling on David and saying, a little sheepishly, "You did say just to drop by ..."

"I did," he encouraged and waved her forward. "Come in."

As they were trooping around to the back door, Neil caught Kate by the shoulder, pointed mutely to Kathy and mimed 'Who?' She hung back with him until there was a sufficient distance between them and leaned into him slightly, murmuring, "Kathy somebody. Used to be Mum's best friend, she stayed with her -"

"Yeah, I remember," he said and straightened quickly, swallowing. "I didn't realise that that's who you were staying with too. I'm sure Rose told me. I don't always listen."

"Are you okay?"

Up close to him, Kate could see that he was not okay, but he gave her an overly bright smile and nodded down at her. "Sure, I'm fine. I'll be fine."

When it was clear that he was going to say nothing further, Kate took the initiative. "Maybe you knew Kathy when she was younger?"

"No, I never met her. Come on, I think she came to see you."

Rose was alone in the kitchen, but was busy with the coffee-maker when Neil held the door open for Kate. While she was struggling out of her boots, she looked questioningly around the empty room.

"I sent them through to the sitting room," fussed Rose, "Well, she's company and this place is nothing but boots and coats. Why David didn't bring her in the front door is a mystery. Hey! Boots!"

Neil held up his hands, looking as if he was finally losing patience with the rules of the house, before sitting and complying with her wishes. He thought better of pointing out the fact that the 'company' and her receivers had not been pulled up on this matter. Kate, noticing Hazel's labelled luggage by the pantry door, frowned. "Does Kathy know what time they are leaving?"

"It should be okay, I think. She's on her way to the other side of Duncan anyway. Work. Houses still need marketing, apparently." Rose sounded unusually abrupt, but Kate was not in the mood to have another concerned question snubbed or dismissed, wanting instead to spend the last hour or so with Hazel and so she disappeared through to the sitting room. Rose, her brow furrowed and her hands busy, glanced at Neil without his knowledge. He seemed to have settled into his usual level of distraction.

Kate sat on the arm of the sofa where Hazel was lounging, not wishing to interrupt the easy-flowing conversation. Although the fire remained unlit, the sun had warmed the room already and the atmosphere seemed cheerful enough. By the time the coffee and biscuits arrived, David had dragged a somewhat reluctant Neil into the conversation about the plans to build two-bedroomed chalets on the edge of the estate. Kate, although interested, wanted to spend time with Hazel and so slipped off the arm and settled beside her sister on the seat. Hazel took her hand and Kate was happy to sit amongst them, no longer the centre of attention.

"So," began Kathy, when the coffee had been given its socially necessary consideration and even Hazel had dried up, "I really just wanted to drop in and see you before you left. But if you're staying on for a while, Kate, I might see you again. As long as that's okay with everybody."

Rose and Kate both nodded and David said, "Sure. Why not?"

Although not the most enthusiastic of responses, Kathy did not take offence. She could think of no other situation where emotions were so near the surface and the fact that there had been any positive signs made at all was a bonus.

"I'll leave you to it," she said, standing. "David, I know many people who would be interested in your chalet plans. Builders, contractors, whatever. If I can help at all, the offer is there."

As the whole company stood to see Kathy out, Rose ensured that she steered them to the front entrance, determined not to have this visitor traipse through the kitchen again. Too late Neil remembered the leak in the roof and he watched, wincing, as they all had to dodge the still dripping water. Rose's face was one of hopeless resignation and so she did not follow them outside, saying her farewells at the doorway before closing the heavy door. She held up her hands in defeat to Neil before heading back to the sanctuary of the kitchen. Neil in the meantime had wandered back to the window, watching as Kathy stood in the midst of the awkward little group, talking to them with sincere gestures. His face was calm again and not for the first time, he felt like a child. He knew his character was flawed; most adults would be out there concluding niceties or getting on with chores, not watching proceedings from behind the safety of glass.

Neil was not stupid or insensitive. Various spells of therapy over the years had also taught him more than the average Joe about triggers and signs and self help. He knew that every time he came back here there was the likelihood of slipping back down, which is why he rarely contemplated it. It was not just the threat of an episode; it was more that it caused this ridiculous change in his persona. It was as if someone folded up his strength and character and shut it neatly away in a drawer, pulling out instead something which unravelled on first contact.

He thought of his life with Andie. He pictured their workshop/office with the flat above, their outbuildings and kennels and their tiny attempt at a vegetable garden. The flat was comfortable and surprisingly cluttered for a designer, with dogs, magazines and tools in need of repair also making the space their home. They had rebuilt the place from scratch at the end of an overgrown track on the east side of Port Alberni and in the last ten years, as finances and time allowed, it had become home. Andie knew everything about him and had observed many of his episodes, but had never once seen him hide or cringe like a child, the way he did in this house. This was one aspect of himself he was quite happy for her never to witness.

He watched David put his arm around Hazel and guide her back towards the house and as he spoke, she glanced at her watch and increased her pace immediately. The last thing he noted was Kathy walking towards her car, Kate's eyes following her movements with interest. He acknowledged the lifting of his spirits which her departure was allowing, and moved away from the window.

Outside, Kate stood with her arms folded, as Kathy rummaged around in the back of her car. When she emerged, she was holding a large buff coloured envelope. Kate smiled at her for a second more before the scrawled black lettering of the envelope's addressee caused her eyes to widen and the noises of the morning to disappear into a buzzing hole. Fiona's handwriting. She snapped her eyes back to Kathy's face which was unpredictably positive and encouraging.

"What is it?" asked Kate, her hand already outstretched.

"She sent me these a month or so ago, but I have to give them all to you."

"All?"

"Look, if there is a way you can get back into the house without anybody knowing about them, then it might be of some help to you. They are letters, Kate. Letters from your mom to all of you. No, no, don't open it just now, *please*. You need to think about it for a second."

Kate's expression was turning from bewilderment to despair in front of her and Kathy pulled her nearer herself and the car.

"Listen, honey. Your mom sent these to me so that you would be able to see yours whenever you needed to. But when you phoned Beth and said you were not going home, she begged me to bring them here now. Maybe she thought it would convince you to go back, I really have no idea. The point is, there is a letter for each of you in that envelope, but your mom wanted you to decide when to give them out She wanted to give you all of her trust. She wanted you to run the show, Kate."

"What?" Kate's shaking hands caressed the envelope but she felt a little nugget of heat forming inside her chest. She could feel the individual envelopes inside the larger one and although the addressee was Kathy, the contents were for her and she smiled in wonder. "Mum wanted this?"

"She did. Look, I want you to have the chance to think about what you are going to do in peace, so I will go. But ring me, Kate. Even if it's just to say hello and all is well, because I will be thinking about you all day every day. I don't even know why I'm going to work!"

"Okay," replied Kate, now hugging the envelope close to her. "I will, I promise. Thank you!"

"Here, hug me, you fantastic young person. One day, we will maybe go for a cup of coffee and talk about everyday things like the weather and my kids' inability to outgrow their clothes. Won't that be wonderfully ordinary?"

Kate grinned and nodded, but already the envelope against her chest had taken priority over every other thought. Before the Honda had disappeared back into the trees, Kate was running to the shed. She allowed herself one last look at the familiar handwriting before diving for its treasure. There were five pale yellow envelopes in total, the one addressed to Kate being the thickest. As she began to unpeel the seal, she remembered how wonderful it had been to hear her mother's voice again through her diary, and now, here she had written directly to her. She hesitated. Did she have time to rush through her words, or did she want to keep them for a moment of quiet indulgence? The contents of her letter would make no difference to whether she stayed here or not, that was not open to indecision any longer. The next step was up to her and she relished that further piece of control.

Carefully, Kate stuffed all the material up her jumper and made her way to the back door.

Chapter 27

David stood with his back to the Check-in queues, arms folded and one leg in danger of seizing up completely. Judging by the compact booth that was the public newsagents, it was almost impossible for him to credit that a person could take so long. Hazel had slipped from his sight more than ten minutes ago, intent on finding some decent reading material. All he could see from where he stood were roadmaps and chewing gum, but who was he to question her motives or taste. "Hey, Hazel," he cried as she finally made her way towards him. "You came back to me!"

Her look as she stuffed three magazines into her little rucksack was scathing. "Was that you trying to be funny, Dad? I should tell you, you failed miserably."

"Guess I'll stop trying then," he shrugged. "Can we check this lot in now, please? I want to buy you a drink and we just about have time. You and I are going to share a beer."

"Excellent! Let's do that very thing!"

In the bar, Hazel had hitched herself onto a stool and was trying to choose a lager according to the colour of the label. In the end, when the infinitely patient barman was on the point of excusing himself to serve another customer, she allowed David to make the choice for both of them. They clinked bottles and grinned at each other.

"So, Dad. Things have changed a bit in the last fortnight, wouldn't you say? I thought we were coming here on holiday!" Hazel's voice was light and her grin remained, but there was no hiding the truth behind her words. David nodded in reply.

"Well, it certainly woke me up! I have to say, that isn't such a bad thing."

"I was just thinking that. Don't take this the wrong way, but it looks to me like you've been lying pretty low for a long time. I'm surprised Rose didn't kick your arse way before now, she usually knows what's best for everybody."

"Easy for you to say, young Wilder," he pointed his bottle at her. "Rose got up every day not knowing how any of us were going to be. You know, it can take years for people to fit back together when there's a gaping hole in the middle. No, it's my fault. It was much, much easier just to work and sleep."

Hazel stopped herself from declaring how big a waste she thought that was. She could see how it had been. Her mother had taken an age to settle her mind, her father had been hurt beyond repair and the pair of them had avoided the possibility of further injury by letting time pass instead. A waste of time, yes, but probably necessary in a lot of ways. Instead, she smiled impishly and said, "Are you really going to tell me that in fifteen plus years you never thought about getting back out there amongst the living? And you know what I mean, so don't give me that look."

"First of all," David began, "Yes, I do know what you mean and as much as I can see you're a woman of the world and know completely *everything* there is to know about relationships, I'm not sure I want to discuss this with my daughter. However, I can say, hand on my heart, that for fifteen plus years, the thought of going anywhere near female company never crossed my mind. No, actually, that's not right. It crossed my mind and I purposely ran it over, then reversed back over it just to make sure. Good enough?"

"Absolutely not good enough, no!"

"And yet, the truth."

Hazel looked at him, glad that on top of everything else, they seemed to be friends. In the last three weeks she had been through a hailstorm of angst with this man and during that time, what had struck as her familiar in the first few days had turned into firm recognition. He had injected himself into her soul and filled the space that had always been waiting for him there. It made her smile every time she acknowledged it.

True, they had missed out on a multitude, but they were equally keen to miss as little as possible in the future. It was gratifying that they both felt that this could be achieved because it implied they would both make a huge effort. But to Hazel it was crystal clear that his family was not the only thing missing from his life and he needed to realise that there were many lonely people out there. He had it in his power to change more than one life for the better, but he also quite clearly needed a helping hand. Suddenly Hazel grinned widely and signalled to the only female member of the bar staff who was free. The girl looked about thirty, tidy and efficient, wiping surfaces as she came over and greeting Hazel with a sharp, "Yes, ma-am?"

"Hi, can you tell me what your name is, please?" Hazel asked politely.

"Georgie, Ma-am." She looked neither mystified nor uncomfortable. David was exhibiting signs of both.

"Georgie," said Hazel, leaning over the bar slightly, "Nice to meet you. My name's Hazel and this is David, he's my Dad. Could you help us out here? David is in his mid 40s, although you know, he could pass for younger, wouldn't you say?"

"Sure," replied Georgie, now beginning to find David's baffled disbelief mildly amusing.

"Well, he's not what you would call a pushy sort of person. Oh, I'll just say it. He's not had a girlfriend in years and I think *he* thinks that there is nothing much there to attract anybody. Could I ask you, as a favour, if you could tell us if you think he is at all eligible? To a woman of a certain age, maybe?"

"Oh, God in heaven," breathed David into his shirt front, unable to keep his head upright. He did not see the grin on the faces of the antagonists, or worse the appraisal that Georgie was giving him.

"Well?" laughed Hazel.

"I can't really see his face, I'm afraid."

"For God's sake!" cried David, but jumped up, stood straight, held his arms out and turned around to give them both the true picture. Hazel was now gripping the edge of the bar, tottering on her stool as she tried to control her laughter. Georgie, in the spirit of the game, took a step back and looked David up and down. She observed, through his resigned embarrassment, his short dark hair, stubbly chin, jeans, boots and windcheater. When she looked at his eyes in that face, she smiled and turned to Hazel.

"Well, I can genuinely say, there looks like there's enough there to work with. I mean, I'm not free myself, but I have many friends who go for that Clint Eastwood, man-with-no-name look."

"And my Dad's younger than him!" Hazel bellowed, barely able to stay on her stool at Georgie's particular reference.

Even David now was smiling as he raised his bottle to Georgie. "Thank you, for making my day."

"Always happy to help," she grinned in reply, and moved away.

"Wrong film, Dad, but still, good one."

David turned his face back to Hazel, who was finally making an effort to hold down her laughter, and looked at her with his best 'you-are-beyond-belief' expression. She spread her hands and said, "Just wanted to make my point."

He nodded his acceptance that she had most definitely done this, and then shook his head again, reliving the whole scene in his mind. Hazel took a long swig of beer then looked amiably around, watching others go about their pre-flight business. There were families, young couples, elderly couples, what looked like a class of youngsters on some sort of school outing, all manner of travellers. She wondered how many were going and how many were staying and felt a small twinge of regret that she was saying goodbye to someone she now regarded as a pal, as well as to the person who had created her. This, in turn, reminded her that she was leaving more than him behind this time.

She had baulked at Kate's idea that she should not come to the airport. It seemed implausible to her still that she was not coming home with her, but she could not deny that she had enjoyed the car journey. David had been cheerful and chatty and they had effortlessly avoided any heavy topics, mutually concentrating on the positives as they found them. On the subject of Kate remaining in Canada, he had understood Hazel's disappointment, but had impressed upon her Kate's physical need to discover all there was to discover and that staying hopefully meant it would be a speedier and more comprehensive exercise. Time was needed and it was not a task to complete sporadically with rushed and disjointed phone calls. This all made sense to Hazel, it was just more than a little bit unexpected and she could see no ending to it. A timescale might have been useful, but nobody was even talking along those lines. She sighed.

"She'll be fine," David assured, "And so will you."

Hazel nodded her acceptance but did not really wish to pursue the conversation further. Instead, she thought of the letter lying asleep in her rucksack. Kate had handed it to her in the bedroom, her eyes like grey diamonds, flashing with excitement. She had made her promise to read it on the plane, when she would have time to digest it and re-read it without others enquiring or commenting on it.

"We've all got them," Kate had whispered. "And of course we'll read each other's when I do come home."

Hazel looked at David as he finished his drink and wiped his mouth with the back of his hand. He had no idea as yet that there were such letters in existence and if she told him, he might screech down the road, tyres smoking and vehicles honking, in his eagerness to rip open his. Better that he got home in one piece, she thought, as he raised his head at the movement of people about him. Hazel looked at her own watch and then back at David, exchanging a look of resignation with him.

"Better get going, I suppose," she frowned.

"Okay," David eased her off her stool, and took the rucksack from her. "Let's go."

As they headed away from the bar, Hazel shouted over her shoulder. "See you, Georgie. Have a nice day!"

"You too, Hazel. Feel lucky!"

Hazel took David's arm as they walked, but she stopped about four or five yards before the Departure gate, not really wanting an audience.

"Two weeks seemed such a long time in my head," she spoke quietly, looking up at his face. He touched her hair for a second then pulled her into a hug. When she emerged, his face was desperately positive.

"You'll have Stuart waiting for you. And Beth. Can you imagine how this fortnight has been for her?"

"I'm coming back, you know," she interrupted, not wanting him to cheer her up just yet. There were words to be said. "Rose and I have not talked nearly enough and there's a lot more to learn about Neil, I can see that. But mostly, I need you to be in my life now. Are you up to it? I can be quite tiring, sorry. But you look big enough to cope and I think, with a bit of effort, we could get you a nice little social life. What do you say?"

"You tell me when you want to come back, and I'll be here to pick you up."

This time his hug was more than a tall body enveloping hers, it meant protection and love and respect. It felt mutual and shared.

"Alright then, I'm going now." She moved towards the gate, walking backwards, looking at him for as long as possible. "Just getting on a plane, not a big deal and I'll see you soon. Could be next week if I wanted it to be. Nothing's impossible. See? Easy peasy."

"Love you, Haze."

As she handed over the documents, she dug down deep and found her most sincere and genuine beam of a smile. "Love you, Dad."

*   *   *   *

210

Hazel looked out at the black night, and then pulled the screen down on her window, the darkness removing all advantages associated with the seat. She had survived the Departures Lounge, the twenty-three minute delay in take-off and the serving of the first round of refreshments. She had paced herself and was proud of it. But, as pleasurable as the anticipation had been, Hazel now wanted so much more. Another couple of seconds, and the pale envelope was in her hands. She looked at her Mum's handwriting and held her breath. She was almost guaranteed to cry and was grateful for the vacant seat beside her. She kissed the handwriting once, and opened the letter.

3rd August 1993

Hello Hazel, my gorgeous, tall girl. Are you angry with me? You probably wish I had had enough guts to talk you through it all, but here we are now, at this place, whenever and wherever this is. I don't have an excuse. Maybe I just couldn't face your disappointment in me.

I suppose you have a million questions. Beth knows everything there is to know, but even better than that, she understands it all. I think probably she and Kathy are the only ones who do. I'll try to explain as much as possible, but they will help in any way they can.

So, you've met your Dad. What do you think? He is such a great person. I bet you were surprised to hear that I have been speaking to him again. I had to, so that I could judge if he had changed. He has not. Be proud of him. Not everyone would go half this distance. I still see him as a young man of course. Does he forget to shave sometimes? I can't imagine him with worry lines and a round tummy from too much good living! Anyway, you must by now see what kind of man he is.

I keep thinking of how much I used to depend on him. I never had a huge amount of confidence in myself, even now I can't believe I had the nerve to go out there. But I coped when I had to and then I met your Dad. He just took me over. Made me feel more important than any other person in his life and invited me in. I've seen you and Stuart grow into a couple. I don't know if you will stay together, who knows better than I do that there is no control over such things, but I hope he will always look at you like he does now. Like he knows how annoying you can be, but loves the bones of you anyway. That's what a good relationship is. And I had it with your Dad. There is a diary in the house, if you want to look at it, Beth knows where to find it. Maybe it will show you how much I loved your Dad. Maybe it will show you how much I lost. Enough of that.

When you were born, I was scared to death! Rose was a complete natural of course, and tried really hard not to meddle. She succeeded most of the time! (Keep in with her, she is a gem). Living all together under one roof was not as hard as you might think, and Pete was completely in love with you, but the best thing of all was that your Dad still loved me as much as he adored you and that is a skill. What happened was nothing to do with being unhappy or frustrated or missing something. What happened was beyond any explanation I can give.

I need you to understand something. I have a very close bond with Beth. Shared childhoods cement you together and I love her dearly. I don't even have to tell her this, because it is just there. I see you and Kate in the same way. I have never had any worries that you will always support each other and indeed feel a bit stupid at even saying it. But this letter I am writing to you does not contain the same as the one I am going to write for Kate. If she wants to share hers with you, then that is fine, but it is her decision. Give her the option to refuse, please. The story of how her life began is for her alone at the moment, it will be up to her who she shares it with. I know you will look after her, but this letter is not about Kate. This is about you, my love, and for you to keep and cherish like I have cherished every minute in your company.

I'm so fortunate that you are my daughter, Haze. When I came back here, all those years ago, I could hardly look you in the eye. The enormity of what I had done to you in tearing you away from your home made me physically ill. I thought about those we had left behind all the time and even though I tried to shut off the feelings I had for your Dad, I saw him in your face every day. The thought of him hurting was actually more painful than me missing his arms. He loved me and he deserved none of what came to him. But because you are you, I know that you will have realised this long before now. I know you never stopped hoping to meet and reconnect with him in some form and of course I expect you would have done it yourself somewhere along the line. But I wanted to do it for you. I have many regrets in my life, Hazel, but one of my biggest is that I cannot see the pair of you together again. I hope it has made you happy to see what you mean to him. Bear with me a little longer.

I do have an apology to make to you. I'm sorry if the truth spoiled your reunion - I just could not think of a way around it. There is something bigger than you and I in this, Hazel, and because I completely trust your beautiful personality, I need you to help me out. The GMP – I know, one last one, eh? – was my project, my penance, my work and there were multiple reasons behind it. I suppose you could roll your eyes and say I couldn't let go of the reins even after I'd gone. And you would be right! But I had caused so much ridiculous pain (even if there had been no intention to do so) to so many people, that I wanted to show everybody that I never ever thought lightly of any of it. Is any of this making sense? If I had thought about it, I could have used the word processor at Beth's work, and then I could have edited it!

The point I'm trying to make is this. I'm sorry your reunion was painful and then shocking, but I hope so much that you also felt it could be the start of something special. Your Dad is going to need you to be in his life. I know that geography will not make that easy, but I've put a bit of money aside for you to travel there when you want to. If you decide to move back to Canada, then you will be able to do so. If you want to stay here, that is also perfectly fine. Just take what I've given you and make the most of what your Dad has to offer. There are

212

so many opportunities for you, Stuart too if that's what you both want. But look, there I go again! Everything you do now will be what you want to do and do it with my love and your Dad's support.

One thing more. Oh, I don't want this to end. I suppose I am lucky, I will see you tomorrow as I wave you off to work. I look forward to it. But I want to say that I loved you before we even met. You know, I thought you were going to be a boy, but I was so delighted when you came out screaming, all hair and fists. I knew you would be beautiful and bright and funny. It was a bonus when you were turned into a bolt of thunder too! All that energy and eccentricity. That's a good word, isn't it? I like that one. When you got your driving licence, I got grey hairs. How you passed that test remains a mystery to this day. But I'm getting off the point.

Hazel, you are the most tremendous source of pride to me and I am blessed as a person that you are mine. I hope with all my heart that when everything settles around you again, when you find some new kind of normal, that you will think of me with love. Trust the fact that I will be missing you wherever I end up. I cannot even speak of how my heart feels when I think of leaving you. So I'm not going to.

Beth is strong and David is strong. Kate may need you. Love each other and it won't matter if you argue or fall out or accidentally hurt each other, because you will know you will survive it. You're my gorgeous, tall girl. Be happy.

Love always

Mum xxxxx

Hazel did not cry. Instead, she held the precious communication to her heart and closed her eyes. She was shimmering inside with the most amazing emotion. Her mother had spoken to her and blessed her with praise and love. Her father had turned out to be a strong and admirable man whom she could call upon at any time, which was as much as she had ever hoped for. She was hurtling through the dark, as fast as was physically possible, back to the hill and the bay and the smell of the bakery. Behind her eyelids, she saw blue sky above the cottage, Beth hanging out the washing and Stuart waving from the driveway. She was going home.

Chapter 28

Kate's eyes roamed over the ceiling of the bedroom, noting the tiny cracks near the window and the fuzz ball of a spider's long vacated home in the corner directly above her. Such a high ceiling did not invite repair or regular cleaning, but in no way was it dirty. It was comfortable. She lay fully clothed, and the sun draping the foot of her bed warmed her feet so that she felt that on any other day she could have dozed into a light slumber. But not today. Today her nervous excitement forbade any such thing as sleep or even rest. She had her hands clasped on her chest, the bulky envelope lying beneath her fingers, forcing herself to lie still and remember this feeling. This was the Before. Soon it would be the After.

Following a moment or two of deep breathing, which ended in a spontaneous chuckle at the prospect of hearing again from Fiona, Kate finally sat up and swung her legs to the floor. Now the bedroom looked huge, empty and a bit on the tidy side, which only went to emphasise Hazel's departure. But before she could begin to miss her, Kate stuffed her camera and envelope into the ruck-sack and clamped her new "Cowichan Valley" baseball cap snugly onto her head. The sun continued to shine and so she jettisoned the scarf but grabbed her gloves from the dresser on the way out.

She found Neil and Rose at the front door. They wore matching frowns as they surveyed the hole in the verandah roof, discussed the problem and questioned the potential of getting it fixed that day. There was much analysing and inspecting, pointing and sighing, before a solution was hit upon. Neil would travel to Duncan for the necessary materials and would patch it up as best as he could, although it would only be temporary. When they headed back into the hallway, they found Kate looking decidedly disappointed.

"What's up, young'un?" Rose asked.

"I wondered if either of you, or both, fancied taking me up to the Lake? It's been days since we last saw the sun and I need some more photos. But if you've got plans ...."

Rose, never altering her stride, headed for the stairs, "Well, that's not a half bad idea, you have to make the most of the sun at this time of year. I'm not sure I'm up to it today, but if Neil has enough gas in his car?"

His face brightened immediately. "So there's no real rush on this repair then? I can live with that. Give me five minutes."

A tiny insecure frown cut through Kate's grin. "Are you sure you don't mind? I don't really want to hang around thinking about Hazel and it was lovely when David took us up there."

"Not a problem. Just need to note down these dimensions somewhere first."

As he disappeared into the kitchen, Kate ran upstairs after Rose. Her heart was fluttering in anticipation of what she was about to do. She was going to give the lady of the house a wonderful gift, the chance to hear Fiona's voice again. It was a feeling akin to when you knew that the Christmas present you had bought somebody was *exactly* what they wanted and they were going to look at you with shining delight.

"Rose?"

"Be right there, honey," Rose's voice sounded along the landing from her room. Kate stopped where she was. There was no real invitation in the statement and in the time she was given, Kate managed to find Rose's precious envelope tucked away under her camera. When Rose emerged, pulling an extra cardigan around her shoulders, Kate had hidden it behind her back. There was no hiding the eagerness dancing on her face however and Rose matched it, pleasantly surprised.

"Which hand?" grinned Kate, the childish question causing the pair of them to chuckle now.

"Left," smiled Rose.

Slowly and gracefully, Kate presented the envelope to Rose as if it were lying on a velvet pillow. She watched the old hands take it, scan the writing curiously and then tilt her head in Kate's direction, no understanding visible in her eyes.

"It's from Mum," said Kate, her voice full of awe. "She wrote it for you, weeks ago. We all have them."

"We all ..?" Rose's eyes were wide and a flush was beginning in the soft folds of her cheeks. "She wrote me a letter?"

"All of us," repeated Kate. "She wanted to speak to all of us again. Isn't that wonderful?"

Rose could not take her eyes off the envelope, but she nodded in response. "It sure is."

Kate gave her a quick hug. "Well, I haven't read mine yet, and David can have his tonight, if he isn't too tired. So, while we're out in the fresh air, you can put your feet up and see what she has to say. I'll leave you to it."

Kate was halfway down the stairs, rucksack slung back onto her shoulder, when Rose halted her progress with her tone.

"Kate! Does Neil have a letter?"

"Of course. I'm taking both of ours with us. It seems like the perfect place to sit, don't you think? And I promised I would help him. This letter will help." Kate remained where she was when faced with Rose's terrified expression, but did not question its meaning or hesitate in her speech. "Look, there's no way Mum would be anything other than supportive of him, whatever the hell happened. And I'll be there to help too."

Rose had reverted to studying the letter in her hands, her eyes genuinely scared. "Oh, Kate. This is truly a dangerous road to travel. What if Neil doesn't take well to what she says? You don't know how to handle him."

Now Kate's face crumpled into confusion. "Can it be that bad? Mum would never want to hurt him."

"It's not the content," Rose had made her way down to where Kate had halted. "It's really just the *revisiting* of the whole time. He always blamed himself for not looking after her. She was in his care. Oh, this is so difficult; I don't want to upset anybody."

Kate studied the face in front of her, not understanding what was happening but not wanting her own pleasant anticipation to be brought down a level. She frowned. Did Rose assume that she had not considered anyone else in this? Of course people would be emotional and certainly some wounds would be re-opened, but surely it was time to face this and deal with it. People were continually *waiting* to act. It seemed to Kate that her brief reign of control was over and that others were going to start making the decisions again, or rather not making them. She felt that more skirting of issues was on the horizon and it made her foot twitch. The time for that was past. Resolutely, she turned and made it to the bottom of the stairs, where she heard the sound of the car engine warming through.

"If you need to come, Rose, then come. But if Neil takes me to the Lake today, then I *will* give him his letter. Some things need to be sorted now, not later."

When there was no response to this, Kate headed off to find her boots. She had located them, laced them up and was pulling on her gloves when Rose appeared from the hallway. Although she still looked shaken, she showed no sign of preparing to join Kate on her quest.

"Just take care, the pair of you. It was very, very difficult for Neil for many years, don't be scared if he becomes upset. And if anything should happen, like it happened the other day? Give him some space and some time. Oh, just take care."

Kate allowed her a final grin. "That's a Mum talking. Don't worry. I'm sure I have more to be worried about than him, if you want the truth. And I'm ready."

As she banged out of the back door, Rose made her way quickly to the sitting room window and watched in wonder. Where did this thin little thing get her strength from? There she was, jeans tucked into her boots, dark brown pony-tail threaded through her cap, ruck-sack swinging rhythmically as she ran to the Dodge, sure that her ability to cope matched her faith in them all. As she strapped herself into the vehicle, Neil spotted Rose and gave her an easy grin and salute. Rose heard the involuntary whimper before she felt it, but she returned the wave and tried to push her fears back down her throat. He was a man. A strong, successful man and he had to accept what the day would bring him. She stood motionless until the Dodge was out of sight. Never had the house seemed so empty or dead.

The clock in the kitchen read just after 2pm when Rose finally allowed herself to estimate the time of their return. The journeys would take, say, thirty minutes each way, they would probably have a drink somewhere and then, of course, there was the rest of the plan, which could take a lifetime if it went badly. All things considered, Rose decided she would not worry until 6pm had come and gone. The entire situation had been removed from her hands anyway, there was not one thing she could do to alter it.

As she poured herself a black coffee, she impulsively reached to the back of her baking cupboard for a bottle of brandy, and sloshed a generous dose into her mug. It was one of those days, when Pete was cold in his grave and not able to visit her mind, and she needed something to heat her own frozen bones. She glanced at the letter on the counter. It was a quality envelope and her name was written in red ink, underlined and formal. Mrs Rose Wilder. Whatever was contained in the pale yellow pages was for her own personal use and she gave a little sigh.

She was under the impression that they had said all there was to be said during their one recent phone-call, a conversation which had concentrated, positively on the future. There was a strong possibility, therefore, that this latest correspondence referred to their distant past and Rose did not know if she wanted to entertain that at this moment. But perhaps its tone and content would reassure her that Neil's letter was also inoffensive and so she seated herself in Pete's chair by the range and lifted the letter out into the open. After another sip of the fortifying liquid, she began to read.

3rd August 1993

Dear Rose

One of my great joys this week was speaking to you on the phone. I won't deny I was dreading it, even though David said it would be fine. You know and I know that circumstances like ours are rare and really, how do you know how people who have been hurt will react given the chance? But you were so easy and warm, and I want to thank you.

Thank you for your thoughts. And thank you for understanding how I wanted to play this. I realise that my family are being accommodating beyond all reason, and of course I include you as part of that family. Beth and the girls seem to accept what I say without question - for the first time in their lives, I should add! But by now you will know what my angels are like. I love them for all that they are, both of them, different though they will always be.

I'm not sure if I ever had the ability back then to thank you for what you did. I doubt I was even speaking in sentences. I don't want to revisit that time, not here with you, because I know it will never leave either of us completely. Just know that I view it as the blackest of nights and if you had not been there, my dear friend, Hazel would have lost her mother long ago. I do need you to know, however, that I have always known what a dreadful position I put you in. It was unforgivable. I also know that it would have destroyed a less compassionate and resilient mother. What an inspiration you are Rose. You were my hero from the day I found out about Hazel, taking me in, organising my shambles of a brain and pointing me in the right direction. Then when our world came to an end, you saved him, you saved all of them.

I cannot express how sorry I am for taking Hazel away. I know she was your life. I dearly hope that you have got to know her again. I want her to visit you as much as your lives allow and I have put some money away for this. It doesn't make up for anything. There is nothing I can do. There are no words I can say. Just consider the relationship we once had and remember that I have nothing to lose by lying or gilding the truth. I never stopped loving David and I have missed all of you from the day I left until this very day.

Please love my girls and appreciate that they love each other. I trust David completely on this one and he has allowed me to make the request to him. I have no right to do such a thing to you, but I will anyway. However it turns out, Kate is a wonderful person and she would be so lucky to be considered as family by you. She's also a lot more guarded than her sister and I'm not sure what her reaction to David might be. I think she may find it just as difficult as he will in the beginning. But that is all speculation, I'm not going to try and guess how she will be, because that might taint your picture of her. Obviously, she knows that none of you have the same bond with her as you had with Hazel, but she is still a very special person. To me, anyway.

I love them both equally, which may almost be impossible for you to contemplate, but I know you love your boys with the same heart, so maybe you can accept it on some level. Please can I ask one more thing of you? Please can you work your magic like you always did for me and try to hold them all together when the truth comes out? David will make us both proud, I have no doubts about that at all. But I'm sure there will be days when his mother's support will go a long way.

I have told Kate the whole truth. I have also left it up to her what to do with it. You may think that is too big a responsibility for her shoulders, but I know she will see it for what it is. It is me putting my faith in her and, trust me, she will be grateful for it. I know her inside out. I have taken everything from her and now I have to give it back. She needs to know that I trust her more than anyone – and I do. In time, she will make it manageable.

I'm sorry that I never saw you again. I'm sorry that David and I did not try to make contact sooner. I am sorry for so many things I sometimes forget that my life with my girls was rich. I am going to stop now. I'm going to lie down and think of all the times my family made me smile.

Thank you for your love when I knew you and for agreeing to help those I love still.

Fiona x

Rose sat forward in her chair. Fiona's continued love and respect for her had created an alien feeling within; a mixture of warm memories, bitter sorrow and a desperate loss of heart. The last emotion was the hardest to deal with, because for years she had thought that one day, when children had become adults and when injured parties had healed enough to make contact, that the situation could be resolved, partially if not wholly. David and Fiona had indeed been able to communicate in the last year, and she hoped that the illness was not the only reason for this ability. But they had never made that eye-to-eye loving connection again, that affirmation that their feelings had not altered, and Rose could hardly bear the fact that this particular option was now closed to them.

On top of these thoughts, was the realisation that the day was upon them, the day which would shape their immediate futures, and bring to the table some answers and most definitely more questions. She dreaded more than anything else, the revelation of the part she had played in the tragedy, and it made her feel quite sick at the thought. She positioned herself firmly against the back of the armchair, willing it to support her while she tried to organise her thoughts. She had the highest regard for Kate, but did not have any clue how she would react to the facts her mother was providing her with. And what of Neil? How would he take to the news?

For all her immobility, her mind was racing, only coming to a nauseating halt when she thought of her oldest son. David, that honest, loyal man who had stumbled from one long year to the next, gradually growing layers of new skin over his open wounds.The same man that had tried to keep his guilt-ridden brother afloat while dealing with his own lacerated heart.And all before the age of twenty-eight. She wondered, not for the first time, what made a man maintain his values to such a standard when life itself was pouring acid on his efforts. Surely it was much easier to blame and condemn and simply howl at the moon? But in the early days, he had sat in isolation, his injuries healing by the day but his heart remaining firmly in pieces.

Even when Fiona had been taken in by a stunned Kathy, in the final days before her departure to Scotland, he could often be found seated on the verandah, awaiting her return. Rose alone had observed him, staring at the same area of sky for hours, sitting at a distance which seemed mutually acceptable. He would watch the heavens fade through blue to yellow to pink, his hands hanging by the sides of his chair, his face inert until some brand new thought would occur to him, when he would frown and lower his eyes to his chest. Rose was the only one in the family who had had the strength to watch this, but she had done it because he was her son and he needed to know that he was worth her pain.

He had begged and pleaded with Fiona not to go, but Rose herself had not tried this approach with her daughter-in-law, because she had understood that no-one could build a solid life on this particular rubble. She had shared so many panic-stricken, traumatised ramblings with her that she had truly feared for her health. Fiona would sit huddled in a ball or run from David's hobbling reach, always with the same agonised face, until the day she had phoned Kathy and begged her to help. His inability to physically or mentally reach her was matched only by his complete lack of understanding. But he had come through it. They had all ultimately survived it. This day would be a further test for them all.

As she sat on the verge of terror, continually amazed that they had ever reached this point in one piece, she began to wonder if perhaps all was not lost. True, things were nerve-janglingly hazardous and seventeen years previously her shoulders had been younger, broad enough to take on the full weight of their troubles. But now, an entirely new individual was also on the scene, one who was more than willing to provide fresh views and support, who thought herself capable of dealing with what was coming. Certainly, Kate had been dealt the heaviest of blows in her time here, and she appeared resilient enough now, but six days ago she had been anything but competent. It was anybody's guess how this day would end and Rose, unable to change even one aspect of this fact, steadied her thoughts and began to read the letter again.

Chapter 29

"Where's Kate?"

Rose looked up from her sewing, her ears sharper than her eyes, but there was little in David's face to accompany the unusually abrupt greeting. She took off her sewing glasses to get a better look at him and immediately, he took a breath and dialled up his smile.

"She's around," Rose replied, calmly. "How did it go?"

David pulled one of the dining chairs out and settled himself in it, trying to look relaxed under Rose's keen scrutiny. "Well, you know. I wish we could have had longer. But wasn't she amazing? She's amazing."

"She's a remarkable person," Rose agreed, letting him assume she was appeased for the moment. "We must make sure she comes as often as possible."

He nodded, rubbing at a smudge on the polished surface of the table. It was just after 9pm and apart from the sound of the television in the sitting room, the house seemed conspicuously quiet. David's heart sank and the restlessness he had brought home with him was now joined by a touch of melancholy. Hazel had been gone from him for just over four hours, and already her presence was missing.

"Have you eaten?"

David shook his head, still distracted then again smiled at his mother to reassure her.

"What is it?" she asked, not a bit fooled and now giving him her full attention.

He toyed with the idea of feigning ignorance but that would just put the whole conversation back by minutes, so instead he folded his arms and looked around the room, safe in the knowledge that she would give him the time he needed to answer. He would have to explain his agitation to himself first.

"Strange days," Neil yawned, not qualifying his words as he wandered in. "She's on her way then?"

"Yip," David replied to both statements, then "Where *is* Kate?"

"She's asleep on the sofa. Been there for about an hour. I think the number of channels wore her out." Neil rubbed his own eyes and strolled off in the direction of the kitchen, one loose sock in danger of tripping him up. David watched him retreat and leaned in towards Rose's still patient gaze.

"D'youthink he's getting thinner?"

"D'youthink that you're trying to change the subject? But in answer to your question, I agree he's looking leaner. He's swimming a lot now. Good for his back. He's fine."

"Yeah, I need to get fitter. Apparently there's still something here to work with." He did not share the meaning of his words, thinking it would make a conversation for a lighter mood. Now, he lay back as far as the upright chair would allow and sighed.

Pushing her materials further into the centre of the table, Rose stood up. "There's some soup I'll reheat, if Neil hasn't already claimed it as his own. Get back to me sometime, please?"

She left him to sort through his emotions, wishing him the ability to bob back up on the positive side. In the kitchen, Neil stood leaning his hands on the sink, staring out into the darkness. At her entrance, he turned and gave his mother a tired but optimistic look. Rose could not remember when his face had last looked so smooth. It did not look younger, it did not look fresher, it just appeared more line-free and relaxed. There was no need to acknowledge the reason for the alteration, they had spoken of little else from the time he and Kate had walked back through the door. Now she was asleep, they could share a little bit more of the hope and respite being dangled in front of them.

Rose now smiled at her grown son, still seeing the mischievous child who had driven her to distraction with his schemes to emulate his older brother. How often had she been forced to split herself in two, as now, trying to appease both of them when they had both needed her at exactly the same time. It surprised her how easily she had fitted back into this role, and so she did as she always did. She addressed them according to who was in front of her at the time. At her smile, Neil allowed himself a grin at last, shaking his head and staring at the floor-space between them. She crossed to him and held him in her thin arms, grateful that after all this time, she could still be a comfort to him. She may be the smallest person in the house, but her capacity to love these men was without measure, and they stood together for just under a minute, feeling no need for words.

Eventually, Neil straightened his back and planted a small kiss on Rose's cheek. In return, she punched him softly on the arm and headed over to the range.

"Well, how do you think she's doing?" she asked lightly, assessing the state of the thickened soup.

"You know her a bit better than I do," he shrugged. "But she seems very sure of what she wants to do. I just don't know what will happen if pressure is put on her - "

Kate appeared at the door, bleary-eyed and crumpled, pulling her jumper cuffs down over hands. She shivered once, looked at their captivated faces and laughed quietly. "Look at the pair of you. All is well, remember?"

Rose turned back to the range. "You look chilled, Kate. Do you want some soup?"

"Oh yes, please," she replied, looking back over her shoulder to the dining room. "Is that David? I want to ask him how she was." Hesitating, she glanced back once towards them. "We're all still in agreement, aren't we?"

Rose acknowledged her by turning away from the question, but Neil nodded. She left them to it.

"Hey, David," Kate put her head into the dining room. "The fire needs you in the sitting room. Sorry, you know I'm crap at it."

When he entered the room, it was to find Kate hopping from one foot to the other and rubbing her arms. He gave her an amused look.

"Come on, it's not *that* cold in here. You want to be out on the road tonight."

"No thanks," she replied, watching his face closely as she allowed him near to the fireplace. "Remember the first time you did this? It seems like a lifetime ago."

"Certainly feels like it to me," he agreed, but he did not sound weary or indeed a lifetime older. His eyes were distracted however and he only a managed a smile in her general direction as he began to settle and revive the fire before them. Slightly rebuffed by his lack of eye contact, Kate took her seat on the sofa and rewrapped herself in the rug Neil had thrown over her earlier.

"Was Hazel okay? Do you think I will ever be forgiven?"

"She was fine," he replied. "She embarrassed the hell out of me, but that's a story for when I'm not so dog-tired." He did not turn to face her until the small logs had ignited and flames were once again dancing in the grate.

Kate nodded, picking at the fringe of the rug. "So, you're just tired. I thought maybe you were thinking that the wrong person had left."

She had not said this to see his reaction, it was simply a statement based on her own thoughts at that time. When he did not answer immediately, however, she looked up, the dreaded feeling of insecurity returning without invitation. What she saw on his face was the same restlessness that Rose had witnessed, his eyes crinkling at his own confusion.

"I just miss her, Kate. I always have," he explained, then held his hand to his brow. "Oh, God, will I ever do anything other than miss people in this life? It's such a useless waste of time, it's pointless and it hurts."

In a second, Kate's mind began to sprint along a more positive route and her eyes brightened as she thought of how she could make this moment better for both of them. She watched as he fought to regain his composure, and felt her own strength growing. He had trusted her enough to share something so basic and personal and he missed Hazel. These were the reasons for the look on his face, not because he wished her gone. And she had the greatest gift of all for him. She stood up and rubbed his arm, willing him to know that she understood completely.

"I miss Mum," she stated. "I can't believe how she loved me, now that I know the situation. But she did and I miss her. My muscles ache with it."

Finally, David put his arm along her shoulder and leaned her against him. "That's the feeling, yes. And I miss her too. I miss talking to her as much as I've missed being with her all these years."

Smiling to herself, she now disentangled gently from his embrace and took a step back, ensuring that she could see his expression.

"David, I have a letter for you. From Mum."

He tilted his head, the question so clear on his face.

"She wrote letters to all of us. Kathy gave me them, they were written a couple of months ago."

Kate watched as his shoulders straightened and his eyes slowly comprehended what this information might mean. She felt completely in control, adamant in her own mind that this news could only be positive and consoling. She and Neil had certainly viewed their correspondence as such and Rose had not appeared unhappy. Yet he said nothing and she felt the need to clarify what she was saying.

"They are personal messages to all of us. Hazel took hers with her. We have all read ours. Your delivery is my last job as a postman."

"Where is it?" he croaked.

"I'll get it."

At her exit, David sank into the fireside chair, his stomach starting to fizz and spin like a Catherine wheel, nothing but questions clouding his brain. What was this? What was coming? Did Fiona have something extra that she needed to confide in him at last? Did he want this tonight, whatever this was?

And yet, Kate obviously viewed it as completely and utterly constructive, her expression one of someone throwing a lifeline. He felt for his heartbeat through his jumper, one more question occurring to him. Could this particular organ, so essential to his being, cope with any more tonight, good or bad? As if to test it, he took in a slow, deep breath and held it. He held it until he could feel pressure building in his lungs and see the odd purple smudge in his vision. It appeared as if it was indeed capable and finally he let it go. His vision and breath were back to normal by the time Kate returned, envelope in one hand and a glass of ice in the other. She handed him the letter to study, then filled the glass with whisky before also handing this over.

"I'm going to leave you to it, you deserve some time together."

He nodded mutely, and was still nodding as she closed the door after her. The envelope did not smell of his wife, it was of no particular design or brand, but it seemed to him the most incredibly precious piece of stationery he had ever held in his hand. Placing the untouched whisky on the floor by his side, he murmured, "Will you ever stop surprising me, babe?"

4ᵗʰ August 1993

Dear David

Well, here we are. I hope you are not spending too much time alone with your thoughts. Since I gave up work, I find that the house is quietly smothering me, so I tend to sit at the picnic table. If it rains, I wear a hat, if it's sunny I watch the comings and goings of people who are much busier than I am, but almost definitely have more time at their disposal. I know how thinking can be a curse as well as a blessing and I pray that I have not burdened you beyond your strength.

I'm not going to waste our precious time now discussing the past few months. Talking to you and listening to you has solidified everything and now I have no opportunity to contribute and indeed, I have no right. You will all sort it between you, because you are all decent, loving, deserving people.

So, dearest Davy, what do you think? Hazel is such a beautiful creature isn't she? That dark hair and that face, the whole package takes your breath away. Beth always commented on how alike we were, well maybe in temperament, but I see you in her whenever she is unaware that I'm looking at her. When she's preoccupied or thinking or even frowning (sorry!) the likeness is startling. At first, it was a knife in my gut, but now I thank God for every day that I had her. I'm so, so sorry I took her away.

I sometimes wonder, (when I feel the need to torture myself until I bleed inside,) if you thought I was just being stubborn by leaving. You offered so much - to put us back together, to overlook my complete betrayal. But trust me, I had to go. I know you disagree with that. Maybe a bit further down the line you will see it as I do, maybe not. I cannot ask for your forgiveness because the idea that you could possibly forgive such a monstrous thing is too childish. All I can do now is give you back what I took away, so many years too late.

I found myself crying the other day. You may be surprised at the reason. It was something you said on the phone about very rarely seeing anybody socially and that Rose and you were like an old married couple sometimes. I lay on the sofa and cried myself to sleep, not for me because I threw that opportunity away, but for all the others who missed out on the chance of loving you. There must have been so many decent young women who wanted to heal you and be with you. You are such a special person, Dave. Were you even aware of that possibility? You always made me feel totally alive, you would have made any good person feel the same and I think I stole that ability from you. You were so beautiful. So striking. I am sure you are just as completely handsome today, you certainly sound no different.

Please do not think any worse of me if you don't find the answers to your questions in this letter. I want you to know everything, because it will show you that what happened was not planned, considered or sought after and that if it could have been altered in any way, we would have lived our life as we should have done. But there is someone who will be suffering even more than you are, and I need to make her see that I still belong to her. Can you see what I am saying? You have Hazel, she has you and Kate has nobody but the idea of a mother who did something so very wrong and injured everybody around her. Kate has to understand that I still regard her as my precious, treasured child and I want to share it all with her first. I want her to feel so prized and special that I would trust her alone with the whole truth. Do you see that? It's the only way I can help her.

If it wasn't for this hideous illness which saps my physical strength and breaks my heart daily, I might think of telling her everything before I leave her. But I am tired and I am a coward. I need them both to love me to the end. I can only hope that you understand this pitiful lack of courage. Beth does. I pray you two can be friends. By the time you read this, you will have met Beth again and seen how amazing she is. She's a juggler and a manager and a supporter. She kept me on the right path. And she finally joined me in your corner when she found out what really took place. She's a good judge of character and has the strength of ten of me. Am I rambling? You have seen what she is like. She will help you I am sure.

You were a gentleman, not asking me about other relationships in the past few years. Whether it makes any difference or not, there was nobody. Do you think anybody could really compare to you, Dave? The thought of trying to connect with another human being, trying to make them smile or creating memories with them still shreds my wasted insides. Why would another man ever mean enough to me, to be able to put you aside? I had my girls and my sister in front of me and you in my mind. Do not be sad for us, my darling, for what we missed. If you believe anything I say to you now, believe this. It was a mistake, a stupid, ridiculous, meaningless error on my part. I missed my footing and fell as far as a person can fall. There was no reason for it and no possible excuse. But that is the last time I can apologise for it, because from it, I got Kate.

I know you will love Hazel to death and she will be so excited by it all. I am even laughing, thinking of the way she will put you in your place! Rose will adore her, there is no doubt in my mind. But I hope you can also see the goodness in Kate. I hope you see that she is worth getting to know, but I cannot ask you to do anything more than what I have already. Literally, I cannot. I trust you to make decisions based on your feelings, because you are not a callous man and whatever you decide to do, you will make it work.

One last thing. Thank you for not coming to see me. I needed to stay strong for my girls and to see your face again would have slaughtered me. Just remember me, wrapped up in your old coat, stamping about in the snow. They were the best days.

I need to finish this. It is almost impossible, because I love you. I love you, but I'm no longer here. I wish you a better life from now on and I dearly hope that you love again. I pray that if you do, that person comes to you with grace and goodness in their heart and can make you feel what you clearly are, the most important and worthy man alive in their world. That is what you were to me.

Do what you need to do, with all my love and gratitude.

Always yours

Fiona xxxxx

The pieces of paper he held had been stiffened by the words carved into them, and he marvelled at the way they lay flat in his open hands. He also smiled at her use of red ink, as if an ordinary black pen would diminish the sentiments in some way. But that was Fiona all over. She had probably taken an age choosing the best paper and easiest flowing pen, because this exercise had been about so much more than writing a letter. He closed his eyes now, the muscles in the back of his neck reminding him of how tense he had become. He could hear her voice and yes, she had revealed something else. She had told him specifically, in the clearest language, that she had always loved him. She had never stopped loving him. She had written down what grief had prevented her from saying over the telephone and now he had tangible proof, something he could pick up and remind himself of at any time of the day or night. It was indeed a lifeline.

As to any other details he may have wished to learn, she had given them to the only person who actually needed them. It was the right and fair thing to do. Only then did his eyes fill with water as he was reminded of Kate's words and hence the extent of Fiona's regard for all of them – 'she was always really fair. Not always right, but always fair.'

Chapter 30

When the house finally felt as if it had disbanded its occupants and tucked them up safely for the night, Kate reached under her pillow and pulled out her letter. So far she had had time to read it only once and although her mother's words to her had opened up yet another door of knowledge and insight, she had not had time to savour them and it was what she longed to do. She wanted to study, to consider and to analyse every phrase, to look at the way she had structured every sentence and put thought into every word, just for her. She opened once more the creased paper, paper that her beloved mother had taken hours to fill, and looked at the letter's simple beginning.

5ʰ August 1993

Hi Katy

How are you, my darling? I cannot really imagine how you are at this moment, but if you are reading this, then things have reached the stage where you need me. Oh my baby, I wish I was there, looking into your eyes so that you could see I mean every word I say. Please believe me, everything I write in this letter is the absolute honest truth and I want you to know it all. Rose knows most of my secrets; Beth not only knows them, but also the reasons behind them. Who else you tell will be up to you, angel. I want you to be in sole charge of this knowledge, because you are at the heart of it.

I am continually sorry that I did not have the courage to tell you face to face the whole situation and I hope so much that now you can grow to appreciate David for what he actually is and not for what you thought he was. Maybe more things make sense now, I don't know. I get so tired of trying to explain the inexplicable. What occurred was so beyond expectation at the time, that all I can really do is tell you exactly what happened and let you make up your own mind. But I will say this, and I am being completely truthful because that is what you deserve, I regret the hurt I caused and I regret my life without David. But I have never, ever regretted having you. You are my precious child and now you are my most valued ally, the person who can make the difference to so many lives. Will you be that for me, Kate? Will you help me put things right?

I need to share with you everything that I can. Be brave, baby.

David was in hospital after an accident which had scared me witless, and everybody thought that we needed to take time out of the worry and the hard work and relax for one night at least. We were going to see a band .....

Nic had his arm around Fiona's shoulder, pointing high above them into the multitude of stars, positioning her head for the most advantageous view. They were both laughing.

"How can you *not* see it?"

"I don't know, what a ridiculous question! It's like saying how can you not speak Chinese? If you can't, you can't!" As always, when she had had more than a couple of drinks, Fiona's voice had taken on a broader Scottish brogue and every time she opened her mouth, one of the company would mimic her. What she usually found annoying just made her laugh all the more.

"Okay, okay. Let's get moving, it's *freezing*."Nic removed his arm from around Fiona without prompting and quickened the pace along the treacherous pavement.

Fiona had huddled herself inside her coat, but her feet and ankles were chilled and she was as eager as the rest of them to reach James' house. Although it was already way past midnight, nobody was feeling the need for the night to end and James had extended an open house to 'all that cared to come along'. At that time, this included Fiona, Nic, Monica, her sister Kristen and James himself. Neil and Judy, the girl he had been dancing with for most of the night, had got as far as putting on their coats, when Melanie, a nurse Fiona recognised from the hospital, arrived through the door all fresh and ready for action. Neil had appeared unsure of himself for no more than a moment, then as cool as you like, he had taken his coat off again and suggested that they stay for one more drink. Fiona had managed to keep her mouth from falling open at his sheer cheek, and Nic had dragged her away before she had the opportunity to share her opinion with her brother-in-law.

It was no more than three streets' walk to James' house and apart from trying to find The Plough in the night sky, it was spent dodging frozen puddles and avoiding the snow-piles which lay every few yards along their route. Fiona's head was buzzing but not in any unpleasant way. It was true that after the smoky humidity of the bar, the bitterness of the Canadian night had sent her swaying against Monica and the pair of them had sniggered and steadied each other until they could both stand upright again. Now the five of them linked and unlinked arms as they felt inclined, sometimes running, sometimes sliding and it reminded Fiona of Hogmanay on Skye, when it mattered not how much noise you made because almost everyone was out of their houses and on the streets. But New Year had been over a week ago and their voices and laughter seemed far too loud for an ordinary morning.

"Ssshhhh," she giggled, as Kristen shrieked with laughter at James' inability to stop sneezing. "People need to get up later today! Oh God. *I* need to get up later today! Where's Neil?"

"S'not a problem," sneezed James. "You can stay at mine. And you're related to the boss, I think you'll be forgiven if you don't make it in at all."

Fiona was about to bemoan how incredibly busy they were, when instantly it did not matter to her and she shrugged and said, "That is so true. James, you are my complete hero. Have I told you that lately? Or indeed ever?"

"I think I would have remembered if you had," he grinned, then, "Here we are. Let's get in from this cold, for God's sake!"

As they filed into the cramped hallway, again something important crossed Fiona's fuzzy brain and instantly became of supreme significance. "Does Neil know your address? Did you let him know where we are?"

"Yes, I told him *exactly* how to get here," James sighed, making sure all coats were folded onto his staircase and not piled in a heap on the floor. "Even made sure that piece he was with heard the number. But don't be surprised if he gets a better offer, honey."

"Piece? Did you say piece, James Benton?" Kristen had wrapped her arm around his neck and was hoping that her admonishment sounded sexy and not irritating. She need not have worried as his face lit up immediately in surprise and turned to face her, slipping further into her embrace. Before he could say anything, Fiona eased past them into the sitting room, not wanting to jeopardise any development with her presence. There she found Nic and Monica, the former positioned on the floor next to the record player and the latter slumped miserably on the sofa, deliberately keeping her eyes away from the hallway. Fiona smiled sympathetically but could not bring herself to comment. She was enjoying the company and the completely unexpected pleasures the night had brought too much to get involved in someone's melancholy. Instead, she dropped down by Nic's side and started helping him to hunt for some near decent music.

"Hey, Jim!" called Nic, "What did you say you had to drink?

Fiona mouthed the word 'Jim?' at him and in a similar response, James poked his head into the room. His face was flushed.

"It's James," he said amiably, "and I have some Labatts, whisky, gin and I think an old bottle of red wine. Or soda, of course."

The entire company with the exception of Monica laughed at the last remark and Nic clambered over Fiona to follow their host through to the fridge. At the door he paused, "Fiona?"

"Oh, heck, I don't know, what have I had already? Oh look! 'One of These Nights'." I *love* the Eagles."

"But, a drink?"

"You choose."

It was only when she sat back against the sofa that it suddenly occurred to Fiona that it was not David she was speaking to and it struck her as the most bizarre experience she had ever had. She had joined this company, enjoyed the chatter and the dancing, had relaxed into a role she had left behind years ago and it had been so incredibly easy. Now she was speaking to a man she had known for two weeks as if he was her best friend and that had come to her as naturally as flopping onto the floor beside him had done. She found herself reflecting on the situation, staring into space, baffled by her own character. But then, whisky had a tendency to make her philosophical and instead of wondering at her own actions for too long, she turned her thoughts back to David and tried to see him sitting across from her, nursing a beer and joining in the ridiculously silly banter. It was unsettlingly difficult to picture.

"Scotch for the lady. Come on Fiona, you haven't chosen anything yet? This night is heading into a steep decline."

She shook herself to life. "Well, if it's my choice, I will have the Eagles, thank you. Side Two has got 'Lyin Eyes' on it"

By the time James and Kristen had joined them once again in the sitting room, Nic was in deep conversation with Fiona, outlining his plans for the summer and Monica had folded herself into the corner of the sofa and was snoring quietly. James looked on her sleeping form with genuine fondness. "Oh, bless her," he said softly and went to find a blanket. Again, Kristen followed him out of the room, grabbing his hand as they left.

"So, Seattle," murmured Fiona, her eyes roaming around the comfortable room, "What's in Seattle?"

"A car lot owned by my mom's best friend's husband. It's purely and simply a money-maker for me. I mean, David will be better by then and I've got to get more in the bank. I want to go to Europe next Christmas ..... Hey, sleepy-head, I'm so interesting you felt the need to rest your eyes?"

"Sorry, s'the whisky. So actually it's your fault."

"Okay."

It was a minute or two before either of them moved or spoke again, content to lean back and sip at their drinks. However, gazing around the room a second time, Fiona began to focus on objects and pictures and her eyes came to rest on a gigantic framed map.

"Never on this earth!" she exclaimed and rolled onto her hands and knees before stumbling to her feet. Framed in gilt and placed safely behind glass was a map of Scotland which measured about three feet by four feet and took pride of place above the oak bureau. Impatiently, Fiona struggled to find the switch on the standard lamp, but when eventually the bulb snapped into life, she was delighted with what she saw. Carefully, she traced the perimeter of her own little island off the western coast, smiling broadly.

"James!" she cried over her shoulder, not even thinking that he might be occupied elsewhere. "This is beautiful! Can you get me one?"

There was no immediate response, but it mattered little as Fiona was mesmerised by the sight.

"What is it?" slurred Nic, not quite finding the energy or inclination to see for himself.

"Map of Scotland.A big one. Wow, I love it!"

James at last appeared and, after draping Monica in a tartan rug, hurried over to where Fiona stood engrossed. He put his hand on her shoulder, steadying himself as he reached to also switch on the bureau lamp.

"There, better still," he said, the map now illuminated from both sides. "Great isn't it? People would be surprised at the perks available to librarians."

Fiona was still shaking her head in wonder, trying to think of the last time the shape of her homeland had been so clear and defined in front of her. She leaned closer, concentrating specifically on the sorely familiar outline of Skye. She followed the coast closely, as it moved north-west from Kyleakin to Portree and she placed her finger on the miniscule bay just south of the town.

"There," she whispered. "That's my home. Was. Was my home."

"Right on the coast, then," James' voice was equally as soft, sensing the change in her mood as she was engulfed by nostalgia. "Must have been special."

"Oh, it is. It's been nearly two years since I saw it last."

Swallowing the remainder of her whisky, Fiona now moved around the room. She could not afford to think of Skye at that moment. Her experiences of the last fortnight had left her ragged around the heart, guilty, upset and tired to the bone. To allow her mind to visit the bay and all of its precious residents would not be a fitting end to this one good night. She would absolutely not *allow* herself to slip down inside of herself and she faced James.

"Your house is lovely. You seem to be a ... collector."

"Not really," he mirrored her smile, pleased that she was once again grinning. "More of an inheritor. Another drink?"

Fiona grimaced, eyeing her empty glass and said, regretfully, "I've probably had enough. Don't want to become all gloom and doom on you."

They both jumped as Nic snorted himself awake. Instantly he was on his feet, glass in hand and eased Fiona's from her's before she could object. He bumped into Kristen in the doorway, whose face was as unreadable as it was pale. Whatever was going through her head, she looked unwilling to share it as she pulled her coat briskly around her. James's face was unmoved.

"You're leaving?" he asked, amiably.

"Oh, I think so," she replied, her eyes appraising Fiona darkly as only a woman can do. "Monica! Let's go."

Fiona excused herself and hurried after Nic. She found him searching the freezer for more ice and closed the kitchen door behind her.

"Trouble in paradise," she explained, pointing her thumb back over her shoulder. "Thought I'd just leave them - oh Nic, I don't need any more alcohol!"

"Snifter," he winked, and then widened his eyes at the raised voices coming from the hallway. Fiona looked back at him silently, both of them trying to judge the cause and hear the outcome of the dispute. Nic crept closer to the door, his eyes never leaving Fiona's, the pair of them not the slightest bit ashamed of their eavesdropping, but rather enjoying the shared secrecy. When at one point Fiona's name was mentioned by Kristen in a less than friendly tone, her eyes widened and she held up her hand to show off her wedding ring, shaking her head in disbelief. Finally the front door banged and as Nic cautiously eased them both out into the hallway, it was to find James standing alone, folding the tartan rug into a neat cube.

"Well, that went about as well as usual," he smiled, completely accepting of the situation. "Can't *wait* to see Monica again later today, which is entirely the reason for keeping work and pleasure in separate boxes."

"But James," Fiona empathised, "If something had happened between you and Kristen it would have been a lot worse. She's her sister and it would have killed her."

There the conversation stalled for a few seconds and during that time, Fiona felt suddenly and completely out of her depth. It was the early hours of the morning, her daughter lay sleeping soundly at home, her husband was probably coughing up phlegm in his hospital bed and she was stuck in the middle of town, exhausted, drunk and on the verge of serious misery. She bit her lip against the anxiety knocking at her door and was for some reason relieved when Nic downed his final drink, moved towards the stairway and reached for his coat.

"Look, talking of work, I'd better be getting myself home. There's still enough to be done tomorrow and I've let the boss down as it is. Are you okay staying here, Fiona?"

In truth, Fiona had never craved the wooded isolation of The Edge more than she did at that moment. She no longer cared if the bed was big and cold, it was her place of rest and sealed her off from the world outside. But the option was not open to her. She tried to look completely at ease and was about to reassure them both when James stepped in.

"Look, it's not a problem. I have a really fabulous quilt that my mother made when she was – well, anyway, I can make up a bed on the sofa and if Neil turns up, he can have the armchair. I would offer you my bed, but I haven't actually done the laundry in a week and –"

"The sofa is perfect, thank you. And Nic, I had a great time tonight. Thanks for your company."

"Pleasure was all mine, Mrs W." He gave her a quick peck on the cheek, and then shook James by the hand.

"Nice to meet you, Jim. I owe you some Scotch, I think."

"So, buy me one the next time you see me. Oh, and good luck with the exams."

"Yeah," sighed Nic and, turning up his jacket collar, headed out into the night.

Before the door had even swung shut on its hinges, James was tackling the stairs two at a time, muttering about pillows and the famous quilt. Fiona, eternally grateful for his sensitivity, wandered back through to the sitting room and eased off her shoes. Her feet had at last thawed out and by the time she had used the loo, pausing to frown at the drawn face in the mirror, James had created a little cocoon of sheets, blankets and quilt. The only real cloud in her brain was how she was going to cope in the morning. And where was Neil?

"I've left the door unlocked for him, because I won't hear him once I'm asleep. If either of you want anything to eat, well, what's mine is yours."

"Thanks James. This looks just the job and I really need to sleep. It's been a great night but I need to shut down my brain for a while. Can I have a hug?"

Smiling, he folded her in his arms. He was warm and solid and although his body felt unfamiliar, the feeling of an adult hug did not and she was grateful for it.

"Night, honey," he said, releasing her and waving as he retreated from the room. He closed the door behind him as Fiona hugged the remaining heat to her for a final second, and then pulled off her skirt and stockings. Her silk shirt was long enough to double up as a short nightshirt and she could not bring herself to remove that one last ounce of warmth. Climbing into the carefully constructed crib, she had a strict word with herself. She would not wallow any more in sad reflections, she would simply close her eyes and think of David and Hazel. Or, she would concentrate on stopping the room from spinning, by shutting her eyes for a few seconds, then opening them every time it spun too fast. Eventually, this method would allow her to step off the roundabout.

When Fiona was next aware of a movement in the sitting room, it was still dark outside and her mouth was so dry she had to peel her tongue from the roof of her mouth in order to lick her lips. She had left the bureau lamp burning and she could see Neil's tall form, boots in hand, creeping across to the blanket-strewn armchair.

"Good night, was it?" she croaked, not daring to move her settled head just yet.

"Sorry," he apologised, "Was trying to be quiet."

Fiona finally raised herself on one elbow, peering at him through the dimness. Even in her woozy state, she could see something was different about his face, but he turned his back on her as he struggled out of his jacket, one awkward arm at a time. His hair was back to its usual pre-groomed mess and his shirt was completely untucked. The jeans he wore were soaked from thigh to ankle and the left leg was black with road grit.

"You okay?" she was now completely awake and had pushed the heavy ache in her head back to her subconscious for a little while longer. "You don't look it. And you need to take those jeans off."

"I know that, *Rose,*" he snapped. "So you need to quit watching me."

Mortified, Fiona hid under the quilt then smiled to herself before chuckling as silently as she was able. It seemed suddenly and hugely ridiculous that she should be hiding under a hand-sewn quilt in James's house, waiting for her brother-in-law to conceal his unclothed body beneath blankets on a chair.

"What's so funny?"

His voice was distorted by the layers of flannelette and cotton and she unwrapped herself to assess his mood better. He was still in his shirt, but had tucked a couple of blankets around his lower body for discretion. The lamp behind his head shaded his expression so that was of no help whatsoever. She tried once more.

"So, what news? You're here on your own obviously. Want to share anything?"

Fiona waited. He gazed at her for a couple of seconds more, his eyes still obscured from her, then leaned his head back and stared at the ceiling. It was then that the lamp illuminated the swollen left eyebrow and growing discolouration on his forehead.

"Shit," murmured Fiona and had miraculously untangled herself and was switching on the central ceiling light within five seconds.

"Jeez!" exclaimed Neil, throwing an arm over his eyes against the blinding light and catching his wound in the process. "How about some warning?"

By the time his retinas had recovered from their assault and he had massaged his eyebrow back to an acceptable level of discomfort, Fiona had wrapped a sheet around her waist and was standing over him. He shrank slightly from her frowning scrutiny.

"Two questions," she sighed, breathing warm whisky fumes into the air between them. "Does it hurt? *And*, what the hell happened?"

He hesitated long enough for futility to kick in.

"Yes, its smarts. *And* I'm not sure I want to tell you. Don't touch it!"

"Okay, okay," she pulled an occasional chair nearer to his armchair and sat as near to the wound as he allowed. It was really just a deepening bruise with a tiny horizontal slit in the skin. If there had been any bleeding, there was no evidence of such. Fiona sighed again. "Well, you'll have to at least tell me what you're going to say to Rose. We have to have the same story."

Neil groaned and turned his face away from her. He appeared so young to her at that moment, in spite of his height and his physique. He clearly did not want to discuss the situation which showed an unacceptable level of immaturity and although Fiona desperately wanted to be tucked onto the cosy sofa, where her headache could be lost in slumber, she needed answers. She tried a different angle.

"Why do you Wilder men insist on ruining the looks God gave you? D'youthink it makes you roguish and exciting?"

He had closed his eyes, refusing to take part in the almost certain interrogation, so she took her opportunity and reached, slowly and silently, towards his injury, still intrigued.

"Do not touch it," he growled, not opening his eyes or moving an inch.

"Oh, for goodness sake!" she hated being caught out.

"Well, how is touching it going to help in any way?"

"Fine," she sighed and took herself back to the sofa, returning the room to semi-darkness as she did so, "But you'd better think of a story before morning. And make it believable. *Rose*-believable."

The last phrase had Neil scowling enough to re-open the little abrasion and he dabbed away the one spot of blood with his shirt cuff. Fiona, well and truly rebuffed, turned on her side, facing the sofa rather than her child of a brother-in-law. Sometimes she could slap him he was so infuriating. And yet, if she was to give it some honest thought, she knew it was because he did not have to tell her anything. He was not David and there was no easy consent to share everything.

However, at that particular moment, she was dealing instead with the wave of nausea created by her frantic movements around the room. She cursed that whisky had been introduced into the evening's proceedings, at the same time admitting full responsibility for the idea. But the warmth of the quilt soon began to soothe her and she was almost on the point of relaxation when she heard her name being spoken.

"Mmm?" she acknowledged.

"You still awake?"

"Just. S'up?"

"Can I ask you something?"

This was more like it and Fiona turned slowly in his direction, trying to appear sleepy and nonchalant so as not to discourage him. She threw him a 'what-do-you-want-to-know' look and was surprised how quickly he picked up on it. He spoke as soon as she was seated upright.

"I keep messing things up. I mean, important things, life-changing things. I can't seem to do the right thing anymore, or at least I misjudge things badly. Is that normal?"

Fiona was momentarily lost for words. She had observed him for the entire evening and was now astounded at his obvious lack of faith in himself. He had danced, laughed and chatted up the booth-blonde Judy with ease and charm. He had proved himself a protective ally and an amusing companion, so either he was an incredible actor or this descent into self-doubt had just occurred.

"What are you talking about, you daft man?"

"Me." He replied. "My instincts are crap all of a sudden."

She looked over at the despondent face, managing not to comment about him feeling sorry for himself, as it invariably offended the subject in question, and there on his face was the expression he had worn the day after Christmas. Fiona's brow now cleared.

"Is it Cindy?"

He sighed, his eyes rolling in his head, and Fiona tried to recollect how much he himself had drunk. He too seemed on the edge of self-reflective misery.

"I was just so sure that's what she wanted. It's what I wanted more than anything. It was bad enough being humiliated by my girlfriend, but now I'm back to making a fool of myself with people I barely know."

"So, what did happen tonight?"

"Not worth even thinking about, except that it proves I am a total idiot." Cradling his head in his hands, he leaned forward and related the story. Melanie had joined himself and Judy for another couple of drinks and they had all sat around smoking until even the band had packed up and left. As the three of them had spilled out into the car park, discussing the 'party' at James's house, Judy had finally taken severe exception to Melanie's presence and during the argument that had followed, she had slapped him across the face and flounced off. What she had not seen was that the slap's momentum had sent him sideways into the nearest lamppost and from there onto the filthy tarmac. He had stood, holding onto the metal pole and cursing, until Melanie had declared him unlikely to be concussed and had wiped the trickle of blood from his face. She had also, however, declined the party invitation as well as the offer of an escort home and had disappeared back inside to call a cab. Her parting shot had been for him to ring her if he ever decided what he actually wanted.

Fiona, having listened to the sorry tale with a sympathetic frown, now watched hopelessness return to his face. She could understand his frustration, but tonight's debacle could not be compared to the end of his two-year romance with the lovely Cindy, who had not simply removed herself from his life but had taken with her his budding future aspirations. This latest drama had obviously floored his confidence yet again and her heart went out to him as his handsome, injured features became so clearly pained and lonely. She could not watch it any longer and, wrapping her quilt around her entire body this time, she knelt by his chair.

"I'm sorry," Fiona stated, "I took it for granted that you were over Cindy and that was really stupid of me. As if I could get over your brother in the space of a fortnight. I'm so sorry, I could have helped more."

He leaned back in the chair and rubbed his weary eyes with both hands. "It's not like any of us have had a minute to do anything but work," he excused her.

Fiona now sat cross-legged by his chair, the quilt folded and clenched to her body. It was infinitely comforting and soft and she felt like a squaw, patiently waiting to hear if she could help her man in any further way.

"I'm tired," he sighed.

She was about to agree and suggest that they sleep on it, when he qualified the statement.

"I'm tired of the way things are."

Not knowing exactly which aspects of his young life he was referring to, Fiona remained mute but allowed her face to question him.

"I was sick of school, so I left. I wanted to work and to earn, but I'm always going to be third in line, you know? And that's not even the problem, because there is definitely a future there. It's complicated," he looked back at the ceiling, despair killing his train of thought momentarily. Right then, Fiona's eyes became more alert, her fuzzy and sleep-deprived head clearing as she saw the man before her and not the boy. He was a man with thoughts and plans and this had escaped her until now.

Neil was a man, yet to all of his family at The Edge, he was the youngest son, the kid brother or the playful uncle. He was the back-up man, the one with the fewest responsibilities and was handsome and charming enough to fill that particular role with ease. A hard enough worker from a secure family business to attract prospective fathers-in-law, but also a guy with enough of a winning smile, lithe young body and loose change in his pocket to have girls waiting in every bar booth in town, if not the state. Now that he had shown that he was missing something more, Fiona was ashamed that she had labelled him as a Jack-the-lad so easily. She gently touched his knee through the blanket.

"I'm here. Tell me."

When he looked in her direction again, his lips were slightly parted and his eyes glazed, but when at last they focussed on her face, he shook his head.

"You won't be able to help. No, don't disagree. You won't be able to help because you're part of the problem and you'll try to change if it will help. I don't want you to change."

"Me?" Fiona's face was burning at his words.

"Not just you. You and Davy. And even Hazel to some extent. You see," he leaned forward, elbows on his knees, his hands animated to express himself. "David is an incredibly hard worker, throws himself into it completely, well you know that. What you maybe don't know is that he does it for the best of reasons. He gets satisfaction from every decision he makes, every tree he fells, because every cent he makes is for you and his daughter. Every day's work is a step towards what he wants for you both. D'youknow how often he talks about you and his plans?"

"He has plans?"

He waved away her question. "Short-term, long-term, oh he has plans. The point is, he doesn't even have to talk about you, I see it for myself every day in life. The way you are with each other, sharing it all, smiling at each other."

"Oh, Neil, you can have all of that and you absolutely will have it! You must know that's true."

He shrugged, obviously not acknowledging the existence of any such fact. "Cindy would have been great. She would have fitted in perfectly and ... she was really pretty."

Fiona was again reminded of the discrepancies in his maturity, but did not smile. "Hey, Neil," she said gently. "So, maybe she had plans too and maybe she didn't want to stay around here and live with our family in the woods. Doesn't mean she wouldn't want it in five years time. Or maybe you'll find another gorgeous girl who only wants you, all day every day."

"Not if I keep doing what I did tonight."

"So, don't do it! Start going out again, but let them come to you. They will, you know. Look at you with your blue eyes and your ridiculously messy hair. Some girl is going to want to take you in hand. Just make sure you concentrate on one at a time!"

He grinned down at her and she reached to squeeze his hand, glad that his smile had been spontaneous and genuine.

"I think," he began, holding her tiny hand in his, "Maybe I need a complete change. If I can't have what you and Davy have at the moment, maybe I need to stop trying to follow him. What would you say if I said I wanted to go to College, learn to do something else with these hands?"

Fiona sat forward, the quilt slipping from her shoulders, "Oh, that's brilliant!"

"Are you sure?" his voice catching some of her enthusiasm, "I don't trust any of my own thoughts anymore."

She took both of his hands now and turned them over, allowing them both to study his slim fingers and bitten nails. Their heads were almost touching.

"I think that these hands were made for so much more than felling and bucking. They shouldn't be stuffed into gloves each day; they should be carving bookends and table inlays and loads of other beautiful things. Oh, and you would be tripping over girls at College! You could be as messy and artistic as you liked." She reached up to ruffle his hair and he pulled her into a hug.

"Thank you," he breathed.

"You're going to be fine," she whispered, resting her head against the side of his face. Again she felt the intense comfort that only contact with another beloved human can bring, his arms around her back, hers around his neck, not moving, not thinking, just being there, sharing warmth and reassurance. It was what she had craved for days and days and it seemed that this man needed the same thing, for he held her close for a long time, not tightly but respectfully, gently adjusting his arms around her to give her the most support. She did indeed feel secure and could almost have drifted off to sleep. Instead, she sighed into his shoulder, focussing on three tiny drops of dried blood on his shirt. "We're all going to be fine."

When Neil pulled away from her, he was on the point of smiling his gratitude but one look at her face brought a concerned question to his eyes. Was she okay? He continued to look at her as she sat back on her hunkers, herself no longer aware of anything else around her, not the quilt, not the unfamiliar room or anything beyond the face of this young man. This man who had held her close and shared his warmth and affection with her, the same affection she held for him. Her heart felt so tight in her chest that she could barely acknowledge what was happening. Whatever reaction was taking place, it was so far beyond her control that she was scared sober in seconds. Out of the blue, tears began to pour from her. She could feel that her own face matched his horrified one, but she could not speak, clueless as to what she was feeling. She put her hand over her mouth, staring desperately at him, until he joined her on the floor and took both of her hands in his.

"What the hell? What did I do?"

Her heart constricted even further. Of course he was going to blame himself, and he had done nothing but communicate with her. But his face was breaking her heart. She looked at his eyes, so mortified to have caused her tears, the cut on his eyebrow which looked so tender up close and his lips which kept trying to form the correct words, but constantly failed. She jumped to her feet and turned away from him, both hands over her mouth, where she stood, shaking, until he came up behind her and wrapped the quilt around her. Even now, he was trying to protect her modesty, at the cost of his own.

"Please look at me. What is it?" his voice cracked in desperation.

"We need to sleep. I'm not well. Let me lie down."

"Sure. Sure, here you go."

He folded her onto the sofa and she lay, engulfed in the quilt, staring up at his face as he tried to make her comfortable and safe. When at last it seemed that he might have succeeded, he looked down at her once more. He tried a tentative grin.

"You scared me to death. Are you okay now?"

Mutely, she gazed up at him, her heart now thundering in her chest. Was she having a heart attack? She nodded, but would not let go of his arms. All that was on her mind was the sensation of his frame pressed against her own, where she could feel the beat of his heart through his shirt and sense the shared emotion within the act. She wanted that again. She wanted to feel warm and secure and loved.

"Neil, can you lie here with me? Can you put your arms around me?"

She knew the risks in that question as surely as she knew the betrayal in the act, but she needed it more than air at that moment. She was not in the slightest bit surprised at the shock registering on his face, but the words had been said and all she could do now was await his response.

"I'm not sure that I can," his words were deathly quiet in the dark room.

"Please?"

"No, it's not what you think. You don't know how I feel ... about you. Oh Jesus."

What surprised Fiona the most about the statement was that her heart did not sink at his revelation and she did not worry about the implications for their future relationship. She did not think about anything much at that moment except that she wanted to make things right.

"It's okay, it's okay," she soothed. "I just needed a hug. I'm sorry. We'll put this whole thing down to too much whisky and my needy nature. Tomorrow it will seem –"

When Neil kissed her, Fiona's breath arrested inside, caught somewhere between her lungs and her throat and from nowhere her hands were on his face, not pushing him away, but pulling him down to her. She would never forget the taste of him. Whisky and smoke and electric tension and she dared not stop, because that meant acknowledging their actions. She would not stop. She would kiss him until someone removed them from this treacherous scene, wiping it from their memories and planting them back where they had been the previous day. Safe and guilt-free and clean.

Fiona was now kneeling on the sofa, Neil similarly positioned on the floor and his hands were on her body, reaching and hugging and sliding beneath her blouse. His hands were not David's hands, they were not hers to use, but she could not, would not halt their progress. She kissed his neck, his lips and his face as he trembled against her. Her hand felt the leanness and strength of his stomach muscles as she eased his shirt aside, neither of them daring to breathe a word. They must not speak. The treason was too great. But as her lips touched his wounded eyebrow he whimpered and the sound jolted them apart.

240

No two people could have looked more shaken to the core, their eyes matching black coals of despair replacing desire. What in the name of God was this? Fiona's chest rose and fell visibly beneath her creased blouse, her unfaithful arms and deceitful hands limp and hopeless by her sides. Neil's face was sheer confusion, no lust and no guilt, just utter disbelief at the events of the past minute. Not only had he lost himself in her sweetness, tasting her and holding her curved body against his, but he had told her of his feelings. There was no road back from there. He turned from her, unable to credit the enormity of his folly, accepting that he had finally crossed over into bleak insanity.

He searched in vain for his jeans beneath the strewn blankets on the floor, his face pouring sweat and tears, each moment stretching into a black eternity before him. It took about ten seconds for his brain to remind him that there was another person worth considering in this disaster and his movements became less frantic. When he looked again in her direction, she was standing in the middle of the room. It seemed she had been waiting to see if he would run or stay. He turned his body to her in submission, his face a mess of streaks and frown lines and looked to her for the answer. She was so beautiful. Had he damaged her forever?

Fiona saw his thoughts on his face and accepted immediately all responsibility. For as long as they both kept company with each other, she would make sure he knew that this had not been any fault of his. They had stumbled into each other, taken something they had both needed and they would never refer to it again after this night. But he needed to understand this now, before he piled any more rocks onto his back. She moved over to where he stood unable to keep his head upright, and placed her hands on his upper arms.

"We will *not* speak of this. Not tonight, not tomorrow, not years from now when we think it doesn't matter anymore. We will never talk of this to anybody. Yes?"

He nodded.

"I'm in love with David. He is my love. But I needed you. You, Neil. Not just anybody, but somebody who felt love when they thought of me. I am incredibly selfish."

"No," he whispered, still unable to meet her gaze. "No, you're not. I wanted everything. You're so special."

Fiona looked up at his face. She put her fingers to his lips in one last bout of curiosity and felt herself sway as he closed his eyes. He held her hand against his face, tears falling again and she knew that if his fingers laced through her own, there would be no question of halting their mutual longing a second time. His free hand dropped his located jeans and placed it on her waist. Her last coherent thought was that his eyes were the bluest, most desperate she had ever known them to be.

Chapter 31

Kate's hands had let the pages slip onto the floor as she read them, aware that later she would pick them up carefully, fold them tenderly and stash them away. They would be a treasure forever at her fingertips and she would cherish them completely. But for the moment, she lay in a trance, trying to imagine her mother as she had been. It was so evident that she had been full of love. She had seen love every day in her life at The Edge and she had reflected it back without effort. Kate had seen it herself back home.

Fiona had never been pushy with either herself or Hazel, never trying to make them take dancing lessons or learn how to the play the recorder. If they came home with letters, excited and begging to be allowed to take part in the latest school opportunity, she would listen and ask questions. If neither of them could provide sufficient information, they would be sent back to school with a list of answers to find. Fiona's view was that if they were still interested at the end of the process, then they could take part. It had worked brilliantly, the only exception being the swimming club which had aggravated Kate's childhood eczema beyond what was bearable for a nine-year-old. Ultimately, both girls had sung in the choir and Hazel had become an above-average archer. They had both enjoyed trips to the mainland as members of the clubs, Fiona funding these because it made them happy and their smiling faces had always been her goal.

Because Fiona's love had been accepted so easily by all in the house, it was sometimes difficult to list specific examples of it. She had loved Christmas and for weeks would be planning and discussing, writing endless lists and creeping along the hallway with bags stuffed inside her coat. In December, when Beth and their granny would attend the various Christmas bingo nights, she would turn off all the lights in the house apart from those adorning the tree and the three of them could play at 'Christmas morning'. It had involved her knocking softly on their bedroom door as they lay giggling and trembling in the pitch darkness. From there they would creep into the sitting room and sit by the tree, pointing at imaginary parcels and declaring that Santa had appeared to have left *even more* presents than the previous year. It was a game that they had never tired of playing, and although it was never referred to at any other time, all it took was for the word 'bingo' to be mentioned and three knowing grins would always appear. All of this had stemmed from her unstinting love.

They had also known her full attention and, latterly, her friendship, but now Kate was learning of so much more, and from the woman herself. Of course, it was almost impossible for most people to imagine their parents as young, vibrant beings, searching for excitement and affection, taking opportunities when they appeared and basking in mutual infatuation. For Kate, who had yet to crave any serious male company, it was harder still. But reading Fiona's diary, and now her mother's unreservedly honest account of her own conception, Kate began to wonder about emotions and whether they stemmed from what you hoped for or from what was actually available to you. Her mother had spoken of needs, the meaning of which Kate was still not aware of; all she really gleaned from her Fiona's words were that some feelings were stronger than sense or even morality, which was incredibly scary to accept.

Kate had had a few crushes since puberty had come sidling up to her, but it had always been safer and easier to pin her hopes on the unattainable. These had included Dr Macallum who had diagnosed her appendicitis, Kevin Costner in the role of John Dunbar and, of course, Mr Ellis. Each one had filled her hours before sleep, where they found her to be a great conversationalist and an amusing friend. In the past year, she had graduated to looking at some of Stuart's mates, but had lost all interest when Fiona had become ill. Kate had witnessed Hazel lean on Stuart and saw how he had learned to support her over time, but she had wanted only Fiona to occupy her thoughts. Nothing was more important to her than every cherished minute spent with her mother. So here she was at the age of seventeen, completely out of synch with the rest of her peers. She was years behind in terms of sexual experimentation and years ahead when it came to reality and the bullets it was capable of firing. She sighed.

Fiona had known what love was, had suffered all of its phases and had shared them with her daughter through deeds as well as words. She had, after all sent her here to meet these people, putting all of her trust and faith in her. Faith that she would understand all of them and give them some peace. On paper, it looked possible. In reality, Kate felt that she had been dropped into the vortex she remembered from 'Journey to the Centre of the Earth'. She needed to compartmentalise each of these people, including her newly exposed mother, and apply what she had learned to all of them individually. And she needed time to do this.

Kate thought back to that afternoon at Lake Cowichan, before she learned of Neil's connection to her. They had chatted all the way in the car, Kate asking about Andie and where they had met, he asking about Skye, but avoiding direct discussion about Fiona. At the time, she had imagined he had been scared of upsetting her, but now it seemed that it may have been for his own self-preservation. They had found a free picnic table where the view had filled their conversation for another five minutes or so, but when Kate had finally presented him with his letter, there had been no sound other than the water lapping nearby.

She remembered his stare as she located her own envelope, not really sure of what his expression was saying to her. Two vertical creases appeared between his eyebrows and she watched his throat move as he tried to swallow his anxiety. She scrutinised him, her letter forgotten for a moment, fearing that he would lose control again. But he never took his eyes from her face, drank in her apparent optimism, and eventually exhaled slowly. She had smiled even wider then and held up her prize.

"This is mine," she had boasted, as if indeed it was a rosette, "We all have them."

"How?" his voice had tried so hard to hide his alarm, but she had not been fooled.

"Mum wrote them weeks ago and Kathy gave me them yesterday." When he said nothing else, but began to twist the envelope between his fingers, she had taken it gently from him and laid it on the table. "Neil, Mum would never send you anything bad. You know what she was like. She's giving you something to remember her by, that's all."

He had seemed incapable of holding her gaze and instead had begun to scan the lake, his slim fingers drumming on the table's wooden slats. She had felt an anticlimax creeping like a mist between them and had wished to halt it there and then.

"Well, I've waited for most of the day to read mine. So, you can read yours now or you can take it back home and wait until you feel you can face it. There are no rules." As Kate had unfolded her letter and begun to listen again to Fiona's sweet voice, she had sensed his movement away from the table and slyly watched as he wandered over to the edge of the sparkling water and stood, kicking at loose stones and turf. His envelope had gone with him.

So involved had she become in Fiona's world of recollections that she had had no idea when he had begun to read, but when at last she had raised her head in his direction, damp-eyed and clammy, he had been sitting on a rock, studying her, the letter open in his hand. Never had she felt so misplaced. What in God's name was she doing here in this country? She remembered the sun winking on the water, far out in the middle of the Lake and she remembered how dusty his boots appeared as they made their way back to her. For the second time in her young life, she had been meeting someone of true significance and she had pondered how much a human mind could be stretched and tested before it either snapped or became loose and useless.

When he had taken the bench opposite her once more, they had both sat motionless, daring the other to offer their thoughts. She had looked on his face, the eyes so much more authentic than his scruffy hair and unkempt beard. Up until that point, she had wondered if he had spent years cultivating that look or whether he had really not cared about such things. Perhaps there had been far deeper and more fundamental issues on his mind.

"What are you thinking?" he had asked, his hands quivering until he had physically held them still.

Kate had managed a mild 'well' before realising that her next words were crucial to both of them, and so had sat trying to look positively thoughtful. She had understood what had taken place, even how the circumstances had created it, but the magnitude of Fiona's confession needed to be appreciated and treated with tender respect. There were so many people in danger from it. Perhaps he had simply meant their own present relationship.

"I'm thinking that I've been in this position before, meeting somebody important" she had breathed. "Feeling a bit wobbly actually. This is it though, right? No more surprises?"

"Not as far as I know, Kate. This is it. Are you okay with 'it'? With me?"

He had needed reassurance. After all the years of hiding from this monumentally awful situation, he had been looking for some sort of pardon, not from Fiona nor David, but from Kate herself. He had needed to see that she had not despised him, and of course she had not. He had not injured her directly in any way, and she had not known him well enough to be disappointed by his actions. It had been easy for her to take his hand across the table and hold it tight. She had even given him a smile of reconciliation, inwardly laughing at the cruel tricks the heavens continually played on all of them. It had been an odd few hours and when the breeze had brought with it the bitter taste of dusk, they had driven home in virtual silence.

Rose had met them, astounded by the quiet dignity they had both appeared to bring back to the table. They had not acknowledged much at all, Kate feeling no particular need to extract every historical detail from either of them, which had been both unexpected and a relief. As she herself had said, she had needed no other opinion than her mother's on this. There had been only one stipulation, voiced by Kate in so adamant a tone that no objections had been raised.

"I'm not going to tell David. He has no need to know."

"You're sure, Kate?" Rose's had been incredulously hopeful.

"For now I am. Yes. It's too cruel and we all know that's true. He doesn't deserve it and neither do you pair. He won't hear it from me, not after what he's done for Haze and I."

Kate now lay wide awake, having replayed every conversation of the day, surprised at how often her thoughts crept back to David. Neil was her father, he was essentially a decent man and had pulled himself up from his own personal hell, managing to forge a life alongside his demons. She hoped that one day she would get to know him better. But David was something far more than that. He had taken charge; he had burdened himself with their lives, when he could have stayed an ocean away quite acceptably. There was no way on God's earth she was going to give him this information, not if he was okay with leaving the past unturned. What could possibly, *possibly* be gained by hurting this family so bound together by their own scar tissue. She would think of a way to protect him, she would make something up to ensure that he was okay. She owed him that and much more.

There was a soft knock at her bedroom door. Kate lay as a stone for a second, the blood pounding in her ears, unsure as to how to react. She was almost certain she heard her name being whispered, but could not put an owner to the voice. Still, whoever it was thought it essential enough to creep about after dark.

"Yes?" she tentatively enquired.

"Can I come in?" It was Neil.

"Just a sec," she replied, almost falling out of bed in her attempt to gather up the paper lying all about. So much for placing them carefully back together. Instead, they were shoved under her pillow in a crumpled mess. She frowned, dismayed, but that was preferable to having to refer to them. She opened the door to find Neil standing, still fully dressed, sheepishly hugging his arms around him to retain as much heat as possible. The sight of him made her own pyjamas seem woefully inadequate and she opened the door wider, before hopping back under her duvet. He appeared unsure of the intimacy of the scene, but she waved him in, trying to keep her voice to a whisper.

"It's okay. It's too cold for me to hang about out there."

He stepped over the threshold but came no nearer, even when he had closed the door behind him. She looked at him questioningly.

"I'm going home tomorrow. I have to. But I didn't want you to think I was running away."

She frowned once more, shrugging slightly.

"You know," he continued, explaining, "'He got what he came for and then took off back to his easier life'. It's not like that; I do need to get back to work. And Andie gets nervous out there on her own."

"It's fine. Did you think I would mind? I can see how it is."

"Okay then. Well, how long do you think you'll stay? You could come up and meet her, she knows all there is to know."

"She does?" Kate frowned suddenly, then, "Has it ever been difficult to keep it from David? Did you ever reach the point where it would have been easier to get it off your chest? Because I can't do it, Neil, not right now. But I don't want that to be something I will regret later."

He ran his fingers through his hair while he gave her words the consideration they deserved. He had one advantage over her and that was that he had had months to prepare for such a conversation.

"It was like this, Kate. Your mother absolutely refused to tell her own husband who was responsible, because she thought his and my relationship was worth more than theirs. She thought she had ruined theirs and would not do it to ours. *That's* the kind of person she was, but you know that already. Rose understood her motives and went along with them. We all took the easy way out, except for Fiona and David. None of us are proud of it, but out of respect for her, we carried on as best we could"

On the verge of despair at his first words, Kate's heart now filled to the brim with utter love for Fiona. Once again, it looked as if she was encouraging and consoling her, showing her that her instincts were correct. Kate nodded. "She was right. He won't ever hear it from me. Not ever."

He hovered by the door, watching her marvel at her mother's courage until her brow cleared, then crossed to where she sat in bed. She did not flinch at his approach.

"Here," he said, handing over his own letter. "Whatever that mother of yours put in your own letter, she said it in exactly the right way. I couldn't have predicted your level acceptance of it in a million years. So, I want you to read mine. I'll get it back from you before I leave. It's just another angle on something that shouldn't ever be forgotten."

For a second, Kate's nose prickled at the generous gesture and she looked up at his positive face, gratified. But as she reached up to hug him, he promptly moved himself out of reach, hands raised between them.

"Too soon," he apologised, looking at the floor. "I'm sorry. You mean too much. See you in the morning."

He was out of the door before she could protest, but perhaps he was right. Things had to develop at their own pace to mean something. She opened the envelope.

4ᵗʰ August 1993

Hello Neil

When people have lost touch or when they have something to apologise for, they often start letters with "I don't really know where to start" or "What can I possibly say?" Stuff like that. This is my third draft and I'm still not happy, so I'm going to say you're a special case and I'm just going to start writing.

I am sitting here trying to imagine the man you have become. I made David tell me as much as he wanted to - he is a very loyal brother. The worst thing for me is that you and I never really said goodbye. Let's face it, we never said very much at all to each other after that night. But I have to believe to this day that my leaving was the right thing to do. You agreed with me. We acted to save the lives of those who meant the most.

Don't think I disregarded you in all this time. I left you to deal with your shock and your fears and your guilt and I'm not proud of it. It's very difficult for me to think of your hurt and your trauma. I cannot forgive myself for that. When I finally started to make sense of my life again, I thought of everything and all of you. Pete and Rose without Hazel, David sitting by himself wondering what the hell happened and you thinking, thinking, thinking. The word sorry is a pitiful five-letter word that cannot even pierce the surface of the regret I feel. It can't be measured, but I will say it anyway. I am so, so sorry. Let's not pretend we don't know who caused this downfall. I took that step when there was a perfectly easy alternative. I'm sorry I did this to you and to me and to every one of us.

I want to remember you as you were, Neil. Friendly, hard-working, funny, decent. And you are still all of these things. Of course you are. You could never be anything else. So, without diminishing the way your life was affected, I want you to try and forget the worst, deadly dark days and think of something else instead. You could argue that when you have little time left, then the worst has already happened and you can indulge yourself. So I suppose that is what I am doing and I am asking you to do something similar.

247

I want you to think about Kate. I want to tell you all about her and I hope that you will take what I'm saying and only think about her in the most positive and loving way. You have seen her. I don't know if you've had enough time to see what kind of adult she is turning into. I know mothers are biased, but believe me, Scottish mothers find it very, very difficult to praise their own children. It's like saying to the world 'look at my wonderful child, I am so clever to have brought up this child so well' and nobody amongst us has any time for big-heads, so instead we smile and let other people pile on the praise. We might occasionally mumble agreement with red faces, but most likely we will turn it around and say, 'oh she has her moments' or 'try talking to her first thing in the morning'. Well, you get my drift I'm sure.

But I'm going to tell you exactly what she is like. Oh, where to start? Well, you've seen how pretty she is. Those grey eyes of hers are beautiful. But I'm sure it's the little things you are interested in, so here goes. She can happily spend time on her own but is not anti-social. She will smile at people, but likes to assess them a bit before forming opinions – the opposite of her sister. She has a handful of friends from school but I would say that Hazel is her closest ally, mainly due to where we live and the fact that she can't drive yet. She and Hazel spar continually, just like Beth and I used to – still do!

She babysits for a couple along the road and takes next door's dog for walks, so she is perfectly happy talking to adults - I think she will have found all of you easy enough to get on with. She tries hard at school, excels in English and Geography, and does her best in Maths and Science! She has an oddly deep singing voice and she likes to read a lot. I hope this doesn't make her sound dull because she is anything but. She hates nail varnish and doesn't wear lipstick because she feels like her nails or lips are being smothered. Who knows what she means?? Before I was ill, Kate and I used to climb our hill in all weathers and she is great company. She goes up there alone now, but I think it's more to wonder why life has thrown this at us and to rage at the sky. If I had the strength, I would be doing just that.

She is a very understanding when people get hurt, likes to make sure everybody is in agreement at the end of the day and gets a bit annoyed when people take her for granted – 'you know I would have said yes, but I like to be asked'! She cannot stand unfairness and just won't tolerate it. She struggled with that aspect of my illness. What can you say in that situation? The fact is there is nothing fair about it! I don't seem to be mentioning any faults, do I? She likes to understand situations in the first ten seconds, which can lead to frustration, and she also likes to get things sorted as soon as she sees what the problem is, which can be a bit unnerving for everybody else! I don't know how she will react to David's presence but she has a lot to learn. Oh, I love her so much. I have always loved her.

What do you see in her face? Sometimes I think I catch one of your wide-eyed 'what-the-hell' expressions, but for the most part I can't see either of us much in there. And do you know what? I'm going to let you discover the rest for yourself.

248

What you two decide to do with your relationship will be up to you. I am going to tell Kate everything and I know that this is the right decision. I cannot let her spend her life like I have spent the last seventeen years – wondering why and how and what and where and could I have done things differently? My time is up with them - and all of you. I find that the saddest thing I have ever had to accept. What keeps me going today is that I am giving everybody I love the chance to gain something, to find something more than they have at the moment. And if it involves you fantastic people, then I know you will make it a great 'something'.

Stay with me for a little while longer. I've tried to tell you what your daughter is like and I've told you that I love her very, very much. I have always loved her. You see, when she was born and I saw the fine downy hair on her head and kissed her so soft cheeks, I could not bear the thought that people might resent her or label her. That is why I never told anybody over here that she was not David's child. Beth knows now, of course, but she has never judged me. I wanted my family and friends to see 'Fiona's two gorgeous girls' and nothing else. That part worked well enough. But I have always thought of them in terms of who they really were. I always thought of Kate as yours because you deserve to have her. What you've got to realise is this. That night, I needed to be held by someone who loved me and of course it was wrong. It was so completely wrong. There, in that room, I loved you for what you were – someone who cared deeply for me. That means that Kate was made from love. And that's why she is as special as her sister.

I truly hope you have a future that includes Kate. But I have no right to make such a request. You will find a way between you, if you want to.

Be happy.

Fiona x

Chapter 32

On the Saturday before Halloween, Kate was up and dressed by 5.47am, her walkman turned up as high as she could stand whilst Runrig sang about the unbelievable news from heaven. Never having been a particularly early riser, she now found the knots in her stomach allowed her little sleep past 6am and today she had decided to do something constructive and enjoyable. She would make breakfast for everybody and feel pleased with herself for doing so. Rose had mentioned a trip to Duncan to see the 'Jack-o-lanterns' and have a bit of lunch, which Kate had immediately declared a brilliant idea and that David should definitely be in attendance. His face had suggested that window shopping did not appear high on his free day activities, and so a compromise had been agreed of a visit to the 'hippy gift shop' *only* and lunch at the venue of his choice.

In the period following the departure of Hazel then Neil, David had spent as much time at work as possible. Kate could see how pale his face was on the more hectic days and the way Rose knew when to ask questions and when to leave him alone. He always seemed interested in Kate's day, however, and to their credit, neither he nor his mother ever asked her if she was ready to go home.

The truth was, Kate was in the process of drafting her own Master Plan, the first she had ever attempted and was finding it a satisfying pastime. She was not sure how much of it was fantasy, but she was prepared to indulge her thoughts because it kept her panic at bay. Panic at the thought of returning to a home bereft of Fiona, to a school full of *children* who knew little of life and to a sister who crept around her, studying her reaction to every word spoken. Of course, she missed Beth and the sea and her own messy room. But here in this house, all three of them now spoke openly to each other about everything. It felt better to be here for the moment; she was learning about her father and she had work to do.

When they had first arrived, Hazel and Kate had been visitors and their days had been filled with trips to the lake and surroundings, meals out and a visit to the timber yard, but this level of holiday activity could not be sustained long term. David was a working man and Rose built her days around his needs, all of which was evident to Kate as they settled back into an ordinary routine. Now, she had begun to feel restless on his behalf. Was this how it was to be for the rest of his life, coming in from a long day to a house which could do with updating, with only his mother/housekeeper to talk to? By his own admission, he was 'not that old' and yet apathy seemed to have taken the place of enthusiasm. When he had eventually related Hazel's airport 'eligibility test' to Rose and herself, Kate had laughed along, but somewhere inside she had felt a twinge of sorrow. There was no reason why this man was stagnating, not now, when he had been taken by the heart and shaken free of dust and detritus.

Kate thought of David now as she filled the coffee percolator. She tried to recall her first impression of him, without the apprehension involved at the time, and what kept coming to mind was his height and his desperately hopeful face. She also remembered his affable temperament and, with some shame, his ability to withstand criticism, usually directed from herself. Now when she thought of him, it wasn't just his physical appearance and initial patience that struck her, it was strength and his care. He cared, in spite of everything, and he was still trying to accommodate her feelings and state of mind.

His letter had left him subdued for one full day only, but he had not appeared gloomy or disheartened, merely reflective and calm. She had made a point of sitting with him at the end of that day, knowing that Rose would be occupied with dinner, to see if he needed to talk about anything. After sitting through two channels of local news without comment, she had taken up a seat on the sofa, only a couple of feet from him. When he had looked in her direction, his eyes were wide in a sort of 'hows-things' question, his mouth turned up slightly at the ends.

"Hello, how are you?" she had asked, as if they were meeting in the street. He had smiled but his brow had creased slightly.

"I'm doing fine. How are you?" he had replied, mildly amused.

She had leaned back on the sofa. "Oh, you know. Still here. I mean, still alive as opposed to still imposing on you."

"It's really not an imposition. We like your company, Kate."

Her heart had appreciated the message, and in a way it had boosted her confidence for the next part.

"David," she had sighed. "I was wondering what you were expecting me to tell you - "

"You don't need to tell me a thing. Really. It's irrelevant to anything we have now. I don't want to know. I mean it, Kate. Unless," he had swallowed, looking up at the ceiling, "unless it will help you to talk about it. But only then; it means nothing to me."

"Are you sure?" she had asked, quietly, noticing the way his hands were resting on the arms of the chair. He had seemed so unflustered and certain of his needs, but she had been compelled to ask him for confirmation, even though it mirrored her own wishes.

"She gave me everything I needed in that letter. Who cares about something you can't change anyway? I'm happy with what I have."

Kate remembered how he had let his eyes connect with hers for a moment or two and how good it had made her feel inside. She and he were no worse off than they had been previously; they still had a friendship and would always have a connection through Hazel. She knew who her father was and he seemed a decent man. Rose, Neil and she were happy to let the past remain undisclosed and now David seemed to be of the same opinion. Maybe, just maybe they would all survive this, merely grazing themselves on the walls enclosing the truth as they scraped past it. It was possible, and with it safely negotiated for the moment, Kate was adding to her Master Plan by the day.

As the coffee began to sigh and bubble, Kate cleared the laundry from the airer, set the table and then tried to find the ancient pad of recipes Rose occasionally referred to. Somewhere, at some time, the lady must have written down her pancake recipe, which produced pancakes like none Kate had ever known. When she had tried her hand at them at home, they had ended in a twisted slimy mess in the pan and she had vowed never to attempt them again. But it was a staple breakfast in this house and really, how difficult could it possibly be if you were following instructions? She was rooting around in a drawer, singing not so softly along to the tape, when David appeared. He watched her pick her way through several loose leaves of paper and wondered how to make his presence known without frightening her to death.

"Kate?" He tried, to no avail and had to pad, barefoot, across the room, willing her to be aware that she was not alone. The closing of the drawer coincided exactly with his standing beside her, but she did not jump. Instead, he saw only a pair of startled, wide eyes gradually dissolving into relief. She laughed as she removed her earphones.

"When did you appear? You're not supposed to see any of this until its ready."

"It's not even six-thirty, honey. And it's cold."

Her face faltered for only a second. "Well of course it's cold, if you walk about in bare feet." She held up two books. "I'm looking for the pancake recipe. Although to be honest, I would call them drop scones. They're too thick for pancakes. You want a coffee?"

"Sure," he watched her move around the room, "although I hadn't really thought about getting up just yet."

"Oh, come on," she teased, pouring them both a mug. "Don't tell me I woke you. There's no way you could have heard me from the top of the house. And you're dressed. Seems to me like you've been awake for a while. Couldn't sleep? Or maybe I stole your thunder. Maybe you were hoping to be the one to treat us all to breakfast."

"Yip, that's exactly what I had in mind. You have ruined my whole day. What happened to the clean socks?"

"I put them in the pantry. What about porridge? I can make a great bowl of porridge."

"Coffee is fine for the moment," he replied, gasping at the cold air whistling through from the pantry. As he sat once more, pulling on some socks, Kate stood awkwardly, stalled in her mission. The clock read seventeen minutes past six, Rose was not likely to be up for an hour at least and she had done all the preparation there was to be done. All she could do was sit at the table beside him. He grinned at her.

"What?"

252

He spread his hands. "This. Us. It's almost six-thirty on a Saturday morning and I'm sitting where, okay I admit it, where I usually sit at this time. But, I'm not alone."

Kate felt her heart slump a little. "I'm sorry. I thought I'd got up early enough."

"God, Kate, I'm not looking for an apology! I'm amazed, that's all. This is my amazed face."

She grinned in response. "Hello, amazed face. I'll remember that one. Is that your relaxed face, now?"

He had leaned back in his chair. "It just might be."

They sipped their coffee in unison.

"Why amazed?" asked Kate, disentangling herself from her walkman and placing it on the table in front of them.

"Amazed at how things have taken a change for the better, even in the worst of times. Oh," he faltered, "Kate, that's so selfish. I shouldn't have said that."

If he had uttered such a statement three weeks ago, Kate might have hated him for it forever. Now, she could see why he felt blessed in a way and tried to reassure him with a smile. After all, Hazel was back in his life, Fiona had told him what he needed to know and even she was still keeping him company. He was no longer alone. Before he could lose his optimism on this cold, dark morning, she grinned and said, "I'm glad we've made a difference. I'm more glad about that than anything else at the moment. It means something."

"It does?"

"It does. You know what else? Hazel was right, we are going to have to get you a social life. I'm going to finish what she started."

Kate could not prevent a smirk as his face registered genuine alarm. "What?" she laughed, standing and handing the walkman to him. "You just said things were looking up, so let's keep it going. You more or less admitted that you need to get out more?"

"When?" he objected, studying the walkman, turning it over in his hands. "When did I say that?"

She waved his protests away, reaching into the breadbin. "It's what you meant, I'm sure. Here, you're making a right mess."

She took the tape player from him, untangled the headphones and placed them over his head. Leaning close to him, she pressed a button. "Right, this is rewind. You should really start at the beginning, because the first two are my favourites. Press that one to play and that's the volume. Remind me to get some more batteries this afternoon. Will Canadian batteries fit?"

"What am I listening to?"

"Real music.Runrig. I'm going to cook now and you can sit there and not be alone. You've got me *and* Runrig. And this afternoon we are going to get you some new gear. You'll need your wallet."

* * * *

253

Rose, having inspected the depth and content of the fruit scone before her, reached for the jam. It was just after 3pm and Duncan had been bypassed in favour of Victoria and its greater choice of shops. Lunch had also been jettisoned due to Kate's infectious enthusiasm for achieving their goal – a range of new clothes intended to transform David into an irresistible prospect to the 'thousands' of women out there, a figure he had felt compelled to dispute. So, having left David to pay for the pile of shirts and jeans, Rose and Kate had gone in search of a table in the store's own coffee shop. Kate could not stop smiling. Rose was less impressed.

"You know," she frowned, "He was always good-looking. If you ask me, all he ever needed was the will to go out and to shave regularly. Nothing more attractive that a clean-shaven face and some good After Shave."

"No, I think he gets away with that rough look. It's all the rage apparently. Designer stubble it's called."

"Designer idleness," Rose replied, watching David's approach.

"Right, that's it. No more." He dropped the bags by the free chair, then noting Kate's imminent protest, said, "No, I mean it. Much as I don't object to any of this stuff, it's still just going to be me inside it. If I can't get anywhere with this lot, then there's no hope."

"I still liked that jacket," moped Kate, pouring him his coffee.

"It looked ridiculous. *I* looked ridiculous."

"Okay," she conceded, biding her time, then, "Well, I think it's been a successful day. Here's to David Wilder and his rosy future."

They clinked coffee mugs and began to eat. Every few minutes, Kate caught Rose glancing in her direction, but at her silent questioning look, Rose would simply smile and turn away. The fourth time it happened, Kate put down her cup.

"What is it, Rose?" Had this woman learned nothing? She must know by now that Kate was not prepared to play games of any kind. Startled, Rose swallowed her coffee the wrong way and choked for a second or two. At David's concerned face, Kate suggested he fetch her some water from the counter and as he departed, she leaned forward.

"What's wrong?" she enquired, mystified.

"It's just," she began, wiping her mouth, "I can see Neil's face in yours. Do you seriously think *he* can't?"

Kate's eyes widened, her face beginning to flush. "You only see it because you know it!" she hissed. "I am *not* telling him and I can't believe that you, who have protected him this whole time, want to open this up! Please, please don't."

David was turning back towards them, glass and jug in hand.

"I'm just so scared," explained Rose.

"Well don't be. Just leave it alone."

The remainder of the meal was spent ensuring that Rose had recovered and agreeing that they were done with shopping for the day. If the return journey was more subdued than the outward one, David put it down to fatigue and the satisfaction that came with the purchase of necessary goods. While Rose chatted in the front seat, Kate sat in the back, her head against the window, watching the darkening sky. Did she resemble Neil? She could not see it, but perhaps it was something that should be worried about. Maybe she should go back to Skye before her face caused any problems. Out of sight, out of mind. Perhaps it was right to put their safety before her own fears of return. She closed her eyes against the dilemma.

"Kate? We're back."

She awoke to find David standing at her open door, ensuring she opened her eyes before moving around to the back of the vehicle. She leaned forward, out of her seatbelt but was unaware that her right leg was asleep and ended up in a cursing heap on the driveway, staring at the cracked hard standing a foot from her face.

"Oh, shit," David hissed, dropping his purchases and helping her to her feet. "Kate! I thought you were awake! You okay?"

"You mean apart from being really embarrassed?" she snorted, wiping grit from her hands and knees, "Yes, I'm okay. How ridiculous was that? Oh, and now I can't actually walk."

Rose, who had managed to emerge from the car totally unscathed, patted her shoulder on her way past. "Hang fire there for a while then, girl. I'll give him a hand."

By the time she had stamped her leg back into life, shaking inside from the laughter trying to escape and grimacing at the painful tingling, they had emptied the car and David was now appearing again out of the gloom to help the invalid. At that point, she was holding onto the side of the car, other hand over her mouth, gradually learning to breathe again.

"Kate?"

"I'm fine," she hooted, "I just wish I'd seen it, rather than done it. No, don't look like that or I'll never stop laughing. It was bloody funny though, wasn't it?"

Completely lost, David now helped her limp back to the house. "Hazel would have loved it," she sniggered, hopping up the steps into the kitchen. "Do you mind if I ring home tonight?"

"Not at all."

"Okay, I'll wait until a decent hour."

After dinner, Kate immediately began to look through all of David's purchases, laying them on the dining room table, matching up possible combinations and suggesting what would be appropriate at what function. He had stood for the first few minutes, genuinely interested, but this had gradually evolved into him fidgeting, folding his arms and yawning and culminated in his seating himself by the door.

"Tell me if I'm wrong, but I'm thinking you might be bored." She looked at him mildly, over her shoulder. His face was indeed part boredom, now also part guilt.

"Actually, there's a Canucks game that I would really like to catch. Do you mind if we do this tomorrow?"

Kate now turned to face him. "I have no idea what you are talking about, but it looks like it might be important. Don't worry; I'll get this lot upstairs. You've indulged me enough for one day."

Grateful, he disappeared. Later, as Rose dosed by the fire and Kate lay on the sofa, he tried to interest her in the joys of ice hockey, but she declared that there was no need for her to know the rules and that he should just enjoy it instead. Meanwhile, she was thinking about what to do for the best.

The whole thing was a balancing act. She wanted to stay here and see what happened. She longed to see David happy and she hoped that one day Neil would be confident enough to let her into his life. But, as Rose had pointed out, her very presence was a threat to this. So, she should go home to what she knew, the cosy comfort of her beautiful island, where everybody there accepted her as she was and awaited her return. But she was scared. Scared that she had altered so drastically in her outlook that she wouldn't be able to settle back into babysitting and playing cards on a Saturday night and her family would get all morose and regretful because they had allowed it to happen. She needed to decide what was best for the majority of them. She needed to talk to Beth.

By midnight, Rose had retired and David was flicking through channels. She appreciated the fact that he was waiting up with her. He always liked to be around when she called home in case she became upset and needed to talk afterwards. And yet he looked tired.

"I don't mind if you go to bed, you know."

"I'm fine."

"Oh, do you want to speak to Hazel? She might get up if it's to speak to you. I'm still on her 'take it or leave it' list."

He smiled and accepted the invitation.

"Okay, I'll give you a shout when she's on the phone."

David watched her roll off the sofa and stretch as she wandered out into the hallway. He stirred the last glowing embers and sat back in his chair, reflecting on the past few hours. He thought of the way Kate had taken over the day, anxious to please but determined to be in control. Fiona had never been so sure of herself, not when he had known her, but then she had been missing from him for so long. Perhaps she had become just as focussed and certain, characteristics born out of desperation and unwillingness to give in. She had, after all, created the Grand Master Plan and they were all here to witness its partial success. Partial in so far as some knowledge had been shared and friends had been made. She had certainly sounded secure enough on the phone.

Both Hazel and Kate had more self-belief than she had at their age, and he liked to think that she had nurtured that very thing in them because of the way she had been. She had done the best job possible, all without his aid. He wondered if he had managed to make *any* amends in the last month. It had been intense and at times agonisingly cruel, but they were all still talking to each other and all seemed on the verge of something more hopeful.

From his seat, David could hear the tone of Kate's voice, subdued in deference to Rose, but still light and swift. He smiled to himself. He could picture her face, the way she formed her words around a smile or a frown, and how her eyes would widen or crinkle depending on what she was sensing. It was an attractive face.

"David? You still awake?"

"I am."

"Sorry, Hazel spent last night at Stuart's house, so she's not there." She sat on the arm of his chair and he did not flinch from her. "And, I think it's time I made plans to go home. Would that be okay with you?" She was staring straight ahead into the dying fire, not trusting herself to look at his face. She did not want to witness either his relief or regret, both of which would make her feel sad.

"I suppose at some point you have to," he accepted, sighing, "I can't monopolise your time forever."

"Well, it will take a few days to organise the ticket, I'm sure. We'll still have a little while, and I need to see the reaction to the 'new you' before I go. Hazel will want details!"

"We'll see."

She got up, yawning, then turned back to face him. "Don't think I won't miss you. All of you."

"Hey," his voice was soft as he stood and touched her shoulder. "You come back as often as you like. There are people here who need you just as much as they need Hazel."

She looked into his eyes, trying desperately to read his meaning, but he turned to place the fireguard firmly in place. Her heart was pounding. The air was silent and thick. When he turned back to her, he touched her face.

"You're so like him, Kate. You'll be good for him."

She reeled as he walked away. "You know?"

"I saw it on the first day. But that's between you and me. Night Kate."

Chapter 33

"Wait!" she cried, forgetting to keep her voice down, "Wait a minute, please."

When David turned in the doorway, his face was guarded and it did nothing to temper her astonishment. On top of his revelation, she felt all the closeness and empathy from the past few days evaporate in that one expression. She could not stop herself reproaching him.

"Please take that look off your face. It makes me feel on the outside again."

His face did indeed soften then and he shook his head against her constant anxiety.

"You mean," she continued, "You spent all that time with us on Skye, alone with this shock? How could you stand it? How did you do it?"

Suddenly, his mouth straightened and he rested his hand on the door jamb. "Skye was about you pair, not me. I wanted to be there more than anywhere, because that's where your mother and you had been. I didn't let myself think about anything else. At least, not during the day."

He looked at her horrified face and tried to break into a smile. "It's okay, Kate. It was okay."

But she could not accept this. How in God's name could it have been okay? She began to think in dream-time, countless realisations bombarding her in the mere seconds which passed between them, before David recognised her eyes losing their focus. He lowered his arm to his side and leaned towards her.

"Kate?"

She heard his voice, clear in the silent room, but she could not have formed a coherent sentence in that moment, for she was thinking of all that had taken place on Skye. She remembered their stilted conversations, her hostility and his attempts to be accepted on any level. He had been patient and borne her negativity and Hazel's ever-optimistic enthusiasm equally well. He had talked to them, encouraged them and throughout it all, he had been looking at her, recognising something in her expressions, convinced that he was on the right track at last. How long had it taken him to come to terms with it, when he had had nobody to talk to? And how had he gone to bed each night, knowing that his thoughts would torture him until sleep eventually came. Unless there had been doubts sewn before. Now, she stared at him.

"Had you ever considered such a possibility *before* you saw me? Had you thought that maybe - "

"Listen to me, Kate," he grabbed her hands and sat her on the sofa. She put up no fight, more than anxious for him to explain it all to her. "I want you to *really* listen, because I'm not going to dress it up to save your feelings or try to sweep anything under the carpet. What I'm going to say is the complete truth. D'youunderstand?"

They were sitting about a foot apart, turned towards each other and still he held her hands, ensuring she concentrated on him. She nodded, her lips slightly apart, her breathing inaudible.

"On my worst days, every man she had ever spoken to was the man responsible. It was the most God-awful time because not one of us could understand what had happened. Fiona was completely vacant. Lost. She couldn't even hold Hazel without losing control. It was pitiful and unbelievable and eventually, when you're breathing that kind of toxic air every minute, you start to ask a different kind of question. Not why or who, but how can we possibly solve this? Your priorities change." He paused, trying to see if any of his words were getting through to her. She seemed calm, her pupils large but alert, only a row of tiny sweat beads visible on her upper lip. "I wanted her to stay, I didn't care about anything else and that was all that mattered to me. But she couldn't do it and that wasn't like her. And Neil. He was broken in two, in treatment for years. But hindsight is a great thing and to answer your question, I can honestly say it never entered my head, even when Neil kept blaming himself. There was never anything like that between them and I would have known."

Kate, anxious not to halt his words, was equally eager to reassure him that he was right about this, but that would remain in her power for a later time.

"He was so ill," continued David, "and I was buried in my dark hole for so long, that by the time we realised we had managed to survive it, the details became irrelevant."

Kate now leaned back on the sofa, easing her hands gently from his and placing them palms down on either side of her. She was indeed listening and was glad of the truth, stripped of sentiment, because she was seeing David as he had been years ago and was still. Strong and resilient. She remembered with shame that she had once considered him careless and unfeeling and made a promise to herself to judge people less readily in the future. As he spoke, she watched his face, his feelings, his actions and savoured the fact that at last she knew this man's true character.

"It took a long time for Neil to talk to me about anything, perhaps something else I should have picked up on. He said he needed to leave. He put Rose through the wringer by suggesting that we'd be better off without him, rambling on about looking for his biological mother. We'd had him since he was two weeks old, for God's sake! But as I say, he was screwed up and in the end, we all pulled together. That's why this goes no further. The door has been firmly shut on that time and your mother must have agreed with this, because even now she did not tell me. She was protecting us all."

When he finally stopped, willing her to comprehend something if not it all, Kate took the opportunity to speak and it heartened both of them to hear that her voice was still positive.

"She was right, you know, not to tell. I understand that bit completely."

Perhaps he had been expecting more questions or the need for further clarification, but Kate simply sat there, seeing how it must have been, astounded at how much stress and pain human beings could actually withstand. "Do you think you and Neil are okay now? I mean, I don't think he could have faced talking to you about it. You're still his hero, I'm sure."

David gave a little smile of acknowledgement and looked over at the photographs on the wall, which tracked the family's progress over the years. The one he was especially fond of was the College graduation photograph taken of Neil and Rose, both of whom were smiling. It had been a long journey for Neil; he had been years older than his College peers by the time he stepped back out into the world, and David was proud of him. Now, more than anything else, he was grateful that Kate had confirmed the subject closed. They might all know as much as each other at last, but there was no earthly reason to acknowledge it.

"You're a very big man," Kate said, unable to keep the admiration out of her statement. "A special man with a big heart."

David shook his head, always amazed by her frankness, but modesty not allowing him to accept the compliment. "People make mistakes. I make them all the time. As long as there's no malice, we should be allowed to get over them in peace. Now," he stood, beckoning her out of her seat. "It's been a long event of a day and I need some sleep. Come on."

"Well," she replied, passing him as he switched off the lamps, "I'm going to bed, but I doubt if I'll sleep. Will you?"

As he followed her out into the hallway, his yawn went unnoticed but when he tripped over his own feet whilst rubbing his eyes, Kate turned and laughed. "Yes, I think you probably will. Sorry for keeping you up."

"See you in the morning, Kate," he called, taking a detour to switch off the kitchen lights.

Rose was seated by the range, wrapped in a fleecy blanket, eyes large and brimming in her face. He swallowed the initial instinct to speak and slowly closed the kitchen door on the retreating Kate. When he finally heard her creak across her bedroom floor, he made his way towards his mother's chair, his face resigned to whatever was coming. She stood immediately, the blanket falling to the floor, and put her hands on his shoulders, head against his chest.

"Don't say anything, ma. Please don't. I know why you all did it and I understand. That's all that needs to be said."

He could feel her quiver against his chest and silently begged her not to try to justify anything. He was tired, so tired of the past. It had shaped far too much of their existence already and now there was a real opportunity for a positive future. He truly believed that, but it had to start now, right at this very minute. Perhaps Rose felt his resolve, it might even have seeped through his shirtfront into her own heart, for she merely looked up at him, squeezed his arms and kissed his cheek.

"Sleep well," she said and left the room.

David glanced around at the familiar room, chilled now that the range had cooled down, and sighed. He figured he would start in here. Maybe take out the wall units and have some free-standing furniture. Kate could choose the colour scheme before she left. Then, if that was successful, he would return to his plans for the chalets and get some serious financial advice. He would ask Neil if Andie would be prepared to be professionally involved and hopefully they would all spend some more time together. It would be good to be involved in something new and fresh again. Finally, his bones now shouting their fatigue loud enough for him to take notice, he made his way upstairs.

As David was dragging his shirt over his head, dreading the icy sheets awaiting him, Beth Mackinnon was standing by the picnic table, willing Kenny to return with the Sunday papers. There was a blustery wind blowing down the hillside, which the house only partially absorbed, but she would have stood in the same spot had there been blizzard conditions, because her heart was singing and she wanted to share her news. Where was he? And why, of all days, was Hazel not in the house? Kate was coming home as soon as was physically possible and she could look at her face once again and hug her close. Just to hear her voice and watch her expressions as she told her tales would be the best pre-Christmas present she could have wished for. She doubted if she would ever let her out of her sight again.

Since Hazel's return, Beth had put her best effort into remaining calm and making sure that Hazel knew that she was more than delighted to see her. But everyone in the house knew that she was in agony, fretting with each passing day and squeezing every last drop of information from Hazel until the girl eventually began to spend more and more time at Stuart's house. Kenny, more patient than Job himself, had only lost his temper once and declared that either she stopped tormenting them all or she got on the next available flight. Beth had been surprised by the tone he had used, but it had also shown her the extent of his worry and so she had managed to curb her anguish on the surface at least.

Just the night before, she had lain in a bubble bath, calming her breathing, telling herself that Kate had to find her future path without her. After all, Fiona had been forced to relinquish her love and care, so there was no reason to assume that she still had that privilege. She had almost accepted this and had taken her soothed and cleansed body and shown Kenny what he had meant to her. She had then slept soundly until the phone had roused her and now she could not wait to share her news.

Initially, Kate had sounded a bit sheepish, apologetic even, but that had soon given way to firm assurances and upbeat promises that she was fine and that she felt life might even be coming out of its nosedive and levelling off. No, she did not want Hazel to know about Neil yet; she would tell her if she ever felt it necessary and yes, David had proved to be a man worth knowing. But it was best that she came home. They had been her words and in spite of Beth's delight, they had sounded oddly empty.

Now, as Beth waved at a couple heading up the hill path, she allowed her joy to be tempered slightly, trying to imagine Kate as she would be on her return. Hazel had said she was thinner and Beth guessed that some of her newly acquired knowledge would be evident on her face. She simply hoped that they would still communicate as they always had, well aware that Kate now knew of the conspiracy Beth had taken part in. All she needed was for her to be in front of her eyes. From there she could cope.

A gust of wind blew Beth's sweatshirt hood from her head and, cursing, she placed herself further against the house. How long would it take David to get Kate's ticket organised and how long did it take a man to buy two newspapers and a packet of firelighters? This last question had no more occurred to her than she saw Kenny's Land Rover begin its bumpy descent from the top of the hill. She did a little jig in anticipation, before running down to the foot of the driveway, her total enthusiasm returned. Not even the thought of aircraft wings tipping in gale-force winds could take the smile off her face.

It was just this smile that Kate was picturing, lying in the darkness, hands behind her head. It was obvious from the phone call home that she had done the right thing and from the point of view of Beth's sanity, her decision had been necessary. But still Kate could not rid herself of the anxiety involved and grew frustrated as to the unknown cause of it. She had never felt at home anywhere other than her cottage and her bay, it had been the most spectacular place to grow up in and everybody she loved was there. In the winter it could be arduous, the road not always negotiable, but it was also brain-clearingly picturesque and inspiring. In the summer, it was a place of paddling and climbing and lounging on the grass, watching tourists begin their trudge to the top of the Ben, knowing that they envied her home and her lifestyle. It was an easy place to live and she knew that she loved it. But she could not reconcile herself completely to returning there and it mystified her.

She had come to Canada, unaware of her mission but felt, even in the short weeks they had been together, that she had accomplished something. Fiona had trusted her and she thought that maybe, with a bit of time and a lot of goodwill, this family could really enjoy each other again. So that was something to be pleased about. Sighing, she turned over and switched on the lamp. Something was still chewing at her brain. Was it simply that she saw no clear path for her to take, or was it that she really could not contemplate island life without her mother's presence? She had certainly felt Fiona here in this house.

Kate sat up, plumping the pillows behind her and realised that maybe she had discovered the problem or at least a part of it. Fiona was still here in Canada. Not the Fiona she had known from birth or the one who had slipped away before their eyes, but a different person. A person who had touched everyone in this house and who had left her mark. This Fiona intrigued her. She had been an individual not a mother and for the time being, she did not want to leave her side. Yes, that was the reason behind her reluctance to go. And of course, the fact that she needed to set David on his new and exciting life adventure.

She laced her fingers across her abdomen and thought of David. He surely must seem like a great prospect to many. True, he had made no effort whatsoever to put himself on any type of social radar, but he was not a hermit. He didn't have a long beard or live in a shack. His business brain was sound; he owned property and his colleagues and associates must have wives and partners who knew of 'someone who would suit David Wilder down to the ground'. Perhaps he had made it clear to them that his heart was not for the seeking. Well, to Kate's mind, that all had to change and she had a few days at her disposal to ensure it did. She needed to get Rose on side and she needed to get him out in public. It was that simple.

But as Kate switched off the lamp once more, a strange heat began to spread up her spine and she lay there, truly scared. Her stomach was now fluttering and she replaced her hands where they had been, trying to press the feeling into submission. As soon as the knot began to ease, she felt her legs begin to tingle and in response, she shoved herself as far down the bed as she could, leaving only her upper face uncovered. She was hiding. Hiding from her own feelings and she knew it as well as she knew the futility of the action. David. He was the problem. One huge, almighty problem of her own making.

Even picturing his face was causing a light-headedness that she had been purposefully ignoring for God knew how long. She remembered his eyes from the very first day, how sad they had seemed. Since then, they had watched her and aided her recovery. They seemed to sit perfectly in his perfect face.

Kate groaned into her pillow, rubbing her face against the cold cotton, recognising that she was opening the floodgates. She wondered if these feelings went back as far as the day he had 'rescued' her, but she wasn't sure how to handle the thought that this might be true. Surely that made them desperate and misplaced, a reaction of some sort. She was confused. All she really knew was that she had begun to look for him at the end of the day, waiting for him to come stamping into the kitchen and throw her a 'how's-things' grin.

Now she had acknowledged her feelings to herself, she wasn't sure if she could keep them concealed, which was going to make the next few days almost unbearable. She had been fooling herself, wondering why she didn't want to go back to Skye. Yes, her mother would be missing and yes, there was no point in entertaining the idea of returning to school. But as she lay there, the tingle of realisation affecting every part of her from heart to fingertips, she knew exactly why she wanted to stay here. David.

She reached under the bed for her walkman, which had been kicked there accidentally on her return from Victoria, and turned the volume up high. She needed to bring herself back from wherever she was headed and she needed to halt something she had never experienced in her life before. But how did you do that? The way she understood it, desire was always something a person struggled to control. And, honestly, at that particular moment, she did not want to try.

Chapter 34

"Okay, I agree," consented Kate. "But _"

"I knew there would be a but," laughed David. "So what particular 'but' would this be?"

"Well," Kate wandered over to the window of David's office. "It's not a huge 'but', it's just that I only have one half smart thing I could wear and I'd hate to spoil the overall effect, when we spent that *whole day* searching for the new you. Do I have to go?"

He was sitting at the desk, rearranging papers in what looked to Kate like a completely random and complicated manner, yet he appeared to be listening with the back of his head. Indeed, he countered immediately with, "Kate, it's a monthly dinner, not a state banquet. I'm not even sure I can be bothered ..."

"Okay, okay, I'll go. You're not exactly subtle, are you?"

"Never claimed it as a quality," he held up his hand, still engrossed at his desk.

Kate wandered about, happy merely to be in his company. She glanced through to his bedroom where some of his new purchases were lying on the bed and some on the chair. Immediately she grinned to herself. He had been trying them on again, so there was some level of interest in the evening being shown. She waited until he stood, threw some balled up paper into the bin and scratched his face, then said to him "So, I know what *I'm* wearing, what about you?"

He shrugged, pushing his chair under the desk and switching off the desk lamp. "Not given it any thought really."

She laughed in his face, then, "You fibber. Look at the mess in there!"

Moving over to where she stood, he glanced over her shoulder then gave her a sheepish grin, "Well, I couldn't really remember what went with what. Didn't want to let my date down."

Feeling a burning flush taking her over, Kate quickly walked into the bedroom, hiding her face from him. She picked up and began to fold all the clothes she could find and did not stop until she felt him by her side.

"So, what do you think?" he asked, lightly.

"Right," she forced herself to sound businesslike, "Well, how posh are we talking? Not a suit, surely. More a shirt and jacket type thing? I'm telling you, we should have got that jacket I liked."

"Kate, it was leather. Are you kidding?"

"Right then. The jacket you wore to Duncan would do, with.... this shirt." She handed him a white long-sleeved shirt, cotton with a thin, grey stripe running vertically through it. "And these. I mean, I know they're jeans, but new black jeans look really smart."

"Sweater?" he enquired.

"No need, unless you want to try it with this one."

"Sure," he grinned and without the slightest hesitation, pulled his worn jumper over his head and began to unbutton his shirt. Thankfully, he was the type of person who concentrated on any given task, and so watched himself undoing the buttons, whilst arguing the case that Rose was unlikely to agree that jeans were *ever* smart. It allowed Kate to retreat to the door without his noticing her mortification, although he did call after her retreating figure.

"Just need the loo. Back in a second!"

As she leaned against the closed door of his shower room, sliding the lock into place, her head began to spin. She could feel the familiar prickles of heat on her throat and neck and desperately tried to calm down her flushed skin with cold water. She had to get through this unscathed, but it was tough. At least his lack of modesty implied he was unaware of her burgeoning feelings towards him; that was something to be thankful for. However, it also proved that he thought of her as he thought of Hazel. He was comfortable in her presence, she was safe company. She found that a little disappointing.

As she now took a flannel to her livid skin, she thought of what she had seen before she had the ability to escape the room. His chest had been broad and smooth, his frame lean, his collar bones visible beneath his moving hands. She closed her eyes. This was ridiculous. Beyond ridiculous and she grew furious with herself. "Get a bloody grip," she hissed. "Get a grip before you completely ruin it all! Come on now!"

When her face and neck had finally calmed down enough to cause no comment, she flushed the loo. Surely by the time she had negotiated the space between here and where he stood, her eyes would have returned to normal from the black holes that had stared at her from the mirror. She began to make her way cautiously back to his room, but he met her in the doorway, looking adolescently pleased with himself. The slim fit shirt was undone at the collar, snugly fitting under the V-neck sweater and he had donned the black jeans and black jacket. He could have graced any restaurant at that very moment, were it not for his bare feet.

"Well?"

"Excellent" breathed Kate, halted on her journey, then "Shoes?"

David's face fell momentarily then did a strange little twisted how-about-a-compromise turnaround. Kate was genuinely surprised.

"You don't have shoes?"

"What about a really good pair of boots? Hardly worn?" he ventured.

Kate's awkwardness was suddenly shelved in light of this disaster and she only just stopped herself from putting her hands on her hips. Instead, she walked over to him, shaking her head. "You know, there were lots of shoe shops in Victoria."

"Agreed," he said, as she bypassed him in search of the boots in question. "But they were never actually mentioned. Anyway, here's a fact, if ever I do come across this elusive female who thinks I am the man of her dreams, she will never see me in a pair of shoes. It's boots or nothing."

Kate was barely listening, regarding the footwear before her, trying her hardest to distinguish the old from the 'hardly worn'. Finally, she glanced in his direction and then back at the boots. "There's a problem?" he asked, innocently.

"But, they're all *ancient*. That one doesn't even have laces!"

Sighing, he crossed behind her and squatted in front of the wardrobe. "Well, it's just as well that the pair I'm talking about are still in their original box, then. I'm not a complete hick."

He pulled open the drawer just as Kate turned to look and they both found themselves gazing at the offensive brown folder Hazel had stored there for safekeeping. David seemed truly taken aback, halting all movement for a second, before slowly looking up at Kate. She was also motionless, her eyes crinkled slightly in recognition, but an instant later she was smiling down at him. She reached in and pulled the folder out of its confinement. "It's okay, David. Actually, I'd like to look at them again. They'll probably be quite funny, now that I'm not so worried about... well, you know. *But* for the moment, let me have a look at the boots which are going to win the lady."

The mood was slightly subdued as David brought out the pristine Timberland box, but by the time the deep brown suede boots had been analysed and added to the ensemble, the crisis appeared to have passed. The folder now rested undisturbed on his bed.

"Okay, they are very nice boots," said Kate. "It would have been better if they'd been black, but you look great."

"Wow," he grinned, "not nearly as painful as I was expecting. Looks like we're all set then."

Kate could not ignore the optimistic expression and so, testing her resolve to the absolute limit, she gave him a quick hug on the way to the door. It had been a friendship hug, a mutual satisfaction hug and she had managed not to shiver as his arms enclosed her and then released her. "Tomorrow night we introduce the new David Wilder to the world," she cried, leaving him to ponder the concept. "Hope the world, or at least Duncan Rotary Club, is ready ..."

David watched her wander out of the door, her work for the day obviously completed. He wondered how she would react if her plans for his future did not come to fruition and even worse, how he would react if they did.

On the floor below him, Kate threw herself face first onto her bed and considered the logistics of remaining there for the rest of her life. She could just wither away, her head buried in her pillow, and never have to consider what games her heart was playing at this moment. She could feel her face burning against the pillowcase and imagined a brown imprint of her features branding itself there. Before the smell of singed cotton could also torment her, she flipped herself onto her back and tried to cool her blush with her icy palms.

So, here she was, completely immersed in the greatest emotional mess that, even on her most creative days, she could not have imagined. The crisis had so many aspects to it, each sewn into place by threads from different lives, all equally important and most still current. Kate let her mind run with the idea of a patch made up of brightly coloured strands, marvelling at the pretty patterns it made and was almost hopeful, until the words 'patch' and 'frayed' brought her back to reality. As she rubbed her temples, Kate tried to look at each problem separately, second-guessing how those who mattered could conceivably react to her present dilemma.

Foremost on her list was her own self-doubt and the actual feelings she harboured for this man. There was the real possibility that she merely ached to mean *something* to him, anything; David had known the bliss of loving her mother, he had his bright spark of his daughter back in his life and now Kate wanted to claim a little of his heart for her. She closed her eyes to see his face and jumped. God, no, it was so much more than that. Kate wanted to clasp her hands in his and stand so close to him that his eyes focussed on her alone. She wanted to feel his breath on her hair and feel the thump of his heart in his chest as he pulled her against him.

Kate was up and off the bed in one swift movement, wringing her hands and breathing against her utter despair. There was no hope for her. This was the definition of the word hopeless and she found herself at pacing pitch. Should she visit the rest of the problems, just to ensure she accepted the futility of her desires? It was certainly a less dangerous option than thinking of David Wilder and his beautiful face. She picked up her walkman from the chest of drawers and sank onto the floor, leaning against the solid wood. From there, Kate took David out of the equation. She could not bear to think of the countless objections he himself would have.

So, Rose. Rose would be scared to death, anxious for her son to be spared any further hurt from someone who was too close/too young/too damaged. She would be sympathetic, but adamant, and would make such a watertight and sensible case to put to him that that would be the end of the matter. Kate would be sent home and never encouraged to return.

Then there was Hazel. Kate's stomach did a little roll as she thought of her sister's face and her total disbelief and horror. She doubted her own ability to even form the words to tell her. It would be like some giggly, heads-together-over-milkshakes conversation where a twelve-year-old tells her best friend how 'cute' she thinks the other's Dad is. Only so much more deadly.

"Jeez," muttered Kate aloud. It was *beyond* impossible. Just to compound her misery, she closed her eyes and pictured Beth and Kenny standing white-faced and open-mouthed. Then there were her classmates, Mr Ellis and even the neighbours' dog, turning to her, their faces contorted with disgust. Finally Neil appeared before her, standing against the door of his ancient Dodge, his arms folded. For some reason, his face only registered calm recognition.

Kate opened her eyes, frowning, wondering what to read into that last expression and was startled to find Rose standing beside her, about to tap her shoulder. She hauled herself onto her feet, pulling the headphones from her ears.

"Oh, sorry. I can't hear a thing when I'm wearing these."

Rose waved away her protests. "I thought I might get me one of those for gardening. What do you think?"

"Great idea!" beamed Kate. "Makes any chore bearable, especially hoovering. It uses a lot of batteries, that's the only thing."

They stood there for a second longer before Kate, fearing that Rose would ask her why she had found her frowning, smiled and handed her the walkman for her to look at.

"That one isn't great quality, but I've never had any problems with it."

"Thanks," Rose replied, then, "David has nipped out to put some air in the truck's tyres. You fancy coming down to keep me company?"

"Sure," smiled Kate. "I tell you what I do need to do, and that's to iron my one dress, for all the good it will do. I'm going to show him up, without a doubt."

As she followed Kate downstairs, Rose suddenly snapped her fingers. "Well now, why didn't I think of it before? Andie is about your size, she's far too thin for a woman in her thirties, but that seems to be the way of it these days. Why don't you ring her and ask her to bring some bits and pieces over?"

Halting on the stairs, Kate could not keep the surprise out of her voice as she turned to Rose. "But why would she do that? It's at least eighty miles away; it took forever when we went the other day. That's far too big a favour to ask."

"Well, maybe Neil could bring her. He knows you're leaving shortly."

Kate now felt her resolve crumble completely. The visit to Neil's amazingly bohemian house three days before had been the most nerve-wracking experience so far, when there had been many to choose from. She had wandered from room to room, acknowledging Andie's deliberately surreptitious 'My-God-you-do-look-like-him-a-bit' expression with a smile, whilst watching David and Neil talking timber and furniture and chalets in light and unassuming voices. Rose had sat in the kitchen, nursing her coffee, paler than usual but upbeat when spoken to. It had been horrific, but they had managed to hide their varying degrees of knowledge and say their goodbyes without giving any secrets away. Kate's head had ached all the way home. There was no way she could face it again, but she hated to offend Rose. Truth, she reminded herself. Nothing but the truth. As they entered the sitting room, where the fire welcomed their chilled bodies, Kate waited until Rose sat and then purposely sat right next to her.

"I've said goodbye to them, Rose. I don't want to do it again, even if David isn't in the room. I don't want to have to hide things from him. I don't like knowing things and hiding things from anybody, but especially not from him. It's not fair. And that's me being honest with you. Sorry"

Rose looked at Kate's face and knew that her words were genuine. It had been a cheap trick on her part, suggesting that Neil and Andie visit, for she

268

wanted to hear Kate's thoughts on the subject. She had witnessed her discomfort at Port Alberni, and had no wish to see her go through it again, but she also wanted to open up a conversation, in which Kate might reveal what Rose suspected. And she had been right. Kate was becoming increasingly attached to David and Rose had no idea what to do about it. What she did not expect, even from a person who had shown that truth was now the only way forward, were Kate's next words.

"Rose, I need your advice. And I really don't know what you're going to do or say, so I'm very scared. Could you be nice to me?"

Rose did not even pretend to be surprised by the request. She just took Kate's hand "Of course. What is it?"

Kate closed her eyes for a moment, not believing that she was going to share her thoughts, but to her mind, her future depended on it. "I need to go home to Skye, but I don't want to. Well, of course, I want to see everybody again and its home, but I don't want to leave here. Not now."

She paused, unable to look at Rose, but desperately hoping that her face was as understanding as her hand was comforting. She heard Rose take a breath in, but paused before finally speaking.

"Well, it's only natural that now you've met Neil that you would want –"

"It's not because of Neil," Kate cut in, finally looking Rose straight in the eye. She watched Rose's face take on a resigned look, but she did not frown or take her hand away from Kate's. Instead she squeezed it, causing Kate's newly formed tears to roll silently over her flushed and worried cheeks.

"Oh Kate," was all Rose managed to say. Her voice was kind, but Kate recognised fear. There was no way she was going to start justifying her feelings to this woman, because she barely comprehended them herself. She only hoped that her actual voicing of them to a third party was testament to the commitment she felt.

"I know. Believe me, there is not one thing in my favour," she sobbed now, causing Rose to listen in the air for any sign of David's return. "But I just can't bear the thought of leaving. What would I have?"

"Kate, you would be going home to people who are waiting-"

"I don't mean that. I mean, what would I have with him? There's no actual connection at all, no blood ties. He would lose touch. He might think of me when talking to his *daughter*, but only as an aside. I would be that person who looked a bit like the love of his life and who wasted his time for a month or so. I can't stand it."

"Oh, God, Kate stop," Rose was actually now shaking. Not because she considered Kate's feelings as anything more than a desperate lunge for recognition, but because there was a real risk that David might learn of them before she left. Could any of them take any further clawing and tearing at their hearts? "You cannot tell him. Please. Think about what you are doing. How can you possibly bring him into this?"

"You're right. I can't. But it's not fair." Kate got up, swiping at her eyes and face. "I had to tell to you, because somebody needs to help me. I can't think about anything else and I can't go home, because nothing makes sense without him. I'm so scared." Pause. "Can I have a bath? I can't see him again tonight."

She did not wait for a reply and as Rose heard the back door slam, she also listened to Kate's feet pounding on the stairs. What was the girl thinking? She was not even an adult, and yet, in little over a month, she had formed some sort of a bond which she viewed as worthy of discussion. Rose had taken a real shine to Kate, had admired her buoyancy and also her ability to still look for the good in people. She had been astounded when she had wished to keep her parentage from David, an admirable decision, and yet one that had first alerted her to the current situation. But how on earth did she think that any of this was feasible?

David appeared in the doorway, drying his hands on a tea towel. "Where's Kate?"

Rose turned on her seat in his direction. Why did those words seem so familiar coming from David's mouth? She looked at him steadily. "She's gone for a bath."

His face took three seconds to change from an enquiry into a frown then settle on a resigned raised eyebrow. "Oh, well, it'll keep," he stated and returned to the kitchen.

Rose now slowly reclined herself against the support of the sofa and sat there, her mind reacting far quicker than her body. One by one, she thought of all the conversations she had witnessed between David and Kate and accepted, without a doubt, that she would get little sleep that night.

Chapter 35

Just after dawn, Kate was aware of someone knocking at her bedroom door. She had slept reasonably well after sobbing her heart out in the bath, but had been wide awake since the colour had begun to seep back into the black/grey objects in her room. There had definitely been a knock, but she doubted she had the strength to speak to either of the other residents. They had never disturbed her this early before and so she waited, her face growing hot with indecision, until finally the door handle turned and Rose crept across the threshold. Kate heard her own breath being exhaled into the silent room.

"May I come in, Kate?"

Kate fought the temptation to point out to her that it was her house, fearing it would sound petulant. After all, she had sought her opinion yesterday and therefore had to accept it, whether or not it was what she wanted to hear.

"Yes," her voice was thin and frail. She cleared her throat immediately, hauling herself upright and pushing the hair back from her face. She could not smile. She had never once considered that this woman would be the cause of her ultimate defeat. But as Rose sat on the bed, she looked white with exhaustion and Kate now frowned, more worried than resentful.

"Oh, Rose," she whispered. "You look so tired. I'm sorry if that was me and my insane little attempt at getting you to understand. Here."

Kate peeled the comforter from the duvet and awkwardly wrapped it around Rose's shoulders. The woman's hair hung loose, mussed up at the back, further evidence of her restless night, but she took the blanket and clasped it at her throat. "Thanks honey. These bones never used to feel the cold, and it's only the beginning of November!"

As Rose made her way across to the window, the blanket trailing behind her, Kate eased the duvet up to her chin, also acknowledging the cold air around her, but really it was a defence against the lecture that was surely coming. She watched Rose open each curtain, letting the dead white light into the room and recognised that silent brightness immediately.

"No!" she whispered in wonder, clambering over to stand beside Rose and watch the flakes float past the window, completely oblivious to their scrutiny. "Oh how beautiful," Kate breathed, the clearing and driveway instantly cleansed by its pure white covering. No muddy tyre marks were visible, no stony puddles, no stick-dry shrubs. Just various shapes dusted with icing sugar, the trees settling and relieving their branches of their burden, while they still had the strength. Kate stood inches from the glass, anxious to view as much as she could and commit it to memory. "I wonder how much film I have left."

"It started about twenty minutes ago, just after David left. It may only be a shower or we may be watching this all day."

The significance of Rose's words took another moment to penetrate Kate's thoughts and instantly she felt her childish delight at the weather dissipate. She leaned her head against the glass, eyes closed, but allowed herself only two seconds of gripping frustration before standing straight. Instead, she felt anger creep into her chest and she refused to turn towards Rose. So, it was true. Rose had now chosen her side of the fence and had to be viewed as an adversary. Basically, she had come to suggest that the furthest David and Kate would travel that evening would be the front door and surely it was for the best. It was the safest option, stay within the confines of this place and best avoid a situation where you could make a fool of yourself. That was what Rose was saying.

Kate folded her arms, the stretching silence between them not awkward but empowering. Kate would be gone from this house in a matter of days. She could be civil for that length of time, but there was no real need to be friendly, not when this woman had knowledge of her feelings and possible future humiliation. She hoped that her posture was sending out this message and that Rose realised she had been rumbled. Finally, the silence was broken by the older woman.

"I'm not sure if he could survive it again."

Kate felt heat spread across her shoulder blades, but did not move a muscle. Instead, she spoke to the window, her breath appearing and disappearing on the cold glass.

"So you want him to fester in this place still. Look, take me out of it altogether if you have to. But he needs a life."

"I know he needs a life," Rose's tone was sharp and Kate finally turned, her own demeanour unchanged. She had one chance to put her case to this judge and she did it without a second thought.

"Then stop acting like his protector and be his friend." Kate paused, thinking herself a little harsh, then, "Well, now, that's not fair. Sorry. Before you say it, I wasn't there in the bad days and I didn't see it. But you still think he's like that, when he's so, so much better."

Kate dared her to respond in a negative manner. Instead, Rose said blankly, "Go on."

"I will, but tell me this first. Is it yourself or him you are actually worried about? I'm not saying you're selfish, you know how bad it was, but I *am* asking you to admit it's the truth. Because if you think *David* couldn't handle another attack on his heart, you're wrong. He's not weak and he's not dead."

Kate paused, wondering if indeed Rose would hold her hands up to this accusation, but she merely said, "What are you saying?"

Kate let out a jagged breath, anxious to do David justice with her words. "On Skye, I was horrible. I didn't want him there and I didn't spare him. But he never gave up on me and he put me right on a few things when I needed to be told. I had no idea at the time what he was going through but I do now, and there is *nobody* who has strength to match his."

Rose sat as a stone, her eyes wide and brimming, as Kate continued.

"You saw it for yourself when we came here, he never flinched from anything, answered all our questions and I loved him for it. You have to agree. After this horrendous year, we had a person willing to help us through it all. And then," Kate swallowed to prevent her voice from cracking, looking away from Rose as she did so. "Then, he was ripped away from me and I was in this place I can't even describe. He tried to pull me out, even against my will and he kept pulling at me until I was back where I was wanted. He did that, and I don't care what his motives were because he *wanted* me here, safe, in one piece."

Tears were pouring down Rose's face, recognising her son's traits for what they were and even appreciating Kate's depth of feeling for the first time. But surely there was no possible foundation to this? Surely this girl could see that she was teetering at the mouth of another dark tunnel

"Let's face it," Kate continued, wiping her own damp cheeks. "That *could* have been the start of my endless nightmare, one that you have lived with for years, but it wasn't. Because he was there with his answers and Mum was there with hers. They got me through it together. I don't ever want to forget what he did or lose this feeling."

Kate, suddenly aware of how much she was shivering, reached into the chest of drawers for a jumper and some thick socks, the room temperature and her own words reminding her that her body should not cool down any further. As she sat beside Rose, who had no apparent desire to speak, she pulled on the extra layers then handed her a tissue.

"He is such a strong man, Rose, and there are things that even you don't know about him. But I know them and I love him. Of course, how can I ever tell him?"

Kate allowed herself a second to see if a solution miraculously presented itself, but it did not. She stared at the floor. "*Because* he is decent and because he is thoughtful, he will never accept this. Us. Me. Even if he doesn't doubt my feelings, he will see it as me wasting my life. I can hear him saying it."

Rose now took her hands, thankful that at least this youngster had visited these facts, even if they brought her pain. Perhaps this would only ever go as far as this conversation, with Kate herself seeing the futility of it. Rose remained mute, willing this to be the case.

"Of all the unfair things that have happened to us," Kate looked from the floor to their linked hands, "This is what takes away all my hope. I just wanted to be something more and, let's not kid ourselves, all this 'get David out among the living' it was just a way of testing the water. I wanted to see if he was even interested in looking around him. The irony is, I only want him to notice me, nobody else." Kate shuddered at the pointlessness of her wishes. "But how can it possibly happen? What on earth would people make of it? How would they understand any of it? Well, they wouldn't, because you don't. It's time I went home."

Standing, she pulled her hands from Rose's and lingered once again by the window. The flakes were as big and as light as feathers, but had lost all their magic. Her mother had loved the snow and hated the snow in equal measures, for reasons which were now a bit clearer to Kate. She sighed from the pit of her stomach.

"If my Mum can live most of her life without him and still make ours a happy home, then I can give it a go. I just wanted someone else to know the way I feel about him and for you to appreciate that whoever comes next for me will always be second best to him. That's a bit sad for them, don't you think?"

Rose who had not spoken in minutes, had managed to prevent any more tears falling by concentrating on what she was going to say, but now none of her words seemed anywhere near as articulate as Kate's and she simply took her hand and led her to the doorway.

"Breakfast." It was the least controversial statement of the day, and Kate followed Rose's lead without argument.

Kate had spent the remainder of the morning ironing her dress, although the evening no longer held any interest for her, and sorting through gifts and souvenirs, forcing herself to acknowledge that she was going home. Rose had occasionally sought her company, but neither of them wanted to revisit the early morning discussion and so their exchanges were short and reasonably sweet. Just before lunch, Kate entered the kitchen, camera in one hand and gloves in the other.

"Do you mind if I don't eat anything, Rose? I'd really like to go for a walk. On my own."

She could see Rose trying to fathom her mood, and deliberately kept her expression neutral. She held up her camera.

"Hazel wanted to see the snow. Now I can show her. I won't be long."

Nodding, Rose turned back to the worktop and hastily began to wrap one of the toasted sandwiches she was preparing for the table. "Sure, but take this anyway. Your stomach might disagree with you while you're out there."

"Have you seen my walkman?"

"It's on the hall table. Where are you planning on going?"

Kate shrugged,walkman and sandwich both shoved into the winter coat David had insisted on buying her. "Probably just the usual loop, as long as I end up at the end of the driveway. I really want a photo of Neil's gateposts. You know, a little reminder of who I am." As she laced up her boots, Rose suggested a flask of coffee, but Kate declined it. "I'm not taking my ruck-sack, I'll be fine. Rose," she hesitated, unsure if she should ask, then, "Was he okay this morning?"

"He was in good spirits," Rose patted her arm, vexed to see the bleakness in Kate's eyes, "A bit concerned about the snow for tonight, but it should be okay if it stays off now. Please don't be long. It's cold out there."

Rose stood at the back door, watching Kate struggle first with the intricacies of the walkman and then the bitterness of the air. As she trudged further into the distance, she saw her wrap her scarf around her head and face for extra protection. Gloves on, she then continued on her way, her posture suggesting relief at being out of the house. Rose sighed at her inability to help but accepted, for a change, that she could not.

The wool of her scarf had begun to tickle her nose by the time Kate had left The Edge behind her, but she ignored it. She could also feel the heat of the toasty bouncing against her thigh as she walked, but still had no appetite. This walk was her gift to herself and she didn't need food or comfort or even music. Her walkman lay switched off in her pocket as she picked her way through the trees, snapping hidden twigs beneath her boots and crunching through semi-frozen puddles. Yes it was cold, but it was oh so clear and light. No sun yet filtered through the clouds, but neither was any more snow falling and if she listened carefully, she could hear the odd truck trailing through the slush on the main road.

Kate no longer cared if they made it to the dinner that night or if they spent yet another evening in the sitting room with Rose knitting in the corner. God, how had he stood this for so long? She liked Rose, but to Kate's mind, she was letting him rot here, and thought that perhaps he was also beginning to realise it. Hazel had pointed it out to him and so had Kate herself. He had not argued with them.

Kate's feet were now beginning to chill and suddenly, her hands were out of her pockets and she was running. Not just jogging, but running through the wood. The chill slid down her throat like an icicle and her walkman bumped and bruised her leg as she increased her pace, but it felt so good. So good to test your breathing and ability to remain upright as you slithered and side-stepped your way along a barely recognisable path. Even better was the way your heart raced and your fists clenched, letting you pound all your demons underfoot and leave them stranded in the snow, wondering how they had offended you. Oh, it was glorious to be outside and running.

By the time Kate reached the gateposts it was after 2pm and the sun had at last broken through onto the driveway. She had run along the ancient pathway until black spots had appeared in the snow before her and for the last half hour or so, she had walked, enjoying the wobbly, dazed sensation in her legs. Now she stood as close to the posts as she had ever been and they truly were a work of art. She removed her gloves and ran her fingers over the grooves in the rough wood, fascinated by the travelling contours and the way they formed their continuous loops. They were steaming in the sun now, and she leaned her face against one of the sides, ignoring the traffic passing on the main road, mere feet from where she stood. She wondered if, in all the hours he had spent crafting and constructing, his mind had wandered to the daughter he had created but had never seen. From what she now knew of him, Kate imagined that he had done this very thing and it suddenly vexed her that, in all her own life, she had not given him a moment of her thoughts.

She gave the post a quick kiss, then fished her camera out of her inner jacket pocket and wandered back down the driveway to take in their full height. It was stunningly beautiful here, the snow revealing its diamond sparkles wherever she looked. She ripped off her scarf and laid it carefully on the fence running the length of the driveway. It felt wonderful to have released her lips into the fresh air and allowed her to position her camera better. She noted that she had only three pictures left on her last film, so stood in the middle of the drive, determined that one shot should include both posts. She had just clicked the shutter when David's truck came easing off the road and onto the drive. Kate had plenty of time to jump back onto the verge, but he still braked quite sharply, as surprised to see her as she was to see him. She felt her face glow red at once and was grateful that she could blame it on the snow brightness. He was early.

David rolled down his window, grinning out at her as she grabbed her scarf and tramped over to the vehicle.

"Hey, Kate!Nearly flattened you. What are you up to?" His voice was cheerful, and she found it remarkable that he had no conception of what was going on in either her own head or Rose's. He had removed his hat to speak to her and she smiled at his flattened hair.

"I just wanted to take some photos in the snow. How are the roads?"

"Oh, they're not at all bad. We'll have to take this truck tonight though, that's really why I'm early. It's not fit to travel in at the moment."

"Oh. Okay. Well, I don't mind walking back, you go on. It's great to get some fresh air."

"You sure? It's freezing out here."

"I'm sure, but just a sec. Hold that pose."

Before he could argue, Kate had taken the photo. She knew that whatever the outcome of that shot, it would end up in a frame. And nobody could stop her looking at it.

*   *   *   *

Kate watched the trees overhead. In the headlights, she felt as if the pair of them were driving through a lovingly receptive audience, the branches bending to applaud them and then stepping back to let others have a look. Kate swallowed her nausea and concentrated on the road ahead instead. There had been no more snow, but the clearing sky had brought falling temperatures and every now and again, the truck skewed slightly.

"You're not nervous, are you?" David never took his eyes from the driveway as he spoke. They had been in the cab for just under a minute but Kate had not opened her mouth since they had said their goodbyes to Rose and she had been reasonably chatty up to that point. Now she looked away from him into the blackness. Even the lights on the dashboard showed too much.

"Hey Kate?" David glanced in her direction as much as the road conditions allowed, "When I imagined this particular journey, I thought I'd be switching off from your babble quite early. You know, 'you need to do this' and 'make sure you' and 'please don't'. What's up?"

"How are you going to introduce me?"

"What?"

"Well, who are you going to say I am?"

David slowed at the gateposts before pulling out onto the main road. His face was thoughtful for a few seconds before he looked over at her.

"Any ideas?" His voice had a forced levity to it and Kate guessed he was embarrassed at not even having considered the problem.

She let her face fall against the window with a bump, the last of her courage running for the hills. This particular dilemma had hit her while she was brushing her hair. In the mirror, her face had looked ridiculouslyteenage, even with extra eye-liner, and her jersey cotton dress had given her a gawky appearance, no longer hugging her figure like it used to. She had belted it, she had unbelted it, she had tied a scarf around her waist like a sarong, which had then ended up wrapped around the ceiling pendant in despair. In a final fit of frustration, she had dressed it with a cropped cardigan, but still to her eye she looked immature. She tried to think of what Hazel might suggest. 'Lipstick and jewellery. Get you into any pub on Skye. Oh, and put your hair up.'

So, she had fixed her hair into a wooden clip, leaving a few wisps loose and donned some earrings and a necklace. She owned no lipstick, which was irrelevant as she could not have worn it even in this emergency. As her eyes took a last look at the more acceptable image, she saw them widen in the reflection. Had David even thought of how he was going to explain her presence and where had his wits been when persuading her to come along?

Kate now shrugged, goose-pimples racing down her arms. "Friend of Hazel's who stayed on for a bit?" she suggested, placing her palm flat against the glass and closing her eyes. All she really wanted was to disappear into the night, the presence of David now choking her. She had no will to begin explaining either the short or long term problem, but had put herself in this position because it needed to be faced and it was easier than another evening trying to avoid Rose's gaze.

"I'll think of something," he stated, his voice now low and non-committal and Kate once again settled herself into the silence.

As Duncan's lights winked into view, Kate forced herself upright and tried to plump her hair back into shape. She had almost succeeded when David swung the truck across the slushy trails and brought it to a halt in a violently illuminated car park. As he switched off the engine and placed both hands back on the wheel, Kate looked out, confused, at the building fully lit up even at this time of night.

"The Dinner is being held at a bank?"

"It's not a bank and we're not going to the Dinner."

Kate did not know if it was relief at his words or anxiety at what his actual intentions were, but she found herself chewing the inside of her cheek as she stared in his direction. He was already climbing out of the vehicle, but she was unable to move. For the first time in days, someone else was making the decisions and it felt a bit scary. When he opened the door for her and offered his hand, his face was back to its regular open smile. She breathed again.

Chapter 36

"We're not going?"

"Did you really think I would take you somewhere you so very obviously *don't* want to go? Kate, I know you've put a lot of effort into this," he waved his hands up and down his appearance, "but nothing's worth the ordeal you're going through."

When he offered his hand again, she took it and eased herself down to the ground.

"So," she began, never taking her eyes off his annoyingly inscrutable face. "What *are* we going to do then?"

"We're going to talk. Somewhere away from The Edge, somewhere where you can tell me exactly what is going on and why the last two days have been miserable for you. I can't take you to a bar; this is the only other place I could think of. There's a diner and if we're lucky, we might catch the end of a hockey game." Pause. "That was a joke. Come on."

Kate felt her nausea return, but could do nothing but follow him across the car park. "What is this place, exactly?"

"Community Centre.Huge deal.Pool, rink, the Library somewhere. The main thing is, it's got food. I'm starving."

When they were seated, David took off his jacket and put both his hands on the table. Kate sat watching his every move, her tongue pressed firmly against her teeth to stop them from chattering, willing herself to relax or at least to appear relaxed. He looked over his shoulder at the near empty eating area.

"I'm sure its table service. Looks like most people are still in the Arena."

When someone waved to let them know they were on their way, he turned back to find Kate trying to unhook her scarf from her drop ear-ring. She was flushed and frantic, mortified at her own stupidity, but he reached over and deftly loosened the stray wool.

"There you go. Now, Kathryn Eilidh Wilder, what is going on in that head of yours?"

Kate could see a waitress approach and so laughed nervously and said, "You know my middle name."

By the time they had ordered, then waited for the girl to return with the drinks and cutlery, Kate's face was burning to her own touch. David's bemused expression had now turned more serious and he took her drumming fingers from the table and laid them flat.

"Hey, now. What is it?" His voice made her dizzy, and she really feared she might die from the tightness in her chest.

"Okay, okay, okay," she repeated under her breath, before she lifted her head in his direction. He raised his eyebrows to repeat his question.

"Okay," she said, this time to his face. "There *is* something wrong. Something really wrong with me. It's not an illness, it won't kill me, but it's something that I can't see myself ever recovering from. I want to tell you about it, because I can't stand the way people don't talk about what is most important. Will you listen?"

David's face, clean-shaven for the first time in days, looked completely captivated and she had never, in all of her wild imaginings, wanted to touch it as badly as she did right then. She slid her hands under her thighs and smothered them there.

"Yes, I'll listen."

Of course he would. She had known he would. So now, she had to be honest and allow him to express his opinions, just like Rose had done. It felt like she was stripping away her outer layer of skin, showing him what she was actually made of, and there would be no way of re-attaching this layer at a later date. Every judgement, every criticism he made would be like him dipping her raw flesh into salt. But then, that's what happened in her reality. If you were her age, nobody recognised your feelings, nobody took you seriously. Love could hurt just as viciously, but everybody accepted that your wounds would heal. How did they know that for sure?

"A couple of years ago, I got really upset in PE and when the teacher asked me if she could help, I told her I thought I might be in love with this lad. She laughed at me and did this funny sort of fiddle playing action. Fiddle, you know, violin. Anyway, it was the most humiliating thing that ever happened to me, so I'm not great at telling people how I feel. In here. But now, after all we've gone through together, I need to share it with you."

David leaned back in his chair, trying to give her the space he thought she needed. "Fine. Okay. There's no rush."

"I never thought I would be saying this tonight, I thought I might write to you instead and not risk your opinions making me cringe and die. Tonight was about putting your face back on the map of Duncan. It was going to be the best thing that had happened to you in a long time. Now, I'm going to ruin everything instead. Unless, you'd rather I just shut up."

"Kate," David leaned in towards her. "I'm not sure how clever you think I am, but maybe it would be better if you just said what's on your mind. I'm really anxious not to say the wrong thing here, but I have no idea where you are going with this. Whatever it is, I accept that it's important to you, so out with it. Please."

"I don't want to go home."

"You don't?" He seemed genuinely surprised and it made her even more nervous. Apparently, he really had no conception of what was coming.

"Two steak specials. Enjoy your meals."

Kate looked at the mountain of food before her, but instead of excusing herself and running to the loo, she stuffed a slice of tomato into her mouth and forced herself to swallow it down. She watched David unwrap his cutlery, then lay it alongside his plate. He was waiting for her to continue.

"I don't want to go home, because I want to stay here with you."

Kate was trying her hardest to lead him gently to the edge of the abyss and expected much misunderstanding along the way, but something in his eyes stopped her justifying anything further. Instead, she felt her neck prickle and cursed her inability to keep her feelings from announcing themselves to the world. She held her palms to her face, unable to look at him anymore. She had never felt so exposed. He sat motionless, swallowing once, his eyes never leaving her face. "I'm so sorry," she mumbled. "I haven't been able to hide anything and I did try. But, why should I? What am I actually doing wrong?"

The entire speech had been spoken to the floor. She could see a crack in the ceramic tiles and wondered what sort of force could possibly have caused such damage. The question now was whether she should keep speaking or get up and leave. She thought herself perfectly capable of walking all the way back to the house, if it relieved her of this stinging awkwardness.

"Hey, Kate?"

She shook her head. "I don't want to see your disappointment."

Kate heard him push his plate aside and then hers. He put both his hands before her, in front of her eyes. She looked at the lines carved into his palms and wondered what a palmist would see there. All she saw were the hands of the man she loved. Almost reluctantly, she brought her own hands to the table. He picked them up in his, and held them tight.

"Disappointment?" he breathed. "God in Heaven."

Kate was still unsure how much he truly comprehended, but his silence seemed to suggest he was getting there. That same silence was instantly shattered as David's stomach gave an almighty rumble and they both raised their heads. Kate held her breath. David's mouth twitched, his eyes apologetic.

"Wow," he stated. "Timing is an art form."

Kate smiled sympathetically and pushed his plate of food back in front of him. He ignored it.

"It's hopeless, isn't it?" she ventured, hiding her hands beneath her once more. "Somebody, everybody, will tell me that it cannot work, and they'll get their own way because there are more of them. They'll back each other up." She wondered if he would be the leader amongst them.

"Kate. Look at me, sweetheart. You have to make it clear to me now, before I become the biggest, oldest, most ridiculous fool that ever – "

"I love you. That's what I'm saying. And I want to stay here with you."

So, this was David's 'shocked' face. Kate thought she might remember it from Day One, when she had offered him the chance to see Fiona. Now she looked away, ashamed of her childish antics back then, before continuing. "And if that's still a wee bit unclear, you had better know that the thought of you

280

meeting someone tonight or any other night makes me feel sick. I still feel sick. Clearer?"

"Clear enough."

Kate forced herself to find the salt and pepper containers fascinating and decided that she would say nothing more until he asked her specific questions. She had provided him with knowledge, whether he was grateful for it or not, and she needed to let him digest this and make a decision. It was his life she was potentially disrupting and she would not try to persuade him. Love shouldn't be a matter of persuasion.

"Right," he croaked and took a slug of water. Kate sat looking at him, determined not to respond, and he finally met her gaze. His pupils were huge and black. "Okay. Kate, this is something that needs to be talked about. And it's good that we're both here, where …. where nobody else …. Look, you're going to have to give me a minute with this. Is it okay to ask you to do that?"

"Of course," she was on her feet immediately. "I'm just going to the loo."

David nodded, watching her scarf slide from the back of her chair to the floor as she fled. He realised he had begun to sweat in his stiff, new shirt and so he unbuttoned the cuffs under his sweater and rolled up his sleeves. It was not enough. His inner thermostat seemed to have exploded and in a panic he tore the sweater over his head, and pulled at his shirt until it no longer clung to his skin. His mind felt inflated with helium. He tried to think of how this precious person had ever taken these feelings of affection and created something more, without his knowledge. He found himself furious at his naivety and inability to recognise, and subsequently halt, such a transformation.

"Steaks not to your liking, Sir?"

David jumped from his thoughts, noting the waitress's concerned look at his agitation.

"Em, it's fine. Lost our appetites for the moment."

She bent to retrieve Kate's scarf and, leaving the bill beside him, said, "I'll give you some space then."

He did not even thank her. He needed to sort his thoughts before Kate's return, but found his racing heart and angry self-criticism too distracting. "Stay calm," he soothed. He put his hands to his head and closed his eyes.

There was only one road out of this situation, of course. He must take all his experiences of the last few months, the joy of finding Hazel, the survival of the truth and the rescue of Kate, and lock them away safe in his private heart. From there, he could make use of them at any time; whilst driving, when the figures on the page made no sense, or even when he was on a future date with some semi-interested female. He could hear himself telling said date about his amazing daughter and - and then what? Kate. His strange, mutually accepting relationship with someone who had no real claim on his time.His growing dependence on her vitality and company to make him feel like he had a life.

But he must not entertain Kate's emotions. He must not even open his mind to her words, because there would be no explaining to anyone, himself included, how she pulled at his heart and no way in this world that he could ever allow her to love him. Not in the way she wanted.

David now looked at the empty chair opposite, at the flat, inanimate scarf hanging there, thinking how much better it looked when it framed Kate's honest face. He clenched his fists and focussed again on the only path before him.

He must gently disentangle himself from her; the majority of people would be unharmed, Rose would not be compromised, Neil would continue on his own, fairly steady route and there would be no appalled condemnation amongst his few acquaintances and colleagues. Hazel and Beth would still welcome him and time and distance would take care of the rest. She would be hurt but only for the shortest time. She had known him for less than two months and her fragile spirit would recover. Obviously, this was the *only* option.

There was however another road; a road so studded with landmines that only a lunatic would even glance in its direction. A lunatic, or a love-deprived old fool. In his own mind, he was an anti-social, uninspiring man who liked malt whisky more than he liked a shave. He allowed himself a little credit for surviving his own life and getting his family through most of the recent trauma, but really, there was little else to love. A set of new clothes and a bank account, that about summed it up. He had loved once with a passion that had ultimately annihilated him and had only begun to live again since connecting with Hazel and Kate.

His head had sunk lower and he clasped his hands behind his neck. So, it appeared he was allowing himself to recognise that she had made a difference, and that he had begun to look forward to her bright face when he arrived home of an evening. He thought of how long it had been since he had enjoyed talking so much, or even when somebody had had so much to say, directly to him. She sent sparks off in every direction when she was in full flow and he loved it. He also thought of how she had changed since Skye and was proud of her. She was an amazing young person. His fingers slipped from his neck as more perspiration gathered there.

Before he could stop them, he felt all of his emotions suddenly channelling down one course and it almost stalled his breath. Of course he wanted her to stay. He opened his eyes, accepting this as a fact, then immediately screwed them tight shut against it. There was no possible way of this working out happily. He was neither a stupid nor a vain man. Kate loved him for his care and he loved her because she was brave and trusted him completely. If she had only left him ignorant of her own feelings, there might have been a chance of ignoring this indefinitely, but not now. Oh, God, it was indeed hopeless.

He felt a hand on his shoulder as Kate made her way back to the table and although it was a fleeting touch, it took the breath from him. She sat sedately, her face resigned to whatever he was about to say. There was her trust, evident on her face, and his heart died a little as he recognised that she desperately needed protection. Protection from the world's reaction to her wishes.Their wishes.

"It's okay," she said, her face so very pale.

"It's not okay."

"No, but it will be. I'm going back and you'll-"

"Stop talking, Kate. I love it when you talk to me, but you need to stop for a moment or two." Kate's eyes were so wide, he had to reach out and touch her face to reassure her. "Don't look so scared. Not when you're with me."

"That's the only time I'm not scared. Okay, I'll shut up."

David allowed himself a few more moments of clarification. What he was going to say was so very important. He had to give her credit where it was due. She knew that the gods were against them and yet she felt strongly enough to let him know how she felt. He would not patronise her by reminding her of the opinions of others or suggesting that he was flattered, he would just say that he was thankful that she was his friend and she meant such an incredible amount to him. But he needed to point out that she had years to grow into these special feelings, with someone who had her youth and none of his history. He would see her safely onto the plane and -

"Oh, God, Kate. I can't do this again."

He wanted to stand, but the strength had gone from his legs. He gripped the sides of the table, as the memory of losing those he loved most to the sound of tannoy announcements and piped music cut through his thoughts like a chainsaw. He was unaware of the crowds of people now entering the room or the gang of waitresses poised to serve them. All he felt were his wits deserting him and all he could see was the flawless face before him. Her grey eyes were no longer sad; they were just clear discs of humanity, searching his face for clues. Her lips lay still, not knowing how to respond. He had to get through this.

"You're making me tell you the truth and there is no need to. You don't need to know. You can go like you plan to and we will both learn to endure it, like we've had to endure worse." He paused for breath. "I can't stand the thought of you being unhappy any longer, and I'm causing you pain now, but I need to keep you safe from all of this. People would be brutal and what they would throw at the pair of us would hurt you too much."

The mob was in high spirits as they passed their table, very few of them noticing the completely motionless couple sitting opposite each other. Even their waitress had forgotten them in lieu of the arriving numbers. Kate remained mute, listening to his every syllable, wishing him to say more of his actual feelings and dreading that he would keep them safely concealed.

He shook his head against his own words. "But the thought of you leaving, not being in my sight, within reaching distance is also too much. I'm so selfish. I don't want to lose you to the rest of the world because the rest of the world has taken too many of mine already."

There was an interminable silence between them, pierced once by a raucous laugh and a roar as one of the waitresses dropped some cutlery.

"Now say something, please," David begged, wondering how his lungs still allowed him breath to speak.

"Suppose I don't want the rest of the world. Do I get a say? I mean, really, will there ever be a time when I can decide how *my life* is lived? Will it be when

I'm eighteen? Or twenty-one?" Kate's voice was curious and she spread her hands in the air before them. "I'm not asking a rhetorical question here, David. I want to know when, legally, morally or any other way, I can do what I want to do."

David unclasped his hands and wiped his jaw free from moisture. "What do you want to do?"

The jostling crowd remained invisible to him as she in turn sat forward, no fear or anxiety anywhere near her now. Even before she spoke, he saw in her face total conviction and it was beautiful. Neil's I-don't-believe-it expression had gone and so had Fiona's meek acceptance. Her skin was unsullied, but he was sure it concealed a soul older than the earth itself. It was a magnetic combination to him and he found himself convinced that his need was greater than hers. Now she was looking straight into his eyes.

"What I want means nothing if you won't help me."

David knew he was staring at her, but it was almost impossible not to, so great was her faith in herself and in him. He felt his first boot searching for a route through the landmines.

"Sir, I'm sorry. But if you're finished, there are some people still waiting for a table."

Blindly David got to his feet, reaching automatically for his jacket and the wallet it contained. By the time he had left an overly generous tip, Kate had wrapped her scarf in place and was watching him through guarded eyes.

"Come with me," he said, taking her arm. She matched his pace until they reached the foyer, when she slid her fingers down his arm into his hand. He halted immediately, but did not let it go. When he looked down at her with frantic eyes, however, she let his warm palm slip away from hers. Breathing deeply, he led her to a chair near the entrance doors and sat her down. The space was deserted for the time being and this needed to be sorted as soon as possible.

"Tell me what you want," he said, his voice desperate.

"Tell me if you'll help me."

Somewhere a door banged and some heeled shoes crossed a corridor, but nobody appeared. David took her hands. "Of course I'll help you."

Kate's hands gripped his in return. "You must know what I want," she smiled. "I want you. I don't want the rest of the world and I don't want a life without you. I thought you were 'clear enough' about this."

"Okay," he dared to look at her at last, the lump in his throat causing him pain. "I'm clear. But how can you possibly know what you want?"

For the first time in days, Kate's smile lit up her whole face and he looked at her in wonder, amazed at her confidence.

"It's so simple David. I know, because I've watched you and listened to you. Every time I see you think, or smile or take control, my heart just …. grows inside me. I love when you laugh and I feel like crying whenever I see your pain. I also want you to look at me all the time, which must mean something. But mostly I know because when I see your face, it makes perfect sense.

His bewilderment knew no bounds. "My face makes perfect sense?"

Kate traced her finger in the space between their faces. "Your eyes are perfect in your face. Your whole face is perfect."

"Kate - "

"No, listen to me. I don't need you to turn round and tell me that I haven't lived enough and I haven't experienced enough to know what I could 'possibly want'. I don't need that kind of advice, not after everything that's happened in the last year. I've met the man who made me and he seems like a man worth getting to know. I'm sure he will make it okay between us some day. But I want much more than that in my life, and I've never wanted it before now."

David had grown visibly paler and Kate's felt her confidence falter slightly. She had said too much. She was about to be judged for her honesty, but there was no other way to go. Her mother had been an angel, but had nevertheless wasted time away from this man. If he decided that they had no future, then she would fight so far and then leave him in peace, but at least she would know that she had tried her best.

"Kate," his voice was steady, "I don't know of anybody else who speaks as openly as you do. It makes me unsteady on my feet, because if I let myself even think about what this would mean to my life, I might start to consider it possible. But I should take responsibility and do the right thing."

"I agree completely. I'm willing you to do the right thing. The right thing for our future."

Kate sat motionless. There was nothing more she could do and it was not fair to put pressure on a man who had given her so much already. All she could do now was smile at him, showing him how happy he made her.

David in turn felt choked. This unspoiled human being was *inviting* him to be in her life, in her heart and it touched his soul. Whatever the mechanics of the attraction were, they seemed real and he could not deny that he loved her, whether he deserved to or not. He looked at her warm smile, which was so uncomplicated and optimistic that he found himself matching it. Yes, she needed protection from the judgement that was heading their way. She needed protection and love and support, which was exactly why he was there. He would shoulder the burden for both of them. *He* would protect her from whatever was coming. Nobody was more worth the aggravation.

Just when Kate thought they might sit there, smiling in wonder until the lights were switched off and the place locked up for the night, he brought her fingers to his lips and kissed them. In turn, she reached out and cupped his jaw in her hand, marvelling at the way his eyes started at her touch. She held her breath and raised her eyebrows at him, begging him to understand what she wanted. Finally, he leaned forward and kissed her. It was a soft meeting of lips and all that was required in that public place. But it left David with something far beyond hope and Kate with a taste of the future.

"See," she whispered. "You've helped me already."

Chapter 37

For the second time in three weeks, David stood motionless in the public area of Vancouver International Airport, but this time, Kate was by his side. She didn't want anything to read, she didn't want anything to drink, she just wanted to stand holding his hand. She alternated between smiling and trembling and sometimes she would just stand with her head against his chest. David's face was giving nothing away, which would have amused Kate if she hadn't been so uptight. They had tried sitting at a table, but Kate physically could not do it. She needed to be able to put her arms around him at a moment's notice and a table did not allow it, so they stood beside a row of low benches positioned against the wall of windows, her rucksack resting on one of them.

Rose had not accompanied them. Indeed, Rose knew very little other than what her own eyes had seen; David had refused to discuss anything with her while Kate was still in the house. The pair had appeared almost professionally distant from each other since returning from *not* attending the Dinner, the reasons for which were also still obscure. But there would be time enough for an inquisition when she was safely out of the country. Kate had thanked her for her hospitality and promised not to lose touch, but Rose sensed their initial closeness had gone. The girl was probably embarrassed.

David himself had spent his waking hours trying to concentrate on maintaining a regular heartbeat. The day following their evening out, he had gone to work as usual and managed to make two phone-calls and speak to Rob for half an hour, before the sweats began under his collar and he had had to escape into the fresh air. He had found a seat behind the skidder shed where there was no sun and no view. He could not afford to do anything other than stare at his boots and make himself look at the situation he had put them both in. She was going home full of hope for their future. He was staying here to beat himself to death with what he should have said and done that night to crush all such hope.

He had visited these thoughts every day since then, especially after she had smiled at him from across the hallway or had sought him out in his solitary fireside seat, leaning over to kiss him. Each of these moments had jump-started his heart, and he had failed each time to discourage them from happening again, because he loved her. But he could not touch her, she was so beautiful and positive and self-assured that he could not lay a finger on her. He dare not contaminate her with his needs or his hopes. And so he had never gone looking for her and that remained the only aspect of himself that he could still appreciate. His doubts remained in spite of his feelings. She was too precious to waste on him and his need to be loved had gone beyond a rational level. He would overwhelm her.

So he had tried to remain self-contained and detached in order to let her heart grasp the magnitude of its wishes. This had appeared an achievable plan, until he awoke each morning, hours before dawn, imagining how life would return to its grey imitation as soon as she was gone; how her touch and dependence actually made him feel vital again and how she was giving him an opportunity which was almost inconceivably astonishing. And throughout all of his fears and moments of black self-analysis, Kate had never once come forward and asked him why she was not good enough, or what was wrong with him. According to Rose, she had spent most of her time walking in the woods, always returning with a calm, but bright smile. In his presence, she had seen his bewilderment and was secure enough of her own feelings to let him deal with his in his own way. She was either naively manipulative or absurdly astute. Or maybe she just loved him.

"How long now?" Kate asked picking at a loose thread on David's shirt until finally the button fell off. She scooped it up and pocketed it. "That one's mine," she grinned.

David kissed the top of her head and looked around. "I reckon about another ten minutes. Are you sure you don't need a book? It's a long haul."

"Absolutely not. Do you think there's any way I could concentrate on fiction when I've got you, us, inside my head? Nothing could even come close."

He looked down at her face and shook his head slightly. "You did say you would think seriously about *all* the options, Kate."

"I know, and I will. I'm going home for two reasons. One, because I don't want to see my aunt institutionalised and two, to decide where my future lies, without your face making it oh such a difficult decision. As if being apart from you is going to make any sort of bloody difference. Hey, you're not hoping I'm going to bail on you, are you? Now *that* I would have to take very seriously."

"Kate!" he chided, but she was already diving into her ruck-sack.

"Okay Mr Sensitive. I've got something for you. Here. It's the Runrig tape you were listening to and it's *very* precious, so you need to be careful with it." She handed it over cautiously, missing it already, but waving away his protests. "No, it's for you. You can listen to the words and think of me. Oh, and this."

She held out to him a thick, yellow envelope with her own name inscribed on it, startling him into taking a step backwards.

"It's fine, take it. Just promise not to read it here, it requires a whisky and a seat by the fire, I think."

"Why?" he asked.

"Oh there's a question. You pick an answer, I'm sure a head doctor would find many, many reasons for it. But really, it's to show you that I'm coming back. That's probably the most precious thing I've ever owned, apart from my watch, and I'm only lending it to you. See if it makes things easier. I'm coming back to claim it. And you."

287

He pocketed the envelope then stood hands by his side, watching her from a foot away. Kate had just handed him another piece of Fiona, yet amazingly it was not the most important thing to him at that moment. This in itself was a revelation, and one that sparked a tiny hope in his tormented heart. After all this time, the details and motivations he had sought were there to be viewed and possibly even dispatched with. But what mattered most to him in that second, was that someone special was leaving; someone who wanted to stay with him more than anything else, who wanted no secrets between them and who was only going because convention dictated it.

"What is it?" she asked.

He had to swallow before speaking. "I'm not sure I dare touch you. I might not be able to let you go."

Kate let out her breath slowly, then pushed her ruck-sack from its bench and stepped onto the firm wood. She grabbed his coat and pulled him over to her. She was almost now at his eye level and draped her arms around his neck. "So don't let me go."

David encircled her waist and kissed her. There was no doubt that they had progressed since the foyer of the Community Centre, a thing Kate was eternally grateful for even though she had accepted his previous restraint as his way of coming to terms with their feelings. Now, she wondered if they should set up home at the airport, since it was the most passionate and uninhibited he had allowed himself to be. As her flight announcement brought them back to reality, she opened her eyes to find his face so completely *alive*, that she could not conceive that she was about to leave it behind her. He lifted her to the ground, forcing his hands to leave her waist and fold themselves against his chest.

"This is it then," she gasped, desperately biting her lip. "Don't let me cry."

"There's nothing to cry about. Just remember, that whatever you decide to do, I'm on your side. You can't make the wrong decision, but you do have to think about it. And," he lowered his face to hers, allowing their foreheads to caress each other's, "I love you. Never forget that one. I love *you*."

"I love you too, David Wilder. I'm coming back."

They had reached the Departure gate. How long before she could return? Would he let her come for Christmas? Should she suggest it and risk a shake of his head? Should she throw herself at his feet now and beg him to take her home? She was handing over her documents; she was going through the gate. His hand was now out of reach, but his face was still there, all green eyes and rough jaw line. When she came back, she was going to throw out every razor in the house. She was going to burn every new piece of clothing that she had made him buy and she was going to sit and stare at that face and those familiar, worn clothes all day every day.

As the queue behind her jostled her forward, she turned and shouted, "Don't go to any Rotary Dinners while I'm gone. You never know who you might meet there."

She saw him salute her in reply, the open-palmed gesture that was his alone. Then she was forcing her legs along the corridor, completely assured that she would not to cry because he had said there was no need to. Everything was going to be just as they wanted, and she had hours and hours ahead of her when there was nothing to do but think of him, all the things he had said, and all the things they had yet to do. That would be a pleasant pass-time indeed. Maybe it would even make her stronger, clothing her in the armour required to tell her family of how things were going to be. There were battles to fight and she would have to have her most mature and unquestionable arguments ready as weapons. At least she would be near Fiona again and she could do anything with her silent support.

Kate stopped in her tracks, doubt unexpectedly drenching her from head to foot in icy water. Fiona *would* help her, wouldn't she? Her Mum knew what she was feeling and what was needed. Fiona always had her best interests at heart.

As other travellers pushed past her lone figure, Kate felt the first tear fall.

Epilogue
September 2011

For September, the month of anniversaries both pleasant and poignant, it was strikingly beautiful, and Kate felt that it would just be plain wrong to ignore the hill today. It had been frowning down upon her for the last week, offended that she had not visited and it was time to make amends.

Ally had not been overly enthusiastic but had given in at the third round of 'nagging'. She had taken it steady, not only because she did not want to risk recriminations for 'going ahead like a train', but also because one of her knees had begun to give her jip since turning thirty and seemed to object just a little bit more each winter. However, by the time they had reached the escarpment where the land plummeted down to the Raasay Sound, even Ally had cottoned on to the majesty of the Ben. To their left, the land was an undulating, velvet blanket, peppered with sheep. To the right, it was like a different planet. The sheer drops to the sea were broken every now and again by curious crags and pinnacles, each of them a lurid olive green or a deep purple, leading down to the shale beach.

Not for the first time did Kate thank God that Ben Tianavaig ascended in a series of steps. A person could cope with the steep rises if they knew that a gentler gradient followed, allowing them to catch their breath and drink in the landscape. Kate did what she always did – stopped every fifty metres or so and carried out a circular scan of the scenery, to see how the panorama changed as she climbed. These days, she took her digital camera. It meant that she could replay the scenes when the Ben was shrouded in mist and she had no inclination to take it on. Now she marvelled at the peace. They were alone apart from the tiniest figure slowly ascending, a good quarter of a mile below them. Well, it was not *exclusively* her hill.

Ally had overtaken her, but was not rushing ahead. He had the rucksack slung over one shoulder only and tackled the slopes with no real effort. On days like this, when there was so much to see and consume, they talked very little. But since they had known each other, there had never been a time when it was awkward. She followed his every move and for the umpteenth time could not believe how lucky she was that he was hers.

"Hey, Al?" she called, "when you get to the top, there's an Eagle's nest somewhere, apparently. Not exactly sure where."

"I'll look for it - while I'm waiting for you," he replied, throwing a grin in her direction.

Kate did not reply, but beamed back at him, watching as he negotiated the rocks in his path, hopping away from the edge as was necessary. He was amazingly sure-footed for someone who did not always approach hill-walking with enthusiasm.

As she reached the summit, she found the discarded rucksack, emptied of contents, the flask sitting upright waiting to be opened. Kate could see Ally about fifteen feet away, on a lower level, inspecting the terrain and glancing out over the Sound. He seemed content to wander about and pick up stones and fossils, launching them as far as he was able without losing his footing or pocketing them if they held his interest. Kate sat beside the stone pillar, breathing more slowly and easily. As ever, it surprised her how little real effort it took to make it this far, and how the prize always cancelled out any struggle. The only thing still to be debated was the return route and that would depend on Ally's mood. Now, she gazed down at Portree, loving the way the town clung to the edge of the twin bays and the houses followed the roads out as if they were strung together. She imagined that they would look like Christmas lights in the dark and wondered if a night expedition would be a step too far for Ally.

She watched miniscule vehicles heading in and out of the town, making their way past the cemetery at a snail's pace. It had been three days since she had gone to see Fiona and had spent a couple of hours cleaning the headstone and trimming the grass around the base. It had not been in a poor state, but it had been a labour of love to tend to it and she had taken the opportunity to relate all her news. Ally had been the main topic, Kate trying to convey without smiling too much of how much she loved him. She knew that Fiona would have been bowled over by him herself.

"Tea?" she shouted down to Ally.

"Two minutes," he replied, his voice bizarrely gravelly for a non-smoker.

She began to relax, the sun accentuating all the remarkable aspects before her, and highlighting the familiar as well as the new. Her thoughts turned to Hazel, who had occasionally accompanied her up here, and checked her phone to see if there was any signal so far out. Three bars, not at all bad. As she was scrolling through her contacts, Ally flopped down beside her and knocked over the flask. He scooped it up quickly, swearing under his breath and succeeded in scalding his hand, but saving most of the liquid.

"Clever," said Kate, amiably.

"That's me," he agreed. "But then it wasn't me who left it there without its lid."

"I was just going to take a photo of you and text it to Hazel," stated Kate, ignoring the pointed comment, "Would you object to that, do you think?"

Ally pulled a 'how-many-more-photos' face but gracefully posed for the shot, even managing a smile, before leaning back on his elbows and staring into the sky. He seemed genuinely contented to be out here, which made Kate love him even more. It was so important to her that he was happy and truly he was not a hard person to please. He could be moody and intolerant occasionally, but she rarely had to go out of her way to accommodate him. She was grateful for the decisions she had made and for everything that had come her way.

"What do you think of Hazel then? She's my best friend, you know. She helped me through a lot."

"Hazel's great. I have no problem with her at all."

"Hey," she poked him on the thigh, "I'm trying to have a deep and meaningful one here and you are not participating."

Ally, who had pulled his hat down over his eyes to shade them from the sun, now raised one corner, trying to fathom Kate's actual frame of mind before answering. The glint in her eye persuaded him that perhaps the best course of action was to sit up. He hauled himself back upright.

"What do you want me to say? Hazel is great, she seems quite happy with me too. Beth makes great cakes ..."

"Okay, forget it," Kate sighed, knowing that once again, she had pushed too hard. All she wanted was for him to appreciate who mattered and what she had in her life. But not everybody could see it. She herself could virtually smell it in the air. The love and nostalgia, all tied up in the bay below her and on this hill, which had shielded and raised generations before her. She picked at the cropped grass at her side, her nose prickling for the days when her mother and she would clamber down to McQueen's Loch for no other reason than to watch the sun wink back at them in the summer haze.

Ally must have sensed the change in her mood, and immediately put his arm around her shoulder, knowing that this action was enough to have her smiling again. He was about to mention how spectacular he thought the Ben was, when he stopped himself and looked over Kate's head. He squinted for a second while Kate, oblivious, checked again to see if the message plus photo had been sent. Then his face cleared.

"Hey, mom?" he said, in his thick Canadian accent. "Look."

Kate turned to where he was pointing and saw a tall figure appearing over the final ridge. Short, grey hair. She was on her feet in a second, not crediting what her eyes were seeing. Standing a matter of thirty feet away, head down, hands on his hips and blowing air from his lungs, was David. When he lifted his head, recovering sufficiently from his recent aerobic efforts, he raised his hand. Kate turned back to her son, whose fourteen-year-old frame now towered above her. "No way!" she exclaimed. "Did you know he was coming?"

He backed away, laughing, "Absolutely not my doing." He waved down to David while Kate scrutinised his face, "Hey, Dad. That's some hike for an old man."

Kate turned back to see him begin the final ascent, and now she was running, as carefully as the incline would allow. Her heart was pounding, but not from the distance or effort required to reach him. She slowed slightly as she approached, suddenly picturing the momentum of their embrace sending them both flying over the edge. But then she was in his arms and was being held as tightly as she had ever been.

"You're here!" she choked. "You said you couldn't spare three weeks away."

"I did say that," he confirmed, still trying to calm his breathing. He held her away for a second, laughing at her perky face and broad grin. It had been over a week since he had put them on the plane, Ally hunched under his hat, texting the last of his friends to let them know of his departure. It had been an optimistic, cheerful farewell, the only cloud being that David was snowed under with a new contract and had to stay behind. Hazel had been disappointed of course, she had been keen for him to see the new Bed and Breakfast in Staffin she had established in the last year. He had not been to Skye for a decade at least and Hazel had been back to Canada only twice. Now, she would be overjoyed at the surprise.

"Have you seen Haze yet?" grinned Kate.

"No, I came straight here. Found the house empty and took a big, *big* chance that it was you I could see on the hill. I wouldn't climb up here for anybody else, you know."

She touched his face. "What made you come?"

"Oh," his breathing had now evened out and he wiped his stubbly jaw where sweat had gathered, "Well, you were gone and I knew it was only for three weeks, but," he pulled her back to him and mumbled down into her shoulder, "It was too long, Kate. Far, far too long. You may ... you might have decided to stay this time."

She looked up into his face, which although had a healthy glow from the climb and was smiling at holding her so close, contained a pair of pained, green eyes. She was about to dismiss his concerns when she understood where his fears had come from and she rested her hand on his cheek. His skin was warm and familiar and she could not take her hand away. She moved it slowly down to his throat then rested it behind his head. She pulled his forehead down to her own, closing her eyes at the proximity of him.

"You know better than that," she said, so softly that the breeze turned the words into a whisper. When she drew back and looked into his eyes again, they were still unsure. "I made my decision a long time ago, and I have no choice anyway David. It's life with you, or no life at all. Tell me what I deserve."

"You deserve life, sweetheart," he replied, looking at the ground where their feet met each other head on. Matching boots.

"Then, this is it. Let's keep enjoying it."

For the thousandth time, David shook his head in disbelief at his extreme fortune and then said, almost apologetically, "I just had to make sure."

In response, Kate kissed him. She took all the love she had for him, all the respect for what he was, all the gratitude for what he had given her and wrapped them all up in that one kiss. She f elt his hands go to her waist as they always did and she welcomed them, her body still his. There, on her hill, with the sheep grazing ignorantly nearby, and her hands lost in his hair, she continued to kiss him until a voice broke them up.

"For God's sake, parents. I'm right here!"